"A very moving story with plenty of drama, heart-pounding action, and seriously emotional scenes."
—*Romantic Times BOOKreviews Magazine*

# WHAT'S A WOMAN TO DO?

"Engrossing and entertaining...The twists and surprises are both plausible and unbelievable."
—*Booklist*

"A fast-paced, soulful, dramatic story."
—*Sunday Oklahoman*

"A talented storyteller with a knack for telling a convincing story, McGlothin manages to weave an entertaining story that may indeed ring true to many readers...[a] new and refreshing voice in the world of contemporary African-American fiction."
—*QBR*

"Four stars...a superb, true-to-life book. With a masterfully created plot, it explores the turbulent lives of three courageous women...offers a gripping emotional glimpse into the dark world of the unknown."
—*Romantic Times BOOKreviews Magazine*

# SINFUL
# TOO

## VICTOR McGLOTHIN

**GRAND CENTRAL**
**PUBLISHING**

NEW YORK   BOSTON

Grand Central Publishing
Hachette Book Group USA
237 Park Avenue
New York, NY 10017

Printed in the United States of America

Grand Central Publishing is a division of Hachette Book Group USA, Inc.
The Grand Central Publishing name and logo is a trademark of Hachette Book Group USA, Inc.

ISBN: 978-1-60751-125-0

Book design by Giorgetta Bell McRee

To every wife who has or will have to endure
a cheating husband and *the other women.*

# SINFUL
# TOO

# ONE

## *Jailhouse Blues*

Dior followed two paces behind the grim-faced correctional officer who led her through the visitor's gate of the Azalea Springs Federal Prison for women. Dior had been incarcerated before, though only briefly. The desperate claustrophobic and suffocating feelings always returned when she took the hour-long drive to see Billie Rae Wicker, her mother.

Dior refused to count the years they had been separated from each other. She'd spent too many of them hating Billie for not being there, for missing her sixteenth birthday and the first time she fell in love. It took a murder, the passing of Dior's good friend, to prompt her initial trip to the prison camp fourteen months ago. Before Isis was killed in a sordid sexual relationship gone awry, Dior couldn't see past her own pain to care about anyone else's, including that of her mother, who had been locked away over ten years before receiving a visit from her daughter. Now, with four trips to Azalea Springs under her belt, Dior looked forward to reconnecting with the woman who birthed and raised her until age fifteen, when the U.S. Marshals came storming through their front door with search-and-arrest warrants to haul Billie Rae Wicker away. No amount of kicking, screaming, or crying was going to stop the men from incarcerating her. She couldn't do a thing to defend herself once the officers found stacks of stolen food stamps, forged green cards, and hundreds of illegal credit cards issued to people who didn't exist. It was peculiar how Dior had fallen prey to some of the same obstacles that had sent her mother down the wrong path. By her twenty-first birthday, Dior's resentment had shifted from Billie's absence to her having been caught. Carelessness and trust were the culprits Dior blamed for her mother's arrest, reasoning that a more precise plan would have better served her efforts. She also grew to believe that every hustler had to stay on top of their game and keep an eye on their friends, especially when the money was rolling in. Dealing with slipups and snitches was merely the cost of doing business on the streets; even an upset ex-boyfriend's brokenhearted rants to the cops should have been expected. Billie getting trapped by his betrayal and subsequently having to leave two teenage kids behind, due to her own carelessness, was inexcusable. Dior's pain turned to pity when the unfortunate death of a friend proved that not everything that happened in life could be planned for or plotted against. At age twenty-six, she was forced to search her heart for forgiveness and then work on storing away the sadness and lost time where they belonged: in the past.

Inside prison, Billie kept a mental record of the birthdays, and missing out on their high school graduations and various other important coming-of-age events left an indelible mark on her heart. She imagined irreplaceable moments when her daughter and son might have needed guidance, direction, and discipline. Billie would never be able to forgive herself for not being there, even if she dared to try. Keeping track was a painful reminder that her schemes had not only landed her behind federal bars on a twelve-year stretch, but they also displaced her children from a home she'd built with ill-gotten gains but the best of intentions.

While sitting on a metal bench in the inmate waiting area, Billie ran her nervous hands down the creases of her neatly pressed khaki prison-issue uniform just as she did each time her children came to see about her. She inhaled heavily then closed her eyes. *I've missed the best parts of this child's life*, she thought silently. *Ain't nothing going to bring those years back to you. Telling yourself how bad you messed up won't either. Pull yourself together, Billie Rae, and face this young lady you abandoned, the woman you hardly know.*

"Inmate Wicker, B. R., move to the congregation room," a man's voice instructed.

Billie opened her eyes and shrugged on a smile from her iron perch. "Yes, sir," she replied assuredly. "I'm moving." She stood up, straightened the uniform, and then pulled back her long ponytail with outstretched fingers. She stepped into a twenty-by-twenty foot room. Everything was gray, cold, and hard. Metal tables and chairs were situated in three rows to facilitate meetings between the prisoners and their lawyers and loved ones. The walls were painted in a dreary, washed-out hue to match the monotonous décor. Billie was told which bench to take. She did as instructed, placing her thin forearms on the flat circular-shaped metal table, and exhaled just as profoundly as she'd inhaled in the other room. She finger-combed her hair again when she heard two sets of footsteps heading down the long cement corridor toward the visiting area. Billie's heart fluttered when Dior traipsed into view behind a stoutly built officer. Despite her daughter's expensive designer skirt-suit and Prada slingbacks, she still managed to see a child in the woman standing on the other side of the chain-link fence dividing them.

"Remember, Wicker, no contact," the corrections officer bellowed, as Billie arose to greet Dior.

"Yes, sir," she answered, in the standard protocol for speaking with COs. "I remember." The gate slid open. Officers stood on either side of it, and two more lorded over the room itself to assure no illegal contraband passed and no rules were broken. There were many rules. No physical contact during visitation was the most hated of all.

The sweet aroma of Dior's perfume filled Billie's thin nostrils as she approached the table allotted to them. Billie looked her daughter up and down, proudly. Dior's hair was shoulder-length, thick, and shiny. Her makeup was applied lightly, not overdone. Billie smiled at how nicely it complemented her cinnamon-brown complexion and sharp features. She also noted how Dior's taste for clothing seemed to mature with every visit. Her edgy, painted-on jeans and revealing blouses had been upgraded to stylish ensembles. "Hey, Dior," she sang quietly, wanting to reach out and secure a warm embrace. "You look good, baby girl. I don't know if I'd have gone with plaid but it suits you. You look like a million."

"You too, Billie Rae," Dior said eventually, using the same subdued tone she'd been met with. She tried not to stare at her mother's hair, in desperate need of a relaxer, or the tired eyes residing beneath it. Billie would have easily been considered a stunner on the outside. Her angular face, high cheekbones, and evenly tanned skin made her appear younger than forty-three except for the despair her eyes couldn't conceal. Her plight was made evident in the slightly noticeable wrinkles that had begun to gather there.

As she took her seat across from Dior, Billie smiled big and bright to fight off the embarrassment of a subtle insult. "Oomph, for once couldn't you call me Mama, or are you too grown for that now?" She glanced at Dior's manicured nails, then slowly balled her fist to hide her ragged fingertips. "You do look it, but dressing the part doesn't necessarily make it so."

Seeing where this was going, Dior decided to get there first. Billie had an annoying habit of being overly critical, about everything from clothing to the way Dior held her mouth when she was upset. Staying ahead of her mother's nit-picking had gotten to be a chore, one she'd rather do without. "Well, since you brought it up, *Billie*, I do have a job, a house, my own car, and I'm paying all of my own bills. If that ain't grown, I don't know what is." Dior neglected to mention how she was running a welfare housing scam in order to live in her twin brother's Section 8 property, where he was paid two thousand dollars a month by the government for renting it out to an underprivileged family. Dior also left out the arrangement she had with the clothing store owner Giorgio, who paid her under the table in cash for sales and sex on the side. Oddly enough, Billie would have been excited and saddened simultaneously had she been apprised of Dior's street-savvy and skillful knack for making ends meet without breaking a sweat.

"Yeah, you've got a point, Dior. You have grown a lot while I've been locked up here. I'm sorry for missing out on your and Dooney's—"

"Don't do this to me, Billie Rae," Dior interrupted sharply and louder than she meant to. "Don't lay your guilt on me every time I come up here to see you. What's done is done. Ain't that what you used to tell me when I cried my eyes out writing those letters begging you to come home? You can save the history lesson. I don't want it."

Taken aback, Billie smiled anxiously. She realized she was the mother in theory only, and it hurt. "Okay, I see. But what you can't discount is the truth. You know that brother of yours, that boy is doing alright for himself too. He had that case hanging over him but he got up and dusted himself off pretty good. With that boy owning a legit business, the building it's in, and five houses, it seems the best thing could have happened to y'all is this happening to me." Her worried smile fell flat when she saw Dior's cheeks drawing in tighter, like they had when she was a child. "Uh-oh, I recognize that look," Billie said, ill-advisedly. "You used to carry that same smirk when I'd make you wash the dishes or get off the telephone when you didn't want to."

"For one, I don't need your apologies. I've had to learn to do for myself. Two, Dooney hadn't been a *boy* since I can remember. Three, I didn't mind doing the dishes. What pissed me off was the way you spent all of your free time with that punk boyfriend of yours. Sting was weak, I could see that back then, but all you could see was him. Four, I stayed on the phone because me and my friends talked about what was going on with us, what we were going through, and how to work with it. I don't like to dwell on the past, but it's worth discussing since you brought it up. You might not remember how I would come into your room in the evenings to sit up under you and share what was going on in my world with *my mama*, then Sting would call or come over and squash all of that. You pushed me aside and Dooney too, for a man, Billie! You played us cheap, for the same one who turned you in. Now ain't that grand." A few moments passed before either of the women made eye contact. Both of them sat there, quiet and torn. Eventually, Dior grunted to clear her throat. "Look, I didn't come to hurt you and get into all of what didn't go right before you were sent up. You are my mother and I don't want to lose you a second time. Your bid is almost up. You deserve to have something decent to come home to. I'd like that to be a tight friendship with me."

Suddenly Billie's eyes rose to meet Dior's. She'd learned to shield her emotions from others for so long it had become second nature, but hiding what she felt was impossible then. Billie's bottom lip trembled as she opened her mouth to speak. "Maybe when I get out of here, I could make some things up to you as a good friend. I'd like to try." A tear ran down her cheek as she slid her hand across the iron table to touch Dior's. "Shoot, I'd probably find a way to mess that up too." As her fingertips inched nearer to her child's hand, Billie prayed the guards wouldn't step in but for once look the other way. When she felt Dior's soft, warm skin, she shuddered uncontrollably.

"No, ma'am, we can't let that happen, not again." Dior drew in a deep breath then shot a paralyzing glare at the officer who appeared to be a hairbreadth from ending their tender moment. Since he'd watched their tumultuous exchange closer than the others, she was certain he understood how important it was to allow concessions for Billie, if only for that minute in time. Dior held her intense stare on the guard until he looked away. "It's okay, Billie Rae. You and me are going to be alright. You'll see."

Dior exited the visitor's section of Azalea Springs the same way she'd arrived, shaken and stirred. While walking to the parking lot in front of the registration hall, she contemplated the need for prisons, the need to incarcerate those who had transgressed beyond the acceptable limits of immorality. Prisons were instituted to protect the law-abiding from the miscreants of society. Imprisoning the prisoners' families was simply a by-product, she reasoned, sometimes more destructive than the crimes they committed.

After a long cry in the safe confines of her preowned 3-Series BMW convertible, Dior wiped her eyes with a tissue, then pulled out of the gravel lot onto the dusty farm road. Within minutes, she'd put this trip behind her like all the others. She was thankful for the broad leap she made with Billie in building their relationship. After an hour of quiet reflection along the interstate, Dior would be back to the reality she'd worked hard at creating for herself: a decent living in Dallas.

# TWO

## Midday Diva

At eleven o'clock, Dior strolled into the entrance at Hills Peak Mall, where she'd been employed for the better part of a year. Coming in on Fridays often put a smile on her face. Her boss always arrived with a pay envelope stuffed with her nontaxable commissions from the week before. She loved selling fine clothing at Giorgio's, a high-priced men's boutique owned by a charismatic Italian almost twice her age. They shared an understanding on and off the clock. During business hours, Dior lured in male customers by the droves and then charmed them into parting with their money while spending casual time with her. And twice a week, Giorgio carved out niches of her private time for himself. Typically, Dior prepared something light for dinner then served him a hot dessert afterward, on her satin sheets. The arrangement met both of their needs — his for the attention of a young, desirable woman and hers to rack up as much undeclared income as possible. Giorgio Torricelli fit Dior's objectives like a glove accentuated with diamond studs. Not only was he wealthy, he was distinguished, thoughtful, and uninhibited in the sack.

Making her way past corridors of recently decorated windows boasting after-Easter sales placards, Dior was surprised to find the clothing shop nearly void of customers. Suza Esquival, a tall Latina with long legs and a rather despicable loathing for men with children, organized dress shirts on top of a folding table near the back of the store. She glanced up when she heard Dior's heels clicking against the hardwood flooring. "Hey, girl," she squealed excitedly. "I knew that suit would be banging once you had it chopped and screwed."

Dior stopped in midstride to strike a pose. "Yeah, I'm rockin' it. Uh-uh-uh," she moaned jokingly, while popping her hips side to side for effect. "A little bit of this and a little bit of that."

"Why, 'cause this is where it's at," Suza sang, girl-from-the-hood style.

"Ahh, look at Suza. It's got to be payday or else I wouldn't be getting two words out of you."

"Yeah, Chica, I don't do *chatty* when I'm broke. Good thing Giorgio came by and dropped off the paper early. I'm cashing my check during lunch." Suza quickly resumed her task of sorting expensive long-sleeve button-down shirts so she'd be completely finished with the shipment when her break rolled around at three o'clock.

"He already came through, huh?" Dior queried. "Did he say if he would be coming back?"

"He might have but I stopped listening once I got my pay envelope." Suza placed her left hand on her narrow hip and held out her right one. "You think I'll have time for a mini-manicure too? Monty, that cute guy from Sports Galore, wants to take me out."

Dior analyzed the situation thoughtfully before answering. "I'd say yes to nails but no to nuts. That fool from upstairs is nasty. He's got three or four chicks pregnant at the same time and they all work for the Gap. I'd bet all hell breaks loose every time they have a benefits meeting. Unless you plan on helping him start a basketball team, Suza, just say no to janky playas, wannabe-ballers, and dudes who don't lay down with the latex. He's looking to buy four of everything as it is: four blankets, four bottles, and a gang of bassinets. There's no way he can sell enough sneakers, hats, and throwbacks to support that many kids. He should've knocked up some sistahs from the Baby Gap instead. He could use the discount."

"He was kicking it with that stuck-up girl from the fragrance counter at Macy's who we can't stand. And she just had twins," Suza remembered. "You saved me, girl. Uh-huh, see, he is nasty."

"Told you."

Dior left her bewildered associate alone to sort out her next move in the dating pool that mall employees dabbled in on the regular. The main reason Dior refused to overindulge in it herself was purely financial. Although there were hundreds of eligible men just around the corner if she broadened her scope, it was common knowledge that most of those who punched a clock at the mall couldn't afford her. The few men whose pockets were deep enough didn't set Dior on fire like Giorgio. In addition to a charming personality and a laid-back style, he had pockets deep enough to swim in. Dior loved stripping down to nothing for an occasional skinny-dip.

In the manager's office, Dior set her purse on the desk. She flipped on the small clock radio. Tangerine "The Midday Diva" had just begun her daily broadcast from the hip-hop station located inside the mall. "Thank God it's Friday, y'all, 'cause I needs my check," a lively voice proclaimed through the speakers, with a bumping bass beat in the background. "Money ain't a thing until you're broke," Tangie joked.

Dior nodded her head assuredly. "I feel you, Tangie, a girl's gotta get that paper." She hummed along with the music as she thumbed through the pay envelopes for the one with her name written on it. "Ooh yeah, there you are," she said, after locating it. "Come to mama and say ahhh." Dior wasted no time ripping it open. "Thirteen, fourteen, fifteen, and sixteen hundred," she counted, before quickly returning the bills to the envelope. Her grin was accompanied by a musical sigh. By Dior's calculations, Giorgio had padded her commission payout by three hundred bucks. "Oomph, I like surprises. Extra cheddar does a body good. Money ain't a thing *today*."

"Cool, then it won't be no thing for you to slide your rent money over this way," commented Dior's twin brother, Dooney, from the office doorway. When her grin fell flat, he shook his head. "Now tell me, why is it that paying your own way puts that stank look on your face?" Dooney was tall and on the thin side of sexy. He wore his hair close to the bone and neat, like his ever-present starched jeans and pressed shirts. His eyes were almond-shaped and covered by dark, perfect brows. Dooney was a bad boy, street educated and slick. His skin was smooth and a perfect match for his sister's. Dior was quickly reminded how women found him attractive when she noticed Suza had passed by the door behind him more than once to steal candid glances. She'd commented weeks ago how she wanted the hookup, starting with a subtle introduction praising her, of course. Dior wouldn't think of getting Suza in over her head. If Dooney was going to do his dirt, Dior didn't want it to backfire then blow up in her face once he'd gotten bored. And Dooney was easily bored, especially where a sure thing was concerned. Oblivious to the heat rising behind him, he sat three large white shopping bags on the floor in order to retrieve the money from Dior's clutched fist. Her arm was extended but wasn't in the least bit anxious to part with six hundred dollars, not even for her three-bedroom brick home in a quiet neighborhood.

"Come on, Dooney, can't you just ease up for one month?" she whined. "Could I at least hold on to it for a minute? I mean, for real." Dior's impish grin returned slowly as the wheels inside her head spun faster. "What if I told you I'd be a few days late with the cash?"

He chuckled and then smirked at Dior's failed attempt to get over on him. "Then I'd have to tell you how quick your behind would be out of my rental property by the end of the week."

Dior turned up her nose rudely. "You'd toss your own sister out on the street?"

"Yeah, and her stuff out on the curb," he answered in an unwavering manner that she'd seen before. "Stop playing, girl, and hand over the rent. And anyway, you ought to be glad I'm not charging you for painting every room in that house a different color. You got no idea how hard it's gonna be to fix it."

"I don't care. You won't have to worry about fixing anything. I'm in love with that house and it loves me back. I'm not planning on leaving it until I'm ready to get married and upgrade to a mansion."

"Well, until that happens, *Spinderella*, you need to have my money on time, every month. I got a mile-long waiting list of single sistahs begging to get up in there."

"You can take that list and your tired threats back to where you came from," she pouted. "If you keep on, I'm telling Billie Rae how you do me."

"Whaaat, you're going to see her again? When?"

"I was up there this morning. She looks pretty good, I guess. Age is starting to set in, though, around the eyes mostly. She was upbeat and all about you. Dooney is this and oh how I love me some Dooney," she teased.

"That's because I've been going to Azalea Springs to look in on Mama for years. You don't get that kinda love for putting in just three funky visits."

"Five, I've been to see her five times," Dior proudly corrected him. "Anyway, I've got to get my stuff together before she gets out. After all this time, not knowing how to feel about Billie being gone, I'm scared she'll come home trying to clown me because I don't have it going on like you." Dior shook her head slowly in retrospect. "There was a time I didn't give a flip what she thought."

"Then you grew up. Congratulations. You finally came around to thinking about somebody other than Dior. About time. Now pay your monthly living expenses before I have to call the county constable on that...you gonna fool around and make me cuss."

"Dooney, you still have a buck-o-five from the first buck you ever made with your tight behind. Why do you need my measly six hundred dollars?"

"Six bills ain't nowhere near measly," he argued, as his voice raised one octave. "And, since when did needing it have anything to do with getting what's mine? Stop stalling and give it up." Dior held on to the money tightly before he pried it from her hand. "Now that we've got business out of the way, let's talk up on some pleasure. I hear you jamming to your girl's show on the radio. When are you gonna put me down with the Midday Deejay?"

"That's *Midday Diva*, and why would I do that?"

"It won't hurt you to tell Tangy I'm trying to get at her."

"See, uh-uh. Her name is Tangie. Tangie, get it right. And every time I try to be nice and set you up with one of my friends, that's one less friend I have after you bang and bounce."

"Don't blame me when they fall for the Doo-Doo. I can't help it that I get down like that."

"You know what, you're right. I don't blame you. I blame me and I'm tired of doing it. Looks like you've got enough going on as it is." Dior sneered at the large bags from Sports Galore. "All of that gear can't be just for you so don't lie and say it is."

"Most of it is for me," Dooney admitted awkwardly. "Okay, some of it. I was upstairs scouting for some new kicks when this cat named Monty started making deals and busting his tail to lay it out for me. I got mad respect for any dude who works a legit hustle like a rented mule. Everybody's gotta make ends meet."

"You bought all that from Monty? He'd have to sell you one of everything in the store just to make a dent in his debt. This reminds me, you need to go so I can start working on a way to recoup my six bills." Dior shoved her brother playfully, stepped out of the office, then closed the door behind her. "Go on now. I have to get up front and move some product."

He lagged behind when a line of velvet jackets caught his eye. "Hold on, Dior. When are these going on sale? I digs this pinstripe."

"Sale? Never," she hissed impatiently.

"Never-ever?"

"And, ever-never. How many times I got to tell you: Giorgio doesn't do sales. He's convinced that it sets a bad example. We'd have too many people rolling up and through here waiting on markdowns. In case you haven't noticed, this is a top-dollar boutique. Those who can afford it, purchase. Those who can't hate on those who can." She held up five fingers as a challenge to his well-known miserly ways. Surprisingly, Dooney reached into his pocket and came out with Dior's rent money after cursing under his breath. He reeled off three bills then waved the money in her face.

"This ought to do it. Let me try on a forty-six long."

"Don't trip. I do this for a living. Your chest is barely a forty-four." Dior snatched three hundred dollars from his hand before he had a chance to change his mind. She pocketed it and then started off in the opposite direction. "I should have charged you full price. Stay here and I'll pull your size from the front display."

"I'm coming with you. Let me get my bags. Hey, Dior, I want a receipt!"

Dior understood the art of selling. She sold her brother, like she had so many other customers. She would interest them in pricey attire then immediately pound their unsuspecting egos by using phrases such as, "It's nice but *expensive*. And, it costs to look that good." At times, Dior charmed men into believing a lofty price tag was a direct correlation to gaining her approval, whether they thought private time with her was included with their purchase or not.

# THREE

## *He Wants Some*

At five thirty that evening, Tangerine called Dior's cell phone to see what plans, if any, she had for barhopping later that night. "Hey, Tangie," Dior said hurriedly. "Can I get back at you in a minute? I'm on the grind."

"Do your thing. I'll come by when I sign off the air."

"Cool, I've got something to tell you. See you then."

Dior attended to several customers at once while Suza chatted with two men in their mid-twenties, both seemingly more interested in bagging her than the items they pretended to shop for. Seeing as how she'd made a bank deposit during her break, Suza was quite comfortable flirting casually while Dior racked up one sale after the next. Dior's business savvy extended far beyond merely suggesting apparel and accessories; she could give a customer the five-second once-over then correctly guess his pants, shirt, jacket, and shoe sizes. She became the top salesperson after having been at the store three months. She also took every opportunity to learn from the tenured professionals who made a substantial living by providing quality customer service. Practically overnight, she'd acquired meaningful tools of the trade. Using her sensuality to close the deal came naturally.

"Hello, I'm Dior," she said, extending her polished nails to a large older gentleman who appeared to be lost among the athletic-cut Magic Johnson line of business suits. "How are you today?" she added with a perfect smile, although he was too busy to shake her hand. Dior was careful not to push, which was one of the first lessons she had learned. If a customer had the inclination to shop there, he should always be treated like a guest rather than a potential commission. She knew that money often followed a honey-sweet disposition.

"I don't think either of these suits will fit me," the clean-shaven man with smoke-brown skin grunted disappointedly. He continued to sort through them again even though he'd previously examined them thoroughly. His wide behind waddled side to side as he tugged feverishly on lapels to continue his hunt. "It's a shame too," he said softly. "I like this vented look. It takes me back thirty-five years. I'd just come home from Vietnam and…" he started to say before realizing the pretty saleslady was too young to appreciate his postwar rants. "Ah, forget it. Macy's is likely to have something that'll agree with me, but I was hoping for a snazzier cut."

"So you're going to give up that easy?" she asked, with a slight head tilt. "How can an ex-Nam vet like yourself quit at the first sign of frustration? You had to deal with a lot when you returned home, but you didn't quit. I'm sure you must've felt unappreciated and undervalued too." The customer stared down his nose at Dior, undoubtedly trying to understand what was happening and how the young lady seemed to know what she was talking about. "Yes, vented-styled suit coats were very popular in the seventies."

"Where'd you learn that?" he queried, like a proud granddad

seeing a small child color within the lines for the first time. "You couldn't have been a gleam in your father's eye back then."

"No, sir, my granddaddy went over there. He didn't make it back though," she informed him. "He'd be about your age now if he had." Dior's story was true and she'd used it to perfection with men in their sixties. When the aging man's cheeks began to round out, she fired up her mental calculator.

"Y'all got anything in this hoity-toity shop big enough for an old army mule like me?" he asked, showing each and every one of his teeth.

"Your name is?" she said, behind an air of confidence the customer liked.

"Dabnis, Dabnis Keith." Finally he offered his hand to Dior after completing their formal introduction.

"Dabnis, that's an unusual name," she remarked, while walking a small circle around him. "It's Sinbad spelled backward."

"Yes, yes it is," he marveled. "That's the first time in my entire life anyone outside of my family made mention of that. People don't want to take the time to notice things, these days." He continued to stand in the middle of the floor while Dior made mental notes and assessments here and there.

"It's my job to notice things that matter and ease frustrations when I can. Mr. Dabnis Keith, I've noticed that you don't mind spending money for quality and that's good because I'm about to show you something that will make your day. If you don't mind, follow me." Dior led the customer to a cushy love seat then asked him to take a load off. She intended on facilitating his happiness while making it look easy. "Your waist is a forty-eight and your chest is fifty-two. Most suits have a two-inch variance between the pants and jacket. That's when it pays to know a few tricks of the trade." She used a metal rod, bent at the end, to wrangle coat hangers from a tall display. Mr. Keith watched anxiously.

"Wow, you can tell all that about me just from looking? You don't need a tape measure or nothing?" Dior decided to let the outfit she'd selected speak for her.

"Slip this on for me," she said, holding out a fetching blazer. Mr. Keith shrugged it on and buttoned it closed. Dior looked on as he gazed at himself in the full mirror, admiring the cut and fabric. He appeared even more impressed with the fit. "That's a very distinguished look, isn't it?"

"Oh yeah, I look at least twenty years younger too."

"That's the idea," Dior asserted. "While it doesn't have the vented style you came in for, not everything is like it used to be thirty-five years ago." He watched her eyes drift toward his broad waist.

Chuckling softly, he nodded his agreement. "True, true. Maybe vents have passed me by. Where can I try on the pants?"

"The fitting room awaits. These slacks are fifties but on the inside are retractable bands to adjust the size. Now go on in there, get duded up, and then step out and let me see when you're done," she demanded playfully. Five minutes later, Mr. Keith strode out of the fitting room with his chest stuck out. Dior noted how he cradled his wallet in the palm of his hand as she circled him like before. "Wow, I like it," she offered profoundly. "It's perfect, Mr. Keith."

"You definitely know your business. Can't I get another one, in black?"

"Well, you do know, it does cost to look that good. But I'm sure you can afford to."

"Young lady, I have more money than I have suits that fit like this. I'll take one of each color. Can you arrange for alterations? I like a one-inch cuff with a slight break over my shoes."

"Yes, sir. I can put our tailor on it this weekend. Is Tuesday morning okay with you?" When he smiled agreeably, she followed suit. "Good. All five suits will be ready for pickup. And, because you were such a joy to do business with, your alterations are on me." Numbers were doing cartwheels in her head now. Dior managed to outfit a customer who had difficult dimensions to satisfy, and eased him into springing for five suits, two hats, and a boxful of neckties. Mr. Dabnis Keith strolled out of Giorgio's with his head held high and a receipt for twenty-eight hundred dollars in his pocket. Dior's commission, at twenty-five percent, totaled seven hundred dollars. In the time it took to make her last customer feel a little better about himself, she'd amassed next month's rent. Dior wished there were more men like Mr. Keith, those with more money than fine clothing and a healthy inclination to do something about it.

Suza was still fiddling with a piece of paper at the register when Dior returned from the ladies' room at the rear of the store. "Hey, what's that? You've been massaging it since those dudes left."

"I got a guy's phone number," she replied in a deflated tone.

"It looked like y'all kicked it off pretty good to me. All I saw was smiling and laughing the whole time."

"I was about to give my digits to the really cute one but then his friend took it and handed me this," she explained. "I'm wondering if I should throw it out or call him and ask for the other guy's number."

Dior frowned. "No…if his homeboy was feeling you too, he'll make it known. That is, if he's a real man. Let it ride, Suza, let it ride." Suza continued playing with the slip of paper. Dior couldn't stand the sight of a woman beating herself up over a man who wasn't hers so she decided to restock the suits she'd previously pulled down for Mr. Keith.

"Dior, please keep an eye on the front," said Suza, as she marched toward the manager's office. "I'm going to call and fix this right now."

"But it ain't broke yet." Dior counted her associate's actions as a mistake from the word go. She considered racing into the office and wrestling the phone from Suza's clammy mitts. Had it not been for a handsome customer sorting through the neckwear, she might have followed through on it. "Hello, I'm Dior," she announced to the stranger. "How are you today?"

"I'm doing fine, thanks for asking," he replied with a raised brow. "I'm Richard." He gazed at Dior in an odd sort of way while shaking her soft hand. "It's not often you get such courteous service these days. It's refreshing."

"Well, thank you, Richard," Dior replied. She began sizing him up within seconds, like she'd been taught, then she suddenly suppressed the smile trying to climb through her lips. Richard's choice of words intrigued her so she studied him closer than she typically would have. He was a nut-colored man, seemed to be in his early forties, and no taller than six feet but pretty close to it. He appeared to be the professional type, with a tapered haircut, clean shaven face, and nice teeth. Richard's modest brown leather loafers, khakis, and purple short-sleeve golf shirt didn't say much about him though, other than he wasn't one to flash when away from the office. His pleasant demeanor was his best asset as far as she could tell. Then she let her assessment teeter in midair. "What can I assist you with, Richard?" she offered finally.

"I haven't shopped here before and my wife normally puts something together for me when special occasions arise. She was tied up, so here I am."

*Your wife dresses you?* she thought, while laughing to herself. *He has no clue how weak that makes him look.* "Uh, are we expecting your wife to show up and pick out an after-Easter suit?" *Oops, did I say that aloud?* The perturbed expression on Richard's face confirmed that she had.

"Beg your pardon?"

"I'm sorry, I was thinking aloud when I shouldn't have," she said, hoping to calm the waters. "Let me rephrase that. Did Mrs. Richard suggest something in a specific color? Is there a particular designer label she likes to *dress you in*—I mean, see on you?"

Richard peered at the floor for a moment, gathering his thoughts. "There must be a misunderstanding. When I came in, there was this rather enjoyable saleslady. She greeted me. She smiled and even introduced herself. Where is she, the one who wouldn't think of insulting a customer?"

*He's funny. I like that,* Dior thought. *And, he can take a joke. Not bad.* She tossed him a hard smirk while locking eyes with his. When he didn't look away, she broke stride. "Hold on, I'll see if I can find her." In a feigned huff, she spun on her heels and took three hard steps toward the rear of the store before sauntering back with an overripe grin. "Mr. Richard, how nice it is to see you again. What can we, at Giorgio's Men's Boutique, do for you today?" The fake smile she brandished hit Richard in a bad spot, his head.

"Now that's the person I wouldn't mind doing business with." He fought off a chuckle when the time came for him to retrace his steps as well. "I have a dilemma. Next month, we're having a pastor's day celebration at the church and I'm typically too busy to shop for myself. However," he added, with a stern glare that insinuated Dior should probably watch herself, "I'm hoping to see a piece or two that catches my eye."

"That was a lot better," she whispered, loud enough to be heard clearly.

Richard found himself admiring the young woman's spunk although he could have done without her inferences to his being spoiled by a doting wife.

Dior wasn't certain how long Richard would continue to play her game so she straightened up, in the event he did have a permission slip from wifey to make his own purchases. "I see you're drawn to the tie rack. If you own a suit that you'd like to accessorize…also, for the special occasion, we have a broad selection of woven shirts, and a wide assortment of French cuffs and cuff links. Tell me what you have in mind and then we can get started." Dior had made the same spiel so many times, it came off effortlessly.

"I'm really not sure, but I'll know when I see it," he answered in a hesitant tone. He followed her footsteps as she gave him a tour of the store, pointed out several mid-ranged garments, and then explained how dressing well could be costly but always worth every penny if a man's wardrobe adequately portrayed his inner man. "Inner man?" he said, as if asking what she knew about that.

"Yeah, some fellas wear nice clothes that are all wrong for them. Some of my best customers are ballplayers and entertainers. When they first came to me, they were put together like somebody had laid out their school clothes." She smirked briefly to get another dig in at Richard's expense. "I don't see the man as he is but as he could be," she added finally.

"That's deep, spiritual. You learn that in church?"

"Uh-uh, I really don't *do* church. I tried to get my sins washed away once, didn't work. In too deep, I guess."

"If you need God to help you," he said, before Dior slammed that door shut.

"Whoa, Deacon Do-Good! Let's get one thing straight: I will not come to your job trying to do mine and I'd appreciate it if you afford me the same respect. Nothing against you or *the Lawd*," she mocked, "but I got my own ministry. I call it 'paying bills on time.' Standing still for sermonettes ain't even my size. Uh-uh, they don't even fit me." Dior exhaled in a slow deliberate manner in an effort to catch her breath. If she happened to lose Richard's business, then so be it, but she refused to be preached at.

Richard stared at Dior, then he sighed deeply as well. He was taken aback and there was no use trying to pretend he hadn't been floored by her frankness and honesty. For far too long, members of the church's staff and the congregation had walked on eggshells around him, even when they knew he was wrong. Dior said her peace and stood her ground. Richard admired both qualities. He also noticed how her grammar and diction slid when rattled. *In a man's anger, his true identity is revealed*, he thought. Was she a ghetto-girl playing dress up? he wondered. The longer he stood there, reasoning with their incidental meeting, it became apparent to him that this young saleslady had more to offer than expensive suits and overpriced fashion accessories. She was likely a hard case, the toughest soul to win. Dior had undoubtedly been torn by hurtful past experiences. Otherwise, she wouldn't have shut him down so readily. Richard kept that in mind when deciding on how to proceed with their incidental meeting. "While I'm not accustomed to getting heckled like that, you're correct. Although He is everywhere, I should respect your workplace and I do. As the ballplayers say, no harm, no foul. I guess I'd better get back to the reason I came in?"

"Then we could both get blessed," she answered politely, as if there hadn't been a peculiar strand of tension pulling them every which way. Dior judged by the colors and patterns of the ties Richard chose that he was a conservative dresser—solids and stripes down the line. He didn't look twice at the vibrant paisley prints or the funky designs other church leaders clamored for. Once she had a sound idea of what moved him, she began to imagine him in a jazzy sports coat outside of what he was likely to have considered traditional. "Ultraconservative taste," she said, placing the pieces he'd agreed to buy on the counter.

"Hmm, when was the last time you treated yourself to a new sports coat or one of these?" She pulled an athletic-styled suit down off the rack, the same one she had to talk Mr. Keith out of because of his exaggerated girth. "Here's a limited edition; it's new. Feel the softness. It comes in three and four buttons with the vented jacket."

Richard grinned heartily. "I heard these were making a comeback. In the seventies, my father used to look sharp as a tack when he popped the vents. Yeah, let me try it out."

Though she could assess Richard's physical dimensions from head to toe from a distance, Dior didn't let that get in the way of taking the scenic route. "This particular line runs kinda big. I'll need to see where you stand first." She chased down Suza for a tape measure, then made it appear business as usual when she stood behind Richard and gently wrapped the tape around his midsection. He felt her warm breath flow through him but ignored it as best he could. Next, Dior bent over in front of him to measure his inseam. Richard squirmed uneasily the second she placed the tape near his crotch. "Stop wiggling," she jested. "I swear, sometimes the only thing standing between men and lil' boys is a driver's license." Richard relaxed enough to laugh. Dior started to pour it on thick, then suddenly she paused. *I felt something move. Was that lil' Richard flapping around?*

*Lord, I hope she didn't feel my businessman move,* he prayed silently. Richard was afraid to breathe, much less look down. Foolishly he allowed his eyes to see what his manhood sensed: an attractive woman with her face dangerously close to it. "O-okay," he stammered nervously. "That ought to be about it, right?"

*That's all right in my book.* "Uh, yes," she uttered softly. "I'm almost finished." Dior knew she was wrong for the stunt she pulled next. The second time he allowed curiosity to get the best of him. Dior's eyes were staring up at his. "Yep, I found what I needed."

Richard exhaled after she headed for the checkout counter. He felt bad about his untimely arousal, secretly enjoying her arms around his waist, her fingers near his erogenous zone. Dior apologized for going off earlier, citing her inability to accept someone's opinion of what she needed. Richard said he understood where she was coming from then let it go. He presented his credit card for the suit and neckties, spoke as few words as possible before signing for his purchase, and then he nodded goodbye without actually saying it. Dior watched him walk toward the exit. She was willing to bet a full month's pay that he'd turn for one lasting glimpse, one stolen glance to take with him.

"Come on, Richard," she sang quietly. "We both know you want to. Turn around, turn around. Don't pass it up. You'll hate yourself if you do." Her face cracked and hit the floor when he made it to the exit without slowing his pace. As soon as Dior began to fill out the appropriate paperwork for his alterations, Richard's head turned slowly. She was right about him after all. He couldn't pass on the opportunity to capture her image in his mind. Unwittingly, Richard just made his first wrong move.

# FOUR

## *Beans and Corn Bread*

Tangerine Green was almost thirty, a smidge taller than Dior, with supple breasts and curvy hips. Long auburn curls framed her oval-shaped face. Proud of her biracial heritage, Tangie often wore fitted jeans and blouses with intricate Asian prints. Her large round slanted eyes and a tiny beauty mark above her lip on the left side were very appealing. A self-proclaimed dime piece from the south side of Dallas, she had a smooth-talking style that made her a radio celebrity. Tangie whirled into Giorgio's, looking back over her shoulder. She was dressed in tight denim jeans and a T-shirt with a picture of Yoko Ono stretched across her chest. "Dior, was that Pastor Dr. Richard Allamay, PhD, coming out of this shop?" she howled, with both feet motoring nearly as fast as her mouth.

Dior shrugged her shoulders. "Don't ask me. I'm wrapping up this sale for a dude named Richard Somebody. Let's see, he did sign this Platinum American Express card. 'Richard Allamay,'" she read. "Yeah, I guess that was him." Dior filed his paperwork away nonchalantly. "I'm glad you came by because I talked Suza into pulling a close for me. Let me get my bag."

"You gon' get your bag?" Tangie repeated in a ridiculously nasal tone.

"What?" Dior asked. "I'm not leaving it here."

"You don't have any clue who Pastor Dr. Richard Allamay, PhD, is, do you?"

"No, but you sound like the man's talking résumé. All he said was that he needed to cop some new rags for a pastor's day at some church. I wasn't trying to keep up with his flossin' after he admitted his wife usually bought all of his clothes. Oomph, I started to tell him to sit down and be still until she showed and gave permission to shop on his own."

Tangie was astounded. "You didn't actually say it?"

"Nah, but I played him like a chump," she confessed. "He shouldn't have been up on my job talking about which of my needs God could help me with."

"Are you slow?" Tangie fussed, as Dior opened the office door to retrieve her expensive leather handbag. "He is a man of God."

"And…this is my job," Dior replied in the same "don't you know" tone that baited her. "Why are you trippin'? I apologized to him. We're cool now. He bought a nice suit and a gang of props to set it off. Believe me, ain't no love lost." Dior's demeanor caused her friend to dig deeper.

"I'm just saying, Richard Allamay is the shepherd of Method-ist Episcopal Greater Apostolic Church."

"All that can't be necessary," Dior said, put off by the long title.

"Members call it the M.E.G.A. Church for short. The name says it all. There's a ten-thousand-seat auditorium, day care, a life-center building with fifty-five classrooms, a CD and DVD ministry, two clothing shelters, three restaurant-style kitchens, and a full-length basketball court."

"Whuuut? It sounds more like a small town than a church house."

"That would make it the largest black-owned *church house* in the state. I was a member before they bought the new facility. It grew too wide for me, in size and in drama. You know what they say: more money, more problems. Saving souls is big business in the Bible Belt and Dallas is the buckle."

Dior's mind was doing cartwheels again, and this time she had more than pocket money on her mind. She couldn't imagine how much that M.E.G.A. Church paid Richard but it had to be a pile of money, money she would have access to if she cemented an intimate relationship with him. On second thought, becoming the first lady of a spiritual cash cow wasn't a bad situation to be in either; then she'd have the chance to fulfill her childhood dream of financial independence and the unrivaled envy of a church full of chicks looking up to her.

"It's a good thing you're smart enough to keep your eyes and hands off him. It must be hard shooing off those church-house hoochies and preacher groupies throwing panties into the pulpit after every sermon." When Dior didn't respond, Tangie grew suspicious. "Dior? Dior? Tell me you're not getting stupid ideas about getting next to the pastor? Wicked women ought to leave good Christian men alone. I respect Richard Allamay. He's for real, a dyed-in-the-wool man of God."

"See, there you go again. What's with you and him and God today? I stay out of God's business and I hope He stays out of mine." Tangie bowed her head, crossed her chest, and began praying silently. Dior, annoyed and fed up with all of the Jesus-speak, clenched her teeth then folded her arms. After lifting her bag off the office desk, Dior cut her eyes at Tangie. "That's the last I'm going to be hearing about that kind of hocus-pocus or else I'm going out alone to get my sin on all by myself."

"Wait a minute, Dee," Tangie protested. "Let's not be too hasty. I'm still coming with you. *He* isn't finished with me yet. I need to get my drink on, get my dance on, and my dirty deed done too—that's if I run into anybody I used to know. New booty is too much duty. You know how men start out by sending their representative to put in work, sweet-talk you, and play the perfect-husband-material role, then the dust settles and all you're left with is a pile of what? Dust. That's why I sleep with the devils I already know."

"I'm with you like beans and corn bread on that one," Dior concurred. "You're more likely to see a lie coming at you than having one sneak by and slap you upside the head."

Tangie chuckled as they left the store. "It'll have you whining in a box of tissues if you don't recognize it in time."

"Tissues? Uh-uh, in a bottle of Hennessy," Dior said, laughing as an old memory played fresh in her mind. "Speaking of that, where is the spot tonight? We could head downtown and crash the Ghost Bar lounge or hit the north tollway and bust a left on Belt Line." She grimaced as a lanky man with a light complexion, in his mid-twenties, slowed his stroll when they drew near. "Ahh nah, here comes Monty from that jock's box upstairs. Ignore him and maybe he'll keep on walking."

He rubbed his shaved head, adjusted the black belt on his referee uniform, then cracked an arrogant grin. "Hmm, hmm, hmm," he said, ogling the ladies like a starving man eyeing two steak dinners. "I must be sleepwalking because this is my dream come true." He licked his thick pink lips as if someone told him it was sexy to do so. "Pinch me, please, so I can wake up and do something about this. Two of the finest vixens I ever seen in the same place at the same time. It's a miracle. A miracle!"

Tangie seemed amused by his sophomoric attempt at impressing them. "You're pretty brave to be parading around in public like that. Let one of those Foot Locker crew catch you in a knockoff uniform, they're gonna thump that head."

"Ha-ha, Tangerine. This ain't no knockoff," Monty argued. "Where their stripes are black, ours are white and visa versa. Ain't no conflict. All of that's been worked out in court." When it became obvious that Tangie had no interest in him or his stripes, Monty waggled his tongue again, this time to entice Dior. "How come you haven't called me, Ms. Dior? I've dropped off three business cards with that Latin sistah so you could holla at me." She leveled her best poker face then glanced down at her watch.

"I don't have time for this foolishness," she scoffed. "But I got two grown-up words for you: *child support*. Now deal with it." Tangie cackled in the man's face as Dior tugged on her arm to hasten their getaway.

"That sure is cold, Dior," he replied, with a gaping hole in his ego.

"Latex, Monty," she heckled boldly. "Look it up, strap it on, and keep it tight."

After blasting the mall hound, the ladies decided to stay on the north side. They ventured to a popular restaurant and bar called Café Bleu. It was the place for upscale African American up-and-comers to network with corporate climbers while sifting through those who were merely faking it. The fancy watering hole served as a suitable meet-and-mingle joint overall, despite the ever-present male fraternal orders of Hoochie Hawks and Desperate Dorks. *How they kept getting in?* vexed Dior. Tangie was too busy laughing at one man's miserable rejection after the next. She almost fell out of her chair when an overconfident snake approached their table with a bottle of Cristal and three glasses dangling from his nimble fingers. He came within two feet before Dior stuck her palm out like a cranky crossing guard. "Uh-uh, don't," she told him, in no uncertain terms. "We're waiting on someone and you're not him. Sorry." After he tucked tail and turned about-face, Tangie questioned her decision.

"That was a full bottle of Cristal, Dior, a full bottle!"

"He was full of something too. He probably doesn't remember me but about a year or so ago he picked me up for a movie in his brand-new Escalade."

"And?"

"And, the inside of his whip smelled *exactly* like the outside of a woman's behind."

"Ewwh!"

"Exactly."

Tangerine spotted the same guy making another run at two unsuspecting ladies four tables away. She imagined how his SUV must have come to reek as Dior proclaimed it did. "Ewwh-ewwh. That's like three kinds of nasty."

"Told you."

During the next hour, waitresses delivered drinks from a litany of men who witnessed Dior send the first challenger away with the quickness. Neither of them had the gall to follow in his footsteps nor subsequently be shut down without getting a decent shot. Tangie sipped from the assortment of concoctions until she felt a nice buzz easing on. Dior nursed a fruity drink while swaying in her seat to the music, oblivious to the gathering of men downing liquid courage. She watched Tangie flirt with several of the onlookers in the crowded den, daring them to come over and try their luck. It was a game they played on occasion. Tired of being approached by weaklings who lacked the intestinal fortitude to stave off their rejection with a healthy dose of determination, Dior and Tangie held out for real men: alpha males with guts. So far, not one of them stood out from the pack.

"It's thick up in here," Tangie asserted. "Slim pickings though. You want to hit the Ghost?" She watched as her companion gazed over the flock, disinterested and subdued. Suddenly, the club deejay fired up a tune that moved Dior.

"Come on, Tangie, let's hit the floor. 'Soul Brotha' used to be my jam. I love me some Angie Stone." She abandoned the drinks then marched through the maze of people with her friend in tow. "There's room over there," she yelled over the music. All at once, several of the men who previously sponsored their cocktails darted toward the dance floor. The boldest among them won out, as usual. The less assertive were forced to hunt in shallower waters.

Three songs later, Tangie exited the hardwood with the best dancer of the bunch. Dior went to the restroom to refresh her makeup and primp her hair. When she returned to the table, Tangie handed her a business card with a man's name, driver's license number, and home address handwritten on the opposite side from his business information. Dior flicked the card with her finger as she scanned the night lounge. "Ooh, get it, girl," she cackled. "Is this the dude from the dance floor?"

Tangie took a sip from a glass of wine. "Nope, turned out he was undercover. His boyfriend called him out then snatched his hand away from mine. I thought you saw it."

"Okay, it's time to go," Dior griped affirmatively. She held up the business card to read the name on the front of it. "Then who's Tyson Sharp?"

"Somebody I used to know. Here he comes." Tangie slid off the tall chair to welcome him back. "Tyson Sharp, this is my girl Dior Wicker." Dior was impressed. Tyson smelled nice, fresh, and clean. His clothes hung in all the right places too. She was sorry not to have bagged him first. However, he did have history with Tangie so that rendered him off-limits regardless.

"Tyson Sharp," Dior said, holding the card up to her eyes. "You can take my friend home as long as you understand I got your office and home address."

"Yeah, what's with Tangerine taking down my information and why are you holding it?" he queried suspiciously.

Dior sneered at Tangie, who quickly turned her head away. "Uh-huh, I figured you'd have me break it to him. Okay, it goes like this: I'll hold the info until I hear from Tangerine tomorrow. It's insurance, which ensures you don't get her alone and start to trippin' or hackin' her up and then dispose of the body. If she doesn't call me, I'll know where to send our friends to bust you up." Tyson smiled uncomfortably. Dior failed to see the humor in it. "Oh, believe me, there won't be anything to laugh about if she doesn't reach me by noon. Something bad happens to her, the same happens to you. Y'all have a good night. Nice to meet you, Tyson."

Initially, he didn't move when Tangie yanked on him. "What? You scared?" she asked boldly.

"You kidding? Your friend threatened me without batting an eye. That's straight-up Soprano-style."

Dior cocked her head to the side. "Go on and put your best foot forward then. Don't get stupid and you won't get hurt. It is that simple."

Tyson chuckled more easily than before. "Dior, don't stress. You have my word."

"Better than that, I have your info."

"That's cool too." He planted a warm kiss on Tangie's cheek to cement the deal. "I'll take care of Tangerine. I always have in the past."

"Good, that sounds like a plan." As soon as they started for the exit, Tangie waved goodbye. Dior was glad that Tangie netted a nice catch, of whom she caught an extra glimpse. "Ooh-wee, that man is slap-your-mama fine." She raised her fruity drink in celebration. "Here's to sleeping with the devils you know."

# FIVE

## *TV Talking*

Sunday morning tipped in quietly, swiping Dior's last waning moments of sleep. She groaned sorely as rays of sun penetrated through the venetian blinds in her bedroom. She raised her head just enough to read the alarm clock on the nightstand. *It's six thirty. I can't get with this,* she thought. *I'll get up at eight.* She rustled beneath the covers with hopes of drifting off again. Something weighed on Dior, keeping her from the restful sleep she craved. That very annoying something had been on her mind from the very moment Tangie laid out Pastor Dr. Richard Allamay's pedigree and highly touted ministry. Fading in and out of consciousness, Dior replayed meeting him and the rough time she'd put the poor man through. All in all, he stood up for himself fairly well, for a grown-up with what she concluded had to be an overbearing wife.

Thirty minutes into a peaceful dream, where all of Dior's bills were paid on time, the alarm clock blared. Dior slapped at it violently to shut it off but her errant swats at the snooze button sent the digital clock plummeting to the floor. "Uhhh!" she screamed. "I'm still sleepy." Bitterly irritated, she threw the covers back. After shutting off the noise, she sat on the edge of the bed in a pair of athletic shorts and a tank top with the message I LIKE BOYS TOO stenciled on the front. She rubbed her tired eyes, stretched and arched her back, then stumbled into the bathroom. One peek at herself in the mirror made her wince. Dior hurriedly washed her face and brushed her teeth. She collected a notebook, two ink pens, and a Bible. Then she threw on a sheer robe and poured herself a glass of orange juice. Once she'd warded off the notion of crawling back beneath the sheets, she yawned. *Come on, Dior,* she heard herself say aloud. *Pull yourself together, sugar, it's time for church.*

After finding a comfy spot on the sofa, she clicked the TV remote. It took less than a minute to locate the Christian broadcast Tangie told her about. Typically, Dior avoided "Church TV" and held little regard for those who watched it religiously. However, that was before she had a personal interest in how it worked and how much money was associated with high ratings of a successful show. *High Praise* with Pastor Richard Allamay must have been doing well, if a full auditorium was any indication. Dior listened to a mass choir chant "So beautiful His love" in an uplifting song that didn't sound all that bad.

When the cameras panned the audience during the applause and amens, Dior's eyes glistened. "That is one really big church house," she mouthed silently, as if the congregation might hear her if she spoke aloud. She studied the concert-style auditorium, filled with thousands of worshipers and numerous cameramen working hard at capturing the right shots. It was obvious who they all came to see, hear, and praise as the camera zoomed in on a familiar face, Richard's. "Hey, Dr. Pastor Richard What's-his-face," Dior teased, watching him flip pages in a Bible placed on top of a clear podium. She marveled because his Bible appeared twice as thick as the one she rarely cracked, the same one she had to track down that morning. Dior began making notes so she'd have a jump on the conversation when he returned to pick up his suit at the shop. *Lots of people,* she wrote, *lots of needy folk with too much time on their hands. Lots of well-dressed needy folk,* she added. *And, lots of money.* A second look caused her to race toward the television with a pen in hand. She began counting rows and multiplying them in her head. Each time she'd get close to estimating the actual size of the congregation, the camera seemed to flash right back to Richard's mug. *Huh, he doesn't look that bad on TV,* she thought. *Nice suit; blue looks good on him. His makeup is a tad too light though. His wife should have caught that before she sent him out of the house with his lunch and backpack.* She wrote that down as well. *Find wifey in the crowd. Find family,* she jotted as well. *Check them out.* Dior's eyes followed the action as best she could while constructing mental notes to match those she'd written on paper.

Richard wasted no time diving into his sermon. Dior missed the title of the message the first time because it didn't sound important. The way he emphasized it the second time around caught her attention. "That's right, church. *Don't get caught dead in the wrong clothes,*" he proclaimed assertively. Dior put her pen down on the notepad then leaned back into the sofa cushion. His words sounded familiar because he'd borrowed them from her speech to him at Giorgio's. She was in for the long haul then, listening for other references lifted from her sales pitch as he continued. "Now, some of y'all are already thinking of that blessed day of your home going, sisters prepared in fine St. John gowns and brothers dapped in Hugo Boss three-button suits with French cuffs to set it off right. But that's not what I'm talking about this morning. I know we like to look good, dress nice, and so forth, but I'm talking about dressing the spiritual man, the spiritual woman. Listen up, because it's a heaven or hell undertaking. This very day, many of us are proudly sporting somebody else's clothes. We're doing the sort of things that ought not to fit a Christian. We're out there Sunday through Monday carrying on like other folk who we put down time after time for doing the same thing, dressed in the same outfit you do your dirt in. Say amen if you can." There was a loud round of *all right nows* and *tell 'em preachers*. "Oh yeah, we dress the part of a committed Christian by saying the right stuff *while in the Lord's house* although our hearts are saying something altogether different. Nice day, Brotha So-and-so, *with all of them silly women chasing him around*," he mimicked would-be busybodies in the congregation. Laughter resounded in the auditorium as many of the members agreed with the lighthearted rousing. "Sometimes our men are no better. I've overheard some of them speak to a sister in Christ with the utmost respect in her face then tear her down like she was Jezebel as soon as her back is turned. Uh-huh, y'all know I'm right." Again, members shouted their acknowledgment of the truth. "That's why God is interested in how you decide to clothe your inner man." Dior nearly jumped into the television screen.

"Deacon Do-Good! You ripped off my line about the inner man, man. That's my hook," she barked, with a partial smile on her lips. "You're biting my style, Richard. You' bitin'." She settled down when Richard called out book, chapter, and verse to discuss further.

"Those who are prepared with your spiritual swords today please join us at Ephesians, chapter six and starting at verse thirteen." As Richard paused for everyone to find the passage, he looked into the camera. Dior felt a chill scamper down her back. It was as if he were talking directly to her. She sat up and grabbed the Bible, flipping through it vigorously. With frustration mounting, she went to the index to locate the particular book because she didn't have a clue where it was.

"Corinthians, Galatians, Ephesians," she panted anxiously. "I'm almost there. Here it is. Chapter six and verse thirteen." She blew off a layer of dust then followed along in her text as Richard read from his. *"Put on the whole armor of God, that you may be able to stand against the tricks of the devil."* Richard raised his head then patted his face with a white cotton handkerchief.

"Don't nobody know your weakness like the devil. He's got some of us so messed up that we're going out of our way to make our friends think we're too cool to follow Christ. Stop trippin'! Put on the whole armor of Christ. Verse fourteen through eighteen reads, *Stand therefore, having girded your waist with truth, having put on the breastplate of righteousness and having shod your feet with the preparation of the gospel of peace; above all, taking the shield of faith with which you will be able to quench all of the fiery darts of the wicked one. And, take the helmet of salvation and the sword of the Spirit, which is the word of God. Praying always with all prayer and request in the Spirit being watchful to this end with all perseverance for all the saints. Amen.* Who can see that there is a holy war going on in your life every day, for your soul? Paul wrote this letter to the Ephesians a long time ago and it still stands necessary today." Richard closed the Bible and proceeded to engage the audience. He strolled closer to the end of the broad platform covered in plush royal blue carpet. "It's important, church, that we get dressed in the proper spiritual clothing before we leave the house because it's a battle waging on for your eternal life. Wrap your waist in truth, slide on the coat of righteousness, cover your feet with the preparation of the gospel of peace, grab hold to the shield of faith, take the helmet of salvation and your Bible, the sword the spirit, and be watchful!" Richard had the crowd on their feet then but he wouldn't let up. "Be watchful! Be watchful! Fight for your soul, church. Don't let the devil trick you into giving it up, getting too tired, growing too weary, feeling so low that you'd rather hand it over without fighting to the death.

Persevere, church! Stick it out! Grow up! Wake up! Stand up! Stand up! Stand up!" Richard marched up and down the aisles with his hand clutching a microphone. Dior was amazed that hordes of people shouting and wailing like the devil had them and they demanded freedom. It was nothing short of remarkable, the effect his sermon had on them. She reached for the remote control to lower the volume when the choir started in low with another song. Then Richard started in again, with subtle humming in the background. "Church, I love you, but a lot of us have grown up in the Lord and are out there fronting like we haven't come into His knowledge. We don't want our drinking buddies and bed-hopping buddies—yeah I said it, our bed-hopping buddies—to know that we've grown up! Woke up! Got dressed up! Climbed out of the sewer and stood up!" Dior watched the crowd boil over excitedly as Richard shouted with each exclamation. "Uh-huh, don't you know that you're not tricking anyone but instead the devil is fooling you into believing a lie? Listen to me well, friends. If you have grown up, woke up, and have stood up for the Lord then later turned around and tried to hide it, you shame God. And if you are not filling out your spiritual clothes, you ought to be ashamed of yourself. Don't get caught dead in the wrong clothes. Dress your inner man daily with the 'whole armor of God' because the devil is out there and he's prowling, looking for weaklings to devour. Be strong in the Lord, be battle-tested, be watchful, and most of all be faithful in the Lord. Amen."

When Richard returned to the stage, he sat off to the right side in a magnificent chair with a high back and wide armrests. It looked more like a throne than anything else, Dior thought. He had his very own kingdom, she reasoned. His queen couldn't be far off, so she approached the television that exploited the fervor he'd caused. The camera stayed on a woman with a fair complexion seated on the end of the second row in the middle section. Next to her were two girls. Both of them favored Richard. One was clearly a teenager and the other, somewhat younger. Dior scribbled a note to herself. *At least two kids...no boys to speak of. Wifey has seen her better days. She might be tougher than she looks. Bet she ain't tougher than me.* Dior clicked off the television and then paced back and forth in her den like a general on the battlefield. She had been involved with married men before, including her part-time romance with Giorgio. She was also tired of watching other women have it better than she did. Although she experienced less than favorable outcomes when previously taking shortcuts in life, she convinced herself that she'd simply gone about things the wrong way before. Dior regretted not putting herself first. She'd assumed that second place in relationships was just as good because it came with half the drama. Now that she'd seen the diamond life, she reasoned there was only first and last. Dior was way past tired of finishing last.

# SIX

## *Don't Push*

Two days had passed since Dior began making plans to change Richard's life by implanting herself into it. She wasn't in the least bit concerned about his family, the potential complications that an affair could introduce, or his soul salvation. Assuming the "first lady" title of Methodist Episcopal Greater Apostolic was her goal, period. She spent Tuesday morning at the local library, Googling Richard's name and that of the church he helped grow from a few hundred to an overwhelming multitude. Ten thousand loyal fans, as Dior thought of them, made for a very stable career, unlimited income, and loads of perks. She left the library then headed to a posh day spa for a Brazilian bikini wax followed by a deep-tissue massage. Giorgio left three messages during her spoil session. Each time he called, she read his name on the tiny screen then ignored the phone as if he'd never called. When she did return his summons, she made up an excuse about being busy with her landlord. Giorgio went for her lies and she went on plotting her steps to snag a local celebrity with a bank account she wanted her name on.

Mr. Dabnis Keith was so eager to pick up the articles of clothing he'd purchased at Dior's behest that he was sitting outside of the shop when the store opened at ten o'clock. Suza fiddled with paperwork in the office while Dior raised the metal gate. "Look at what the cat drug in," she hailed pleasantly. "It's Mr. Sinbad Keith in the flesh."

"Good morning, sweetie," he chuckled, grunting when he stood up. Getting his heavy body moving all at once was a task, Dior thought as she watched him shuttle into the store. His smile was as wide as his belly.

"Wait a cotton-picking minute. Stop right there," she barked playfully. "If you keep losing weight like this, my tailor is going to get a bad rep."

He laughed so hard his stomach shook. "I can't believe you noticed that right off, Dior. I've been so excited to see myself in some fine vines I couldn't eat a single thing all weekend. My wife thinks I'm crazy but a man my age has few things to look forward to. I've been telling all of my friends about you. Maybe they'll come in and let you spruce them up too."

Dior's grin matched Mr. Keith's inch for inch. "I'm glad to help when I can, Mr. Keith, and thank you so much for sending referrals my way." She went into the back to retrieve his altered suits. He followed behind her, beaming from ear to ear. "Why don't you wait over by the fitting room and I'll bring them out. I know you'll like what we've done." Dior asked Suza to watch the front while she entertained her customer. Suza informed her that Giorgio called to verify she had made it in to work. Suza couldn't satisfy the awkward expression Dior tossed her way, the one questioning why it appeared he was checking up on her. Dior quickly dismissed it then hustled toward an anxiously awaiting war veteran. Mr. Keith's suits were so large that she had to carry them out in shifts.

When he stepped out of the changing room in a light brown outfit, superbly customized to fit his unusual build, the older man held his arms down by his side then shrugged. "Well, what do you think?"

Dior gushed like a doting granddaughter. "I think you look very handsome. In fact, you make that suit look good." It was easy to fuss over a grateful customer who appreciated the way a woman's touch made him feel like a better man. She snickered when he had finally noticed a monogram stitched on the bottom of his left sleeve. He held it up to his face, seemingly confused.

"What's this? I didn't pay for anything this special and how'd you know my middle name was Elston?"

"I called your wife from the number on your alterations ticket. I thought it would add an extra touch of class to something that meant a lot to you. Mrs. Keith agreed." Dior thought he was going to well up and cry. "Don't go getting all sentimental on me. You made my day when you came in last week, so I took care of it. Now, if you make me ruin my mascara, I'm going to charge you for the work I had done on the other jackets too." When he realized she'd gone out of her way to please him, he reached out to hug her. Dior cooed gleefully. She almost disappeared within his massive bear hug. Richard had just walked in to see it. He also saw something else he didn't expect, a woman who seemed hard as steel commit a random act of kindness at her own expense. As soon as the gentle giant realized they weren't alone, he released her and took a calculated step backward.

"You're one of a kind, Dior, thank you. You didn't have to go through nothing extra but you did. That says a lot about you. Most young folk see an old man and they see pity and uselessness. You saw something different." In such a hurry to race home to share his gratitude with his wife, Mr. Keith forwent trying on the other garments. "I'm sure I'll like them just as much," he said in parting. "I could never say thank you enough."

"Bravo." Richard applauded. He admitted overhearing their interaction. "You're different, very...very different. How long has that gentleman been a customer of yours?"

"I met him the same day you came in," she answered with a soured expression. "How long have you been stealing people's lines and using them in your Sunday morning praise sessions? Come out with it, Brotha Pastor. Don't clam up on me now."

Richard blushed. He was actually at a loss for words. "I thought you didn't *do* church?" was his clever response.

"I don't; Church TV doesn't count and do not think that avoiding the question with a question works for me because it don't," she fired back, with both hands parked on her hips. She caught his eyes resting on her tight black slacks for an extended beat. He'd peeped the chest cleavage from the jump. Dior pretended not to notice. An accomplished actress in her own right, she'd ease in and out of character so often that it was difficult to know where she ended and pretending began. "Well?" she said insistently.

"Okay, I did use a couple of exchanges from our conversation in my sermon but that's what ministers do. We use everyday experiences to help the flock. Day-to-day application benefited the first-century church and it still works today."

"What-ever," she smarted, behind a hint of a smile. "Tell your inner man to have a seat while I get your clothes." Dior sauntered away with a natural sway to her hips. She could feel the pastor's eyes remained locked on to them like a heat-seeking missile. Taking the time to have her favorite man-catching pants dry-cleaned was a great move, if she did say so herself.

*Oh my Lawd, that woman is fine,* Richard's carnal man confessed to him. He sat on the cushioned love seat outside the fitting room, fidgeting uncomfortably. *Whew, I'd better get my stuff and leave before I embarrass myself again.* He wiped his sweaty palms on his slacks, refusing to admit to himself that Dior had been running circles in his mind since their previous meeting. He thought he had successfully wished her out of there but she reappeared when he crafted his Sunday morning message, again when he delivered it, and several times when members of his congregation expressed how it inspired them to take a good look at their spiritual wardrobe. Dior observed his restlessness through a crack in the storeroom door. He was sitting on pins and needles and shifting his weight every five seconds. It was fun to see him frying in his own grease and battling with the inner man, who was undoubtedly putting up a decent fight.

Richard stood when she returned with a plastic garment bag. "After seeing what you did for your last customer's ego, I think I'll try mine on too," he said nervously. Immediately, he wanted to rescind every word. He hadn't intended to knock around in a small booth but now it was all he could do to prolong his visit without making his attraction to her painfully obvious.

"I hope you're not expecting monogrammed sleeves like I did for Mr. Keith?"

Richard hadn't considered that but it did present the chance to see Dior again. "Why don't I get the special treatment?" he asked, beaming on the inside.

"I put in for Mr. Keith because he reminds me of my grand-daddy and I *like* him," she quipped.

"Oh, that's cold. I see how you do me," he played along. "And just for that I refuse to accept this suit until you've had my initials stitched into the sleeve too." Dior had released the rabbit and the chase ensued right on schedule. Richard wasn't all dog but he was a man and that qualified him in Dior's book. She counted on her ability to pique his interest and her competence to have him sniffing around her in due time. When she took a deep measured breath, her breast heaved forward. Richard's tongue almost fell out of his mouth.

"Okay then, I'll get you squared away but it's coming out of your pocket, not mine. Besides, you owe me for inspiring your *message*. I ain't, I mean I didn't, forget that either." Dior whisked the plastic bag over her shoulder in a feigned protest. "It ought to be ready in a few days."

"Why so long?" he asked, too quick to salvage any cool points. "Uh, I was hoping to get it squared away and off my to-do list," he explained pitifully. He felt like a teenaged boy with designs on kissing the cute new girl on the block and there was nothing he could do about it at the moment, not even if he wanted to. Dior was firing pheromones and subtle glances at him. True enough, they had connected the first time they met. What Richard was willing to do about it scared him. The last time he acted against his better judgment where a female was concerned, he had hell on earth to pay. A reckless indiscretion with a church secretary almost cost him a fledgling marriage. Even though it had occurred over ten years ago, the sting was ever-present and he couldn't see traveling down the same bad road twice.

Dior wrote down Richard's initials then grabbed a generic card with the store logo and phone number on the front. He looked away when she scribbled something on the back.

"Here you go, Pastor Dr. Richard Allamay, PhD," she said, as she offered the card in an ultra nonchalant manner. "Yeah, since you carried yourself like somebody, I looked you up on the Internet. I guess you're some kind of big shot?"

"You don't seem even slightly impressed."

"I try to get the lowdown on my upscale customers when I can. You've got a good life and you strike me as an alright dude, when your ego isn't getting in your way." Dior didn't give him a chance to question her comment. She skillfully shooed him away before allowing room for it to happen. "Okay, goodbye. I have work to do. Call before you come. I'd hate for such a busy man to waste a trip and come up empty."

Richard left resentfully, passing Giorgio on the way out of the store. Both men nodded cordially in passing, sizing each other up in the process, then immediately stared at Dior for different reasons. Giorgio was protective, understandably so. Richard clocked the Italian's swagger, his expensive taste in shoes and clothes. Dior waved at her boss amicably then sent Richard away wondering what, if anything, Giorgio meant to her. Jealousy was written plainly on his face. Dior thought it was a good look for him. She liked it.

Giorgio, average height with dark skin, was fifty years old. For a workaholic and proprietor of many money-making enterprises, he was incredibly fit. Dior was reminded of that when he removed his sports coat. She eyed him up and down, admiring how Giorgio's clothes always hung perfectly from his strong wiry frame. His silver hair was a match for the sexy movie star Richard Gere, and his quiet confidence made Dior want to lock the office door and jump him on the desk. The first time she pulled that stunt, a former employee almost walked in on them. Dior grinned at the thought of being discovered straddling the boss. She'd been in a crowded bed before. It wasn't her proudest moment but she garnered no regrets, reasoning that life had screwed her so often that it was time to get paid for it.

"Dior? Dior, are you feeling well?" Giorgio asked, after calling her name without getting an answer. He leaned back in the chair, gazing at her peculiarly. "Where is your mind today?"

Dior smiled innocently, while hiding a stream of guilt running just beneath the surface. "Oh, I'm fine. Just a bit hungry. Next

time I'll get something to eat before coming in," she asserted
calmly.

"Late night?" Giorgio said slyly. His tone was filled with
uncertainty, questions he wouldn't dare ask outright. He wanted
to believe his relationship with Dior didn't rate an interrogation.

"Yes, I was up late last night. And yes, I was alone." She
strutted around the desk and stood between his legs to put him
at ease. "I painted the downstairs bathroom again. The other
color was all wrong, too much mustard." Dior brushed her hand
against his inner thigh. Giorgio moaned under his breath. "You
should come by and check your net," Dior whispered. "It's been a
while." The rise in his gray slacks was saying yes. His eyes argued
against it. She was aware of his other women, those other than
her and his wife. Dior teased him about setting mutually benefi-
cial traps, alluring arrangements with hot singles around town,
which she sometimes called "nookie nets." Giorgio had an appetite for erotic diversity and fostered several financial relationships that yielded casual sex when he had time to get away. It was
a provocative form of solicitation without having to pay for it by
the piece.

Giorgio stroked Dior's behind as air in the small room began
to thicken. "I called over the weekend for some of this but I got
no response," he said, staring coldly into her eyes. "Was that
man, the one I passed out there, the cause of it?"

"Who? That preacher?" she spat, with her lips twisted
disagreeably.

"He left holding your cell number in his hand. There was no
ticket, no purchase, no other reason for his visit. Don't tell me
you're looking for another job?" he submitted dubiously. That
was his way of asking if she was interviewing other men. Dior
caught it right off. She unzipped his pants and slid her hand
inside them.

"Nah, baby, I like this one just fine. I can't give up on a gig that really works for me."

"Glad to hear it," he sighed, with slight reservations. "I'd like to come and check that net later."

"I'd love to work late tonight," she answered seductively. "Should I prepare dinner?"

"No, don't bother. I'd rather have you instead."

# SEVEN

## *You Changed*

Four thirty that afternoon, Richard sat in the pastor's chambers. Moments before, he ended a tenuous phone call with the president of a major construction company, who offered discount pricing on a job to pave one hundred acres of land adjacent to the church complex. Several construction firms submitted bids for the project but the others wouldn't lower their fees as an incentive to be awarded a potential building contract. Richard's shrewd business acumen proved sound in the past; he had saved the congregation millions by brokering the best deals possible. He was overwhelmingly responsible for the boom in church membership, and seven elders and five deacons followed his lead. At M.E.G.A., Pastor Dr. Richard Allamay, PhD, cherished a well-earned reputation for levelheadedness and a moral compass beyond reproach. His opinion surpassed that of all others; his word was bond. It was utterly inconceivable for him to put his own desires before the welfare of his family and friends.

Deacon Phillip Hunter, Richard's closest friend of ten years, was a serious man with a dark complexion, shorter in stature than most and rather thick in the midsection. His full-time position, presiding over the DVD ministry, was a coveted job given to him after his former employer rightsized him out onto the streets. There was an insignificant amount of grumbling when Richard convinced the elders to pass over more qualified applicants. Phillip was happily married to Rose, Richard's first cousin. Although it hadn't been voiced aloud, the leadership board knew that Phillip backed Richard's every decision, without question. Phillip's loyalty had been bought and paid for. "I thought I heard you in here," he said, as he stuck his head into the pastor's office. "How'd the conference call go?"

"We're getting closer to the final numbers. I set a meeting with Tatum and his right-hand man for late next week. You should be there too. I'll get Dawn to send out notices to each member of the building committee. Based on the information I received from our banker, we can also break ground on an elementary charter school without additional paperwork." A church-owned primary education facility was Phillip's idea. He couldn't believe it was becoming a reality.

"A real school?" he asked excitedly. "When, how did all of this happen?"

Calm as usual, Richard grinned. "It was nothing really. Dangling the right carrot pays off every now and then. I thought you should be the first to know. Tatum Construction wants to win our future business, unlike the others who handed in inflated projections because they knew we could afford them. Good stewardship is so important when you're dealing with the Lord's pocketbook."

Phillip rushed over to thank his best friend. "I always said you were the best thing that ever happened to this church. You're a good man, Richard, solid to the core. M.E.G.A. owes you so much."

Richard shook his hand then held it for an extended period.

"Sound relationships built on trust, Phillip—that's the corner-stone of success. It started with the disciples and it still works today. Do us all a favor and keep the school business under your hat. I haven't ironed out all the particulars yet."

"Don't worry, I'll keep my mouth shut but I'll be popping off on the inside. Hallelujah, Brother Pastor, hallelujah!"

"Amen. You mind closing the door for a minute? I have another phone call to make." Phillip left Richard alone in his office, which was nicely decorated with mahogany wood furniture and expensive oil paintings purchased by the church at Richard's behest. His discretionary budget was five thousand dollars a month and attached to a credit card paid by his personal secretary. It was a minimal concession in comparison to the six-hundred-thousand-dollar salary he had demanded after learning two years ago that ministers with far less notoriety and smaller flocks earned more than he did. He considered his previous compensation of a quarter million a slap in the face. The elders had a meeting, then wholeheartedly agreed.

Behind closed doors, Richard slid a platinum credit card from his wallet. He laid it on the desk beside the business card Dior had given him. He stared at both of them, interested in what Dior was really like underneath her tough exterior and somewhat gritty homegirl posturing. He'd seen glimpses of warmth and honest compassion, wit, and an underlying angst toward conformity. She was a complex soul, a solitary woman who posed so many questions. Lured to her like a moth drawn by a flame, Richard was more than curious and he couldn't explain it; not even to himself.

When he heard a car door shut outside, he turned his attention toward the parking lot. His wife had pulled into her personal space. He watched her climb out of her mint-green Lexus SUV, which she purchased because she thought it complemented her eyes. Nadeen waved at him through the partially opened blinds. He did the same. As she stomped down the pathway toward the business office entrance, chatting into a cell phone, he continued watching. Somewhere during their seventeen years of marriage, the torch he'd carried for Nadeen had blown out. He loved her, nothing changed about that. She was his wife, mother of his daughters, and someone who could no longer fuel his passion. Richard collected the cards from his desk then put them away. He realized his dilemma the moment she stepped through the door. He had everything a man could have prayed for. However, he was utterly and undeniably bored with it all.

Richard heard Nadeen's flats clicking down the hall, her feet and mouth moving at an amazing clip simultaneously. He folded his arms and chuckled, remembering how that used to amuse him when she'd tear through a room like a whirlwind. Now, it seemed like a ridiculous way for a forty-three-year-old woman to act.

Nadeen Allamay wore her fair complexion and emerald-colored eyes like fashion accessories. Voted Miss Mississippi Valley College 1987, she still cherished the years when her waistline wasn't so full and her behind didn't sag. Her looks hadn't shifted nearly as much as her shape. Beautiful green eyes, long, thick, sandy-red hair, and high cheekbones still drew second glances from other men. Nadeen held her own as far as carpool moms went, but years had passed since Richard looked at her and saw the beauty queen he'd chased around campus for months before she gave him the time of day. Their marriage hadn't died, but it was limping along the shores of apathy and mediocrity. Richard loved Nadeen and his children enough to stay in it without making a fuss like his father had to provide a safe environment for him and his four sisters. Nadeen loved Richard much like she always did, before the money and fame entered into it. He was a great provider and a good mate, when he wasn't overly concerned with church business at the detriment to his family's issues. Nadeen didn't mind Richard's weight increase or that his midsection had softened over the years. His shifting measurements didn't change the way she felt about him. Unfortunately, Richard didn't share her philosophy. His predilection to overvalue the visual aspects of his relationship had become a problem, although he hadn't voiced it. Now that Dior was on his mind, Richard had already begun to reevaluate his marriage and his needs.

"Hey, Richard," Nadeen whispered, with her hand up to deter him from starting a conversation while she blabbed into her cell phone. "Yeah, Rose, I'll make sure your name is on the list for next Tuesday. I'm still hot over the way they acted like you couldn't be worked in. Uh-uh, girl, me either. Oh, uh-huh, I'm in Richard's office right now. Okay, we'll confirm the details later. Yeah, I will. Bye, Rose."

"Nadeen?" Richard said in a questioning manner. He wasn't sure if she'd committed to shifting gears and conversing with him. "You through?"

"Yes, honey. That was just Rose. We're coordinating our schedules for next week and planning our monthly spa outings. You know, girl stuff. The last time her name didn't make the list or somebody took it off, either way she was not happy." Nadeen could tell by Richard's blank expression that he wasn't interested in hearing about a girl's day out. She placed her designer bag on his desk then leaned in for a kiss. "I'm sorry," she cooed lovingly. "I should have been off the phone but Rose can't keep her mouth shut. You know how she can be. How was your day?"

Richard took Nadeen in his arms like he'd done a million times before, but this one was different. He held her not like a wife but rather as a dear friend. He felt little beyond kinship. Disturbed by the lack of zeal in his heart, Richard pecked her on the cheek. "My day was good. Not anything special. I am hungry though. What's for dinner?"

Nadeen wrinkled her nose, as if dinner was an afterthought. "I had a late lunch so whatever you're in the mood for is alright with me," she answered casually. Had she known what Richard was thinking, she'd have put more thought into her response.

"So, you didn't sit anything out to thaw?" he asked, behind a shroud of discontentment. *So this is the first time today you've thought about feeding your family?* he thought to himself.

"It's no big deal," Nadeen surmised, "I could stop by the Olive Garden and pick up something. The girls love pasta and it's one of your favorite places and—"

"What I really love is when you put your foot into dinner," he interrupted emphatically. When he saw Nadeen staring at him oddly, as if to ask where that came from, he smiled. "Eating take-out is cool too."

"I didn't know you felt that way about my cooking but I'll keep it in mind." Her comment hung in the air so long Richard wished he hadn't brought it up. "Maybe I should get started on dinner then. I'll see you at home, honey."

"Do I need to stop by the store for anything?" he asked, after regrettably putting his wife on the offensive.

Grabbing her purse, Nadeen sighed. "Uh-uh, I got it. Just come on home when you're finished here." She left his office without saying goodbye, one thing she'd never done. Richard wanted to apologize for hurting her feelings, then he thought better of it. Since she was a housewife, well-cared for and lavished with the best of everything, the least she could do was lend more concentration to their household, he reasoned. It would be only the beginning of his disappointments, intensified by his growing admiration for another woman. His scheming heart began to plot against Nadeen, making it easier to rationalize the moves he was making in his head about Dior. He knew it was wrong to conceive such hazardous thoughts. But he told himself that tipping around the fringes of lust was enough of a thrill to sustain his curiosity. Convincing himself of that wasn't so easy.

Later that evening, Richard had dinner with his family. His mind was on the other side of town. Nadeen watched him closely after their discussion about home cooking. It shouldn't have been difficult to feel the hole she bore into him with her eyes the entire time he picked over his meal, but he didn't pay the least bit attention to her or the chicken, macaroni, and cheese casserole she'd prepared. Apparently, something other than her, his children, or the plate of food he allowed to get cold had inundated his mind. Nadeen shooed away her initial thoughts, dismissing them as bothersome notions having no business in a happy marriage. Richard was a busy man, a successful pastor, and a loving father. He wouldn't be foolish enough to let a second affair inside the hedge he'd built after an earlier indiscretion nearly tore his world apart. Nadeen figured her husband was merely wrapped up in church matters. Until there was something concrete to make her think differently, it was best to keep her eyes open and her unsettling concerns to herself.

Richard's restlessness followed him into the bedroom. Anxious ideas had him tossing and turning throughout the night. When he finally dozed off around three in the morning, Dior was there waiting on him. She stripped off his clothes and kissed him aggressively, performing the kinky acts Nadeen reserved for his birthday. It was the wildest sex he ever had, and even though it had happened in the recesses of his mind, it felt real as could be. He smelled Dior's scent, touched, and tasted her. She was sensual, naughty, and sinfully skilled in the art of erotica. Passion swelled between his legs. Dior's provocative maneuvers twisted Richard's body while contorting hers in positions he wouldn't have guessed possible. He gave her all that he had, matching stroke for stroke until he climaxed amid a thunderous boom of emotion. Richard awoke when he heard the sound of lightning clap against the darkened sky. Rain streamed down the windows. He sat on the side of the bed, staring breathlessly at the rise in his boxers and shocked by the accumulation of semen on his lap. Embarrassed by his first wet dream in years, Richard tiptoed into the master bathroom then closed the door. Gazing at himself in the mirror, he realized two things immediately. He'd have to rinse out his underwear and he really needed to get a tighter grip on reality. Confident in his ability to control his interest in Dior, he told himself it wouldn't become a distraction in his home. His inner voice fooled him into believing it hadn't already.

# EIGHT

## *Easy Ain't Free*

The next morning, Richard couldn't wait to get out of the house. By the time Nadeen had gotten dressed, he'd had breakfast, read the newspaper, and disappeared. He left a note on the kitchen table explaining that he had a full agenda and needed to get a jump on it. He checked in at the office, followed up on a few phone calls, and quickly began to plot out the rest of his day, which was centered on seeing Dior again.

Richard stopped by a ritzy car wash to have his Lexus sedan primed and polished. Next, he found himself at the Neiman Marcus fragrance counter. A pleasant sales assistant displayed several gift sets. Richard listened attentively to her spiels, each time imagining how that particular perfume would likely commingle with Dior's natural scent. He smiled when the thought of spraying her shapely body came to mind, then he did his best to chase that wicked wish away. *A gift is just a token to show my appreciation*, he kept telling himself. *Nothing more; nothing less.*

After sampling numerous fragrances and floral bouquets for almost an hour he decided on a pricey French perfume with hints of citrus and teakwood. It reminded him of a college girl he didn't have a shot at nailing before eventually meeting Nadeen. Richard had dreamed about sleeping with Elise too, although he was married two months before giving up on that dream coming true.

With a smile in his heart, Richard made his way to Giorgio's. He strolled through the lower level of the shopping mall, holding on to the twine-strapped department store bag. He stopped at a kiosk in the middle of the pathway to check his teeth in the sunglass salesman's mirror before making the turn into the men's store. Suza recognized him the moment he came in. She smiled cordially, knowing who he was there to see. "Hey, is Dior in today?" he asked. "I'm supposed to pick up something." Richard began to feel a bit sophomoric when Suza stared at his small Neiman's bag before answering his question.

"Dior's tied up in the back, but I remember you. Tell me your name again." While she awaited an answer, Richard held his lips together defiantly. He had gone through so many mental gymnastics planning for this meeting to have it stall before ever really getting started. If Suza retrieved his alterations instead of Dior, he'd have no viable reason to hang around. Returning later in the day occurred to him but he'd cleared his calendar so there was no other particular place to be. "I can't pull your tag without a name," Suza said, teasing him. She'd seen too many men strutting into the store with all kinds of gifts for Dior, and not once did they want her to gum up the works for them.

When it appeared he'd wasted a lot of energy and effort, the office door opened. Dior came out, showering the room with her infectious laugh. "Richard, what are you doing here?" she asked innocently. Suza exhibited her displeasure in the way of a smirk, because her mini-torture session had come to an abrupt ending. She cleared her throat and immediately made herself scarce.

"Hey, Dior," Richard answered gleefully, as she drew nearer. Seeing her legs for the first time, he enjoyed watching how her short sundress showed them off. "Oh, uh, I came to get my suit and to bring you this." His smile waned when Dior's evaporated. "What, did I say something wrong?"

"Come over here," she instructed. Richard followed her as ordered to a section of the store where tall displays helped to camouflage their conversation. "Why didn't you listen to me? You're not supposed to be here today." *All I need is for Giorgio to come busting through that door and catch me up in this man's face*, she thought. "I was going to drop this on you later but you just had to deviate."

"I don't understand. You told me to come by *today* because my monogrammed suit would be ready *today*."

Dior placed her freshly painted nails on her hips. "I told you to call before you came too." Richard couldn't quite read her demeanor. He leaned in to question it then decided to come out and ask.

"You might want to tell me what's going on," he blurted out in a way she understood. "I didn't think it was necessary to commit our last discussion to memory but it sounds like you're reprimanding me." Dior's eyes widened with surprise. The tone in his voice thoroughly exhibited his frustration. It turned her on. Suddenly, she softened her expression to put him at ease.

"Don't be silly, I'm smart enough to know you can't raise a grown man, no matter how hard you try. I asked you to call first because I didn't know if I'd have a chance to get it wrapped in a special box," she lied. "You did say it was for a special occasion." She relaxed when it seemed that Richard fell for it hook, line, and sinker.

"Now I do feel bad about *deviating*." Laughter danced with his words. "Speaking of gifts, I stopped by Neiman's to get a little

token of thanks." When he raised the bag, Dior put on a manufactured smile.

"Ohhh, how sweet," she sang, cutting her eyes at the closed
office door. *I've got to get this idiot out of here.* "Thank you, Richard. That's very thoughtful." She continued propping up the
fake cheesy grin although she hadn't lifted a finger to accept
the bag from his outstretched hands. Actually, she would have
been surprised had he shown up empty-handed. What she hadn't
anticipated was his unheralded arrival with her lover less than a
comfortable distance away. "Okay, this might sound kinda funny
but I was going to tell you that it probably isn't a good idea for
you to come by the shop. My boss was clocking you the last time
you came through and he's real particular. He thinks you're up
to something." *Aren't you up to something?* she wanted to say, for the
pure satisfaction of seeing his face when it rolled off her tongue.
However, it was only a matter of time before Giorgio finished
with the books.

"Who is your boss to be making assumptions about my intentions?" Richard asked. He peered directly into Dior's eyes for
the answer. *I'll bet he's trying to keep you for hisself,* Richard thought.
"I mean, I could speak with him if you want." Again, he was
reading her and she knew it. He was a lot more intuitive than
most men she'd determined. She was forced to kick up her game
another notch. Dior batted her eyes at Richard, tilted her head
to the side like a smitten schoolgirl, then placed her hand on
his wrist. Skin on skin contact, even on the most minute level,
worked adequately when applied correctly.

"Hmm, that won't be necessary. Look, I'd love to accept your
gift. You went through the trouble of picking it out, came in
here smelling like a perfume counter, and I'm very flattered. I
don't need drama on my job though. Besides, your suit isn't here
anyway. I'm working a split shift so I can bring it to you when I

get off in about an hour. Call me?" Richard liked the sound of that. He had to close his mouth to keep from drooling over the thought of an off-site meet-and-speak. "So, would you please do us both a favor and hold on to my—what did you call it?—my token until I see you in about fifty-nine minutes?" Pensively, Dior marched Richard toward the exit then waved goodbye. The moment she spun on her heels to head back inside, Giorgio called her name. She cussed under her breath because it didn't look good. "Yes," she answered hesitantly, as Suza took a phone call at the cash register.

"That was the preacher man again?" he asked, using the title she'd given him when questioned about Richard before.

Giorgio knew what he saw, true enough. Dior figured there was no use in trying to smile her way out of this one. Drastic measures were required to hush his stormy apprehensions. She forced him to choose, his eyes or her lies. Once again, she turned her nose up to insinuate Richard had nothing she wanted. "This needs to be the last time we go here. I like our arrangement and I would not disrespect it by hooking up with other men in your shop," she lied continually. "That would be like getting with someone else in your house and I'm not like that." Though she *had* slept with her own cousin's husband in their marital home. But what Giorgio didn't know wouldn't hurt Dior…she had him on the ropes. Now it was time for the knockout. "Preacher man wasn't up to anything. He did bring me a little something for getting a rush on his alterations and initials stitched into his coat sleeve. I told him his payment was enough and sent him on his way, with whatever he brought with him. If that don't feel like right to you then I can bounce. Better yet, you can. I'm not the one who's married." Without giving it another thought, Dior sighed and walked away as if she couldn't be bothered with any more of his insecure rants.

Minutes later, Giorgio awkwardly apologized for suggesting she could be remotely interested in that sort of man, the boring type. Dior huffed, feigning frustration. She demanded an end to questions about her life outside of the clothing store. Giorgio agreed. He had no other choice. They said their goodbyes on even terms, as he grabbed his keys and left with a bank deposit tucked under his blazer.

With an hour to kill, Richard drove to a small sandwich shop across from the mall complex. He ordered a fajita wrap but barely touched it. Instead he played with the business card Dior had given him. Richard had committed her cell phone number to memory by the time he'd actually dialed it. Oddly enough, he couldn't get himself to toss it into the trash can along with the half-eaten Tex-Mex entrée. He wanted to savor his association with Dior, discover what made her tick and what exactly made him want to be near her so bad. Richard had no idea she was two steps ahead of him, lying in wait to spring her trap. She was accustomed to playing the mistress, weekend girlfriend, and the occasional back-office sneak freak. Each of them paid dividends in their own way, but a chance to live the square life with a prominent minister was too big to pass up. Dior wanted top billing and the limelight. This time around, she was set on playing for keeps.

Richard waited until he was certain Dior was out of the store before he returned to his car to call her. His chest tightened as the phone rang. When she answered, he had to suppress the cheerfulness buzzing through his entire body, so as not to appear what he was: an old bee chasing young honey. "Dior, this is Richard."

"Hey, you, hold on." She backed her car out of the mall parking lot then glanced at her watch. It was ten after four. "I'm glad you called. Where are you?" she asked in a sultry tone more suit-able for private grown-folk conversations.

"I'm not far from the mall. We could meet at this sandwich shop across the street if you like."

"Uh-huh, I know the place but I don't have your stuff with me. Do you have something to write with?"

Richard rustled through the console of his car for a pen and pad. "Yes, go on." Dior gave him directions then asked if he could be there within fifteen minutes. He recognized the area then concluded that the place she'd selected was about ten min-utes away. "Sure, but it sounds like directions to a residence," he said, staring at the piece of paper.

"You're right; that's how you'll get to my house." She hung up without offering a closing salutation, wheeled down Monfort, then hooked a left onto the freeway feeder road. Her radio blasted hits between Tangie's comical inserts during the intermission. Dior raced to her house, pulled into the garage, and then flew inside. Richard had already popped up once without calling so it wasn't far-fetched to think he'd overstep his bounds again and arrive early. She opened her hall closet and pulled out an assort-ment of gift boxes. The largest was two-by-three feet, big enough to hold the garment Richard had been waiting on. Dior opened another box filled with ribbons, wrapping paper, and everything else that wrapping services used to beautify a cardboard con-tainer. Skillfully, she strung a thick felt bow around the box, tied and taped it perfectly, then set it on the sofa table in her den. Another glance at the clock warned that she was running out of time. *I know he'll come early,* she thought. *I just know it, with his impul-sive, impatient behind. Men with money are all alike.*

When Dior noticed a black Lexus had parked in front of her house, she began to take off her clothes. "That is him," she said to herself. "Sometimes I hate being right." It took Richard what seemed like forever to get out of that sixty-thousand-dollar car. Dior couldn't fault a man for taking his time to climb out of a fine automobile. Her brother, Dooney, once told her that a nice whip was the next best thing to a fine woman. She figured that was the reason men ran out and pampered them every chance they got. "Boys and their toys," she said after the doorbell rang. She wasn't in any rush to answer it. Richard wasn't going anywhere. And once he laid eyes on her treacherous trappings, it was likely she'd have to put him out afterward.

Richard was impressed with the outside of Dior's home. It was a small two-story redbrick starter home trimmed in black, well-kept, with a neat lawn and manicured shrubs in the front. Assuming it was more house than she could afford, he wasn't sure if she lived alone. Hence, the lengthy time he'd spent in his automobile against the curb. "Hey, you found it," she offered warmly, after finally answering the door. She pretended to be in such a hurry and oblivious to the spell her sheer negligee and sexy golden slippers put on him. Richard was thrown for a loop. A woman dressed in what he'd always called "entertainment skivvies" was flitting about as if she didn't care whether or not he could see her hot pink panties and bra underneath. "Come on in. I'll be back in a minute," Dior said, strolling in the other direction. She needed him to be off balance, early and often, so she left the door ajar. That way, he had to make himself at home without realizing it wasn't his idea. "Sorry, I spilled some pop on my dress and I was about to change. Let me get your box."

Sweltering emotions boiled within Richard's head and heart. He couldn't steer his gaze from Dior's shapely attributes swaying sensually in her tiger-print robe. "What the," he mouthed from the doorway, totally lost in the confusion she created. While stepping into her lair, Richard observed that the inner confines were very accommodating. Each room was painted a different color and decorated with bone-white leather and rich earth-toned accessories. *Expensive contemporary furniture*, Richard thought. *She's got taste.* White ceramic tile placed throughout the foyer added to the contemporary appeal. It was clear Dior had spent quite some time and a great deal of money to make it just so. Richard was honored to be invited in but it wasn't clear why he took a seat without being offered one, why she came to the door dressed like a high-priced call girl then dashed off seemingly uninterested.

Eventually, Dior came down the stairs carrying a full laundry basket. Richard stood when he heard her approaching the den. The moment he saw her load, he rushed over to help with it. "Thank you, Richard, but you didn't have to get up. I'm used to doing for myself." He took the laundry basket despite her objection. Once again he was following her steps. He'd have stayed on her tail to the end of the earth.

In the utility room, Richard set the basket on the floor then shrugged his shoulders. "Is this alright?"

"I told you I'm used to doing everything for myself," she reiterated. "Thanks though, it was getting kind of heavy." She chuckled, giving him a quick full-frontal view. It was exhilarating to watch him fantasize about her breasts. "Well, I know you're a very busy man and I do need to get dressed and back to work."

"Oh, yeah-yeah," he answered, on her heels again. "Dior, do you always dress like this when you're home?"

"All the time. I get hot so easy so it's either run up a high utility bill or shed some fabric. Plus, I'm free-spirited so this works for me nine times out of ten." She stopped in her tracks. "You're not one of those extra-inhibited-type brothas?"

"No, nothing like that," he answered quickly. "Uninhibited is good. Everything has its place."

"I agree and up in my place, this is how I roll." Dior picked up the box she prepared for him. "I hope you like it." She folded her arms when he stood there, unsure what to do next. "Well, what are you waiting on? I've got to get changed and you've got to go, so scoot."

Richard thanked Dior for the trouble she'd gone through to provide optimum customer service. He graciously took his wrapped gift box and placed it on the front seat of his car. After sitting out in front of the house for the longest time, struggling with his horny inner man and asking himself what just happened and why he was feeling guilty about it, he started up the car and pulled away. His palms sweated, his zipper stretched under the force of a massive erection, and a fire burned deep within him. He was thankful that nothing transpired he'd have to ask forgiveness over, although he wasn't willing to admit how thankful he'd have been if things had turned out differently. Richard hadn't encountered anyone like her before. Dior was a free spirit like she said, being near her caused him to want some of it for himself. Halfway home, Richard calculated his chances of seeing her again. Since Dior's boss had all but banished him from the clothing store, it would have to be privately. Richard exited the tollway wearing an impish grin the devil himself would have envied.

# NINE

## *Bait and Switch*

Two days had passed since Dior enticed Richard at her home. Through the power of suggestion and a drop-dead gorgeous body, she tugged at his morals and aggravated his inner man to no end. He went to bed with the image of her sultry strut and sinfully sheer robe indelibly stamped on his brain. Sleeping wasn't any easier. Dior had traipsed her way through his dreams again. This episode far exceeded the last. Richard woke up at two fifteen in the morning with another stiff rise in his shorts and Nadeen staring upside his head like she'd read his mind and condemned him to hell. He turned his gaze from hers, hoping he hadn't said anything incriminating in his sleep. When Richard built up the nerve to address the evil glare she'd flung at him, he pushed out a labored yawn. While catching his breath, he licked his lips and then cleared his throat. "Baby, why are you looking at me like that?"

"Why is your chest heaving in and out like that?" she replied sternly. His answer didn't come forth directly so Nadeen sat up against the headboard, flicked on the lamp on the nightstand, then adjusted the nylon bonnet wrapped around her head. "Something's bothering you, Richard. Now is as good a time as any to tell me what that something is." Nadeen examined his face and tense shoulders. Obviously he was putting up with a formidable entity, one strong enough to trouble him even at rest.

Richard rubbed his eyes and faked another unconvincing yawn. "I can't really call it. Just tired, I guess. Why don't you put out that light? It's late." She didn't accept that lame answer but there was no point in trying to pull it out of him then. Another opportunity would present itself to get at the truth, she'd decided. On the other hand, they were both awake and behind on sleep, presenting the perfect opportunity to catch up on a major benefit of being married.

"I remember a time when you'd wake me up and insist we keep the lights on so you could see what we were getting into," she asserted seductively. "But I can be persuaded to do it in the dark." Nadeen raised her behind off the bed to wrestle her granny panties down past her full thighs. Once they were off and on the nightstand beside the bed, she climbed to her knees and began planting openmouthed kisses on Richard's neck and chest. If she had seen his worrisome expression, she would have climbed into a deep hole instead. "Ooh," she moaned, when her hands found the bulge in his shorts. "This isn't tired at all. Let's see if we can wear him out." Richard's lips parted but nothing came out when Nadeen sauntered over to lock the bedroom door. He examined her body, significantly thicker than it was when they married. Before seeing Dior in all her glory, he was always up for a bout of slap and tickle with his wife. He realized then it was a mistake to compare her figure to another woman's. Nadeen recognized their relationship had taken a turn when she slid beneath the covers to Richard's limp excuse.

"Sorry, baby, I don't know what to say. I guess it's not—"

"Uh-uh, Richard, don't even try to explain!" she hissed through tightly clenched teeth. "I knew something was wrong. Since you're bent on keeping it to yourself and letting it come between us, I'm holding you responsible."

"Nadeen, I'm sorry," he apologized sorrowfully.

"Just fix it!" She snatched her panties off the nightstand then stomped into the bathroom with them balled in her fist. Although she locked the door to shut him out, Richard considered trekking behind her like he had when keeping step with Dior. Knowing Nadeen needed to be touched in ways that mere words couldn't, he thought better of it.

Inside the bathroom, Nadeen wiped tears from her face. She paced back and forth in front of the mirror, terrified that Richard had lost his affection and desire to be with her. Nadeen heard hundreds of stories about men growing tired of being with the same woman but that didn't make it any easier on her. When she thought Richard had finally fallen off to sleep, she put on her nightgown, got in the bed, then pulled the cover up to her neck. "I love you so much, Richard," she whispered quietly. "Don't let that *something* tear us apart."

Although Richard pretended to be asleep, he'd heard every syllable. *I know and I am sorry, Nadeen*, he almost said but didn't. After cheating on her over ten years ago, Richard couldn't put any stock into cheap and empty promises. He'd have to reaffirm his commitment to Nadeen in a manner befitting a loving husband through his actions, thoughts, and deeds. If he was going to be a do-right man, there was no room for Dior in the life he built with Nadeen, no room at all.

Morning came so soon that neither Richard or his wife seemed adequately prepared to meet it head-on. Nadeen dressed and showered with the bathroom door locked. Richard used the upstairs guest suite to do the same. Like two bulls in a china shop, both of them avoided smashing things, said very little, and stayed out of the other's way. Finally, around noon, Nadeen collected her briefcase and then hit the door. Clueless as to how to proceed with Richard, she'd had enough of the awkward feelings permeating throughout the house. He blamed himself for what didn't happen the night before and for sounding the alarm that he wasn't there mentally any longer. Nadeen had the right to be upset, he reasoned. It wasn't every night she managed to kill an erection simply by sliding out of her panties and strutting across the room. Richard sat in his home office, kicking himself for letting things go unresolved for so long. After another hour drifted by, he came up with a hundred better ways to have handled the situation. And he wished he had used one of them, if for no other reason than Nadeen was his mate and his friend. There were a number of methods available to satisfy her, had he been interested. Penetration was off the table and oral satisfaction was out of the question. How quickly times had changed. A few months ago, he'd have sopped Nadeen like a hot buttered biscuit and then licked the plate.

Richard puttered about the house as if a neighborhood bully stood on his front porch and dared him to set foot outside. He regretted having to see Dior for more reasons than one. Since she had previously seen the gift he bought her, he had to follow through on delivering it. Richard realized how his fantasy of befriending the attractive minx for the sake of a semi-harmless association now bordered on obsession. He also recognized the undeniable need to step back and move along once he did. Calling Dior to squelch the fires he'd begun to fuel was harder than he expected. He dialed the number twice then hung up each time. Saying the right things hadn't come easily in the past ten hours so Richard determined that a cell phone text message would set the ball in motion. Then he'd set up a short meeting with Dior when and if she made time to respond. *This is Richard. I forgot your gift. Where and when do you want to get it?* He pressed SEND then set the phone next to his car keys. During the time he slipped on a pair of leather loafers Dior transmitted a very simple but naughty response.

*I want it now... my house. Call me.*

Richard grabbed his keys off the desk and flew out of his garage like the house was on fire. With so much at stake, he was understandably worked up over facing his latest demon. *Better sooner than later,* he thought, while carrying the department store bag toward Dior's passion pit. *Do what you know is best and leave it where it belongs: on her doorstep.* He rang the bell, intending to see her one more time while keeping his feet firmly planted on the welcome mat, where they were on safe and solid ground. Richard should have saved the deep breath he took when someone opened the door from the other side. He'd need it the moment he started to sink.

Even more alluring than Richard predicted, Dior's outfit gave him cause to rethink the deal he'd make with himself. She baited him with a sexy pair of low-rise denim shorts, high heel pumps, a sleeveless crop-top pullover, and a fresh application of shimmering body lotion to glaze her skin. "So you just gonna stand there like the pizza man?" she asked in a subtly seductive voice.

"Hey, I came to tell you that it was a mistake for me to come here. But, since I do want you to have this and since it's not acceptable to stop by the shop, here I am again." He held out the small bag. Dior turned up her nose. Richard couldn't be sure if her disdain was aimed at him or the perfume.

"Come in for a minute, Richard. Had me putting on out-side clothes inside my own house and trying to be respectful of your hang-ups. Come on, it's the least you can do." Again she turned and walked away, leaving him with a perfect view and little resolve to deny her. Richard shook his head while staring at Dior's perfect frame.

*This ain't no kind of right, Pastor,* he said to himself the minute he stepped into her house. *Get her out of your system now. It's not too late to turn back.*

"I can tell you don't want to be here so I'll make it fast," Dior said, motioning for him to take a seat on the sofa. She sat catty-corner on the love seat then slowly crossed her legs. "You're strange, Richard. This is strange. And when I think about you, it makes me feel strange."

*You think about me? Wow!* "I don't get it. You think about me? Why? About what?" he asked, amid a pack of other questions.

"This isn't about stroking your ego, but I dig you and I sense you're feeling me too. If I'm wrong then maybe you should go right now, act like I never brought it up." She leered at him, to heighten his dilemma. *Don't even fix your mouth to say goodbye to me.*

Richard shifted his weight uncomfortably on the sofa. *It's not like I'm in a hurry to go either,* he thought. "I'd be lying if I said you've read me the wrong way. Yes, your body is amazing, you're a beautiful woman, and I am very attracted to you. Equally so, I feel just as strange when I lie in bed thinking about you." *I know I didn't just admit to that.*

*How sweet, I've got this brotha creaming in his drawers and he ain't even much sniffed the panties yet.* "Okay, we agree the interest we share is real and *strange.* Now what?"

"Earlier you said I was strange, what did you mean?" Richard asked, not sure if he wanted to hear the answer.

Dior analyzed the question for a brief moment. If she played it right, Richard would be wagging his tail like a happy dog, a good dog. "I don't know how to explain it. You're a nice man, smart, even powerful. Yet still you're humble and don't carry your title pinned to your chest. I guess that's where the *strange* part comes in. To be as successful as you are, you've got to be a take-charge type but I see lil' hints of insecurity that don't make sense to me." Dior spread her legs open then leaned back against the love seat knowing that Richard couldn't stop his eyes from wandering to the place he wanted to cram those insecurities of his. "Maybe if you told me about yourself," she suggested, utilizing a technique she acquired when working as a stripper: *Get a man to talking about himself so he can open up then it won't be long before his wallet follows suit.*

Richard's eyes roamed every inch of Dior's thighs. He'd forgotten the question momentarily. "Uhm, is this an interview?"

"I'm curious. But if you think I'm trying to get into your business, I…" Dior cleverly crossed her legs again to insinuate that he wouldn't get in if he kept his guard up.

"No-no-no," Richard stammered, with his hands raised in a defensive posture. "I don't think you're trying to pry. You should know something about the man sitting in your den. Where should I start?"

"Right here, today," Dior answered assuredly.

He shrugged his shoulders then leaned back. "I'm a minister, married with two daughters, ages sixteen and eight."

"Now that I'm up-to-date with the family dynamics, why don't you tell me about Richard? I mean, what do you like to do? What kinds of things make you laugh, happy, get you mad and show your tail? Here's your chance to impress me. Isn't that what the fellas do, try to impress women to get us hot, bothered, and naked?"

Richard chuckled when the word *naked* flew out of her mouth. "Whewww. You're bad, very very bad. I'm way too old to waste time with that whole trying-to-impress-people business. Besides that, I'm married. Life for me is what it is and that's as far as it goes."

She bit her bottom lip to keep from saying what was on her mind. *Men are never too old to floss and the married ones are the worst. They'll say anything to get their freak on.* Dior stood up, then walked over to her wet bar. She poured two measures of wine then grabbed a bottle of water from the refrigerator. "I have another question since you half-answered my last one," Dior said from the other side of the room. When she returned, she bent over to set both glasses on the coffee table, making sure that Richard's face was less than a foot away from her tight behind. She wanted his full and undivided attention. "You scared of me, Richard?"

Dior's mischievous whispers dazed him. His mouth was as dry as cotton when it popped open. "That's an understatement," he admitted. "There's no use in lying when the truth will do, right?"

"No need for lies at all. Listen, Richard, because I need you to hear this. Honestly, I'm not trying to be your future," she lied. "The present has always been more of my size. If it decides to flip on me, I can deal with that today better than I can tomorrow."

Richard was further impressed with Dior's simple yet cerebral thought process. "Hmmm, well said. Where'd you pick that up?"

"The same place I get all of my little sayings: from the streets. I signed up for college one year, that's about as far as I got, though." She snickered. "Drink up, it's pretty good."

Richard glanced at the wineglass nearest to him. "I don't usually drink unless I'm having it with dinner."

"I could whip up something if you like. Yes, I can cook so don't be looking at me like that." Dior reached over and brushed her hand against his leg the same way she had to Giorgio. She laughed inside when Richard reached for the wineglass then hurriedly gulped down a swig. "You're really thirsty. Let me get you some water." Dior was glad she had the bottle on standby.

"Thanks. I told you I don't typically drink," he said, somewhat uncomfortably. "You're right, you know, about my insecurities. Most of the time, I am the decision-maker. It's my nature. With you, I'm not the one in control. You hold all the cards and that's sort of tempting. Okay, it's turning me on. You've got me feeling like a youngster, goofy and giggling. No one has thrown me off my game like this, until now. With you, I don't have to be serious all the time or put on my best face because members are judging me. It's been a long time since I felt normal." Richard squinted when a question entered his mind. "Dior, I know it's not polite to ask a woman this, but I have to know how old you are."

"I don't have a problem with answering that. I'm twenty-six. And you?" Richard's eyes widened. He threw on a befuddled expression. "What? Don't tell me you forgot?" she teased. It was easy to see Richard had a problem digesting the realization that she was younger than he thought.

"No, I remember," he chuckled nervously. "I'm forty."

"Oh, I see. You're still having issues with letting go of your thirties. Let it go, then laugh about it. Forty looks good on you."

"Good, not great?" he joked, while fishing for a compliment.

"Don't push it. Good is good enough for me. I don't know what I'm going to do with you, Richard. Maybe I'll figure it out before I see you again."

"So, I've earned an invitation for a return visit?"

"Who said we were finished with this one?"

# TEN

## *Trust Me*

Dior lifted Richard's wineglass from the table then handed it to him. "Here you go, sugar. Sip on it and relax." She winked at him then strutted past. His head was on a swivel as she closed each of the window blinds in the den to darken the room. He was still tracing Dior's steps with his eyes when she cleared the floor by shoving furniture aside. Richard didn't know what she was up to. Her peculiar behavior intrigued him.

As Dior paced the floor like a model down a runway, her confidence kept him glued to her every move. The thought of asking what she had up her sleeve occurred to him, but the old adage about looking a gift horse in the mouth warned against it. Besides, he'd rather imagine himself mounting that horse for a long ride.

After clanging pots and pans in the kitchen and then taking a quick jaunt upstairs, Dior returned to the den. She stared at the lump in his slacks, blatantly undressing him with her eyes. The naughty expression she wore embarrassed Richard. Her carnal leer shattered the pillars he'd counted on propping up his principles.

With utter disregard to his marital status or professional prominence, Dior flirted shamelessly. She was in total control of the situation and of their association. She'd learned the hard way that a woman should hold on to control like a grudge. Richard was on her playing field, wounded and wanting. Giving in to his desires would cause an eventual shift in momentum, which was the natural order of things. Dior fully understood that men were wired to hunt until capturing their prey. She was careful not to relinquish that control too soon because it was extremely difficult to restore, if at all. Keeping Richard off balance and out of his mind was her recipe, two heaping helpings of both. One quick glance at his hungry eyes was a clear affirmation that he'd already begun to simmer. She chose the most opportune moment to turn up the heat and bring his curiosity to a steady boil.

Dior reached into the back pocket of her tight denim make-him-want-some shorts she'd picked out just for the occasion. Holding his gaze, she pushed the power button on a tiny remote control. Richard chuckled when soulful sounds from the entertainment center permeated the room. "Dior, I don't, I don't dance," he said awkwardly, hoping she wouldn't insist he did.

"Ain't nobody expecting you to neither," she replied slyly. "Something about you being all up in my space put me in a playful mood." There were no visible signs of trepidation when Dior's hips began to sway in perfect rhythm with the music. "If you got anywhere to be, now is the time to get going," she offered sensually, with her head tilted back and both eyes closed.

Richard sat there for a second with a constipated expression, shaking his head feverishly. "Uh-uh. I'm good." *You kidding me? Ten strong men couldn't pull me off this spot.*

Dior raised her left hand above her head and then eased the right one down inside the front of her shorts. She rotated her pelvis in a slow calculating manner certain to grind out any leftover apprehension Richard couldn't shake off by himself. When his mouth fell open, Dior moaned passionately. *You'd better close that thing before I put something in it*, she thought to herself. *It's on now, Deacon Do-Good. You messed up and walked into the House of Dior. You should've left when you had the chance.*

Richard wasn't going anywhere. Dior's saucy gyrations and provocative performance had him transfixed in the worst way. When she unzipped her pants and shimmied out of them, his heart rate quickened dramatically. *She's actually coming out of her clothes*, he thought. *A private striptease, for me? Hallelujah.* Richard leaned forward to sneak a closer peak at Dior's black thong as she adjusted the thin patch of cloth covering her shaved pubis. Richard was flabbergasted and uncertain whether to fish around in his pocket for loose singles or hand over his wallet outright. Whatever Dior demanded would have been within acceptable limits as long as she didn't stop dancing, gyrating, tempting. She readily recognized the shroud of desperation on his face. It played the same on Giorgio's and all the other men who came before him. Dior was intoxicating, carefree, and wild. Men wanted to touch that side of her and tame it simultaneously. As far as she was concerned, they were all the same, with slight deviations of course. Trading tit for tat seemed like a fair barter in the past. However, Richard would be handled differently, she decided. Considering how his ego was bigger than most, it was likely to be more fragile as well. She was resolved to stringing him along slowly and patiently, so he wouldn't buckle beneath the weight of guilt and grandiose sex. The only thing more predictable than married men was their susceptibility to a bad case of remorse after steamy episodes of unbridled pleasure with Dior. She'd saddled Richard with the abridged version so he wouldn't fall apart the first time his wife looked at him sideways. It would have been a shame to let him off the hook so soon after getting him to take the bait. *Nice and easy,*

Dior thought, while sauntering nearer to him. *Be careful not to bruise his inner man. It can't take the strain, yet.*

The same sex-starved expression Dior recognized earlier was still plastered on Richard after she pulled the thin shirt over her head. When she flung it in his lap, his mouth watered. He swallowed hard. His eyes said a multitude of things he wasn't prepared to voice openly although Dior heard them loud and clear above the music. He wanted to tell her that she made it impossible to see past her toned thighs and firm breasts. He wanted to convey his fantasies, which always resulted in him driving her crazy in bed with her high heels on. Dior tossed the small remote aside when she'd heard enough silent whispers. Richard took a deep breath then pushed out a heavy sigh instead of uttering a single word. "You like the way I move?" she moaned tenderly, sliding her moist tongue along his neck. "You like the way I move you?" Before he could muster a response, Dior massaged the stiff monument he'd erected especially for her. "Ooh, is all that for me?" she purred seductively. "Impressive."

Richard nibbled on Dior's neck then and lowered his head toward her breasts. When she pulled back, he pleaded quietly. "Come on now, you know that's not fair. How am I supposed to be this close to those and not be expected to sample them?" Dior offered no immediate answer. She stared longingly into his eyes, pretending to qualify him for the next phase. Richard didn't comprehend that she'd sized him up for bedsheets during their first conversation. She took so long to answer, he almost repeated the question. His eyes, suddenly saddened, closed momentarily. "Too much, too soon?" he asked after opening them.

"It's about trust, right? I need to know I can trust you," Dior said, with her hand extended toward him. "Some men can't take no for an answer. Can you take no for an answer and still be down with me? Can I trust you, Richard?" Dior was one step ahead of him. She knew the kind of man he was, cautious and respectful even in the hole he'd dug for himself. He couldn't spend any time thinking of all he had to lose if she appealed to his need to prove himself. Reverse psychology rarely failed her because of men's predictability.

Having been stamped by Dior's wickedness, he reacted in the manner to which she was accustomed. She had actually anticipated his every reaction to this point. His next question was no exception. "What are you going to do to me?" slipped out of his lips in one helpless groan.

"Honestly, I haven't figured that out yet. Thought I'd just let it ride," she answered, shielding the truth with a lie. "Come on, sugar. It's time to get wet." Dior started up the carpeted stairs with Richard in tow. Following closely in her steps, he marveled at the curve of her behind and the rich cinnamon hue in her skin. There wasn't a scratch on it, no stretch marks or blemishes. Dior was a crafty chameleon who carried all of her scars beneath the surface, hidden from plain view. She'd learned to disguise the pain and reinvent herself at a moment's notice. Had Richard caught a single glimpse of her past, he'd have reconsidered her suggestion to ride it, much less stumbling over himself to do it.

At the top of the stairs, Dior waited until Richard was within striking distance. She pulled his arms around her waist then leaned back against his chest. "Hmmm, I've wanted to do this since you rang my doorbell today. I knew it would feel so good." She looked over her shoulder to survey his reaction. He was falling, off balance, and rapidly losing the slight grip he had on his mind. "Let's get in there before it spills over."

Richard hadn't noticed the sound of running water before Dior mentioned it. Two doors on the second level of her modest home were closed. The entire floor was covered in a light-colored carpet. He couldn't tell how long she'd lived there, only that she'd taken good care of the house. Her bedroom furniture was a chestnut shade of oak, more subtle than the downstairs furnishings. Except for the fancy royal blue comforter fashioned with gold trim and flat-panel screen television, it reminded him of his oldest daughter's room. *Tasteful* is the word that came to mind. "I like your style," he whispered, as she gestured toward the bathroom.

"Thank you. It's not much, but it's home." She shut off the water then opened a slender closet door. Dior passed two thick bath towels to Richard then smirked at him oddly. "Unless you like to air dry, you'll need these."

Richard's grin evaporated when he caught her meaning. Candles surrounded the bathtub, flames flickering slowly. He gawked at the satiny bubbles floating atop the bath she'd drawn while arousing him downstairs. "That's supposed to be for me?"

"For us," she informed him. "I thought we'd spend some quality time getting to know the ins and outs, so to speak." Richard didn't have a clue what that meant but it sure did sound good when she said it. He went to unfasten the second button on his golf-style polo shirt until Dior stopped him. "Uh-uh, I'd like to do that if you wouldn't mind." She grabbed the tail of his shirt and pulled it over his head in the same manner she'd removed her own. She ran her fingers through a thick nest of hair on his chest. "I like this; it's very manly." Dior didn't mention how she also liked Giorgio's as well. Richard watched as she fluffed his shirt before placing it on a hanger. He enjoyed it even more when she unfastened his belt and zipper. "Step out of your pants, sugar, so I can put them away too." He gladly did what he was told then looked away as she knelt down to relieve him of his red silk boxers. Richard dropped his eyes with a grimace that made Dior giggle. "This is not the time to be modest. Let's see what all the fuss is about," she jested sensually. Dior, eye-level to the pastor's penis, inspected it closely like she'd always done after hearing too many horror stories about men who let their equipment get out of whack. Richard didn't appreciate being examined. The broad frown masking her face gave him pause.

"Is something wrong?" he grunted uneasily.

"Nah, not with me, but that big ol' thang of yours looks like it hurt. How long it's been swollen up like that?" Richard fought off the urge to laugh, but it still came pouring out.

"I hope you're getting your kicks. Got me standing up here like some kind of nervous patient?"

"Uh-uh, we'll play naughty head nurse next week," she moaned. "Don't worry though; I'll go ahead and work on that little problem you got today."

Dior eased her thong panties down past her knees then stepped out of them. Richard leaned against the vanity counter with his arms folded. He observed the clinical manner with which Dior checked the water temperature, tied up her hair with a long multicolored scarf, then sprinkled in a powder substance from a glass canister resting on the back of the bathtub. It didn't appear to be rehearsed but he could tell she did it the same way every time, whether or not she had an audience. Dior didn't let his presence affect her routine. He doubted she'd let any man change her beyond the person she intended to be. There was something to be said for that, something to be admired.

Against his better judgment, Richard climbed into the water facing Dior. "Ouch, it's kind of hot!"

"Ouch, you kinda sound like a punk," she smarted. "Big old baby. Stop crying and hand me that loofa so I can relieve some of that tension of yours." Dior lathered Richard's body from head to toe, bathing every inch in between. He enjoyed the time she spent on his *in between* the most. Afterward, he tried his best to reciprocate but was all thumbs. Dior gave him a pass then told him she'd expect a better effort in the future if he wanted more of the same from her. "A man who's bathed daughters before ought to be more accomplished at this sort of thing," she hissed jovially, while nestled against his chest.

"Believe me, I wasn't any better at it then," Richard admitted. He caught himself before saying something stupid to bring his wife into the conversation. There wasn't enough room in that tub for all three of them so he redirected the discussion. "Hey, you told me at the shop you'd looked me up on the Internet. If I Googled you, what would I find?" Not that he expected to run across articles written about a young salesperson who was more than likely shelling out her entire paycheck on a charming little house, expensive clothes, and a small luxury car to keep up appearances. He'd been wrong before.

Dior shrugged tenderly. "I tried it once myself but nothing popped up," she lied. "Really didn't think anything would, since I'm no big-time celebrity like someone else I know." Dior was such an accomplished liar that it came just as easily as breathing. She could have been up front and told Richard how she'd been arrested more than once for boosting clothes before getting paid under the table by Giorgio to hawk them in his store. She neglected to mention her former employment as a naughty nanny, the mobile escort service she built on her back, or the fact that it got her girlfriend killed when one of the clients went too far during a bout of sexual acrobatics. Dior also could have added how she almost ruined her favorite cousin's marriage by climbing into the bed with her husband after splitting them up. She merely acted as if her answer to Richard's question was sufficient and then she left it alone.

He bought it. Without a reason to distrust her, he held Dior close, wrapped snugly in his arms. He'd quickly grown to respect her brand of quality time. He wouldn't have thought it possible to transcend the awkward sexual phase in a relationship without actually having any. On the other hand, she did take care of that swelling problem of his, which was no small feat.

Lounging intimately like old lovers instead of newly acquainted hedonists out for a sporty fling suggested to Richard there was more to Dior than met the eye, although she was quite nice to look at. She was also deliberate in her actions when pleased and quick to snap otherwise. Dior was unlike any woman he'd ever met: self-assured, outspoken, and skillful enough to back up a gang of attitude if cornered without provoking an all-out war. There was definitely more to her than she allowed him to see thus far. Richard was respectful of that. He was a guest in her home, a visitor in her life. She trusted him and asked for the same in return. Unfortunately they were playing with two distinctly different sets of rules, both adequately justified in their own mind.

# ELEVEN

## *What-ever*

During the twenty-minute drive home, Richard had a long time to think about his fledgling relationship with Dior. He leaned on the fact that he hadn't actually had sex with her much in the way a former president denied having relations with a female intern. Richard laughed at himself because it sounded just as preposterous as when he'd heard Clinton's flawed rationalization on CNN. Wrong was wrong regardless of how he tried to slice it. Richard spent the last five minutes of his drive deliberating just how far he was willing to go with Dior. He honestly believed he could resolve his curiosity with a taste before getting it out of his system. Unbeknownst to him, steamy bubble baths were only the beginning.

Loud chuckles poured from the family room when Richard closed the front door. His home sounded happy, full of love. Hearing laughter warmed his heart and put a grand smile on his face. The smell of chicken frying in the kitchen snatched it off. "Hello, Daddy's home," he shouted over the television. His oldest daughter, Mahalia, sixteen, paused the movie on the big screen.

She was a pretty girl with a honey-brown complexion and eyes a shade lighter than that. Mahalia's slight frame had been a sore spot for most of her life and she'd often complained about being too skinny. Richard hadn't noticed that her rants of self-pity were now nonexistent; neither did it occur to him that her body had recently undergone several flattering developments.

"Hey, Daddy" she said with an effortless wave. "Mom is almost finished with dinner."

"Where's Roxy? I could have sworn I heard her in here with you." Richard grinned when he felt someone sneaking up behind him. He remembered a time not so long ago when Mahalia tried her hardest to do the same. Now it was his eight-year-old's turn. Joyful that someone was excited about him being home, Richard played along. "I wonder where that Roxy is. Maybe she's in the backyard, trying to dig her way to China like she did last year. No, maybe she's on a magic carpet ride. Trips around the world can't last forever."

"What-ever," Mahalia scoffed. "I don't have time for this. I'm getting back to my movie."

"Boo!" yelled Roxanne, plowing into him from the side. "I'm right here, Daddy!" Roxanne giggled as he hoisted her over his head. "I scared you. I finally did it." She giggled gleefully through a gaping hole where two teeth used to be.

"Uh-uh, you didn't," he debated playfully. "I ain't scared of nothing."

"Uh-huhhh, you got scared when Mama thought she was having a baby." Richard lowered Roxanne to the floor after the wind had suddenly been let out of his sails.

"She got you there, Daddy," Mahalia seconded. "When you overheard Mama telling Auntie Rose about it you looked like you just ate a bug."

"*What-ever*," he said, mimicking the same annoyed tone she'd used earlier. "Y'all ought to be ashamed, double-teaming your old man like that."

"It's okay, Daddy, fifty isn't so old," Roxanne offered on his behalf.

"Fifty?" Richard howled humorously. "Who's fifty? Tell her, Mahalia, I'm barely forty."

"Yeah, and that won't last forever either."

"I think I liked it better when you didn't have time for us. Nadeen! Come in here and whoop my oldest child please."

"Go on and do it yourself, I'm busy!" she snapped from the kitchen. "And get it done before the dinner rolls come out of the oven."

Richard began to creep toward Mahalia just as Roxanne had done to him. When she heard her younger sister snickering, she peered over the back of the sofa. "Stop, Daddy," she said, inching away from his tickling tentacles. "I'm too old for this." Richard chased Mahalia around the den, to Roxanne's delight.

"Catch her, Daddy!" Roxanne yelped loudly. "Catch 'Halia and tickle her until she pees her pants. Pee pants, pee pants, pee pants," she chanted.

"I'm just the man to do it, too," Richard threatened.

Mahalia leaped over the love seat to get away. "I'm not playing with y'all. This is not funny."

Roxanne frowned miserably when it was clear her sister had no plans of giving in. "It would be if you peed your pants."

For the first time, Richard realized that Mahalia was no longer the darling little girl who craved his attention and his indefatigable tickling. She scowled at him, fled from his affection and, more so, his desire to keep her forever young. "Let's get washed up for dinner," he asserted finally, "before it gets cold."

Assembled at the rectangular kitchen table, Richard sat across from Nadeen with the girls on either side. He said grace over the food, giving thanks for blessing and health, then forked three helpings of vegetables onto his plate. When he neglected to remove any of the chicken from the meat platter, Nadeen questioned it. "Is something wrong with the way it looks?"

"It looks scrumptious like always," Richard answered.

"You used to love my pecan-crusted fried chicken."

"I still do, Nadeen," he replied insistently, to strongly suggest she drop her passive-aggressive assault. "Fried chicken will always be my favorite but I could stand to lose a few pounds."

After he'd eaten an extra helping of peas and a second salad, Nadeen started up again. "Richard, that's barely enough food for a child. Since when are you eating like a rabbit?"

"Since today. I'm forty, a hard age for a man. Taking account of my life up until now made me realize I'm on the other side of the bridge. I need to look and feel the best I can from here on out." Mahalia opened her mouth to crack on him until Richard cut his eyes at her, stifling the opportunity.

Roxanne built a pyramid out of corn in the center of her plate, oblivious to the tension mounting around her. Nadeen felt that Richard's reaction toward Mahalia was a bit harsh, then she determined his restrained animosity was misguided and meant for her. "You've been a forty-year-old for five months, and I think you're making the best of what you got. It's good enough for your wife."

"Thank you, sweetheart, but it's not nearly good enough for your husband." Richard cringed when his self-assessment came out like one of her slick snipes previously leveled at him. "I need to do better when I can. It wouldn't hurt me to get fit and fine."

"Mahalia got a crush on a *fine* boy at her school," Roxanne sang, as if it was her turn to contribute to the discussion.

"Mahalia *has* a crush on a fine boy at school," Nadeen corrected her.

Mahalia growled at her sister. "You little snitch."

"Skank!" Roxanne fired back.

"Excuse me," Nadeen huffed, taking offense at the conversation and to Richard's apparent decision to stay out of it.

"Oh, not you, Mama, I was talking to Mahalia," Roxanne apologized, as if that made what she said any easier to take.

When Richard passed on another opportunity to discipline the children, Nadeen jumped in again. "Hush up with all of that vulgar talk. Where'd you pick up such a dirty word anyway?" Everyone's eyes were glued to the eight-year-old, who couldn't muster up the gall to tell them. Instead she pointed at Mahalia.

"I heard her say that Trevy Dempsey was a sk—one of those, for kissing two boys behind the building after a basketball game."

Mahalia jeered at Roxy as if she could have strangled her. "Ooh, I can't stand you. You run your mouth too much."

Richard wiped his lips with a cloth napkin once he'd had his fill of dinner and their assault on one another. "That's not nice, Mahalia. Apologize to your sister. And next time watch the name-calling." He dismissed the girls with a soft suggestion that they try harder to get along. Nadeen began to collect the dishes from the table. Richard appeared puzzled about something. "I could be wrong but last I heard Mahalia and Trevy were best friends."

"Yes and maybe one of the boys that *skank* kissed was the fine boy Mahalia has a crush on," Nadeen surmised. "Then all of this would make perfect sense."

"You think Gloria knows about her daughter Trevy being with boys? She couldn't be sexually active? Could she?" he asked as an afterthought.

"With too many of the girls in the congregation growing up too fast, I'm surprised Mahalia isn't."

Nadeen continued puttering around the kitchen as if she didn't just drop a bomb on Richard's head. He wasn't ready to concede that she liked boys or happened to be turning into a vibrant young lady, although both were transpiring right under his nose. "What makes you think she's halfway mature enough to run behind boys, kissing and all that?" he questioned frantically.

"It doesn't have anything to do with maturity, Richard. It has everything to do with hormones. Young or old, it really doesn't matter. Hot in the pants is hot in the pants." Richard's eyes fell toward the floor. "I don't know why people get all bent out of shape over sex. It's been a problem since before Genesis and more than likely will be long after Revelation. Some folk can't seem to do without it and others can't give it away."

Richard wasn't 100 percent certain that was a dig at him but it stung nonetheless. "Are you suggesting that I'm getting it somewhere else because I wasn't in the mood one time?"

"You tell me what was behind it. I couldn't reach you at the church today. Nobody could remember seeing you, then you come strolling in the house with liquor on your breath, Brother Pastor."

"For your information, I was buried in my office behind closed doors and a pile of papers. I left early to hit the gym then stopped by Chili's for a bowl of low-fat clam chowder and a glass of wine." Richard's explanation sounded credible enough so he remained on his soapbox. "Need I remind you that according to the Word: First Timothy, chapter three and verse eight: *Leaders of the church must be reverent and not given to* much *wine.* I only had a glass of merlot." Richard cleverly omitted the part about not being double-tongued. "Besides, Jesus' first miracle was turning water into wine. Obviously, he didn't have a problem with it so why should you?" His indignant attitude bothered Nadeen. She set the dishes on the counter and stared at Richard.

"Okay, so you want to put this on Jesus? You really want to take it there?"

"Where's that, Nadeen?"

"To the cross," she spat venomously. "First off, there's not one mention about Christ taking a nip for himself. And secondly, Jesus never once came home smelling like Bath and Body Works."

"I can explain that." *The bubble bath with Dior,* he thought. *I've got to be more careful.* "That's nothing but your imagination. I told you I went by the gym to work out. I showered afterwards with some of that citrus bath gel they're always trying to sell you when you sign out." Richard was thinking quick on his feet and plucking lies out of the air just as fast. He forged ahead, playing on Nadeen's insecurities. "If I didn't know better, I'd say you were jealous. It's kind of getting me going too." He snuggled up behind her and wrapped his hands around her thick waist, thinking how Dior's was much slimmer.

"Go on now, Richard, don't start anything you aren't willing to finish. I can't take rejection twice in one week."

Richard said he was sorry about that then lied about being mentally drained at the time. "My mind is pretty clear now though," he whispered in her ear. "There's only one thing on it: what I want to do to you."

"Can you do that thing I like?"

"You know I can."

Nadeen quivered when she felt a twinge shooting up her thighs. "Well, what about the girls?"

"Don't get so loud, they won't hear you." He convinced her to leave the kitchen in disarray, which was extremely uncharacteristic. Then he locked the bedroom door and turned the television on just in case the girls came snooping around for them.

In a ravenous display of passion, Richard practically tore

Nadeen's clothes from her body. She couldn't remember the last time she felt so desirable. Richard ran his fingertips along the ridges of her breasts, tracing his fingers with tender kisses, just the way she liked. Even though Richard envisioned Dior's body instead of his wife's every step of the way, he put his all into their early evening rendezvous.

Nadeen bit down on the pillowcase when she could no longer battle the fervent cries welling up inside of her. She sank her nails in his back as a renegade scream roared from her mouth. "I can't get enough, baby!" she panted loudly. "Shhhh, the girls will hear us. Okay, okay. I'll be quiet. Ooh! Here comes another one!" Nadeen kept on panting until Richard was convinced she'd been pleasantly persuaded to drop her suspicions and alter her attitude about the night before.

"I love it when you take your time and drive real slow," she cooed afterward. "I'm going to take a shower before I fall asleep. Richard? Richard?"

He pretended to have dozed off already. *At least one of us got what they needed,* he thought. *Driving slow? I hate cruising in the geriatric lane. Dior, that girl's a freak. I know she can keep up. I'd bet on it. Shoot, I'd be willing to pay for it too.*

# TWELVE

## *Deep Dug Ditch*

R ichard stayed up half the night thinking. He lay in bed, next to the wife he loved but didn't care for her like a good husband should. Sure, if Nadeen had fallen ill, he'd have been there day and night by her bedside praying for her full recovery. Sympathy wasn't what she needed now and he couldn't find it in himself to shower her with adoration the way he used to. Dior was renting space in his head, in every available room. Although they hadn't known each other for any substantial length of time, his best was hers for the asking. Deep down inside, Richard never stopped thinking about having a woman on the side, a younger woman at that. He couldn't believe it was now staring him in the face. He'd counseled couples on the mend after the husbands thought they were handling their business on both ends. In time, the affairs grew out of hand and too much to manage. He knew what it would take to sustain a full-fledged romance. He decided against the strain of pleasing two women simultaneously. Someone had to get the short end of the stick. Someone had to lose out. There were no two ways about it: heartbreak and misery traveled the same roads with cheating spouses. He'd seen enough upheaval in rocky marriages to know that pain and suffering was the cost, to be paid in full every time. Once Richard had thoroughly evaluated the magnitude of adultery, hanging out near the fringes was as close as he was willing to get. He smiled to himself when it made perfect sense. Dior was extremely tempting but not worth eating the whole apple. Nibbling around the edges, as long as she allowed him to, felt like a safe and satisfying alternative. Confident that his after-dinner romp was a satisfying deposit in Nadeen's quality-time bank, Richard determined he deserved a couple of days off for good behavior.

Richard was up and out of the house at six o'clock the next morning. While en route to the health club, he diagrammed the next forty-eight hours of his life. Allocating every spare minute to seeing Dior was his top priority. He hoped she'd be willing to reciprocate by setting aside time for him too. She agreed to meet him on her lunch break after he sent a third text message. "So when can I see you?" he asked, once she answered his sixth phone call.

"You have to stop blowing up my cell, Richard. You know I got to work. These clothes don't sell themselves," she cackled playfully. "Are you trying to get me fired?"

"Of course not," Richard replied quickly. "I wouldn't think of coming between you and your independence. Every woman needs to have her own."

"Good, then let up off the phone calls and meet me on my lunch break in twenty minutes." Dior agreed on an out-of-the-way place to meet where he felt at ease and not likely to run into members from his congregation. She told him about Casa Blanca, a Mexican restaurant south of the freeway. It was a small place, converted from a family residence by immigrants. Dior appreciated the owners' ingenuity and their authentic chicken enchiladas even more.

Richard parked in front of the tiny white house then laughed at the sign with CASA BLANCA stenciled on it, remembering that white house was the Spanish translation. *A clever name for a hole-in-the-wall*, he thought. *I'd better not catch anything in there.* Leery of the old neighborhood, Richard locked his car manually then armed the alarm as a secondary measure. Surely none of his esteemed church members would be caught dead in a hovel on the wrong side of the tracks. Unfortunately, he underestimated Casa Blanca's reputation for outstanding service and famous fajitas. No sooner had he opened the door to enter, a familiar face caught his attention. His secretary was seated at a table with another woman he didn't recognize. When he tried to duck out before she saw him, Dior strutted in through the entrance.

"Where do you think you're going?" she asked with a suspicious expression. "I'm hungry and only get forty-five minutes." Richard leaned in toward her, purposely shielding his face.

"Let's find another place. My secretary is in there."

"And what, ministers can't break bread?" she argued, without moving an inch. "Look, Richard, you seem to be really twisted over seeing your friend in there. Maybe we should make other arrangements."

"Cool, I'm glad you understand. There are plenty of other spots up the road. I'll hop in the car and call you on the way."

Dior was visibly irritated despite trying to conceal it. "Uh-uh, you don't have to do that."

"Really, it's no bother," he answered, after glancing over his shoulder.

"No, it won't be necessary because I'm not leaving," she informed him. "I love the food *here*. And I don't go jumping behind bushes for *nobody*." Dior read her watch while Richard deliberated sorely. "Maybe this was a mistake. You can't be out with me, ducking and dodging like this. I told you I was hungry and I can hear some chicken enchiladas calling my name. Excuse me." Dior stepped inside the restaurant alone.

Richard realized it wouldn't be as easy as he predicted, operating from the fringes. Dior left him standing on the sidewalk, stuck in a tough position. He'd planned his morning around the slim opportunity of being in her space. He'd called her repeatedly until she conceded. With his back against the wall, Richard held fast to his reservations. Overwhelming distress in regard to explaining who Dior was and why they were together in the middle of the afternoon needled him. Richard disarmed his car alarm then jetted down the street before potentially being hit with leering eyes questioning his integrity. He couldn't have known the secretary witnessed his entire interaction with the attractive lady through the restaurant window. Subsequently, there were two women wondering what the pastor was doing there—Dior was the other one.

Anxious to overcome the lunch date debacle, Richard employed a personal shopper at Nordstrom to assist with a shopping spree for Dior. He imagined how it must've looked, his neglecting to follow through after insisting she see him. It made him feel inadequate and weak. He couldn't blame Dior if she thought less of him. His second mistake was using the credit card tied to his church expense account to charge over eleven hundred dollars in trendy designer jeans and fashion accessories to save face. Getting out of trouble was a lot like filling a deep hole: There would always be dirt left over afterward. Buying his way into a deep hole was just plain dumb.

Dior refused Richard's phone calls for two days so he'd get the message. She had gotten over his gutlessness by the time she returned to work that day but there was no benefit in telling him. She was resigned to keep him scratching at her back door until he made it worth her while to open up and let him in. When

Dior received a special delivery from the department store, time had come to unlock that door.

On the way home from work on Thursday night, she called Richard knowing he'd be standing by the phone. "Hey," she said cordially. "I got the package from Nordstrom's this morning. You didn't have to do that." *Yes you did*, she thought to herself. *Next time stop by the Prada store while you're at it.* "You have a good eye for fashion. Thank you."

"I didn't think I would hear from you again after bailing on lunch. It was the least I could do." Richard listened for signs of forgiveness in her voice.

"About that," she answered with a lengthy pause, "I was really disappointed. Maybe I shouldn't have been but I expected better from you." Richard sat in his home office with the door closed, holding the phone to his ear. If she planned on resolving her feelings toward him, he couldn't tell. "I'm almost at the house. We need to talk, in person." Again, Dior pulled his strings like a veteran puppeteer. She didn't ask if he was available or if he happened to be in for the night. He'd find a way to meet even if it meant cooking up an excuse to sneak out. How he managed it was not her issue; that would fall solely on him.

Richard weighed his options briefly then settled on the one response that would allow him to get some sleep later that night. "I'm on my way," he replied quietly. "Give me twenty minutes."

Dior hung up the phone then put her game face on. *He must be at the house*, she reasoned. *Huh, probably has to tell a string of lies to get loose. That's what he gets for punking out on me. Spending on a shopping spree was good for him, when he could've gotten by with a twenty-dollar lunch. Weakness—it's so disappointing and yet so rewarding.*

Richard rang the doorbell, wearing his heart on his sleeve. Dior greeted him indifferently, wearing her sheer negligee with nothing underneath. "Well, I guess you'd better come in before we give the nosy neighbors something to talk about." *They're just getting used to seeing Giorgio come and go at all times of the night*, she thought.

"Hey, you," said Richard, straight-faced and hopeful. There weren't any guarantees she would accept his apology and then agree to continue moving forward with their tryst. Answering the door nearly nude was no clear indication. Dior was an exhibitionist, after all, who admittedly peeled off her outside clothes the moment she made it inside. Richard was a bit surprised she didn't have on a pair of three-inch pumps, which seemed to be her house shoes of choice. "Thanks for calling me," he added, once he'd come in and locked the door. Richard didn't know where to go from there. Not willing to jinx things, he followed Dior into the living room with his mouth aptly shut. There was no point in acting as if he had a say in the matter. She held all the cards.

During their quiet stroll past the drawn shades, Dior began to limp gingerly. She took a seat on the far end of the sofa, on the other side of three fluffy white towels and a tray filled with assorted salts and gels. It was apparent that Richard was welcome to sit anywhere, outside of the makeshift boundary she'd created. He took the hint then sat on the love seat positioned perpendicular to her. "Do you mind getting me a bottle of water from the fridge?" she asked indifferently. Richard leaped off his perch, at the ready to fetch. "You can have one too, if you want," she added plainly. "Thanks and oh, could you plug that in over there? I mean, since you're already up."

Richard tugged on a white extension cord attached to a salon-size foot spa then searched for a wall socket. "I saw you limping when I came in. You hurt?"

Dior poured a small measure of cuticle remover into the bubbling water before commenting on his question. "If you saw that, then what took you so long to ask about it?" She didn't expect an answer. The one she got in return threw her for a loop.

"I thought of sweeping you off your feet and carrying you to wherever you wanted to go. I didn't know if you felt like being touched by me, so I backed off." He offered a labored smile, like a man trying to sway the jury with remorse.

"How much time you got?" she asked, looking into his eyes with grave anticipation. "We need to get some things straight."

"I've got as much time as it takes," he replied, oozing with a renewed zeal.

"If we're going to keep this up, there are two rules we need to agree on. If you can't deal, I'll understand." Richard shrugged and nodded that he was up to hearing her stipulations. "One, don't ever come to my house without calling first. I need my privacy, even when I'm alone. Next, do not allow your married life to set foot into mine. I'll get back to you on the remedies, if it becomes an issue." She made sure he was still on board before continuing. "Now, I'll tell you what to expect from me. I won't ask too many questions about what doesn't concern me. I will never talk to you about your wife unless needs be because I won't carry another woman's baggage. That ain't my way. I'll cook for you, care for you, and create a comfortable environment for you to lay your head. And if you're interested, I'll provide some of the things you probably can't get anywhere else and feel good about it." Richard raised his hand slightly, to get Dior's attention. He wanted her to elaborate on the last item but didn't want to wreck her flow.

"Uh, you mentioned providing things I wouldn't be comfortable doing elsewhere. What kinds of things?"

Without batting an eye Dior reeled off a list of no-no's most preachers denounced. "Cigars, cognac, strip shows, pornos, whip cream, hot wax, weed, Viagra, or whatever you might need to take the edge off."

Richard was stunned. Although he hadn't given thought to using a number of the items on her list, the mere discussion was enticing. "Okay, I'm down with that. Yeah, I'm good with it."

"A few more things," she said. Resolve covered her words like sackcloth. "I do for you, you do for me. I will not ask for money. You can contribute what pleases you. However, this is a play-as-you-go arrangement. Start talking to me crazy, it's done. Put your hands on me, you're done." Dior's twin brother, Dooney, put an ex-boyfriend in a mile of stitches for beating on her. That information was on a need-to-know basis so she kept it to herself for the time being.

"Anything else I should know going in?" he uttered hesitantly.

"Funny you should mention that. My vagina has a constant need for entertainment. If I really dig you, I'll show out every time you show up. I keep hot, naughty sex on the menu. I like it rough but respectful. I suck and yes, I swallow." Frozen on the love seat, Richard coughed to clear his throat. He opened his mouth. Nothing came out. "Is there anything you want me to know about you, Richard? Because I don't do boy-girl-boy and I don't roll with boys who get down with other boys. I'm up for an occasional girl-on-girl tag team, if I get to choose the girl." Richard was so excited he almost erupted on Dior's leather furniture. "If you're in, say alright then."

"Amen. I mean, alright then."

"Good, come over here, sugar, and seal it with a kiss." Ever so eager, Richard popped off the sofa. He took one step then clutched at his shoe. "Ohhh, it's a cramp," he yelped, landing butt-first on the floor. Dior stood over him. She eased off his shoes then began massaging his calf.

"Be still and let me work this kink out. You should probably increase your water and potassium intake. Don't be looking at me like that. Just 'cause I've been stocking inventory all day don't mean alls I know is pimpin' clothes."

"Ooh, that feels good. Uh-huh, you can say that again," he seconded. "I'll be okay. Why don't you go ahead and put your feet in there." When Richard went to put on his shoe, Dior frowned.

"You could stand some attention on those claws of yours. I think you stabbed me the other day."

"I'm sorry. It won't happen again."

"I know it won't. Put those in this Soft Soaker 5000." She moved the bubbling spa closer to him then slid over so he could get at it easier. Richard rolled his pant legs above the water level then lifted his feet over the spa. Suddenly, he squinted apprehensively.

"I'm kind of picky. How many other feet have been in there?"

"How is that important if yours are the only ones in there now? I didn't stop to ask how many other places your feet have been, did I?" Dior waggled her finger in his face then pressed her point further. "As long as your feet and my tub are both clean, it should not be an issue."

Richard felt a lump in his throat, somewhat smaller than the one in his pants. "Are we still talking about soaking my feet?"

"Don't trip, Richard. This discussion was never about your feet."

# THIRTEEN

## *Hoochies and Hot Wings*

During yet another drive home, Richard replayed the entire evening with Dior several times. The edicts she laid down concerning rules of engagement and the penalties for breaking them paled in comparison to the hot loving she poured on. After massaging, manipulating, and introducing his body to a debilitating brand of sexual discovery, Richard awoke two hours later. His tired eyes found the digital clock. Panic-stricken, he stumbled over an armchair while wrestling on his underwear. Dior grinned sheepishly despite his petrified expression.

At eleven forty-five, Richard jaunted through Dior's love lair, collecting articles of clothing he'd carelessly flung off when the action started. Dior, nestled beneath wrinkled bedsheets, offered to help find his things but Richard declined. He wanted to remember her the way she was, relaxed and relishing in his affections. Regretfully, he stormed out to the car without locating his expensive timepiece. There'd be other watches if his anniversary gift from Nadeen failed to show up, he reasoned. Since there was no duplicating his initial earth-shattering bout of sensual elation with Dior, he still came out on top. *On top*, he thought, *hmm-hmm-hmm, it ought to be against the law what that woman did to me when she was on top. I know there's got to be a law against that trick she did upside down. Oh, and the way she arched her back against the headboard, I thought I heard a bone crack. As long as it wasn't mine, I'm down for doing it again, and again and again.*

It wasn't until Richard rounded the turn onto his street that his mind hinged on the business at hand instead of the work he'd put in across town. What would he tell Nadeen, if she asked where he'd been? Why hadn't she called his cell phone to investigate? Questions paraded in his head like a high school drill team. So enthralled with finally getting between Dior's legs, Richard hadn't prepared an adequate lie or an alibi to get him out of potential trouble with his wife. He took a deep breath then slapped at his pants pockets relentlessly. A loud growl flew from his mouth when realizing he wasn't only short on principles and plans to conceal his devious behavior. Richard had dashed out of his other woman's house while his cell phone vibrated relentlessly beneath her bed. Like a condemned man facing the moment of judgment for his crimes, Richard slinked from the garage dragging the weight of his shame and remorse behind him.

Richard feared a knockdown drag-out fight if Nadeen challenged the excuse he was still stitching together, so he tiptoed inside warily. Most of the lights on the first floor were off. Two of the recessed lights in the kitchen dimly illuminated his plight. Nadeen had left his dinner plate covered in aluminum foil on the counter. Richard didn't pay it any mind. He scouted around in the muted light for a note or something to clue him in on Nadeen's disposition. He thought it odd when there wasn't one. Richard began to pray, then he caught himself. God already knew what he'd been involved in and wouldn't be interested in helping him out of it. Instead, he shut off the recessed lights then climbed the back staircase with a heavy heart.

The bedroom door was wide open. Richard felt like a desperate man prowling in another man's house. In a disturbing way, he was exactly that. That man—the husband and the father responsible for raising his children, seeing to his wife's needs, and seeing to the general benefit of the family—had gone out into the night on a personal mission that in no way profited them. Richard, now the stranger in his own home, stared into the faintly lit master bedroom, where Nadeen was fast asleep. She'd awaited his return for hours before calling it a night.

In times past, Richard had been known to work late while seeing to the welfare of the congregation. He spent hours counseling young girls and their parents on abortion and adoption issues when their families were torn apart by an unplanned pregnancy. Richard also prayed all night with the parents of young men who had been locked up by the police or, worse, shot down in the streets. In either case, he always came home afterward, showered and then told Nadeen all about it the following morning. It was difficult to trust him when her phone calls went unanswered for hours on end. Although sharing Richard with others during their time of need came with the territory of being the pastor's wife, Nadeen didn't treasure that part of it. The only validation she received was that he'd done the Lord's work. She went to bed on numerous occasions with that in mind. As far as she knew, she'd been wrong about him only once.

When morning came, Richard looked for the clothes he'd worn the night before to hide them in the bottom of the laundry basket in their roomy walk-in his-and-hers closet. Nadeen must've taken them. Richard freaked when he couldn't remember showering before sharing the bed with Nadeen, after what he did with Dior. His eyes darted back and forth then a thought flashed across his mind. Richard rolled his top lip then sniffed it. His shoulders drooped dramatically when remnants of Dior's scent filled his nostrils. He had outdone himself.

Richard stepped into the shower, scrubbed at his face and hands until they started to prune. He'd done it. Certainly he'd gone too far. There was no way Nadeen neglected to pick up on his strange behavior and overwhelmingly peculiar aroma, he concluded. Likewise, there was no conceivable reason Nadeen didn't wake him up with a fist in his mouth. By the time Richard had gotten dressed, nothing about the quiet morning added up. He tried to sort it out while sitting on the stairs, lacing a pair of designer basketball shoes to complement the pricey running suit some thankful parishioners bought for his birthday. He quickly donned a plastic sports watch to avoid potential questions about the one he failed to bring home. Then it hit him: He'd walked off and left his wedding ring at Dior's house too. Richard sighed as he shrugged off feelings of self-pity and imminent danger. *A man this stupid deserves everything he's got coming to him*, he thought. *Stupid, stupid, stupid.*

Cowering under the weight of explaining his whereabouts, Richard strolled into the kitchen. He didn't see Nadeen or her car in the garage. He reached for his cell phone then remembered where he'd left it. Richard raced to the home phone sitting on the counter near the desk nook. He couldn't think of Nadeen's cell number so he scrolled the caller ID list. He wasn't sure if calling her to hasten his punishment was the smartest thing to do. Conversely, he couldn't afford the luxury of not knowing what he was up against.

"Nadeen? Nadeen?" he said when she answered. "Hey, I woke up and you were gone."

"Richard, what's wrong with you?" she said irritably. "I called several times last night, and I left a plate for you. You can't be out there running yourself ragged without eating. I wanted to change the sheets this morning but you were out cold. It's been a long time since you slept that hard. Don't stay so late that you can't come home and shower when you're finished. You stunk."

"Okay" was all he could manage to say. Nadeen was motor-mouthing as usual so Richard assumed he'd made it through unscathed.

"I've been taking your advice. I'm putting in time at the gym. My personal trainer is meeean. I think the attitude costs extra. Uh-oh, here he comes. I've got to go. Call me later. Bye."

Richard hung up the phone, shaking his head. *By the grace of God*, he said to himself. Even a preacher on the take should have readily recognized when God was responsible for pulling the strings on his shiftless cover-up. Pleased by the narrow escape, Richard called Giorgio's clothing salon from his home phone. Suza answered. She explained that Dior called in to say she'd be running late and then something about picking up his personal belongings after eleven. Apparently, Dior had his back and all bases considered. Even though every little scandalous piece of the puzzle fit perfectly, he was more confused than ever.

The mall was quiet for a Thursday when Richard made his way through the maze of boutiques, gizmo shops, and fast-food walk-ups in the food court. He had a sweet song in his heart and a clear conscience. A chance to see Dior, if only for a minute, rattled that moral compass of his. Reality was a foggy detour when he envisioned her lips on his, their bodies slapping together and a whirlwind of passion in the sheets. She was a break from his everyday, the one he'd longed for and cherished before they met.

When he entered Giorgio's, Suza looked up from a clothing catalog at the checkout counter. She smiled cordially to keep from laughing. Richard's grin was more suitable for a small child staring through an ice-cream parlor window. He peered over the store then back at Suza. "Is Dior in? I'm Richard. I spoke with you earlier about something she was holding for me."

"Sure, Richard, I remember you. Dior is in but she'll be tied up awhile." She lowered her head then looked away. The secret she concealed was hard to disguise. Dior was in the manager's office with Giorgio on one of their frequent *sales meetings*. Suza didn't have the heart to tell Richard what was being sold behind the locked door. "Here is what she left for you," she offered instead, handing Richard a small package. Suza's lips were pursed so tightly it looked as if she'd sucked a lemon. "I'll be sure to tell Dior you came by, when she's finished…up…in…the…back." Richard accepted the white envelope, cradled it, and then nodded peculiarly.

"Okay, thanks," he offered finally. "Thanks a lot." With a decidedly slower bounce in his step, Richard left the store with his parcel in hand. The encounter didn't go anything like he'd anticipated. In fact, it was a total letdown. Dior had confided to him that the owner preferred he stayed away and maybe it was for the best. Loitering was bad for business, any business.

Once he'd settled into his car, Richard blew off the lost opportunity to flirt with Dior. He was satisfied with retrieving his watch, wedding ring, and cell phone, which informed him of seven unheard messages. While listening to Nadeen's from the night before, Richard nodded nonchalantly, blah-blah-blah style. He chuckled at the quirky voice mail message Dior sent, bragging about the physical drubbing she put on him and how her offer to provide a full dose of Viagra was still on the table. She concluded the call with a chorus of steamy moans and groans reminiscent of their erotic episode. Richard replayed the message several times before forcing himself to delete it. The last message Richard retrieved happened to be Phillip's, reminding him of their monthly meet-and-munch lunch. Somehow it had

slipped his mind. Face time with his closest friend was important. Phillip had been a constant, through good and bad times.
Richard readily grasped the significance of a sound support system. Phillip had always been a commendable confidant and as
good as gold.

Boscoe's Wings and Things was a modest eatery that prided
itself as a hot wing heaven. Loyal customers waited by the dozens
for the wings. Richard spotted him at the table the second he
walked in the door. "Phillip, you must've gotten here when the
place opened. You see the line up front?"

"Hey, Brotha Pastor. Glad you could make it and yes, I did. I
always get here before the lunch crowd. I'm too hungry to stand
still and watch plates of hot food glide by my nose. God is still
working with me on that one, I guess."

Richard joined him at the table near the window. Whenever Phillip saddled him with *Brotha Pastor*, he knew what to
expect. Phillip was a great friend and a better deacon. He ate,
drank, and slept church business even when Richard wasn't in
the mood to put on his minister hat and spend the entire afternoon church chatting. "Ahh, I know that tone, Deacon. Could
we wait until after I've had some food in my stomach before we
get deep into a M.E.G.A. strategy session? The congregation is
holding up fine despite the elders running scared of growing too
big. Ain't no such thing as too big or too many. Shoot, didn't
Jesus feed five thousand souls with five loaves of bread and two
fish?"

"Yeah, but He could walk on water," Phillip countered.

"I know where some of the rocks are too," Richard jested,
as if he had some tricks up his sleeve to pull off a miracle or
two. Phillip didn't like the insinuation that Jesus may have used
deception to perform his phenomenal wonders.

"Alright, Richard, I get it," he said, heading off a lengthy discussion about faith and fortitude. "I'm ordering my usual: a six-stack with French fries. Rose says I got to get my vegetables."

"Everything fried, huh? That is one way to go." Richard scanned the menu, flipped it over, then opened it again. "They don't have too many low-fat items."

"Who'd come here if they did?" Phillip asked, as if he wouldn't.

"There comes a time in a man's life, he wants options is all I'm saying," Richard mumbled, his eyes glued to the colorful order board.

"Options?" Phillip gave his spiritual leader a shrewd once-over. "I see you're exercising one option. This is the first time I've seen you decked out in a jazzy running suit in the middle of the day. What happened to your stance on church leadership dressing the part? You know, business casual."

"I know what I said but today was one of those days I just felt kind of loose."

"Loose? You've been away from the office a lot lately. That wouldn't have anything to do with your new lease on loose?" Phillip studied Richard's relaxed body language while a waitress took their orders.

"Actually it does and it doesn't. Look, Phillip, I've met someone. She's not a Christian but it's like the parable of the lost sheep. It's hard not to go after the one when ninety-nine are safe and sound."

"This lost sheep, have you ministered to her?"

"Yes and she even watched the televised broadcast afterwards. Said before, she didn't do church. You can't tell me you haven't taken a certain interest in a beautiful lady with a hole in her soul? This woman is rough around the edges and young, sort of."

Phillip shook his head disappointedly. "That depends. How young and how beautiful is this black sheep? She is a sistah?"

"Yeah, man, yeah. I had no intentions of getting close. It just kinda happened."

"What's that?"

"Me being crazy about her."

"You're crazy alright and nothing just happens, Richard. You're a married man and a minister," Phillip reminded him, while controlling his pitch so as not to be overheard by others sitting nearby. "Besides, Nadeen is a good woman."

"Did Rose being a good woman have anything to do with you and that cocktail waitress you shacked up with for a weekend in Denver?" Richard warned him not to throw stones when his house was also made of glass.

"That was different. Me and Rose were on bad terms and I was snowed in. Couldn't catch a flight out for two days, and anyway Sharon was a bartender."

"So! You couldn't keep your pants zipped either but it's not my place to chastise you. Men do wrong all the time, always have. David plotted to have a man killed so he could get at Bathsheba."

"What is this, Bible trivia? Richard, don't tell me you're comparing yourself to King David now, because he really messed his life up behind some new booty. That's not the pattern you'd want to cut out for yourself."

"Look, Phillip, I'm not asking your permission. Just thought I'd tell my best friend what's been going on with me. Life on this side of the table isn't as easy as it looks. I've poured my life into making Methodist Episcopal Greater Apostolic a huge success. Is it wrong for me to back off when I need some private time to rejuvenate?" Richard saw a sour expression gleaming back at him.

"Never said it looked easy, Richard," Phillip asserted regretfully. "We all have to make our own beds, no doubt about that.

Okay, the friend in me will listen while I keep my Christian mouth shut."

"Thank you. That's all I ask." Richard sighed, then smiled as easy as breathing. "Her name is Dior, like the designer handbags and perfume. She's classy and sweet just like that too. Her house is small but furnished real nice. She's a saleslady at the mall."

"At the mall?" Phillip yelled, louder than he intended to. "You're cheating on your wife with a mall rat. God Lawd, help him."

"You can say that again. She's an animal, Phillip, a man-eater. She lets me be me, no pretense, no posturing. She cooks dinner, healthy meals too, because she cares about me. Dior's got a fully stocked bar, wine, weed, a ravenous sexual appetite, and Viagra."

"Viag—what?"

"I haven't popped any little blue pills yet but I've been thinking about it. I told you she was an animal and I'm going to do my best to train her."

"Train her to do what?"

"Be my faithful concubine," Richard answered smugly.

Phillip sat up in his chair then leaned in. "You intend to keep this Dior on the side long-term? So this isn't just a fling, like that woman who almost broke up your marriage?"

Richard pouted. "See, why'd you have to bring that up?"

"Because it's history repeating itself or worse. You were young and foolish then. I don't know how to justify what you're doing now. Anyway, if what you say about this one is true, you know what happens when you hold a firecracker in your hands too long after the fuse is lit."

"I'm not worried about that. I'm busy trying to be all she wants and needs. Life is about investments. Give and take, that's what works for us."

Phillip rubbed at his temples. He couldn't make sense of it no matter how hard he tried. Richard had obviously fallen head over heels for the other woman, a young and dangerous other woman. "Where do Nadeen and your daughters figure in when you're investing in another woman?"

"Nadeen knows my heart," Richard answered boldly. "She also knows which side her bread is buttered on. Push won't come to shove." He stuck out his chest boastfully. "Nadeen ain't going nowhere unless I say so."

"If you could hear yourself talk you wouldn't stand another word. What did that girl put on you? Never mind, I don't want to know." Phillip had heard enough. "When all of this blows up in your face, where are you and this saleslady gonna live, in her tiny but nice house behind the mall?"

"It won't come to that, trust me. I've got it under control. Anyway, here comes the waitress with our lunch."

"Wrap mine up to go. I can't stomach another bite."

# FOURTEEN

## *Pay to Play*

Richard's involvement with Dior had taken on a life of its own. For three weeks, Richard was diligent in her bedroom while shirking his responsibilities at the church. He'd heard Phillip's stern warning about weak morals corrupting the soul. Although Phillip was dead-set against the affair, he continually covered up Richard's indiscretion and stints of inaccessibility. Richard kept telling himself that his tryst with Dior wouldn't affect his position as a pastor or his relationship with Nadeen. He'd determined that a healthy dose of affection when he was at home, coupled with frequent gifts and spontaneous outings, would keep his wife in check and clueless to his philandering ways. Double-duty is the name he pinned to his underhanded double-dealing. Hedging on nearly a month's worth of lies, Richard was thumping his chest. He actually thought he'd figured out a foolproof method for pleasing two women at the same time. However, he hadn't counted on Nadeen doing quite a bit of figuring herself.

While Richard executed his scheme to perfection, maintaining a comfortable home life and a mistress who drove him wild at every turn, Nadeen was privy to the flip side of the same coin. Richard had been uncharacteristically absent when she stopped by to visit him at the office, and he avoided answering his cell phone for hours at a time. He disappeared late in the evening, then he'd drag in tired from what he called "seeing to the needs of the flock." Since he had been true to his word in the past, she wanted to go on trusting it. It bothered her when Richard came home late then continually ignored the dinner plates she'd set out for him. He used to look forward to sitting down to a meal set aside for him, sharing what he'd been doing, and for which member of the congregation. That was often a highlight of Nadeen's day as well. Their daughters were typically in bed so she had her man all to herself. Richard recapped the struggles and triumphs he witnessed so vividly Nadeen felt as if she'd been on the front lines with him. Helping people sort out their lives after misfortune came knocking was an admirable calling. Richard was good at building bridges over troubled waters. Nadeen was proud of him. Now it seemed that he was out and about building bridges that didn't help anyone but himself. There was a knot in her stomach every time she allowed herself to wonder if Richard was getting his nourishment elsewhere, intimate and otherwise. She was concerned about his weight loss, rushing off to the health club first thing in the morning and popping vitamins by the handful. Nadeen watched and waited for definitive answers to a slew of disturbing questions. Firing accusations at him wouldn't do anything but put him on the defensive, ignite arguments, and widen the divide currently looming in their home.

Having been married to Richard for eighteen years and listening to hordes of women crying over their relationship ills armed Nadeen with more than a few tricks of the staying-married trade. Despite her suspicions, she decided to utilize what she learned to make the best of what she had to endure. Whenever Richard found his way home past what she considered an acceptable hour or had been missing longer than she deemed necessary, Nadeen demanded sex the minute he walked in the door, just in case he'd been thinking of sowing seeds in another woman's garden. To conclude he had really gone through with it was unthinkable. Nadeen wasn't ready to give up her life as the M.E.G.A. Church first lady or trade it in for the doldrums of single-motherhood. She was a wife and a good one. It meant a lot to her but so did her sanity. Nadeen was well aware that being a preacher's spouse required a certain amount of commitment and challenges, but she refused to be anybody's fool.

Early one morning, Richard was getting dressed. He hadn't said two words to Nadeen the night before. Despite his silent and late arrival, she managed to get thirty minutes of intimate whispers out of him during his mandatory performance. Richard knew the score: Putting in at home was just as important as putting out at Dior's. Thus far, his execution merited a sound grade but his health was beginning to fail.

He came out of the bathroom coughing and wheezing. Nadeen rolled over in bed rubbing her eyes. "Hey, you alright?" she asked, really wanting to know. Richard sat on the edge of the bed with his back to her. He nodded that he felt fine then started a pathetic chorus of snorts and sniffles.

"Yeah, just a little run down."

Nadeen looked him over casually then smiled to herself, deep down inside. "Spreading yourself kind of thin, aren't you?"

A wicked chill came over Richard's entire body as he shuddered wearily. *You don't know the half of it*, he thought, as he reached for the box of tissues on the nightstand. "You know how it can get. There's so much laboring required," he said, thinking mostly of the energy required to keep up with Dior. "I can't let up on it."

Nadeen didn't appreciate his choice of words. "Neither can I," she replied, to even the score. Richard blew his nose, sneezed again, then turned toward her.

"Was that supposed to mean something?"

"You're a smart man. Doesn't everything mean something? Have a good day, Richard. Oh and by the way, if you plan on coming in late again, you might want to pocket some of your energy. You'll need it."

Later that morning, Nadeen read her Bible for fortification. She felt comforted when studying the fifth chapter of Ephesians. She nodded her head affirmatively when her eyes scanned across verse twenty-two through twenty-four in the Life Application edition. *Wives, submit to your husbands as to the Lord. For the husband is the head of the wife as Christ is the head of the church, his body, of which he is the Savior. Now as the Church submits to Christ, so also wives should submit to their husbands in everything.* Nadeen sighed when she realized that every word of that passage was true, even if it happened to be Richard's favorite. The next eight verses put a hint of a smile on her face. They were the cornerstones with which she'd built her marriage and the words she drew on when hard times put her on her knees the most. *Husbands, love your wives, just as Christ loved the church and gave himself up for her to make her holy, cleaning her by washing with water through the word, and to present her to himself a radiant church, without stain or wrinkle or any other blemish, but holy and blameless.* Nadeen wanted to be cherished and held in the same high regard that Jesus had for the Church. She could scarcely remember a time when she knew beyond a shadow of a doubt that Richard couldn't eat, sleep, or breathe without thinking about her. The children came, his ministry grew, and life happened. Nadeen tried to push the loss of his once-abundant love clear out of her mind by getting back into the Good Book. *In the same way, husbands ought to love their wives as their own bodies. He who loves his wife loves himself. After all, no one ever hated his own body, but he feeds and cares for it, just as Christ does the church; for we are members of his body. For this reason a man will leave his father and mother and be united to his wife, and the two will become one flesh.* As tears welled up in her eyes, Nadeen read the end of the chapter aloud. If Richard had lost his way, bonded physically with another woman, she had to know. How she'd handle it worried her but that was a bridge to cross when and if she came to it. "*This is a profound mystery—but I am talking about Christ and the church,*" she read, nodding slowly again. "*However, each one of you also must love his wife as he loves himself, and the wife must respect her husband.*" She sighed, offered a silent prayer of thanks, forgiveness, and discernment to get her heart right with the Holy Spirit. Then Nadeen closed her Bible. She picked up the telephone for human reinforcements to help get her mind right before dealing with the evil spirit she felt was tearing at the seams of her marriage and had the audacity to crawl in her bed.

Rose, a medium shade of brown, was as tall as most men and built like a battleship. At age forty-five, her face was full, but the glowing features that drove her husband, Phillip, crazy fifteen years ago were still visible. Large round brown eyes sparkled beneath the perfectly tamed coif framing her face. Two almond-shaped dimples anchored a joyful smile, and her full lips bolstered attractive accents. Rose knew she looked good, regardless of forty extra pounds of voluptuous womanliness she'd padded on over the years. "*Fine is fine,*" she told Phillip on more than one occasion, when he strongly suggested she diet. "Don't bring up should've, would've, and shortcomings because I'd like to alter you a few inches in one place in particular but I don't beat you over the head with it." After shutting Phillip down, she prayed for repentance although she meant every word at the time.

An inviting aroma of freshly brewed coffee guided Rose into

Nadeen's kitchen. As usual, she dropped everything when receiving a call from a sister in need. And, as usual, she broke her neck getting to some juicy gossip and a pot of expensive Colombian blend. Rose let herself in, which was par for the course. She didn't see herself as a visitor in the Allamay household for two reasons: Richard was her first cousin, and Nadeen had become her dearest friend. Despite strong family ties, Rose's alliance lay elsewhere. She often cited how women had to stick together, "especially when men started to feeling themselves at a sistah's expense."

"Nadeen?" said Rose with a careful grin, walking softer through the room when her high heels click-clacked too loudly against the imported tile. "Ooh, sorry."

Nadeen raised a glass dome then eased half of a pound cake from beneath it. She glanced at Rose peculiarly with a question in her eyes. "Why are you apologizing? I'm just a little troubled. I'm not asleep." She almost asked why Rose's blue jeans and blouse were so tight but reasoned it wouldn't change the way her friend dressed or the fact that Rose didn't care what other people thought about her somewhat provocative attire.

"Because I can see you've got a headache from here. I came as fast as the good Lord would allow. Now that I'm here, why don't you get me some of that coffee I smell so we can talk about the reason you called me away from my stories." She set her purse on the granite countertop gingerly, carefully watching Nadeen's every move. "God knows I don't want to rush you but this has all the signs of a heavy heart. You might as well go on and cut me a thick slice of that cake too." Nadeen moved at a slower clip than Rose was accustomed to seeing. "You sure Richard didn't try to make you do anything you said you wouldn't?" Secretly, she wished Nadeen would take an occasionally broader step on the wild side so she'd feel better about sharing her own sexploits openly.

"Not everybody is all wrapped up in alternative sex, like someone I know," she answered with her nose in the air. "Besides, one day you and Phillip might get stuck doing that thing the Bible says you're not supposed to."

"Huh!" Rose laughed. "You don't have to worry about that. I got a bottle of oil by the bedside. Never needed it yet but I keep hope alive." She blushed over the lewd comment then motioned at the saucers Nadeen took from the cupboard. "I wasn't playing about the cake either, so come on now. I ran three red lights and a stop sign knowing what you had sitting under that glass."

Nadeen poured two cups of coffee, set the sugar caddy in the middle of the breakfast table, and then picked at her slice with a fork. She didn't have any conclusive evidence of Richard's wrongdoing and didn't really know where to begin. "Maybe I shouldn't have called you, Rose. It's probably nothing."

"Probably nothing?" Rose repeated. She was disappointed when it appeared Nadeen was stalling. "Don't make me guess what's got you looking like you just got fired off a good job."

"Funny. In a way, that's exactly how I feel." She sipped from her cup then held on to it like a crutch, as if she'd lose the courage to speak her mind if she set it down. "How many couples have we known to break up over the past five years?"

"Hmm, too many to count," Rose replied with a disappointed sigh. "It's like the flu. When it gets around, it touches a lot of people in the same house. What goes on in the world is bound to touch those we love. M.E.G.A. is a great place to worship and grow in the Lord as any but it's also a reflection of what goes on outside the church doors. Off the top of my head, I can recall twelve or thirteen families that split for some reason or another. Since most of the wives come to us for a shoulder to cry on, you know as many as I do. Sad, how we seem to get hit by one flu epidemic after the next."

"Yeah, there's no getting around it. That's for sure." Nadeen lowered her head as if it weighed a ton. Rose's eyes narrowed. With grave distress, she waded away from church talk and farther from shallow waters.

"I hope you're not trying to tell me you think you're coming down with something?" Rose made it a point not to use the word *divorce* unless it was pertaining to people she either didn't know or didn't like.

Nadeen fiddled with her cake awhile longer before diving into the deep end with Rose. She forced an uneasy smile on her lips, dreading the conversation about to ensue. Discussions regarding potential wayward husbands were the most troublesome to initiate so Nadeen jumped right in. "It's hard to say and even harder to imagine but I believe Richard is seeing someone," she whispered, as if others might hear her words and judge them. Nadeen stared into her coffee cup, filled with a muddy hue, matching her suspicions. "I can't prove it but there's something going on with him."

"Oomph" was Rose's quiet response. She remained uncharacteristically silent. She'd held her marriage in the highest regard, even after learning of Phillip's indiscretion in Denver. Cheating husbands was such an ugly business so she knew to tread lightly. "Well, maybe it's not what you think," Rose muttered, her mouth taut and dry.

"I don't know Richard anymore. He's staying out late, in meetings, he *says.* Most mornings, he's up and out the door before I can say hi good."

Rose didn't want to ask the natural question begging to be released from her pursed lips. "Where's he going so early?"

"To the gym, I guess. At least that's what he tells me," Nadeen added. The expression latched to her face was blank and empty. "There must be some truth in it because he has been trimming down. He really looks good, when I think about it." She took a brief sip of coffee, still neglecting to make eye contact with her confidante.

"I'm not one to tell you what to do, but this unrest isn't healthy for you. Richard is a busy man with lots of things on his mind. The church pulls at him something awful at times. People count on him for so much. And so far you haven't told me anything that sounds like adultery." Rose wanted to believe her friend's marriage was safe. Early morning workouts aside, it seemed all else was well. "Has anything else changed?" When Nadeen heard the loaded question, her eyes drifted up to rest on Rose's.

"What hasn't changed? Richard hardly answers his cell phone anymore. When I phone him at the office, he's either on a call or out running errands. He's distant mentally, the times I do get to speak with him. We used to share so much, about life, about the kids. Mahalia's friends are at that age where they're playing with fire. You know, flirting with sex and seeing how close they can get to it without actually getting burned. Richard used to be so in tune with her. Mahalia is becoming a young woman and he doesn't realize it. I feel like a single parent, like I'm going it alone."

"Have you told him how you feel? I mean, it's clear you're hurting over this."

"I started to sit down with him several times but our rhythms are off. He's tired, I'm sleepy, it's late, or he leaves too early. It never seems like the right time to talk." Suddenly the corners of Nadeen's mouth rounded into a playful smile. "I could make time but then I'd have to loosen the bridal reins when the rides have been pretty good lately." She almost laughed at the befuddled look on Rose's face. "Girl, I'm so bad I'm too ashamed to say."

"Oh yes you will say or I'm moving in to see for myself."

"Okay but I wouldn't advise trying this at home. It could get tricky."

"Nadeen?" Rose said, raising her voice. "Hurry up now. You know I like tricks."

"Yes, I am well aware of that," she mused. "Well, since Richard spends so much time away from the house doing God knows what, I make him pay a toll when he gets in."

"A toll? You got your husband paying for sex?" That sounded like a great deal she didn't mind working on her end.

"No, I make him pay *with* sex. See, I'm alone and worrying about what he might be getting into so I tax his behind for coming in late, staying away, and leaving early. He's got to compensate me for my pain and suffering."

"Ooh, sexual healing is the best kind," Rose agreed wholeheartedly.

"Hallelujah. God is good."

"Raise your hand and say amen." Rose was laughing so hard, she didn't notice right off that she was laughing alone. "What's the matter, Nadeen? Seems to me that freak fee you got going on is working out fine. Shoot, you have me thinking up a way to tighten the bridal reins in the Evans bedroom. I'm due for a good ride too."

"I'm making fun of a difficult situation, but it isn't as fun as it sounds. For instance, I taxed him last night. We made some good, long, loud loving too. It felt sort of strange though, like somebody was watching us."

"Uh-oh. Look out now. Y'all got it on video?"

"No, Rose, it's not that kind of party. It was Richard. His eyes were open the whole time. He held this cold blank gaze on me for darn near an hour."

Rose jerked uncontrollably, spilling coffee on her hand. "An hour! Sixty minutes? God sure is good! This is turning out better than my soaps. I wish Phillip could hold it straight for that long. I'd let him stare at it, videotape it, and take a picture too. I wouldn't give a flying flip what he was doing as long as he kept it going, okaaay."

"You are so crude."

"Me? Uh-uh, you're like those slim cigarettes from Virginia. You've come a long way, baby, and I'm proud of you. Look, if Richard isn't living up to his vows the other signs would be there. Men get evil when they mess around. They pick fights, stay on their periods, and cannot be satisfied with anything you do for them. I can't tell you the stories I've overheard while women figure it out a little at a time at the beauty shop. If something is going on, it'll show itself. Satan always does. Otherwise you just keep raising the taxes until he gets his act together or gets too whipped to leave the house."

Nadeen pushed the cake saucer aside then peered into her tepid cup of coffee. "You're probably right. I'd just hate to sit back and be made a fool of like so many other women I know. My mother was a prime example. Remember, I grew up in a minister's house and was raised by a minister's wife; who often got the scraps after Brotha Pastor had spent all night *seeing to the concerns of the church*," she said, mimicking her father's pious justification for creeping. "What he was seeing to were his own concerns. We found that out when two sisters from the congregation turned up at the maternity ward on the same day, both claiming my daddy was the one who done it." A solemn sigh passed between her lips as she thought back on that miserable era in her life. "I saw my mother's hair fall out, in clumps, over church mistresses. I will not let that happen to me, and my girls don't need to know it's possible for a woman to hurt that bad because her husband can't keep it in his pants. History won't repeat itself here," she asserted adamantly. "I'd leave him first and take my children with me."

Nadeen huffed violently and lifted the fork from the table. She stabbed it into the slice of cake then stuffed a big piece of it into her mouth.

Rose watched in awe. Nadeen looked like a breath of fresh air. "Whew, I feel better already," she announced emphatically.

"I see that. Got milk?"

"Uh-huh, got more than that too. Got my dignity and I got my friend Rose."

# FIFTEEN

## *Pulpit Pimpin'*

Friday evening found Dior in the middle of a bragging session with Tangie. "Yeah, girl, I got that brotha tossing and turning," Dior boasted over cappuccinos at the nearby coffee bar. "He said, *baby...you got me reaching for you in my sleep.*"

Tangie howled at the tiny table and didn't care who cut their eyes at her for doing so. "Whuuut? That's my ace. That's what I'm talking about. I figured you've been up to something since it's been taking you three or four days to return my calls. So, out with it. Who is he? What does he do?"

"He's into marketing. You might say he's a public speaker," Dior said, after wiggling in her seat to feign false excitement. "I heard him do his thing too. He's real good. People get all excited when he gets to going."

"Public speaker?" Tangie said, like those words stunk. "What kind of product is he pushing?"

"Books, motivation, and stuff," Dior answered, wishing the subject changed all by itself. "Tangie, I don't want to spend a lot of time getting in his business. I done already got where I really need to be with him."

"In his heart and in his head?" Tangie questioned, like a hopeless romantic.

"Uhhh, in his pants and in his pockets. You don't hear me."

Tangie leaned back in her chair then sneered down her nose. "Dior, I thought you were really feeling this one, having been stowed away for days at a time and him wanting you in his sleep and whatnot?"

"I never said we stowed away," Dior pouted defensively. "Not yet, anyway. He's got a lot going on but my time is coming. I'll get my hands on more than just his money. I want the whole enchilada, the platinum package, big house, kids, and a diamond ring."

"Are you sure someone hasn't already booked that very exclusive trip? Why haven't I met him and have you ever been to his house?" Tangie queried skeptically.

"No, but thanks for asking how I'm handling mine. I haven't seen his house and don't want to. His father's house, that's what I want. It's a mansion." Dior felt her chest swelling with resentment for having to discuss Richard's personal business. "I'll be sure and let you know when I get all moved in. I might even let you be in the wedding," she offered, to move the conversation along. "That's right. I'm going to be his wife. It's still early so he hasn't asked me yet but he will. I got him stuck on my stunts. That upside-down thing I do off the edge of the bed, it turned him out. I keep him weak. He didn't even care that he left his cell phone and gold watch under my bed."

Tangie leaned in closer. "Ooh, for real? You rocked your best move like that? I tried to pull it off but it did not turn out right. I stuck the upside-down part but then I slid off the bed and right onto the floor. All I ended up with was a bump on my head and this. See, look at that carpet burn. I'll leave all of that cartwheel-ing foolishness to you."

"How many times have I told, it's a handstand, not a cart-wheel," Dior scoffed playfully.

"That's why that fool Tyson kept dropping me," Tangie sighed. She began to reevaluate her decision to give up on pulling stunts of her own. "It was good seeing you again, Dior. I'd love to stay but I got to make a private call. I owe Tyson an apology and another shot at getting it right." Tangie sprang from the table with her cell phone in hand and poised to press SEND. "Don't be a stranger. Okay, bye." She bent over for a quick cheek-to-cheek embrace then darted out hurriedly. "Handstand, maybe I should write that down."

Dior remained at the coffee shop for a long while. She spent most of the evening sipping on overpriced chocolate syrup concoc-tions, flipping through wedding magazines, and marking the pages with the prettiest bridal gowns. She didn't mind that Tangie had full knowledge of her sordid relationship with Giorgio. Her affair with Richard had potential, she'd decided. Selling men's apparel paid the bills but she also envisioned herself living the lavish life-style afforded many of her client's wives. She dreamed of jewelry boxes filled with exquisite stones and customized closets loaded to the gills with designer dresses and shelves aligned with imported handmade shoes. Dior had grown tired of faking it, rummaging through bazaars for knockoff gear and scouring department store clearance bins for cubic zirconium accessories. Richard was her ticket out of just scraping by and it was time to catch that train.

On Sunday morning Dior pulled her baby Beamer into the M.E.G.A. Church parking lot. She stepped out of the 3-Series BMW loaded for bear, with her mind set on bagging the top prize: Richard. Privately, he belonged to her. When they were alone, manipulation was easy. He fell for every sleight-of-hand maneuver, insistent whisper, and soft-talking proposition. Taking her merry-mistress show on the road was a first. If she adequately executed the plan to perfection, this opening act would be her last.

Dior sauntered past a slew of Mercedes and Lexus sedans littered throughout the vast parking lot on her way into the main foyer. White-gloved ushers greeted her as she viewed the broad area just outside of the auditorium entrance doors. After she captured the attention of several ushers bidding to accompany her to the balcony overflow section, Dior objected delicately, insinuating the balcony was simply unacceptable. She'd gone through too much trouble engineering the exact conditions to introduce herself to the other side of Richard's world, the holy one he'd kept hidden from her. Dr. Pastor Richard Allamay, PhD, in all of his splendidly spiritual glory—that's what Dior came to see. Of course she'd witnessed his charismatic stylings on the local television station since meeting him exactly twenty-seven days ago. Watching Richard on TV was a start, she'd determined, but this was his day, pastor's day. Successfully unseating the current first lady called for taking a closer look at what could one day be hers.

When Dior batted her soft brown eyes just beneath her pink wide-brimmed hat, the male usher who had been awaiting her answer pursed his lips to keep his tongue from falling out of his mouth in the Lord's house. "Normally, I wouldn't mind sitting in the balcony," she whispered, just this side of seductive, "but I'm a special guest of Pastor Allamay's and he said I should be taken down front, no matter what time I arrived." Dior flirted with the man again. She ratcheted up the heat with pouting lips and a come-hither leer. Like most men, the usher was defenseless against her sensual sighs humming in his ear like a sultry siren's song. "I know you don't want me to be late for the pastor's message. He wouldn't like that, not at all," she contended finally. *So hurry up and get me within kissing distance*, she thought. *My man is down there and you're in my way.*

The young man watched as Dior ran her hands down the sides of her tight pink dress. It was a calculated measure to remind him that she wasn't in the mood to be refused, on any level. With his eyes trained on her hips, the usher responded just as Dior knew he would. He treated her like a VIP when opening the doors to escort her down the main aisle. Heads swiveled when she followed the amicable attendant toward the second row, which was in direct opposition to protocol and seen as discourteous so close to the beginning of the minister's address.

The auditorium at the Methodist Episcopal Greater Apostolic Church was filled to the rim. Dior's first impression was that it didn't appear nearly as ostentatious as it did on television—until she noticed the plush carpeting instead of worn-out linoleum she remembered as a child when being forced to attend Sunday service with her cousin's family. *It sure is packed up in here*, she couldn't help thinking. *Too bad there isn't a cover charge. There must be 8,000 people on the hook. Let's see, at ten bucks a head...that's $80,000 a week, easy money. What if they threw in with the whole 10 percent thing? Oh man, that's a lot of money.*

In Dior's estimations, the church was raking in close to two million dollars a month, not including cable TV rights and weekly DVD sales. Had she known membership contributions alone were four times as much and that Richard's salary, including bonuses, exceeded $20,000 a month, she'd have fallen and bumped her head in front of all those people giving her a peculiar once-over.

Despite the host of video cameras and countless production personnel filming every movement in the pulpit, Dior had a feeling something was missing until it occurred to her. There were no rickety old hard-as-stone wooden pews—instead, the room had been custom-fitted with endless rows of comfortable, cloth-covered, stadium-style chairs. It appeared the business of the day was entertainment, and she was being afforded a ring-side view. She imagined that becoming a woman of the Word, as opposed to the woman of the world she'd always been, might require some stick-to-itiveness and a couple of No Doz tabs because those cushioned chairs presented a surefire challenge to stay awake. That was before the curtain went up and the gospel hour began.

An enormous eighty-piece choir rose like a military platoon, on the command of the director of music. Dior, impressed with their pretentiousness and colorful robes, settled in for the concert. Anticipation grew as a very large man approached the microphone. Dior kept an eye on him amid intermittent glances to her immediate left. Nadeen occupied her designated throne in the front row, in the adjacent section. Dior buzzed inside when she recognized Richard's wife, heavier than she envisioned and adorned in far less flamboyant regalia than she would have guessed. She caught Nadeen twice sneaking a peek at her. Each time, Dior returned the fleeting looks with subtle smirks. By the end of the choir's second number, Nadeen's glances grew increasingly more constant. Casual curiosity bordering on insecurity eventually morphed into unsettling contempt. Dior found it extremely amusing: a woman near her mother's age obviously bothered by the presence of a beautiful stranger. *Let that be a lesson to you. You shouldn't have let yourself go,* Dior wanted to shout in Nadeen's direction. *It takes a bad chick like this to keep a man like yours.*

There were some choice words popping into Nadeen's head too. Because she was there to worship, other more productive thoughts quickly replaced them. She told herself to train her focus on the man and the message, not some tight-dress-wearing disruption. As the choir completed a stirring number, Richard came forward with unrivaled confidence. It lit a fire in Dior.

With thousands looking on, he didn't seem nervous at all. She would have hidden herself behind that podium like a frightened rabbit, but not him. He strolled into the limelight where he belonged, where he was adored, and exactly where Dior wanted him. *Hey Richard*, she said with her eyes when he flipped through the Bible for a specific passage. *You're gonna be my babies' daddy as soon as your marriage to that cow falls apart. The new and improved first lady, yeah that's just my size and I love the way it fits.*

Richard started in with his normal greeting. Nadeen was attentive as usual. She had her Bible open and at the ready to follow along with the sermon, but something gnawed at her, keeping her from concentrating. It surprised her when Richard nodded to the usher that it was alright with him to oblige the pretty lady in pink by sitting her among the most prominent members of the congregation and so close to the pulpit. Typically Richard was the consummate professional orator. He detested unnecessary interruptions when he preached, although he hadn't actually begun his delivery then. The more she analyzed the odd occurrence, other things started appearing out of order as well, but Nadeen couldn't resolve them without rehashing ugly business she had encountered previously.

During the past month, Richard had been distant to the point of acting out of character. He'd also been unseasonably tired and aloof. The week before, Nadeen said she could have sworn her husband was involved with another woman because nothing else made sense. Although she wasn't certain of it, there was a knot the size of a softball tearing at the lining of her stomach and it was the one time she would have easily accepted having been wrong. Earlier that morning, Nadeen had complained to Richard about his behavior and restlessness, and a lack of romance in their relationship. After he'd almost convinced her that she was overreacting to what he called "a pampered woman's guilt," he balked at wearing his favorite red silk necktie. Since he'd worn the same colored power tie for the past six years on pastor's day, his uncharacteristic banter about going in another direction and opening himself up to trying new things made her even more leery of the shaky ground supporting their marriage.

Unwittingly, Nadeen's gaze drifted back to the woman in pink. She admired Dior's figure and her style. The cut of her clothes was a tad too provocative for Nadeen's taste, although she once understood the rationale for flaunting. Now she reasoned that not everything worth having had to be wrapped in a size-six frame. She had a husband, a God-fearing man, who had been satisfied with the full-figured woman he was married to—until lately. Richard was a good provider, who, in spite of a busy schedule, reserved quality time for his family—up until about a month ago. Nadeen had begun to draw some stark conclusions when she noticed Richard's eyes glossing over the woman sitting in the fourth seat of the second row. Suddenly Nadeen found herself scoping out Dior's toned legs and full breasts, sitting up too perfectly to be natural—at least that's what envy forced her to believe. When Richard held his gaze on Dior for a fraction too long, Nadeen determined that this younger mystery lady, adorned in expensive labels, had pulled off a fashionably late entrance with a specific purpose in mind. It wasn't long before Dior's intentions became too obvious for Nadeen to overlook, try as she may.

Richard, standing tall and polished from head to toe, reached for a handkerchief from his inside breast pocket. He panned over the audience, welcomed them for the second time, and then made the extra effort to thank the crowd for helping him celebrate his day, the day set aside for the appreciation of his hard work. With his eyes now trained on Dior, he gestured toward her like an old friend. Dior's lips rounded into a barely noticeable smile, and then she quickly tilted her head down, using that wide brim to shield her eyes. That sneaky move didn't make it past Nadeen. She caught it like a bad cold.

Moments later, Richard sauntered nearer to the side of the aisle where Dior sat. She peered up at him as if they were the only two people in the entire arena. Richard placed his hand on his chest with his fingers outstretched, proclaiming how much he loved doing the Lord's work. Nadeen felt her heart tighten when his gesture reminded her of the pink necktie he just had to wear that day, which happened to be the exact pattern and shade of Dior's dress. Nadeen was utterly floored as the realization of what Richard had been up to and with whom became painstakingly obvious. It was hard to reconcile, but there it was. Her husband, the father of her children, was craving the attention of someone else. So much so that he didn't mind parading her around his church family, in front of God and everybody.

Dior's curiosity had gotten the best of her. She drew in a relaxed breath and turned her head partially to the left for what she thought would have been a stinging glare. Nadeen, forty-three last May and hiding the extra unwanted pounds with sturdy, quality fabrics, cast an inquisitive evil eye simultaneously. It resulted in a staredown of the ages. Neither woman blinked during what Richard later called the cold front to freeze hell over. Nadeen was appalled by the brazen disrespect of the vixen she assumed Dior to be. On the other hand, being the kind of woman who wasn't all that quick to lie down and roll over, Nadeen winked then tossed a leer across the aisle to signify what she thought: *You need to go and find another sandbox to play in, little girl, because I don't plan on sharing mine.*

Although Dior blinked first, her resolve appeared impenetrable. Her lips tightened ever so slightly to hold in what she wanted to pledge aloud. *Oomph, all of that winking is gonna look mighty silly when you realize I took your man. Be nice and maybe I'll let him come home at a decent hour when I'm get finished.*

Nadeen was seething now. She lowered her eyes, contemplating the changes in Richard's demeanor and the way he looked at this mystery lady with a sizable level of interest. His glance lasted an iota too long. There was certainly a haughty degree of recognition. He knew her. How well, Nadeen was afraid to guess. Richard had chosen this woman's necktie over any of the previous gifts purchased by his wife. Nadeen felt sick to her stomach at the thought of being pushed aside for a newer model. Although Richard began his dissertation, she couldn't get past her internal discord to hear it.

Spending Friday afternoon with Rose, philosophizing on the topics of love and life over coffee and pound cake, seemed like such a waste then. In a playful manner, Nadeen had allowed herself to theorize about the kind of woman Richard could have been drawn to. Later, she comprised a mental list of potential church hoochies low enough to invite him into their beds while smiling in her face. There was Tina Williams, a single sister with lots of baggage. Tina had four abortions by three different men, none of whom were inclined to take a paternity test to narrow the candidates for fatherhood. Next was Rosalyn Bates. She was nearing forty, never married, and rumored to flip onto her back easier than a flapjack. Patience Jackson was also a likely contender because she would do anything to get a man and just about anything to keep him, including occasional threesomes with his friends. Nadeen laughed when Rose's list far exceeded hers, then they both decided to let it alone for the time being. As it turned out, they were merely wasting time. Dior happened to be a devil she didn't know.

# SIXTEEN

## *Run Tell That*

F or those of you still shaking off your nightclub buzz," Richard huffed when he noticed people in the audience dozing in their seats, "let me say it again. Lack of faith will fail you. Lack of faith will burden you down and numb you to the power of the Lord." After a round of applause, Richard raised his right hand as if taking an oath. "With God as my witness, my voice mailbox overflowed last week with church members asking for prayer. Jobs are hard to get. Friendships are hard to maintain. Families are splitting up every which way you turn. I know you're heavy-laden, downtrodden, and doggone tired, but we still need to remain faithful to our calling. If you thought it possible to get up when the clock struck, climb out of bed, step out of last night's lust and last night's lies without God's help, you are what they call 'some new kind of fool.' How else did you get here, considering all of the things you've been through? People, you'd better listen and hear me well. Without a goodly amount of faith, Satan will have his way with you. He'll get you crossed up, tripped up, and that's jacked up. Y'all aren't used to Brotha

Pastor taking it to the street, but tough times call for tougher measures. Faith is a necessary key into the Kingdom of Heaven. How else would you get into your own home? God's house is no different. Some of us are tried and tempted, thinking we're making out just fine without the Lord's help. That's a lie you shouldn't be telling yourselves." Richard paused to wipe his forehead with a white cotton handkerchief. When returning it to his inside breast pocket, he caught a glimpse of Dior hanging on to each syllable. He was upset that she'd crashed his party without mentioning it beforehand, but it also excited him. He relished the idea of having a dirty little secret so close to home base. It didn't hurt that she was a head-turning stunner.

Richard beamed when he hopped back atop his soapbox. "If you believe in your heart that God promised deliverance and salvation and that He has the power and intentions to save you from yourselves, your dilemmas, and your sins, then you've come to the right place, because this house was built on those promises. Now then, if you are not a believer nor have any good intentions for yourselves or anyone else, then you'd better check yourself. I'll just be honest with you: People who brought Satan in with them this morning, those who've come into God's house looking to do harm and take advantage of our tempted and tried, you should get up right now and get out! You heard me. Go to hell, without running through the church on your way there. I mean it, get your fake behinds out of here because we came to be about Godly faith this morning!" Richard absorbed a thick shower of cheerful affirmation. Nadeen's pensive expression stood out like a sore thumb. Richard was slightly concerned, failing to understand the magnitude of Dior's presence around his wife. He shrugged off what he'd determined to be nothing worth worrying over, then quickly marched to the left side of the stage, waving an open Bible above his head. "Since nobody stood up and bolted for the door, I'd have to guess we all came here for the same reason: to share in His Word and seek His Kingdom. Faith is vitally important but faith alone won't open the door. In the book of James, chapter two, starting at verse number fourteen, it reads a little something like this," he said, reciting the scripture from memory. "*What good is it, my brothers, if a man claims to have faith but has no deeds? Can such faith save him? Suppose a brother or a sister is without clothes and daily food. If one of you says to him, 'Go I wish you well, keep warm and well fed,' but does nothing about his physical needs, what good is it? In the same way, faith by itself, if it is not accompanied by action, is dead.*" The crowd applauded at his recollection of the passage. Many shouted with affection. Still, Nadeen appeared unmoved. Clearly her mind had taken a trip to some other place, where Richard's showmanship paled by comparison. "Let me finish, let me get back to it," he yelled above the excitement. "Verse eighteen furthers the point. *But someone will say, 'You have faith; I have deeds.' Show me your faith without deeds, and I will show you my faith by what I do. You believe that there is one God. Good! Even the demons believe that, and tremble.'* Mark it down, church. You've got to walk the walk when you talk the talk. Amen?" Richard stormed to the other side of the vast pulpit as the auditorium erupted. Men and women leaped to their feet. The organist chimed in on the heels of a stirring message. She played along masterfully, wringing emotion from the congregation while the pastor brought his sermon to a close. "Just like a body without a spirit is dead, faith without actions to validate it is too. The doors of the church are open." Richard sat behind the podium in a chair fit for a king. It was hand-carved from deep rosewood and decorated with dark crimson fabric. Someone brought him a gold-plated chalice filled with water and another handkerchief to dry his face.

*What a gift*, Dior thought, clapping excitedly.

"What a mess," Nadeen said under her breath.

Strangely enough, they were both right. Richard had undoubtedly utilized his talents to help restore faith to many enduring tumultuous times. On the other hand, he boldly directed his life toward disaster. Assisting others to find peace in the midst of prickly predicaments was one thing. Locating some of it for himself wouldn't be nearly so easy to orchestrate.

After the church service ended, Nadeen played the minister's wife although her heart wasn't in it. She assumed others had witnessed what she did: the cute little pink thing openly flirting with the pastor. It was difficult to imagine otherwise. Her ego had taken such a beating. She excused herself, then shot off like a rocket toward the pastor's chambers. Nadeen was fuming, pacing back and forth in Richard's office. She couldn't wait to question him about his viperous visitor and whether she was the inspiration for his drawer full of new underwear, the hours he reported having been at the fitness center, and a host of disappearing acts. She also questioned the discussion turned debate from earlier that day when Richard reacted like a defiant toddler. He pouted and hissed after Nadeen laid out a collection of the red neckties, which had traditionally been his preference for previous pastor's day services. His adamant determination to wear pink annoyed her then but now she was infuriated. *How could I have been so stupid?* she thought. *Richard said he wanted to step out of the box he's been living in. Had me listening to all of that nonsense about it taking a real man to wear pink. He must think new kinds of fools are born every day. Wait until I see him. Just wait.*

Nadeen waited in Richard's chambers for as long as she could stand to. When he didn't show up, she set out looking for him. Zooming past members without batting an eye or raising her voice to acknowledge them, Nadeen trekked down the sidewalk from the business offices to the main auditorium entrance. She had blinders on until something caught her eye. She recognized a pink dress and wide-brimmed hat heading her way. Disregarding the horde of people milling about, Nadeen guarded the pathway with her arms folded. As Dior drew closer, Nadeen began tapping the toe of her shoe against the cement. Dior stopped less than three feet from the woman blocking her way. "I don't think we've had the chance to meet," said Nadeen, definitive and daring.

"I *know* for a fact we haven't," answered Dior in the same tone she'd received. "I surely would have remembered you."

"Then let me make it plain. I'm Mrs. Richard Allamay."

*That's a silly name for a girl*, Dior wanted to say. "Okay, is that supposed to mean something to me?"

"Look, little girl. I don't know who you think you are," Nadeen challenged, unaware of Dior's street pedigree.

"Ma'am, I haven't been any kind of girl for a long while now. And as for who I am, you'd have to ask *Mr.* Richard Allamay where I fit in with him. And a word to the wise: You might want to get your business straight before stepping to me again."

"Just in case you don't know, the pastor of this church is married, happily married, with two adorable daughters. You're not welcome to come back here."

Dior tilted her head to shield her eyes from the midday sun. She wanted to see Nadeen's face when it cracked. "I came here to worship, not be driven out by some insecure female with her butt on her shoulders. I thought Christians were supposed to invite people into God's house?" Dior asked with a questioning expression that ruffled her adversary. "Don't tell me you're one of those fake-baked ones pretending to be a holy roller?"

Utterly appalled by what she viewed as disrespect, Nadeen looked around to see if anyone heard Dior's verbal assault. "I'm as real as my wedding vows. Maybe we should get Richard out here and see if that wipes the cheesy little smirk off your face."

"I don't answer to you or him, lady, and unless you got

something real to get off your chest, best move to the left." Nadeen observed passersby taking notice. She relaxed her stance then eased over slightly so Dior could squeak by without creating an outright incident. They parted ways, both upset at how the introduction played out.

A month ago, Nadeen would have thought it was inconceivable that a woman would stand up to her when confronted about moving in on her husband. Meeting Dior was extremely unsettling. Richard had a lot of explaining to do.

After Nadeen caught her breath, she stomped into the office building wearing a plastic grin to hide her real emotions while aggravated beneath it. When she rounded the corner past the third-floor elevator, Richard's voice poured out of his open office. Nadeen flew in with both barrels blazing. "What do you think you're doing? Huh? I talked to your lady friend, that pink thing, who just had to sit down front. Yeah, I saw the looks between y'all. Now you're going to tell me what all of that is supposed to be about." Richard glared at his wife for raising her voice at him when others could have easily overheard her rants. Calmly, he collected his keys and wallet from the desk drawer.

"Mahalia, Roxy, I need to talk to your mother," he said with a manufactured smile on his face. "Why don't y'all meet us downstairs by the car in a few minutes." Nadeen was so full of fury she didn't see her own daughters standing between her husband and her wrath. Both girls quickly exited the office as instructed. Nadeen slammed the door so hard the walls shook.

"I hope you're proud of yourself," she spat. "It takes real nerve flaunting your backdoor woman around your wife and friends, Richard."

"Watch your mouth, Nadeen!" he shouted with measured restraint. "You're in the Lord's house."

"You cannot expect me to stand here and listen to you lecture me about respecting the Lord's house after half the church is probably wondering the same thing I am."

Richard sat on the corner of his desk with both arms folded across his chest. "Ahh-hhh. I'm not concerned with what's on the minds of half the church, but I would like to know what's got you acting like this at my office and in front of our children."

Nadeen stared him down. She was highly upset that he would even try and flip the script so easily. "That's just like you, Richard, massaging the issue until it benefits you. Not this time. I know what I saw and it sickened me. The woman all but confirmed what's going on but I want to hear it from you. No lies and no double-talk. Just shoot it to me straight up so I'll know what to tell the divorce attorney."

Richard shrugged his shoulders, stared at his wife of eighteen years, then offered her the truth, his truth. Richard wasn't stupid. On the contrary, he was treacherous. He was lucky enough to catch the interaction between Nadeen and Dior from his office window. Although he couldn't hear a word of it, their body language told him everything he needed to call the outcome correctly. He could tell that Nadeen approached Dior on a fact-finding mission. Dior confirmed that she knew him but under what circumstances was still unclear. She must have said something to send Nadeen reeling because she threw her hands on her hips to protest it. When they didn't come to blows, Richard was sure that Dior held her own while getting a few digs in somehow, leaving Nadeen with a bad taste in her mouth and a full quill of ruffled feathers. "I'm almost afraid to ask how badly you embarrassed me, yourself, and the church, for that matter."

"See, there you go," Nadeen hissed. "Negro, please. Unless you're coming clean, you can save all that for somebody who hasn't been sleeping by herself and waiting up for you to find your way home."

"I'm sorry to disappoint you but one thing has nothing to do with the other, Nadeen," Richard said casually. "Dior is a lost lamb. She sold me this suit and threw in this necktie. I've seen her do a lot more for other customers. That's right, you just insulted a harmless salesperson who said almost a month ago, 'I don't do church.' Thanks to you, she may never *do church* again. I did what I was supposed to. I got her here and was really looking forward to introducing the two of you," he lied to save face. "She could use a seasoned mentor to help get her feet wet in the Lord. However, based on your actions, I wouldn't blame her for running in the other direction and never thinking of reentering another church of any kind. Look, you need to take your sneaky suspicions and that un-Christian attitude to God and seek forgiveness for what you've done. I'm through." He breathed a long labored breath then stood up. Nadeen replayed her conversation with Dior, thought on it some more, then wiped a tear from her eye.

"I'm alright with God, Richard. I'm not alright with you though, nor with how that woman's presence and brazen carrying-on made me feel. She's got designs on you. I saw those looks. I recognize it when hoochies and groupies undress my man in front of my eyes. She couldn't take hers off you."

"You mean, she couldn't take her eyes off my suit," Richard asserted. "I made a deal with Dior when she sold it to me. You probably didn't even notice the monogram on the sleeve." He held it out so Nadeen would feel even more foolish by the time he finished spinning his deceitful web. "I promised her that if she came to M.E.G.A. as my guest, I'd wear this ridiculous pink tie on pastor's day. I didn't think she'd hold up her end of the deal. And yes, I was proud when she did. I always said the journey of a thousand miles begins with a single step. Today, that young lady made perhaps the biggest one of her life toward salvation. Hopefully, it didn't result in two steps backward." When Nadeen's eyes fell toward the floor, Richard knew he'd done another masterful job of adequately clouding the issue. Nadeen didn't know what to believe, so Richard tipped the scale in his favor by using her words against her. "Oh yeah, I'd love to hear how Dior all but confirmed what you thought you saw happening between us?"

"I told her who I was and asked the same of her. She said to ask *Mr.* Richard Allamay where she fits in," Nadeen said reluctantly, as a sinking feeling came over her.

"She used to fit me for suits, although that might not be the case any longer," he said in passing. "Come on, ain't nothing we can do about it before the Lord does so let's get some lunch." When he opened the door, Roxy and Mahalia quickly leaned against the opposite wall. They had undoubtedly heard a great deal of the conversation. Richard didn't feel the need to address their wandering eyes and itching ears, so he grabbed his eldest by the hand and quietly started for the elevator.

Nadeen was torn asunder, not sure if she'd done the right thing by confronting a person who appeared to be a very dangerous wolf marking the shepherd's moves. Then the thought of potentially committing the unthinkable sin of chasing a lost soul from the church door made her head hurt. Richard's explanation sounded plausible, but she couldn't completely take his word for it. Confused and darn near cross-eyed, Nadeen decided to put her feelings on hold until she could firm up her suspicions or cast them away altogether. Despite how mixed up she felt, Roxanne's snaggletoothed smile helped ease the strain, until the child's inquisition began.

"Mommy, why are you and Daddy fighting over that pretty lady in the pink dress?"

"We aren't fighting, baby, and that lady isn't so pretty," Nadeen sniped irritably.

"She looked like a movie star to me," argued Roxanne. "I

heard so many people fussing over how pretty she was and how her face looked painted on."

*Her makeup and tight dress were painted on,* Nadeen thought to herself. "People are sometimes excited to see a new face. It happens all the time, even at the zoo."

Roxanne missed the boulder her mother threw at Dior's head. She didn't miss the opportunity to share what she'd heard earlier. "Mommy, what's a stank-butt gold digger?"

"Nothing, Roxy," Nadeen answered firmly, guessing what other terrible things were said about Dior. "I thought I talked to you about not repeating what you heard said about others. It's not nice."

"I just thought it sounded funny," Roxanne countered. "Herman was telling everybody his daddy called that pretty—uh, not so pretty—lady lots of names. Some of them didn't make me laugh, though." Nadeen began to feel sorry for attacking Dior without knowing all the details. Perhaps it was Richard's prior actions that put her on edge, on the offensive, and ready to pounce. She was reminded that a minister's wife should act considerably kinder toward visitors than Herman's foul-mouthed daddy. Nadeen stepped off the elevator unsettled, but she couldn't find an ounce of regret in her heart for protecting what was still hers, as far as she knew.

# SEVENTEEN

## *Too Many Husbands*

All afternoon, Nadeen followed Richard around the house with her eyes. She tracked him into the bedroom, counted his steps into the kitchen, and later stared him down when he said he was leaving early for evening service. If it hadn't been for Roxanne's sudden stomachache, Nadeen would have grabbed her shoes and followed him out of the house. Mahalia was old enough to look after her younger sister, but it bordered on psychotic behavior trying to keep Richard under constant surveillance. After the heated discussion they had in his private chambers, he would have been brain-dead to do anything remotely ominous, which would potentially spark another venom-laced attack, whether it was warranted or not. Nadeen felt justified when she watched him walk out the door without his typical confident stride. She breathed a labored sigh of relief, feeling she had put him in check but good.

Over the next hour, Nadeen read bedtime stories to Roxanne while checking her temperature intermittently. The child couldn't understand why her mother chose nighttime reading material when the sun hadn't gone off to bed yet. Although it was merely wishful thinking on Nadeen's part, the precocious eight-year-old fought off her trip to dreamland as best she could, playing the sickly patient to the hilt all the while. Roxanne asked for ice cream to soothe her sore throat, then she pleaded pitifully for chicken soup to take the chill away. Nadeen met each request with a motherly there-there followed by a heaping dose of love. She'd all but forgotten about Richard and that "treacherous thing" dressed in pink who disrupted morning worship and caused her to repent for the terrible mischief she imagined having gone on behind her back. When Nadeen investigated the reason why Mahalia had been cooped up in her room for hours, behind closed doors, she realized how derelict in her duty she was regarding her oldest daughter.

Down the hall from Roxanne's room, Mahalia lay sprawled across her bed as well, only she hadn't spent most of the day demanding her mother's time and attention. Mahalia took full advantage by burning up the second phone line she convinced her parents was necessary and well deserved for being a good student and a part-time babysitter. Reluctantly, Richard caved in to Mahalia's constant petitions. Nadeen however, was not fond of the idea from the very beginning nor had she softened her stance in the two months since her husband buckled. She held legitimate concerns about the intimate conversations very likely finding their way to Mahalia's private line.

Nadeen tiptoed up to the bedroom door quietly. She leaned in, carefully placing her ear against it. Stifled by muffled sounds, Nadeen had a difficult decision to make. Spying on Mahalia wasn't the coolest mother move, but she felt compelled to keep tabs on her daughter, who now had budding breasts and a swelling interest in mannish, smooth-talking boys. With that in mind, Nadeen squeezed the doorknob gently. She turned the handle and held her breath. As she pushed it ever so slightly, Mahalia's words became clearer. "Yeah, girl, I'm telling you. All Dwayne wanted to do was get his dirty fingers in my panties. No, I didn't want him to...until he washed his nasty hands."

After hearing her child's recognition and admittance to participating in a sexual act, Nadeen gasped. Her knees trembled and her fingers tingled. She wanted to barge in, rip the phone from Mahalia's hot little hands, and commence running a bar of soap through her filthy mouth. Nadeen felt her chest heave in and out. Where was Richard at a time like this? she wondered. He wouldn't be able to shrug off this incident as if it hadn't changed everything about their relationship. Nadeen was a breath away from busting through that door on a mad tear but something stopped her. She heard further appalling language spewing from her daughter's lips.

"I don't know, Trevy, they say you can't get pregnant if you're on top, so next time Dwayne can get some without the condom as long as I ride. I'll tell him that he can bring his big brother, who's home from college too. I hope he can show me some new moves. Girl, yeah, I'm ready for a threesome. I can handle it."

Nadeen couldn't hold her place or her tongue any longer. She ripped through the door, tortured. Her daughter sat casually at her desk, seemingly unaffected by her mother's sudden appearance. "Mahalia! Hang up that phone!" screamed Nadeen, loud enough to peel paint off the walls.

Mahalia rolled her eyes. "I have to go, Trevy. Told you my mama was at the door," she said knowingly. "Yeah, she knows I was playing." Mahalia tossed the telephone onto the light-colored desk, next to her personal computer.

"Uh-huh, you were playing alright? Am I supposed to believe you knew I was standing out there?"

"Yeah, Mama, playing. I heard you coming down the hall from Roxy's room. These walls are thinner than you think," she said as a warning for Nadeen to watch what she said behind her own closed doors.

"You must think I'm stupid."

"You must think I'm a ho," Mahalia snapped angrily. In the blink of an eye, Nadeen hauled off and popped her across the face with an open hand.

"I will not be talked to that way in my own house, much less by my own child. I won't stand for it. You hear me!" Nadeen watched as her daughter massaged her face bitterly, gawking with contempt-filled eyes, which held no tears. "If you want to keep your phone privileges, be mindful of what you say on it and watch your mouth in *my* house." Nadeen trembled all over. She'd never been sorrier for anything in her whole life. The anger that caused her to strike Mahalia was misguided. She'd been storing it up for Richard.

"Since you really believed what I said to Trevy, then why don't you take the phone, Mama?" Mahalia huffed. "You don't know me any better than you know Daddy." Nadeen clenched her teeth as she lunged furiously at her daughter like before. Only this time was different. Nadeen froze when Mahalia jutted the opposite side of her face toward her mother's outstretched hand. "What's the matter, Mama? I'm just turning the other cheek!" she hissed proudly. When a single tear streamed down the large swollen red welt in the shape of her attacker's hand, Mahalia scowled. Nadeen understood then she'd made a dreadful mistake. Her daughter wasn't crying because of the stinging blow. Mahalia was hurt far greater and much deeper than a mere slap could create. She shared her mother's concerns while dealing with her own issues regarding her father's deficiency of time and attention. It had become devastatingly evident to Nadeen that she wasn't the only one in the room missing Richard and the way things used to be.

Nadeen stepped toward Mahalia with her arms open wide, but her efforts were not received in the spirit they were offered. Mahalia stiff-armed Nadeen then turned her face away. She wasn't ready to forgive her mother's backlash or reluctance to do what she felt necessary to fix her marriage. Nadeen backed away, feeling sorry for harming Mahalia and worse for allowing her unrest to damage their friendship. She wanted to apologize. She craved reconciliation. She needed forgiveness and a long conversation with her husband.

Nadeen stomped into Richard's home office, tossing drawers and digging through his files. She didn't find anything that appeared inappropriate. After duplicating her steps a third time, she noticed the corner of a white card sticking out from beneath the black leather desk pad. Intuition forced her to ease it out with her fingernails. Nadeen felt foolish when she discovered it was simply a business card from a clothing store, Giorgio's Men's Boutique. The name Dior Wicker had been written on the bottom in blue ink, but it didn't raise an alarm because Richard explained how she'd sold him a suit and a couple of neckties. Just as Nadeen made a move to return it, she remembered what Dior said earlier that day about how she fit into Richard's life.

Giving in to her sixth sense again, Nadeen flipped over the card. Her head wobbled wearily when the numbers written on the back were underlined twice with the words *cell phone* jotted beneath them. *There it is*, she thought, *hidden in plain view*. Since the abbreviated evening church service had concluded more than two hours ago, Richard should have been home by then or at least have called to check on Roxanne's condition. Seeing as how neither had occurred, Nadeen sat in the leather high-back chair, staring at the telephone.

While punching in the numbers, she imagined saying things she wouldn't be sorry for or have to repent later on. She'd meant them, all of the vile rants entitled to a wife whose husband had found comfort in another woman's bed. Nadeen rehearsed a tirade of words in her mind, a wall of them, and each one more putrid than the last.

Fifteen miles away, Dior's cell phone rang repeatedly. She ignored the annoying summons from the nightstand next to the bed as her evening companion lapped heartily between her thighs until she erupted thunderously in unbridled cataclysmic ecstasy. "Okay, okay," she muttered, pushing his head away once she'd had enough. "I don't have nothing left. Go on now, lay down or something." Dior slid off the moist sheets then scurried into the bathroom. She groaned when the phone began ringing again. "I'll turn it off in a second!" she hollered from the darkness.

"Someone wants you almost as bad as me," he replied. "Why don't I answer it?"

"Because you're not that crazy," she teased, returning to the bedroom. Dior tried to steal a peek at the incoming call before shutting it off, but the number wasn't familiar to her. "Somebody must have the wrong number," she said dismissively.

"Go ahead and take the call," he insisted, putting Dior in a prickly spot. She did not want to risk it being another man asking for quality time she didn't have to spare. She was forced to answer the call in order to throw off the suspicion of juggling lovers in a crowded bed.

Dior grimaced when the ringing continued. Smiling uncomfortably, she picked up the phone. "Hello? Yes, this is Dior. Who's this?" she asked, frowning at the woman's ugly tone. "How'd you get this number? What? Oh, it's like that?"

Although Nadeen worked hard at controlling her emotions, she found herself shouting belligerently while demanding to speak with her husband immediately. She had fallen so far, stooping to the level of the bitter wife snooping through her man's things in a desperate attempt of grasping at straws. Nadeen held her tongue when she heard rustling noises and whispers in the background.

Dior was boiling hot when she shoved the telephone in his face. "Here, it's your wife," she said, sitting on the edge of the bed with her legs crossed and arms folded angrily.

He put the phone to his ear and then grunted calmly, as if it hadn't been the first time he'd gotten jammed in the middle of two women. "Yes," he said. "No, no, no. How should I know? I'm sorry too," he uttered softly, with a slight grin on his lips. Dior stared at him oddly, wondering what had transpired during the brief phone call. She was almost afraid to ask — almost.

"Tell your wife that type of behavior will not be tolerated. Who she think she is, coming at me like this?"

"An even better question is: Who's Richard?" Giorgio asked, handing the phone back to Dior. His voice was calm and even. "His wife was really pissed. She sounded rather determined to find her husband," he added devilishly, then headed for the shower alone.

Dior sat in silence. Giorgio was certainly on to her about Richard, although she would emphatically deny it all the way to her grave. Nadeen thought she'd found the answer to her husband's extracurricular activities before her theory suffered a major collapse. It was only a matter of time before Dior confronted Richard, making him aware of Nadeen's errant phone call to the right woman on the wrong night. Richard had explained to Dior earlier how he would be working late at the church to prepare for a very important meeting on the following day. Apparently, he did not have the same talk with his wife. Now Dior held the trump cards. Still, she'd have to play them decisively in order to win the entire pot. Getting Giorgio to disregard that phone call was her first and most immediate move. Sharing a steamy shower in the dark wasn't a bad way to start cleaning up a hot mess. Actually, it was the perfect place to begin.

Nadeen, on the other hand, was in a world of confusion. Richard wasn't with Dior as she suspected. To make matters worse, Dior put her boyfriend on the phone to embarrass her. After making mistakes all evening, Nadeen waited by the door to tell Richard what happened with Mahalia and later with Dior. She prayed for enough apologies to go around when her explanations were done.

"Are you all right, Nadeen?" Richard asked the moment he saw her sullen expression. "Is it Roxy? Why didn't you call me?" He laid several rolls of architect plans on the dining room table then placed both hands on her shoulders. "Why didn't you tell me she wasn't feeling any better?"

"Roxy's fine. Just a stomach virus and some companionship issues," she answered uneasily.

"Maybe you ought to tell me now what you should have hours ago," he said firmly, figuring something had taken place she wasn't too happy about or proud of.

Nadeen lowered her head shamefully. "I didn't call because I can't remember the last time you answered readily. So, I got my own ideas about catching up with you."

"Catching up with me?" Richard repeated. "I was at the church. Phillip and the other deacons were there going over those plans for the charter school." He gestured toward the kitchen table. "We talked about it in the car today. I thought you were listening." Richard took a seat next to Nadeen on the love seat. "What's going on? What happened tonight?"

"I thought Mahalia was fooling around with boys and getting interested in all kinds of God-forbidden three-way sex games with some college kid."

Richard pounced up erratically. "What do you mean, you thought? How did something so ridiculous even get into your head?"

"I heard Mahalia on the phone. She knew I was eavesdropping from the hallway so she started talking dirty, just loud enough so I'd hear it and get all worked up."

"So it was a bad joke. She got her digs in. You realized what she was doing so it's all good, right?"

"Wrong, Richard! Way wrong. I overheard our daughter talking about sex and letting boys touch her. I lost it. She said some things. I said some things, then I smacked her."

Richard was beside himself. Mahalia was a good girl, not one who needed to be punished with vicious blows from her parents. "You smacked Mahalia, where?"

"I slapped her face."

"What! You didn't! I leave for a meeting at the church and you're here beating on our child like she's some woman in the streets. Where'd this anger come from?"

"From you, Richard!" she spat scornfully. "You caused me to distrust my daughter and then I jumped on her when she stood up for herself. You're the one who got Roxy playing sick and me on edge with everyone around me. If I had known you weren't with Dior Wicker, I wouldn't have had to call her looking for you."

"Dear God," Richard grumbled. He stumbled back to the love seat, wearing a wearied expression. "You put your hands on our daughter and accused the same woman of having an affair with me twice in one day then you have the nerve to blame all of this on me—who, might I add, happened to be at the church. If you'd had half a mind to call, you'd have known that." Richard was on his high horse then, with no plans of stepping down anytime soon. "Please tell me how my doing the Lord's work caused you to act like you did. Because from where I sit, you've got it twisted."

"Oh, do I? I admit going off half-cocked when I shouldn't have. I can even admit to snooping in your office to find Dior's number. But I will not let you put the weight of this family on my shoulders. That's your burden to carry, Brother Pastor, yours and yours alone. Try staying home sometimes and seeing to the well-being of your children before the cares of the world. They need you, your time and your attention. I can get by with the crumbs you leave me, they can't. Now, if you're finished patting yourself on the back and condemning me for my shortcomings, maybe you could look in on the girls." Nadeen struck out toward the kitchen to put away the plate she was accustomed to setting out for him. "Oh, by the way, when you do talk to that tramp, and I know you will, tell her I'm sorry for interrupting her date. The man lying next to her had reason to be irritated by the misstep I took but he handled the situation like a gentleman. Maybe he'll get over it like I just did."

# EIGHTEEN

## *Please, Baby, Please*

Bright and early the following morning, Richard pulled another snatch-and-grab before rushing from his bedroom. He dressed quickly and left a trail of smoke down the staircase, through the kitchen, and out of the door. Richard kept trying to convince himself he could handle Nadeen, explain what happened to Dior, and manipulate the outcome. There was no way to predict what Dior would say after she answered the telephone with a graveled voice. Richard didn't try to guess.

"Hey," he said, strained.

"Hey, yourself," she whispered, tired from Giorgio's extended stay through two a.m. "Who is this?" The question was meant to rattle Richard's cage. Dior was a veteran at pulling a man's chain then leading him around by the nose.

"It's Richard. Are you alone?" His question was plain and simple with no covert underlying meaning. He honestly wanted to know if the man Nadeen mentioned, in an undeniable attempt to rub his face in it, was still there warming Dior's sheets.

"Why wouldn't I be alone?" she answered with another question.

"Sorry to wake you. I know we need to talk and I know you like to sleep in on Mondays but…"

She groaned testily. "But what, Richard? If you really cared about my beauty sleep, there'd be no buts about it. And I'd be getting this call around ten o'clock instead of"—Dior reached for the digital clock resting next to her bed—"eight nineteen?"

"It couldn't wait until after my meeting with the building contractors. I didn't sleep a wink. There's no chance of maintaining focus without hashing out what happened last night. Nadeen told me she called you while looking for me. That was unacceptable. I recognize it and I want to make it up to you." There was a long pause on the other end. Richard wondered if she had drifted off to sleep. "Dior, you there?"

"For the time being," she answered eventually. "Now that you got me up and you seem so determined to get into what your crazy wife did, tell me why I'm still holding this phone."

"I'm not too far from there. Can I come and visit for a minute?"

Agreeing to see Richard before his meeting, Dior pretended to be more agitated than annoyed. "Man, I guess so. Stop by Starbucks and bring me something sweet. Hurry up." Dior ended the phone call without another word between them. Richard was clueless. The young woman he'd planned to train had just shortened his leash and yanked on it for good measure. In addition, Richard was glad to fetch her coffee and then drag in with his tail between his legs. Dior had him right where she wanted him: in a precarious predicament and scratching at her door to get in.

Seven minutes later, Richard rang the bell. A million scenarios danced around in his head but only one appealed to him. He wanted things back the way they were, before Nadeen contacted his mistress. He'd worked hard formulating a tasty setup, a secret piece on the side with all the trimmings. As he waited for Dior to answer the door, Richard submitted an unthinkable prayer request. "God, I know it's wrong for me to be here. I don't even know how to fix my mouth to ask but I need this woman in my life. Please help me salvage this. In your son, Jesus,' name, amen." Richard felt like a drug addict standing on the crack house steps, preparing to give over the last of his rent money for one more ten-dollar hit. There wasn't any reason to continue with the empty self-talk he'd begun spouting to himself every time he drove home with a guilty stone around his neck. Those days had passed him by. He was in it now, waist deep.

Dior opened the door ever so slightly. She wasn't certain about letting him back in. Richard could barely lift his eyes from the cement porch. Dressed in navy slacks and a soft brown blazer so he'd be comfortably business casual at the meeting, he was all dressed up with no place to go. "We have to do this right here?" he asked sullenly. "What about your nosy neighbors?"

"I don't give a——" she said, catching herself. Dior had more respect for Richard's position as a pastor than he did. "I don't have time to be concerned about my neighbors this morning because of what went down last night. See, my phone kept ring- ing. There was this woman on the other end, a very loud woman who was bananas about finding her husband. It doesn't even matter how she came across my cell phone number. The fact is, she did." Richard hated being talked to like a chump. However, Dior had him literally on the outside looking in. He stared at her through the crease in the door, wrapped in a flannel housecoat he didn't know she owned. "You told me you had her in check," Dior continued. "I told you what would happen if you weren't up to task. I don't stand for men bringing drama up in here. I can't afford to. That's why we discussed the rules up front, which leads me to my next point, the remedy for breaking rule number two. Since you let your married life seep into mine, I'll expect a gift or cash in the amount of five hundred dollars. That's if you expect me to carry on with this. Weakness on your end almost shamed the hell out of me last night and it'll cost you today." Dior saw the question in his eyes then tackled it before he mustered the nerve to ask it outright. "After your wife jumped on my chest, my brother started trippin'. He listened to her yelling about this and that, then he got all up in my business, asking if I was into kicking it with married men now. You have no idea how that felt. Should've seen the look on his face when he asked me who Richard was and why his wife thought he could be cocked up in my bed."

"Your brother?"

"Yeah, Dooney. I told you I had a twin brother. He came by to fix that rack in the guest closet. It keeps dumping my winter clothes on the floor. You almost met him the other night when he rolled by to see about it. He said he saw your car, noticed the lights were off upstairs. Said he decided against killing my groove. Now how am I gonna look confessing that I was getting my freak on with you?" Richard bought the persuasive explanation she'd dropped at his feet. Dior could have told him it was Santa Claus making a surprise spring visit. Richard would have believed it because he wanted to keep his fantasy alive. Sharing her with another lover wasn't part of it. Accepting lies for shades of truth had become an essential component. Nadeen accepted Richard's fabrications and he later swallowed Dior's baited deceit in one big gulp. He wasn't any closer to manipulating those circumstances than Nadeen was to stopping him from sneaking off and satisfying his earthly lusts. From the small rented house across town, Dior was practically running the Allamay mansion by the seat of her panties. Control was merely a by-product of giving Richard access to them as often as she saw fit. He was whipped and practically begging to pay for more.

"I didn't mean you any harm, never did," Richard offered sorrowfully. "I'll take care of home but in the meanwhile, I do owe you this." He pulled a roll of fifty-dollar bills from his pocket, with a bright red ribbon tied around it. "Just wanted to let you know I respect your home and your privacy. Besides, rules are rules. I think you'll like what I picked out. It's not Starbucks but I think it's your color."

"Ahh yeah, it's just my size too," she cooed intimately. "Come on in, and bring your present with you." Dior opened the door wide so he could enter. Richard had the nerve to thank God once he'd been welcomed back into her fold. His hypocrisy knew no bounds nor bore any shame.

Dior held the stack of bills tightly in her clutches. Her enthusiastic smile vanished when Richard pulled her close to put his lips on hers. She jerked away playfully, remembering she hadn't brushed her teeth since going down on Giorgio in the shower. "Uh-uh, you came before I had a chance to brush. Let me deal with this morning breath then we can talk about hooking up after your meeting. I've got some corners to turn but I'm off all day."

Richard backed off. He paced in the downstairs foyer, thinking of all the things he thought someone else was doing to Dior while he tossed and turned during the night. He was excited about resuming their affiliation, close proximity, and the heated relations that always followed. With that playing loudly in his mind, Richard climbed the stairs. He found Dior putting away her toothbrush and mouthwash. "Hey, I have a minute," he said as an afterthought. "I was thinking that we could, you know."

She leered at him like a woman who was fairly interested. "I thought you had to be somewhere."

"There's no place I'd rather be right now than here with you like this." Richard began removing her thick robe. His heart rate quickened when his eyes discovered a naked body beneath it. After spending the night with legitimate fears of never touching her again, he savored it like he had during their first time together. Richard shrugged off his blazer. He perused Dior's breasts with his hardened tongue, traveling the very surface her last lover had done merely hours ago. Swept up in a haze of passion, Richard pinned Dior against the wall. He sucked on the nape of her neck, panting desperately. Her back arched instinctively when he spread her legs with his eager fingers. "I want you so bad," he moaned. "I want to feel myself inside of you." Richard wrestled his pants down with one hand as he probed her wetness with the other. Dior writhed agreeably.

"Don't let anyone come between us, Richard," she squealed wantonly as she pressed herself against him. "Come on, baby. Come on." He obliged, shoving himself into her violently.

"I won't let anything do that, baby," he replied assertively. "I promise." Richard pumped furiously, reveling in the moment. His head was filled with clouds of delusion. Dior's mind was clear and calculating. She gave him what he needed while getting closer to what she wanted. When Dior felt him nearing a climax, she pushed him away.

"Uh-uh, this was a mistake," she brooded falsely.

"What? No, this feels too right to be...to be wrong," he debated heatedly. "Look at how you got me all stranded." He couldn't help but feel betrayed having been taken to the edge of ecstasy then turned away cold. "I thought you said we were good again, I mean a minute ago it seemed as if..." he rattled mindlessly.

"Everything is gravy, baby, but not like this. You were pounding on me like a man with a grudge. If you're mad, then just say so and we'll deal with it. I don't mind it rough when I know where it's coming from. I need to be sure why you're here this morning and that you still care for me." Dior eased closer to Richard, staring at him face-to-face. She ran her fingers down his chest until they were wrapped around his throbbing flesh. "Now then, you get undressed and I'll get the condoms." Previously, she hadn't allowed intercourse without protection, which was yet another method of controlling him. "Business as usual is just that: business. Bareback ain't nothing to play with, sugar. Many things can go wrong and not any of them are worth the trouble." Dior convinced Richard to strap up before they got at it. He fussed initially, then common sense prevailed. It was an easy choice after he realized she wouldn't go any further unless he made the right one.

Richard gave it his all that morning; his stamina was unbelievable. His determination to outlast Dior was legendary. Their bodies flipped and smacked for the better part of two hours. She brought out the tiger in Richard and he loved her for it. There was never a substitute for the way the right woman made a man feel invincible. Richard could attest to that as he climbed back into his clothes, an hour late for his meeting with the contractors at the church. Dior had the presence of mind to stay on top of more than just him. She encouraged Richard to hurry. "You shouldn't have stayed so long but I'm happy you came."

"What are they going to do if I'm late, leave? I'm the reason there is a meeting in the first place" was his arrogant reply.

He sauntered back to his car after ten a.m., weak-kneed and quite a bit more weathered than when he arrived. Dior watched him drive away from her window. She exhaled wearily, counted the money Richard paid to reaffirm his commitment to her, then she counted the few remaining condoms in her top drawer. The past twelve hours had all but depleted her stash. She grinned impishly then made a mental note to stock up.

# NINETEEN

## *Smoke and Mirrors*

While waiting for the elevator on the first floor of Methodist Episcopal Greater Apostolic, Richard stared at his watch. At ten twenty-five, he headed up the stairs toward the third-floor conference room. He blushed over the thought of Carlton Tatum, owner of Tatum Engineering, twiddling his thumbs and secretly licking his chops. He wanted to ink the deal awarding his firm exclusive rights to current and future building projects with a booming church. Richard expected Tatum to be patient and poised to kiss his behind. Arriving well over an hour late for the meeting, Richard found an empty room. He read his watch again, scratching his head curiously.

As he turned to exit the conference room, Phillip blew through the door like a Kansas twister. "So you finally decided to show up!" he grunted, his eyes on fire.

"Yeah, I'm here. Where are Tatum and his head man?" Richard asked with no visible signs of remorse. "You'd think they would have waited."

Phillip pursed his lips then he huffed disappointedly.

"They did wait over an hour for you but you don't seemed pressed."

"Why should I be? They want business from me" was Richard's placid response.

The look on Phillip's face was disturbing. He eyed the plush carpet as if he wanted to rip it from underneath Richard's feet. "That's what I was afraid of," he said eventually, when the temptation to lash out swelled in the back of his throat. "You have the audacity to think this meeting and the school were both about you. Check yourself before you have all of us following you off a cliff."

Richard stared Phillip up one side and down the other. "Look who's stepping out of line now. You need to watch yourself before you say something evil. So I missed a sit-down with a rich white man who wants to get even richer on my back. Yeah, I said it. I'm the reason there are thousands instead of hundreds in the auditorium on Sunday morning. Huh, I'm the reason there is an auditorium. Lest you forget, this was a congregation dying on the vine when I took the job. It wasn't anything more than a leaky roof with old people and children getting drenched."

"Funny you should mention that. You're in danger of tearing apart everything the Lord has done through you, not because of you. I pleaded with the contractors to 'hang around.' I said, 'He'll be here. You can count on Pastor Allamay.' Well, you proved me wrong. We'd be lucky to get a good deal on a sack of dirt now."

After taking a brief moment to calm himself, Richard closed the conference room door. "Alright, we've been friends a long time, Phillip. We've come a long way together and saw some things neither of us thought we'd live through, but you're pressing me and it's about to get under my skin." Several years ago, they were involved in a fatal hit-and-run while on the way back from a tent revival ninety miles south of Dallas. A cargo van struck Phillip's car. Richard was asleep in the passenger's seat. Their vehicle flew into oncoming traffic and crashed head-on with an SUV. The entire family inside of it died in the accident. A man, his wife, and their infant child perished. Richard wasn't sure who was at fault but he knew Phillip was just as tired as he was although he refused to stop and rest. Richard suffered facial abrasions and a broken collarbone. Phillip underwent two weeks in intensive care due to a punctured lung. Both men realized how close they came to meeting God that night. Richard was the only one comfortable with bringing it up.

"Man, don't start with that," Phillip protested with his hands raised in a halting manner. "It has nothing to do with the fact that you're slipping and I'll bet I know what's behind it."

"You don't know what you think you know."

"Don't I? Just last night you were here, busting your butt trying to figure out how to make this project proposal more flattering without giving up safety for the children who we're supposed to be building the school for. Then you turn right around and ditch the whole thing like it didn't matter at all."

"I already apologized for being late and actually I'm getting sick of doing it. I'll call old man Tatum and get him back to the table. He'll jump at it."

Phillip seethed beneath the collar. He didn't believe Richard's arrogance ran so deep and wide. "I wouldn't blame him if he told you to go jump in the lake and kiss his wrinkled behind."

Richard sat on the end of the conference table, staring up at the man who sounded to him like a jilted woman. "Is that what you think I should do, Phillip? Huh? Bend over and kiss that man's butt? I'm starting to see what this is really about. I think you got your hopes up, then got your feelings hurt. Grow up, brother. This is about money, all about money. Tatum is a businessman. He will reschedule." Richard stood from the table, stepped up to Phillip, and then insulted him with a dismissive tone. "If you can't take the heat, you know what you do?"

There was a hint of sadness in Phillip's eyes. "Is that how you're going to talk to me? None of this would have happened if you'd dumped Dior like I suggested. It's time for a reality check, Richard. That sweet young thing has you whipped and she has everybody else standing around waiting on you to show up." Phillip's comments caused Richard to look at him with a discerning eye, thinking he was either overreacting or jealous. He leaned in closer to the deacon.

"You look kind of green, Phillip. Is that a bad case of envy? Don't tell me you're letting my personal affairs jam you up? Maybe next time you can watch. I'll ask Dior. She might be wild enough to go for it."

Phillip didn't back down an inch. He stood toe-to-toe, trading harsh stares. "I'd be surprised if she doesn't," he answered with anger rising in his voice. He found it hard to believe Richard was casually throwing his mistress's sexual proclivities around like a single man on a street corner. "There was a time you'd never speak that way on holy ground. You're moving so far from God it makes me sick."

"Let you tell it," Richard grunted irritably. "Looks to me you got your panties in a bunch over something that doesn't concern you."

"I'm going to pretend you didn't come at me like that. I'm also going to tell you what does concern me and then I'm going to leave before I act like the south side thug I used to be." With Richard standing inches from him, Phillip sneered down his nose as he continued. "Your *personal affairs* are turning me into something I'm not. I've got to deal with Rose looking at me sideways when she knows I'm covering for you. A month ago, I wasn't lying to my wife and you said you'd stopped lying to yours. Wake up, Richard. This is wrong. Wake up and stop it before you let Dior's hold on you take all of us down. How do you think it's gonna look when the newspapers get a hold of it?" The mere thought of that shook Phillip where he stood. "I can't deal with this anymore. Just let it go and forget about it!" He motioned toward the door when he heard someone outside, but Richard wasn't ready to let it end there. He grabbed Phillip by the arm and held it tightly.

"You know what? You made an excellent point." He chuckled rudely while shoving Phillip in the chest. "I don't need you to be there for me anymore. I'm tired of lying to Nadeen, tired of ducking and hiding. Yeah, it's over, but not in the way you want it to be. Since I'm all out of alibis anyway, I may as well let the cat out of the bag. Remember what happened in Denver? If I tell it, I may as well tell all of it. What do you think Rose would say about the action you got into while snowed in?" Phillip's eyes glassed over with disbelief. He opened his mouth but nary a sound came out. "Uh-huh, that's what I thought. You know as well as I do how sweet secret lovin' is. Don't be so fast to rattle my skeletons when we both got plenty of bones buried."

"You'd better let me go before I knock some sense into you!" Phillip shouted viciously.

"You ain't that stupid," Richard snarled. He moved toward Phillip to shove him again but his shoes slipped on the carpet. He landed against the edge of the table. Phillip lunged at him with both fists swinging. "Back the...off me!" Richard grumbled beneath his adversary's weight. Phillip ripped Richard's shirt. He scuffled to get the upper hand. At each other's throats, the friendship they'd built crumbled hopelessly. The moment Richard slammed his fist against Phillip's mouth, all was lost.

Suddenly the door opened. Nadeen, having heard the latter part of their argument, watched her husband and his best friend groveling on the ground. She wanted to intervene but they were fighting like stray dogs. The rage-filled room caused her to mistake their argument about Dior for a lover's quarrel; she couldn't move. Several people gathered at the door before the brawl subsided completely.

Richard griped, assessing his damaged clothing. Phillip massaged his swollen lip, then he glared at the collection of spectators gawking at them. "I'm done with you," Phillip grunted angrily as he staggered by Richard. "Nadeen, I'm sorry," he said to her in passing. "You didn't deserve any of this."

Nadeen was in utter shock. She held out her hand to stop Phillip with the thought of questioning him about the melee. Intuition told her to let him go so he could lick his wounds in private. Unfortunately for Richard, he wouldn't get off so easily. There was something vile behind the fight and she needed to get at it immediately. With a swollen chest filled with exasperation, Nadeen pressed forward. "Excuse me, y'all, but I need a minute with the pastor," she hissed toward the stunned onlookers. She pushed the door closed, locking them out before they had a chance to respond.

Now alone with her husband, Nadeen took a minute to compose herself. She stared at him. He was disheveled and dishonored. Although her stark expression left little doubt how bothered she was by the altercation, Richard didn't appear concerned about her in the least. "You want to tell me what's been going on with you and Phillip?"

"Nothing," he said coldly, avoiding eye contact. "Just a disagreement between old friends that got out of hand."

"A disagreement I'd understand. What I can't process is what I heard before y'all starting going at each other like…like a couple of, oh God, I can't even fix my mouth to say the word." Nadeen told herself to be strong and keep a stiff upper lip because she had to know the truth. "Phillip said I didn't deserve any of this. What exactly is that, Richard?" She watched his feeble attempt at straightening his clothes to regain his composure.

"You'd have to ask him," he answered plainly, as if not interested in speaking on it any further.

"No, I'm asking you!" she shouted, failing to keep her voice down. "You are my husband and what I deserve is to know why you don't need Phillip to be there for you anymore. And...and what lies are you tired of telling me?" Nadeen felt sick when she imagined him in Phillip's arms and their legs intertwined. "I heard you talking about bones and skeletons and alibis, Richard. Tell me what happened and how long it's been going on and everything you did to have Phillip talking about being turned into something he didn't want to be!" Amid Nadeen's hysterical rants, Richard turned a deaf ear. He was overwhelmingly concerned at how the brief skirmish would play out once the congregation got hold of the news.

"I can't talk about this right now," he said, too calmly for Nadeen to comprehend.

"You're going to walk out while we're in the middle of an important conversation?"

Richard felt his pants pockets for car keys then headed for the closed door. "This is not the place to discuss it," he mumbled.

"The heck it isn't. This is where it went down."

"I've got to get some air," he said, showing traces of remorse for the first time since she began interrogating him. "I'm done. We'll discuss it when I get home."

Nadeen huffed furiously. She stood alone in the conference room, ashamed for thinking what she did about Richard and Phillip while drowning in a sea of indecision. Change had always been a strange bedfellow. Having to confront the idea of living with a husband on the down low, as far as she knew, made her shudder. She pondered where she had gone wrong or if his homosexual relationship had anything to do with her. There were far too many questions she wouldn't get answered until she cornered Richard and demanded them. Nadeen almost laughed at how ludicrous it sounded when hearing her inner voice questioning her husband's sexuality.

A soft knock at the door pulled Nadeen away from her muted thoughts where nothing stood to reason, absolutely nothing at all. She sauntered to the door, breathed deeply, then opened it with all of the life drained from her face. Bearing a tentative smile was Richard's personal secretary, Dawn Beverly. She kept to herself more than most, but was quite amicable when the need arose. Dawn was a shade over five-four with a slight frame. Blessed with a smooth medium-brown complexion and soft facial features, she could have presented herself in a more attractive light but didn't feel the need to overdo anything. The hairstyle she wore rarely varied. She liked it low-maintenance and manageable, like her life. A penchant for modest dresses and quality leather flats served her well, as did her determination to raise two grown children by herself.

Dawn Beverly was good people, without making a big deal about it. Nadeen was reminded of that when she saw the secretary's hesitant stance underscored by her subtle and almost apologetic eyes. Dawn offered a sorrowful smile then followed it up with a heartfelt embrace. Both women avoided words initially. None seemed suitable at the time. Since Dawn had worked closely with Richard over the past five years, answering his personal and private calls, Nadeen assumed she was aware of his secret life and thereby merely offering confirmation that she had expected it would come to this. Dawn, on the other hand, held on to various assumptions too. She felt uncomfortable when the pastor's credit card bill arrived with a number of peculiarly intriguing purchases. His spending habits were all over the place. After scanning the charges, an assortment of undergarments from women's boutiques, popular perfumes, outlandishly over-priced designer jeans, and expensive trinkets from a department store jewelry case, Dawn easily presumed the wayward pastor had strayed from home. Furthermore, the woman he showered with fine gifts was holding something over him he couldn't see himself doing without. But it wasn't her place to question her boss about his brief encounter with a shapely lunch date that fell short in front of the Tex-Mex restaurant, or pages of charges from his church-sponsored expense account. Dawn paid the bill, although it was sufficiently higher than in any previous month, and she left it at that. Now, taking in Nadeen's apparent frustration commingled with an obvious case of embarrassment, it wasn't a stretch to further presume recent changes in Richard's behavior also caused uneasy speculation at home as well.

"I can't tell you how much that meant to me, Dawn," Nadeen whispered once she'd let go. "I'm sure you've heard that Richard and Phillip finally had a fight. I guess it couldn't have been anything but ugly when it came out. He won't even tell me what drove him to it or anything about it." Dawn fought off a frown. She wasn't certain how much Nadeen knew about the other woman so she reserved her comments. It was a good thing she did, totally oblivious to the true meaning of Nadeen's supposed revelation. "You think living with a man for eighteen years gives you an inside track to who he really is. I'm sorry to be laying this at your feet. Just talking myself through it. Thanks for listening."

"It's the least I could do. Christians got to stand up for one another, even when we make hurtful mistakes." Of course she was referring to Richard's. Nadeen chuckled when she caught the hint to keep that in mind when traveling the difficult road ahead. "If He brought you to it, He'll bring you through it. Everything in its time, my mama used to say."

"Was she right about it?" Nadeen asked, honestly wanting to know.

Dawn smiled while nodding her head assertively. "Enough for me to share it with you."

"And I'm glad you did."

# TWENTY

## *See-you-bye*

Dior was unaware how interesting Richard's life had just become. Contrarily, she zoomed down the expressway heading south, thinking how her life wasn't interesting enough. She decided to make the best of her day off by mapping out her moves over the next week and setting a few traps along the way. Dior's plan to wedge herself solidly in the middle of Richard's marriage was faring on course. However, it hadn't moved with the speed she'd hoped. Sure, Richard loved being with her, but he didn't love her. She had a number of ideas up her sleeves to remedy that.

Dooney Does It, the barbershop owned by Dior's twin brother, was situated on the south end of town in a building once abandoned by the neighborhood, tenants, and the city of Dallas alike. After Dooney's release from prison four years earlier, he made a deal to rehab the property. Then he convinced big shots on the city council to sell it for pennies on the dollar. Imprisoned for malicious activities, including petty larceny and assault, Dooney walked away from the state correctional facility with his freedom and a new lease on life. While not entirely able to give up his street connections, he steered clear of the most unlawful enterprises. Tight fades and close shaves provided his primary income stream; keeping his hands clean assured him a chance to build more profitable avenues and increase the flow.

When Dior entered the shop looking to see the one man who knew her better than she did herself, she found one of the barbers fiddling with the television remote control instead. "Hey, Tiny, is Dooney in the back?" she asked of the enormously stout assistant manager. He clicked over to a daytime talk show before answering.

"Uh-uh, ain't nobody here but me and Jerry Springer," he joked, eyeing the screen until he caught a glimpse of the show's topic. "Who's yo baby daddy week? *Again?*" He quickly turned the television off disappointedly. Turning his attention toward Dior, who was dressed in a tightly fitting powder-blue Juicy sweatsuit and running shoes, Tiny knew better than to spend too much time admiring her curves. Despite Dior's troublesome past, her brother wouldn't stand for anyone disrespecting her, whether she invited it or not. "What's been up with you? Ain't seen you in a minute."

"Little of this and that. You know where I'm at," she said playfully.

"Yeah, I remember, stuck somewhere in the middle."

"Hahhh, you do remember. It looks like Dooney forgot I was supposed to slide by today."

"He said something about going by the house for lunch. Hit him up on the cell and see if he's still there."

Dior eyed the closed storeroom door when she heard a noise coming from the other side of it. Tiny threw his hands up wearily as she marched toward it. "Just you and Jerry Springer, huh? Then what's with the audience in the back room?" She jiggled on the knob suspiciously, smirking at Tiny's failed attempt at putting one over on her. "Dooney?" she called out when the door finally popped open. To her surprise, there were rows of neatly stacked boxes where old loungewear had previously been kept. "Tiny!"

"Don't even ask, Dior," the giant barber discouraged. "Dooney don't feel too good about holding boosted gear as it is. I am not getting into it with you. Uh-uh. Close the door, let it go, and walk away."

"Ooh, are all of these ladies shoes?" she shrieked, bolting into the room. "Dooney done did it, for real." Against Tiny's persistent pleading, Dior opened several boxes at random, hoping to find something to fit her taste and size.

"Doggoneit, girl, you sho' is hardheaded. Nobody is supposed to be in there. If word gets out we have those, it could be hell to pay. I'm a call Dooney."

"*Call Dooney*," she smarted off. "I'm not gonna tell anybody he's babysitting top choice stolen goods."

Tiny paced outside the room. "Hey, Doo', this Tiny at the shop. Garrard 'n'em ain't come through yet but I'll give you one guess who did and then done sniffed her way into the storeroom goodies. Man, yeah! What was I supposed to do? One of the boxes must've fell down or something." He glared at Dior, riffling through several more pairs of shoes at once. "I told her they were on lock. Uh-uh, you talk to her. She ain't tryna listen to me or I wouldn't have had to call you." Tiny waddled sideways through the door and quickly handed the cell phone to Dior. "Here, now let's see you talk your way out of this."

"Hey, Dooney, I didn't know you were fencing boosted gear. I could have been shopping here all along. You got some good stuff too," she said, painstakingly shoving her foot into a knee-high leather riding boot. "Huh? I heard what Tiny said.

He's not running anything but his mouth," she added, goading the big man to his face. "Don't you yell at me. Don't yell!" she hollered into the receiver. "I got *money*. Enough to get me these boots before you and your fat friend go to jail. Okaaay, okay. You know I'm just playing. Yeah, I'm on the way there now. Bye," she spat hastily, while shoving the phone at Tiny in the same rude manner he'd done to her. "Here, Dooney wants to get at you, big boy."

Tiny, annoyed by the game Dior initiated, listened and muttered quiet responses. "Yeah, I know she's your twin. Yeah, I been knowing that too. Alright, I'll do it only 'cause you said so. Bet." Tiny flipped his handheld closed, sighed mightily, and stepped toward the box of boots Dior was about to carry off. Tiny frowned at her then swiftly snatched it from her hands. "Ahh-ha, who's laughing now? Dooney said for me to confiscate whatever you was tryna take and get to puttin' you out the shop." He wasted no time before relishing in his victory. "Well, get to moving. The exit door is that-a-way. It must be getting kinda hard, living right there, stuck in the middle."

"Whatever," she hissed halfheartedly. "I'll take this up with Dooney when I see him. You just make sure to hold those back for me. I don't want to see nobody in my boots."

"See-you-bye," he said, motioning toward the door with a satisfied grin.

"I'm serious, Tiny! And don't eat 'em," she teased. "Not everything dark chocolate *is* chocolate." Dior sashayed to the head of the shop, slinging her behind to further aggravate matters. She threw a glance back over her shoulder and laughed at his sex-starved expression. "Uh-uh, you can't eat this either."

"You wrong for that, Dior!" he shouted after her as she exited the shop. "Wrong! Why she got to be so fine, fine and hard-headed." Dior had shaken off their interaction in the time it took to drive twenty miles to Dooney's home just north of downtown. Tiny never quite managed to get over it.

Dior hummed along with a song on her car stereo when exiting off the tollway. She hit a left then traveled west until she reached one of the oldest African American communities in the city. What once had been block after block of quiet residential districts had morphed into a busy lower-class neighborhood where adult grandchildren never left the homes where their parents had been raised. Although it wasn't exactly clear why new Mercedes Benzes and broken-down hoopdies often shared the same small driveway, she didn't think it made any sense for three generations of family to live cramped in the same house. Dooney was one of the exceptions. He lived alone, kept his vehicle in the garage, and his house was immaculate. Dior eyed the sidewalk suspiciously then armed her car alarm. Not that thieves would have taken a particular interest in a three-year-old 3-Series BMW but she didn't want to go through the trouble of being wrong.

She walked past one of very few lush green lawns in sight as she ascended the pathway toward the one-story ranch-style house, which was constructed with considerably more wood than brick. The reason why a man who owned a lucrative business, the building it operated in, and four other rental properties would actually choose to reside in the smallest and least appealing of them escaped her. There's no way she would think of living in that neighborhood or in that house, if other options were available. The difference was, Dooney had risen from the ashes of his checkered past with his self-esteem intact. What people thought about him didn't matter nearly as much as what he knew about his own successes. Unfortunately, Dior hadn't begun to realize she wasn't the designer outfits she wore or the second-hand car she lied about buying off the showroom floor. She was still reaching for the lifestyle she wanted others to believe she'd already captured. Dooney had his grasped firmly by the neck.

When Dior rang the doorbell, she followed it with rapid thumps on the front door. Dooney whipped it open with his right hand carefully hidden behind his back. Dior recognized the pose he took. She threw her hands up in a defensive posture. "Don't shoot, it's just me," she said, annoyed by the hostile manner with which he greeted her.

"Don't come up here beating on my door like some strung out crackhead, then."

"And put that gun away before you shoot your foot off."

Dooney smacked his lips then shoved the chrome automatic pistol underneath a perfectly starched shirt, which he never left home without. He brushed off a speck of lint from his freshly creased jeans then locked the door behind him. "Why did you give Tiny such a hard time with them shoes and why were you at the shop in the first place?"

"What, I can't get invited in good before you start grilling me?" she smarted, in no hurry to answer his questions. "*Hey, Dior,*" she said sorely. "*How is my favorite sister?*"

"My only sister," Dooney asserted plainly.

"Yeah-yeah, aren't you happy to see me?"

"Since you want to put words in my mouth, no, I am not, nor was I *happy* to hear Tiny ringing in my ear about you showing your, ahh, see you got me wantin' to cuss but I refuse. A great man once said that people resort to foul language because of a limited vocabulary. So, I gave it up. However, if you get your nose caught in my business and jack up my money, I can't make no promises about actin' a fool." Dooney must've said all he was going to about that because he shrugged on a different demeanor. "Now then, hello, Dior. Why are you here?" He walked over to an enormous aquarium and resumed the task her brash entrance had interrupted. Dior pulled an envelope from her purse then laid it on the sofa table. She gave the room a broad stroke, smiled warmly at the modest but tasteful furniture, the largest television she'd ever seen, and several new pieces of original artwork he'd collected.

"Here's why I went by the shop and the reason why I came over." She extended the envelope humbly then took a seat on the sofa.

Dooney felt the package carefully. He furrowed his brow then chuckled. "What's this supposed to be?"

"What it is: my rent without you having to hunt me down for it. For once," she added, with a slight chuckle of her own. "You've been good to me, Dooney. When I got things twisted in the past, you forgave me, although you saw some of it coming and tried to make me behave myself." The year before, Dior worked feverishly at taking her cousin's husband by seducing him with alcohol and late-night trickery. Dooney had warned Chandelle beforehand; she should have listened. "Not too many people would have stood by me then but you came to the rescue, like always. Love like that shouldn't be overlooked."

"Love? That's the first time I've ever heard you say that word when it wasn't tied to a designer bag, fly dress, or some bangin' shoes." Dooney eyed his sister suspiciously. "Now you're bring-ing me your rent money, without discussion and all of it at the same time. Hmmm, what's really poppin'? You about to drop dead or something?"

"No, I'm trying to say thank you," she whispered, bothered by the way the sentiment touched her. "I've never been real good at saying that either." Her eyes drifted from his toward the floor.

"Dang, girl. If you ain't fixin' to die, you must be in love," he surmised. "Is it the dude with the pimped-out Lexus or that cat you work for?"

Dior hunched her shoulders like a small child being asked if she swiped a treat from the cookie jar. "Neither. Both. I don't know."

"You know I roll by your spot to check on you from time to time while on my way home."

"Don't you mean to check on your money? And my house ain't on your way home," she teased.

"Like I said, don't but two cars sit in the cut in front of your spot. So, which is it?" She shook her head, not committing a response to his question. "Okay, be like that. But, if I had to guess, it'd be the baller sittin' on chrome." When Dior sat still, uncharacteristically quiet, Dooney knew she was keeping something to herself. "Dee, don't tell me that dude is mixed up in the dope game?"

"Negro, please, you can get to the back of the bus with all that," she sniped, pouncing up from her seat. "I ain't insane. My man is a square with a square day job, W-9s, vacation pay, a dental plan, and everything." Dior hadn't realized her chest was heaving furiously. Dooney didn't miss it. "Besides, didn't I just see your storeroom loaded with boosted stuff?"

"I'm just holding 'em for a friend," he said, as if that wasn't the lamest excuse on the books.

Dior cackled loudly. "Is that what you're gonna tell the cops if somebody rats you out? I already tried that line more than once, and please believe, you got to come harder than that."

"That's just like you to try and flip it when you're on the hot seat. Consider this though: If your man's an easy-breezy corporate smoe, there's got to be some educated females all up and through his mix."

"So!" she spat viciously.

"So, what's he want with you then?"

"He's a man. If you can't figure it out, I'm not the one to break it down for you."

"It's easy to figure he's got you all knotted up. You'd better watch this one, Dior."

She fanned at him dismissvely. "You worry about a gang of shoeboxes with department store labels still stuck on them. I got this."

Dooney was reasonably concerned with his only sister getting her heart broken, when he wouldn't have previously wasted his time believing she had one to break. "You can't keep running men in and out hoping you won't get busted."

Dior threw her hand up to stop the madness. "Maybe I could take you more serious if twenty different females weren't running all up and through here behind you."

"Oh yeah, I gets mine but this isn't about me. I'm telling you to watch *your* back, so get the wax out of your ears and hear me on this, baby sis. Everything cost, everything."

The expression shrouding her face had several lies hidden behind it even though she wished otherwise. "Thank you for your funky two cents but you ain't said nothing I didn't already know."

A bundle of mixed emotions, Dior returned to her car with slow, deliberate steps. Dooney had his nerve, she thought. He wouldn't think of limiting the number of women in his fan club for the sake of thinning it out. Despite being upset by her brother's meddling, there was no denying his advice came from the heart. Double standards aside, it was in her best interest to sort things out after stringing Giorgio along and dangling Richard from the same rope. The decision to cut one of them loose was fairly easy to make. Bearing the bad news to the odd man out required a bit more fortitude than Dior expected.

The clothing store was quiet when Dior sauntered in. Suza was busy restocking a display rack with imported neckties. "I thought you had the day off," Suza said, surprised by her presence.

"Yeah, I'm off alright. Is Giorgio in his office? I need to speak to him."

"Uh-huh," she mumbled sorely. "Maybe one of those long talks of yours will snatch him out of the foul mood he's been in all morning."

Dior grinned apprehensively. "Sorry, but I'm not looking to have that kind of discussion today."

After making her way to the rear of the men's boutique, Dior stood quietly outside the closed door. She couldn't help wondering what to say once it opened. Giorgio had been good to her. He paid her well for increasing his clientele twofold and paid her extra money off the books. More important, their secret rendezvous enhanced his bottom line. Dior and Giorgio benefited from the relationship, at both ends. Hopefully that would still mean something to him after hearing what she had to say. "Can I come in?" she asked when he unlocked the door.

He furrowed his brow initially. "Sure, sit. It's good to see you, only I didn't expect to today." When Giorgio closed the door, he noticed Dior's pensive demeanor. "You don't look happy, Dior. What caused it?"

She drew in a measured breath then tried to relax. "I am happy, that's the problem." Dior squirmed in her chair uneasily before continuing. "See, it's like this. I am so grateful for all that you've done for me."

His face exhibited a great deal of angst. "Don't tell me you're quitting. You're not going to work for someone else are you?"

"Kinda yes and kinda no. Giorgio, you know I love what I do here, but I think I have a future with someone else." She cast her eyes downward to avoid looking into his. "You've been so good to me but—"

"But you've made room for another man?" He leaned back

in the leather office chair then ran his fingers through his thick salon-styled hair. "So, what are you saying exactly?"

"What I'd like to say, what I'd like to do is keep on working here but without the perks, so to speak." Dior raised her eyes to meet his, expecting to find them agreeable. She reached across the desk with her hands when they weren't. "I'll never stop caring about you. Our friendship means that much to me."

"You want to, how do they say…have the cake and eat it too?" he asked in a noncommittal manner that left Dior hanging by a thin thread. "This poses a crossroad of sorts. You make me a lot of money here. I like money. And I like you. Together it tastes like cake." Eventually, Giorgio chuckled. "I like cake very much."

"Ohhh, thank you so much for understanding," she cooed. "I'll work twice as hard and bring in so many new customers." Dior circled the desk to hug him. Giorgio kept his distance. Slightly taken aback by their new arrangement, she nodded that she understood the rejection. "You won't regret this, Giorgio. Trust me, you won't be sorry."

"That's left to be seen," he joked. "Now go so I can start to get over you." Dior thanked him again and then departed, relieved. She tried to feel sorry for Giorgio but couldn't, knowing that he'd find another midday treat before too long. Men like him always did.

# TWENTY-ONE

## *Silly of Me*

Nadeen remained alone for hours before finally working up the nerve to leave the conference room. She smiled pleasantly while church employees looked at her with apologetic expressions sprinkled here and there. Not one of them had any idea what caused the awful interaction involving the pastor and his favorite deacon. Their best guess: Richard having been chastised by Phillip for arriving late to a very important meeting, in a manner he didn't appreciate. Nadeen wouldn't stop to receive their heartfelt pity or questioning stares too bold to dismiss. She was torn into a million tiny pieces and not any of them seemed to fit. Usually, she'd bounce her concerns off Richard, who was always there with reassuring words and viable solutions. Since he was the root of her crisis, she decided to reach out to the other person she felt was in the same predicament. Surely Rose would understand the hurt she endured. Perhaps together they could find a way to deal with what had happened without either wife being the wiser.

Once in her car in the church parking lot, she dialed Richard's first cousin for a desperately needed chat about their husbands. "Hello, Rose? Hey, this is Nadeen. We need to talk and I mean right now." She held the phone to her ear, expecting to hear a reasonable facsimile to the wealth of anger churning inside of her. Rose's attitude missed the mark by a mile.

"Nadeen, I just finished talking to Phillip and I'm sorry for the fight the fellas had at the church," she said, as if there was something stifling her resentment from seeping out.

"Is Phillip sitting there in front of you?" Nadeen asked irritably.

"Yeah, I'm still dealing with a headache," she said plainly, to throw Phillip off. "I'm going to the store to get some strong medicine so I can calm down."

"Okay, Rose, I understand. Let's meet at the coffee shop near your house, the one over by the supermarket on Belt Line." After Rose uttered in code she was minutes from being en route, Nadeen proceeded that way herself. During the short drive, she cried for a series of reasons, then laughed hysterically because her life as she knew it was over and there wasn't anything she knew to do about it. Thoughts circulated unabated. *What are Mom and Dad going to say? How is the congregation going to respond when they learn their beloved leader is one of those down-low brothas doing who knows what? Black churches are built on character, whether it's perceived or otherwise. There's no way their faithful members will follow him after this, not straight to hell. I wouldn't blame them. How could I?*

Nadeen had other thoughts too, of the violent nature. She imagined her claws digging into Richard's face, ripping at his flesh, so he could share her misery. Nadeen had worked herself into a knotted ball of suspicion and animosity. She was sitting in a small shop, staring blankly into a lukewarm cup of coffee, waiting for Rose to meet her. Disturbing scenarios saturated her mind. She thought about leaving Richard and the life she loved,

about how that would affect the life he'd put together profes-
sionally, and the questions waged war within her troubled soul.
Sustaining their relationship never crossed her mind, not once.
So engrossed in her dilemma, Nadeen didn't realize Rose had
taken the seat across from her at the table she'd commandeered
when arriving several minutes ago.

"Nadeen? Girl, snap out of it," Rose said anxiously when her
girlfriend called her name for a second time.

"What? Oh, when'd you get here, Rose?"

"Apparently not soon enough," she replied, wearing the
same pitying expression Nadeen tried to ignore at the church.
"You don't look so good," she added when nothing else seemed
appropriate.

Nadeen leaned over the small circular table to get a lot closer.
"How am I supposed to look?" she hissed in a whispered tone.
"There's no telling what those busybodies at M.E.G.A. will be
saying about that mess Richard and Phillip got into. I was there
and let me tell you, it was ugly."

Rose shifted her weight in her seat, stalling an inevitable discussion concerning why the fight broke out in the first place.
"Yeah, I heard it all from Phillip. He's done nothing but worry
hisself sick. He doesn't blame Richard alone, seeing as how he
played a part in it." Nadeen bucked her eyes. She looked at Rose
as if her head had just popped off. She was convinced Rose had
known about the affair and wasn't as bothered by it as she should
have been.

"A part in it?" she groaned quietly. "A part in it? If I didn't
know better you were alright with their behavior?"

"No, I'm not alright with it, not any of it," Rose answered,
thinking she was talking about the skirmish that started when
Phillip tried to check Richard about Dior.

"My head won't stop ringing. Every time I remember Richard

kneeling over Phillip, their hate-filled eyes, and all of the anger in the room, I keep seeing them together." She took a deep breath to keep from throwing up on the table. "To be in the same boat, I don't understand how you're taking this so well."

Rose sighed then shook her head, certain that Nadeen was speaking of Richard and his mistress because Phillip had filled her in on the particulars, including the tryst he had in Denver years ago. He was surprised when Rose informed him that she figured as much when he returned home, acting different and unable to touch her for weeks. Rose was able to pray it out of her system and forgive him, as long as he didn't ever go willingly with his carnal demons again. Besides, she'd slipped up a time or two when he was out of town. It was like Phillip told Richard over lunch. They weren't getting along and it didn't appear they stood a chance to weather the toughest time in their marriage. Strangely enough, Phillip's indiscretion helped bridge the muddied waters. They'd been a lot closer ever since. "I was in the same boat. Phillip owned up to the dirt he did. I've dealt with it," she told Nadeen in a way that sounded condescending, although she didn't mean it that way. "I, uh, I'm not implying Phillip is any better than Richard for doing the same thing. It's just that he's not on that road anymore. We've mended things between us. What Phillip is the most sorry for is lying to me about Richard. He didn't have any business covering for Richard all this time." She stopped talking altogether when she noticed Nadeen's face had contorted into one colossal scowl. Suddenly, it occurred to her that she'd said too much.

"Phillip told you he'd been involved with other men, I mean, other than Richard?" she asked carefully.

Rose jerked her head back when Nadeen's words slapped her across the face. "What? Other men? What are you talking about? Is that why you're sitting there about to bust? You think our husbands are gay? That's nonsense. Phillip's thing was with some loose waitress. Uh-uh, you've got it all wrong. The fellas were fighting over..." When Rose's mouth continued to move without a single word coming forth, Nadeen knew there was more to tell, something Rose was privy to or fooled into believing by Phillip.

"You don't have to keep secrets from me, Rose!" Nadeen growled nastily. "You didn't watch them. You didn't. I've seen men come close to killing each other before and every time it was over money or someone getting caught slipping out of someone else's back door. Now, unless there's a lot of borrowed money I'm unaware of, it's about who's sexing who." She bit her bottom lip to bridle her tongue, assuming Rose was either sadly mistaken or dense.

Rose simply felt awful because it was clear that Richard hadn't admitted to what he'd been doing nor with whom. Despite how much she loved Nadeen and cared for her as a good friend, she couldn't bring herself to share what Phillip had confided in her. Although she really wanted to explain everything she had learned, Rose agonized over it not being her place to do so. It was Richard's. "I am sorry, Nadeen. This is messed up, I know that, but I can't say any more about it. I can't."

"You mean you won't!" Nadeen shouted, her voice rising above a normal pitch. "I thought you'd be there for me. I guess all of that supposin' we did at my house when I thought Richard was seeing another woman didn't hold water. It was easy to stand with me when there was a real threat of some...some tramp sleeping with Richard. Imagine that tramp being Phillip, Rose? Huh, where would you be then? I wonder if you'd be sitting all cool, calm, and collected if that thing Phillip confessed was only half the truth? Where would you be then? Right here crying to me, that's where," she said, trembling bitterly as she grabbed her purse. Rose understood where she was coming from but didn't know how she'd arrived at that peculiar destination. All she could do was send her in another direction.

"Speak with your husband, Nadeen!" Rose shouted after her. "Talk to Richard!"

Shortly after leaving the church in a disgruntled blur, Richard briefly stopped by his home to change clothes. If only ridding himself of the actions that led to the dangerous struggle was so easy. With that in mind, Richard hopped back in his car then made a very important phone call. He dialed up Tatum Engineering, requesting a special visit to right the ship that had run aground because of his bad timing and poorly conceived decision to sack out with Dior beforehand. Three minutes of slick maneuvering with a goodly dose of pandering mixed in awarded Richard a ten-minute summit with the shrewd contractor. Thirty minutes after Richard arrived at the CEO's office, he had successfully persuaded Carlton Tatum to overlook the inopportune catastrophe he lied about having been the cause of his absence earlier in the day. Richard's knack for presenting best-case scenarios versus choosing Tatum's top competitor for the multimillion-dollar job inspired the old man to seal the deal that the quick-talking preacher had seemingly blown off for personal reasons. Soon enough, Richard was signing a stack of documents and scouting for the nearest exit. He autographed three sets of agreements, took copies for his records, then tore out of the overly decorated office for more subdued surroundings.

Quite satisfied with landing on his feet, Richard decided that his next course of action should include a heart-to-heart talk with Dior. She answered his phone call while out shopping. "Hey, you," she moaned, still caught up in the afterglow from their mid-morning rendezvous. "I knew you had a lot to do today but I was kinda wondering when you'd get back to me."

"Well, I do need to see you but our workout this morning will have to hold you for a minute. I'm more pressed for time than I thought I'd be but we should talk before I call it a day. How soon can I see you?"

"Didn't I just tell you I was shopping? Who knows how long that'll take?" Dior informed Richard she hadn't planned on returning home for hours. However, she offered to meet for a late lunch. "Listen, sugar, I'm not too far away from the Tex-Mex spot I like. I am hearing something in Spanish and it sounds like enchiladas calling my name again. If you're not scared, you could meet me there."

"Dior, come on now," Richard answered in a backpedaling manner. He hadn't completely dug himself out of the other hole he'd fallen into. "We've already gone over that. What would I say if Nadeen or one of her friends saw me out with you?"

"Oomph, I'd have an answer for that if Nadeen and her friends were *my* problem. But that's a good question. What would you say?"

"Let's not get into that right now," he debated, for the sake of time. "Besides it's probably not a good idea to deal in hypotheticals at this point. You ever hear of speaking things into being?"

"Yeah, I get that, all of it." When Richard balked at seeing her in public, Dior grew increasingly agitated. "What you're trying to say is you're only good with kicking it at my place. Ever think I might want to get out for dinner, a cozy cocktail, maybe catch a jazz set or two with my man?"

"Sure, I've considered taking you out so that's not what I'm saying at all," he argued, with a hitch in his voice Dior hadn't heard before. She didn't like it.

"Know what, Richard? You've already said too much. Why don't you run on home and hide. I must have been silly to think you could hold me down. You're not cut out for this lifestyle,

Preacher Man. Next time, don't come if you can't stay. This is a real big man's game and you just lost." Dior hung up in his face then turned it off when Richard continually redialed, just like she knew he would. She wasn't that disturbed by her role as Richard's private joy or the arrangement they agreed on in principle, an agreement she still intended on honoring. It was the way Richard clamored nervously about the possibility of getting busted by Nadeen that set her off.

Richard grunted violently when Dior's phone forwarded to voice mail each time he persisted in reaching her. "She's dumping me, ending it," he said to himself more than once. "Just like that, huh?" Perhaps it was better this way, he reasoned, since walking away from Dior was unimaginable. He didn't have it in him to tell her no, even if he tried. Richard was exhausted, dejected, and eager to spend quality time in his own house for a change. It had been a tiring day, one he wouldn't soon forget and one that wasn't nearly over. Dreading a difficult and overdue discussion with Nadeen, Richard took the long way home.

Nadeen couldn't busy herself enough while pacing the floor. She wrung her hands nervously when hearing Richard's car pull into the three-car garage. Mahalia sat in the family room with the television locked on the cartoon channel. She observed her mother's pensive actions although pretended not to be affected by it. Roxanne clung by her older sister's side on the sofa. She couldn't have known what was acutely wrong with her mother but she sensed Nadeen's angst only in the way a child could, on the periphery of their bond.

Oblivious to her children's close proximity, Nadeen met Richard in the utility room after he closed the garage door. She realized he had changed clothes and had somehow managed to shrug on a cloak of humility since she saw him last. His eyes were weary and encircled by dark rings. It was understandable that he must have spent hours soul-searching after what she assumed he had gone through and had yet to address with her. Despite the whipped expression he dragged into the house, Nadeen wasn't about to let him off the hook. "It's about time you came home," she said, almost as uncomfortable as the man she thought she knew.

Richard's eyes closed momentarily, then he breathed deeply. "Hey, baby. I thought you would have called my cell today," he replied in a choppy staccato manner as if he was piecing the sentence together as he went along. When Nadeen sneered at him, he cleared his throat. "It was unacceptable what happened at the church today. I feel real bad about how it looked too but that's all behind us now." He tried to saunter past her to enter the kitchen. Nadeen shook her index finger mere inches from his nose, motioning for him to stay put.

"Oomph, you want to talk about unacceptable? For eighteen years, I've carried your name, eighteen. And during those years, I carried your dreams in my chest and your children in my womb. At times, I even carried your burdens and your bad credit. If that's the best you can do in the way of explaining to me what's been going on, I may as well get the girls' bags packed and catch the midnight plane to Georgia. Nothing could possibly be put behind us until I know what's been going on behind my back."

"You're right, Nadeen. You have been there for me every step of the way. I'm thankful for that. Maybe, maybe a few days away would do everyone some good," he uttered foolishly.

Nadeen chuckled with an air of disbelief. "Whew, that sounds just like you, Richard, always trying to minimize things to take the heat off. Got news for you: that ain't gon' get it this time," she whispered fiendishly. Nadeen was unraveling. Richard was surprised when she managed to control herself and sustain a modicum of restraint instead of cutting him to bits. "I already have half a mind to notify Mahalia's and Roxy's schools first thing in the morning, from Atlanta, that they won't be coming back."

"You'd do that to me?" he growled, with a glint of resentment in his eyes. "What's gotten into you?"

"Funny you should mention that. I'm still waiting for you to tell me the same thing. What and who's gotten into you, Richard? Don't lie to me. I know Phillip isn't the only one. How many others have there been?"

"Phillip? Others, other-other-what?" he stammered, his eyes darting erratically to and fro.

"No use in holding back now, I heard you and him talking about sweet secret lovin' and his decision not to be there for you any longer," she mocked. "I heard it all so you can stop pretending!"

Richard stood back on his heels. He'd slipped up and broken his vows more times than he wanted to remember at the moment but what she was suggesting sounded ridiculous, even for him. "Nadeen, you cannot think I've had a sexual relationship with Phillip. Baby, baby, you know me better than that."

She laughed at how funny that sounded coming out of his mouth. "You know, I thought I did until I found myself at the doctor's office today, submitting blood for an AIDS test."

"What! Oh wait a minute. What doctor? Dr. Griggs? Now she thinks I've been fooling around with men?"

Nadeen licked her lips when his last statement smacked her hard. "You care more about what she thinks of you than I do? Negro, you've done it now. If you won't spill it, then keep it. I don't need this in my life. You can hang out with the boys, play poker, or whatever it is y'all call it. Just leave me and my children out of it!" Nadeen turned to abandon the discussion that to that point had failed to compel Richard to admit a single infraction.

"Wait! Wait!" he yelled, grabbing her by the arm. "Wait a minute!"

"So now you want to talk?" she snapped back. "Tell me then. How often have you had unprotected sex? Anal sex?" Richard's eyes flew wide open. He reached for answers but found none. Admitting he had unprotected sex was admitting he'd had relations, and with Dior of all people, the one woman he profusely denied being involved with. In the wake of his silence, Nadeen jerked her arm from his grasp then parked both fists on her hips. "Tell me all about it, Richard. Tell me how long you've been gay!"

Richard looked as if he'd seen a ghost. His ashy lips quivered as a small shadow eased around the corner just ahead of Roxy. She eyed her parents after growing concerned about the boisterous accusations thrown about the room. "I heard y'all fighting," she said, not settled on quite how to feel about it. The pointed question she leveled on them explained why. "Are y'all getting a divorce?"

"No, Roxy," answered Richard without hesitation.

"That depends on what your father says to me next," Nadeen replied flippantly.

"It wouldn't be so bad," Roxy added naïvely, having contemplated the idea when a classmate's parents called it quits. "I could have two bedrooms and a whole 'nother set of toys and dresses if you do."

"Why don't you go back in there with your sister, Roxy," Nadeen demanded sternly. "I promise, you'll be the first to know." She watched her daughter rush off, blind to the situation involving all of them.

"Listen to me, Nadeen. You might have heard me and Phillip fall out over a situation but it didn't have anything to do with me and him caught up in some sort of homosexual, twisted affair."

He scratched his head, trying to come up with an explanation that wouldn't likely force his wife to follow through on her threats to leave him. Richard was running out of options and out of alibis. He coaxed her to come back inside the utility room, then he closed the door. "Okay, you've got to know I didn't mean for it to come to this. Phillip was covering for me when I went to see Dior." He paused when the name circulated in Nadeen's head. "It started out like I told you, me ministering to her, and then I got too close."

"Dior? Dior?" she questioned peculiarly. "Isn't that the same little tramp I asked you about? The one who pranced down the center aisle after service had begun and you lied to my face about seeing? No, that couldn't be the same hood chick who all but challenged me on the sidewalk after church." Nadeen's eyes turned bloodred. She reached up and slapped the taste out of his mouth the same way she had to Mahalia. Only this time Richard deserved it. So much so, Nadeen allowed venom to hang on her bottom lip as she walloped him again. Too mad to let Richard see her cry, Nadeen threw her hands up, wiped her nose, and spun on a dime. While she twisted the doorknob to exit the tiny, angry room, he made a last-ditch effort to explain. Unfortunately, truth went flying off his tongue on the back end of a lie.

"It's not like you're making it," he groveled. "I did develop feelings I shouldn't have and it was immature to think I could get close without stumbling."

"Why do I get the feeling you did more than that? Just how far did you fall? Never mind, I'll wait on the test results to find out."

"Nadeen, it's over," he announced sorrowfully. "I mean it. It's done between me and Dior."

"Don't! You've already brought that woman into our bed. I won't stand for hearing her name spoken in my house. Expect a call from my lawyer. I mean that!"

# TWENTY-TWO

## *Mama, I Lied*

Over the next four days, Dior avoided Richard's futile attempts at closure. She sensed it in the scores of messages inundating her voice mailbox. Richard's hesitant tone warned Dior that he'd experienced a change of heart compelling him to end their relationship. However, she wasn't nearly finished with him. The changes he underwent during the month she'd entertained him played over and over in her mind as she took the country drive to Azalea Springs Federal Prison for women. Richard's weight loss and ever-increasing need for Dior's affection made her smile. The thought of coaxing him to explore her desires while improving his expertise one episode at a time made her tingle.

She stepped out of her car in the federal penitentiary parking lot, firing off pheromones and craving another sheet-drenching session with the man she planned on being hers someday, hers and hers alone. Dior soared through the visitor intake area, turning the heads of several male correctional officers and quite a few female personnel as well. She grinned devilishly when the grim-faced guard, who typically treated her as if she didn't have anything he wanted, gestured cordially for her to walk ahead of him down the long corridor when it was a hard and fast policy for visitors to follow behind by two paces. She felt him picking up her scent and staring at her apple bottom, tight cotton blouse, and high heels. She found it difficult to blame him for finally acting like a man instead of a eunuch.

When the stoutly built officer unlatched the chain-link fence separating the corridor from the congregation room, he stepped aside with his eyes again attentive to her curves. Dior almost giggled. The poor man's innermost thoughts were plainly stenciled on his face. His mouth, hanging open like a gaping hole, irritated Billie Rae just as it would have watching any grown man salivating over her daughter. Her brilliant smile, the one she'd been saving for Dior's visit, quickly faded. It had been months since Dior strutted into the visitation section dressed for a night on the town instead of a heavily guarded early morning meeting at a federal facility. Billie Rae's soured expression displayed exactly how strongly she disapproved of Dior's attire and the response it drew. But Billie Rae decided to suppress any other signs of her displeasure. She decided to hold back other news too: She had recently been informed of her release date to a halfway house in the city. Because the ink hadn't dried on her discharge papers, Billie Rae hesitated to share the good news with Dior, for fear of being disappointed by an unforeseen glitch in the bureaucratic red tape, which could have potentially upset everyone's plans for a homecoming celebration.

Dressed in a starched and pressed khaki uniform, Billie Rae inched forward on the cold metal bench when Dior entered the twenty-by-twenty-foot room. As usual, Billie ran her eager fingers along the creases of her pants after internalizing the jailer's instruction: *Remember, Wicker, no contact.* "Yes, sir, I remember," she

answered in a softer voice than she'd used in weeks. It was nothing short of misery not being allowed to reach out and embrace
her child as Dior approached the gray table constructed of the
same lifeless material as her perch.

"You look good, Mama," Dior hailed pleasantly, much to her
mother's surprise. It was the first time she had acknowledged her
lineage while in Billie Rae's presence.

"And you smell nice," the inmate replied, grinning ear to ear.
"'Mama'—I like that. Thank you for making me a very happy
woman. I—" she started to say before Dior interrupted.

"I met somebody special," she sang sweetly. "He's a good man,
makes a legit living and everything. He's kind of a holy roller but
I've been trying to loosen him up some."

"A good and Godly man? Okay, that's different. If you like it,
I love it. So, how'd you meet him?" she asked, swallowing
yet another hearty helping of surprise. Billie Rae listened inten-
tly as she shared her first such conversation with Dior regarding men in her life. She generally kept tabs by getting the scoop
from Dooney. Having been separated from her daughter for close
to eleven years by bars and barbed wire, Billie promised herself
that she wouldn't exhibit any signs of concern if she heard
something hinky about the man who had Dior buzzing from
head to toe.

"He came into the shop one day, looking for a new suit for a
special event he had to do," Dior said, her smile soft and inviting. "I wasn't really busy so I watched him pick through neckties,
expensive ones. Richard, that's his name, said he didn't often do
business with such pretty women," Dior added, telling the story
with exaggerations thrown in here and there. "Since I bump into
fine men all the time, I blew him off until I saw he wasn't trying
to size me up. He was just being nice; that's his way. Our first
conversation was rougher than most. You know me, always trying

to figure out the answer even if there's no problem to speak of. I actually pushed some of his buttons to irritate him after he told me his wife did most of his shopping."

"His wife?" asked Billie Rae with panic-stricken eyes. By the way her mother's forehead wrinkled with worry, Dior recognized she had slipped up in underestimating Billie's comprehension of the sort of things going on in the free world. She was still a woman after all.

"No, no, not his current wife," she lied. "Richard is happily divorced."

"Oh, I see. Has he got any kids?" Billie asked, now feeling more at ease about Dior's love interest.

"Yeah, two gorgeous daughters. They love them some daddy," she asserted. Dior chuckled as if she'd seen them interact fondly on numerous occasions.

"It seems to me Dior loves her some daddy too," Billie asserted. She glared playfully at her visitor from the corner of her eye. "Watch your back, baby girl. Daughters can tend to be overprotective of their fathers, especially good ones. They're so hard to come by nowadays."

"Wasn't too easy getting good ones to line up on yesterdays neither," she cracked glibly. Dior's father turned out to be a rolling stone, a married salesman she never met. Billie Rae received very little support from him because it was hard to track him down due to a number of fake aliases he kept under his belt. "Richard is the settling down kind but I think I'll let him marinate awhile before accepting his proposal." Dior was on a roll and couldn't see one reason to douse her delusions of grandeur. "I keep the two-carat diamond and platinum engagement setting he bought me in a deposit box for safekeeping. He'll appreciate it a lot when I let him rebound completely from his first wife." Dior's eyes sparkled as she strung lies together continuously. As far as she knew, Billie Rae was slated to be incarcerated another eight months at least. By that time, she honestly hoped that every fabricated word from her shiftless story would have come to fruition. Once breathing life into those empty lies, she became more determined than ever to pull off the slickest man-grab of her life. There were at least two obstacles standing in the way: namely Nadeen Allamay and the married woman's utter repugnance for selfish and scandalous homewreckers like Dior.

With the prison in her rearview, Dior sailed down the interstate on a natural high. After selling Billie Rae a bill of goods that didn't exist, she couldn't see her way into turning back now. She felt as if every aspect of her life had just gotten that much sweeter. Looking down the road in rose-colored glasses, Dior blushed when envisioning her name on the church registry as the pastor's wife, the first lady. She remembered hearing Dooney's heart-wrenching response after being sentenced to jail. He could have thrown himself on the mercy of the court or begged for probation instead of paying his debt to society in the state penitentiary. When the judge glared at him, asking if he had anything to say before they took him away, Dooney glanced over his shoulder at Dior sitting behind his public defender. He'd done the best he knew how to keep the lights on, food on the table, and her out of harm's way after their mother was convicted. "Yes, I do, Your Honor. In a very short time, I've come to learn how a house divided cannot stand and also just how easy the right amount of pressure can bust a steel pipe." It didn't matter if the judge comprehended Dooney's soulful revelation; Dior understood. She had experienced barely scraping by, up close and personal, seeing it develop from the inside out. Years later, an opportunity presented itself to assert her brother's jailhouse philosophy, standing on the outside, looking in.

\* \* \*

Sunday morning, the M.E.G.A. Church men's choir wailed joyously. The congregation clapped along with the spiritual beat,
while swaying and praising to their hearts' content. Rose, sitting next to Nadeen, smiled at her when the chorus rolled into
"I'm Looking for a Miracle" with resounding intensity. It was
as if the entire building and everyone in it were on fire. Nadeen
hadn't gotten over Richard's confession but she was moving
toward it. For days on end, she'd threatened to file separation
papers unless he came clean about everything. Richard apologized profusely but disagreed when Nadeen pushed for marriage
counseling. He said he had a hold on his curiosity, stating that's
all it was, and how he couldn't risk having his business floating
around the medical community after some arrogant psycholo-
gist started digging into the dark corners of his life. Nadeen let
up on her Gestapo interrogation tactics when Richard shed tears
over allowing himself to get drawn in by Dior's temptress ways,
although he wouldn't admit to doing anything past infrequent
intimate canoodling. Nadeen was sorry too. She had vehemently
accused her best friend's husband of engrossing himself in homosexual activity and then concealing it from his wife. Rose said
she understood how Nadeen could have gotten things mixed up.
Overhearing a woeful argument about secret love and the like,
it was foreseeable that misunderstandings would abound, especially on the heels of Richard's flat-out refusal to discuss the
incident initially. Furthermore, Nadeen recognized the difficult
position she'd backed Rose into and why she remained tight-
lipped regarding what Phillip divulged to her in the strictest of
confidence. As the pastor's wife, sustaining silence and a straight
face when crossing paths with members whose dirtiest secrets
she'd been privy to always seemed to eat at her insides too. There
weren't any new transgressions under the sun; most of them
were merely the normal garden variety, recycled and duplicated

a million times over with slight variations. Nadeen was jubilant
when she squeezed Rose's hand thankfully. She was hopeful the
worst was behind her and Richard. What happened next caused
her short-lived jubilation to get snatched up around the collar
and body-slammed.

Nadeen's eyes filled with utter disbelief. Dior came swagger-
ing down the aisle as bold as you please in a short white sundress
with low cleavage and spaghetti straps. Despite another grand
entrance, no one other than those who knew what Dior was up to
appeared to notice. Hymns and spiritual songs played on while
Nadeen's world stood still. She eyed Richard's plaything dis-
approvingly. The fact that Dior's legs were bare and extremely
toned didn't make it any easier. Rose had asked in retrospect what
Nadeen really thought about Richard chasing after a younger
woman. Nadeen replied that the chasing aspect didn't amount
to anything worth worrying over in her book unless he had lied
about catching the skank a time or two while he was at it. Now
that Dior's brazen entrance drew the attention from several men
in the choir, Nadeen had to rethink her position. Suddenly, it
came to mind how wrong she'd been about marriage and the suffering that oftentimes aids in building the institution. Throughout her upbringing, she thought her mother was a fool to let
her father run around off the leash and then act like everything
was going to be alright. In that instant, Nadeen knew why her
mother stayed with a philandering preacher. She wore a cloak of
indispensable commitment like a tattoo, proud and permanent,
because love had a hold on her and it was stronger than pride.

"I can't believe she'd have the nerve to show up here," Rose
whispered, as she looked on with tightened lips. "She ought to be
ashamed."

"But she ain't," Nadeen growled, like a lioness preparing to
pounce on a dangerous intruder circling her cubs. In actuality,

Dior was doing exactly that, endangering the welfare of Nadeen's children. A major breakup over another woman would tear them apart and likely cause deep-seated issues of distrust manifesting themselves in the girls' lives later on. There were far more circumstances to consider than Richard's infidelity and his supposed waning affinity for Dior. Nadeen stared sullenly as her nemesis took a seat on an adjacent pew. In a moment, clouded by ambiguity, one truth was made clearly evident. "It takes a different kind of woman to show her face, Rose, after she's gone to so much trouble showing her tail."

# TWENTY-THREE

## *Daddy's Girls*

Richard entered the stage from the left side, in the red power tie Nadeen had selected for the previous pastor's day observance. Phillip, whose lip was still slightly swollen, trailed behind him. Both men felt awful about the conference room brawl but it was Richard who called his old friend to make amends. Phillip agreed that things had gotten out of hand, citing his frustration about the charter school setback and his favorite pastor putting all they've worked for in jeopardy because of what he called "the devil's daughter" trying to bring down the Lord's house. However, Phillip was relieved when he was told about Richard's make-up session with Carlton Tatum and his decision to squelch the carnal lust burning in his heart for Dior.

Without any additional fanfare, Richard approached the pulpit podium displaying an intense expression. He opened his copy of the Word to the book of Exodus, then peered up from the text, his eyes locked on his wife's saddened face. Because he'd labored over this sermon, he wasn't interested in being distracted in the least. This was a message to himself as well as to the congregation. "Morning, church," he said, forcing a hint of a smile. "It's a great day to worship the Lord, amen?" There was a resounding assurance from the audience. "Today is special in many regards. I'm not sure where to begin so I'll just get right down to the lesson and pray it all falls into place. Now, I know that oftentimes Christians feel as though our sins are so big, so bad, and so bountiful that there is no way we can continue to go to God and have Him be there at the ready to pick us up when we fall." A smattering of applause emanated from the audience. Not all of them wanted to openly admit their sins had drawn them so far away. "Oh, I must be stepping on some toes this morning because I know that in a man's, a woman's, and a child's life there are moments, days, weeks, months when the storms seem insurmountable, meaning…the problems we've faced, the wrongs we've done, the hurt we've caused is so high that we can't get over them, so low we can't get under them, and so wide…you know the rest." A thunderous roar rang throughout the crowd. Richard pointed his finger at the congregation then toward the television cameras. "I knew it. I knew. You can't hide the truth. I can't hide the truth. God knows all, sees all, and is able to do all. Now, this brings me to my point. Praise God and serve God in your *brokenness*. I'm not sure that's even a word you can find in the dictionary but it's certainly a word God understands, and it makes a whole lot of sense to me. Listen well, church, the human soul is the only thing I know of that can still be of great worth when it's broken." Richard flipped pages to find the scripture he wanted to lead in with. Oddly, his attention was pulled in another direction, to Dior's cleavage. He glanced up from the Bible, froze for a brief moment, then took out his handkerchief to dab at the sweat beading on his forehead. Seeing Dior unexpectedly sent a bolt of emotion through him. Simultaneously, he found himself morbidly uncomfortable, sad for Nadeen, and extremely excited Dior had returned.

Nadeen could barely stand to see the way Richard's countenance changed the second he saw his mistress batting eyes at him while he was attempting to spread the Word no less. When she was no longer able to watch Dior's blatant display, Nadeen bowed her head so she wouldn't have to. Richard saw that his wife appeared to be taking the brunt of Dior's presence. For the first time in his marriage, he was truly sorry for having hurt Nadeen. Before, he'd said or done things in the heat of an argument or as a result of a discussion gone awry but this one was blaringly mournful. Immediately, he reverted focus to the text and held his finger there to secure the precise passage. "The Lord had proven time and again that He does not put more on our narrow shoulders than we can handle. He knows what your breaking point is and every now and then lets you get there, only to be reminded of who He is and what His place in your life should be." He heard Phillip's voice howl above the others after being reminded himself.

"Amen, Brother Pastor!" he cheered, having seen what can happen when people lose their sights on the importance of keeping God where He belongs.

"If the Lord is not on the top, supporting you from the bottom, both sides, and in the middle, something is incredibly wrong with the way you're doing business with Him. Let's take Moses, for instance, in the book of Exodus, starting at the second chapter somewhere around verse number one. Most of us have read the story of the burning bush or have seen it on TV during Easter movies week, but I'm here to tell you right now, God went out of His way to get Moses to see things His way by first getting his attention and proving beyond a shadow of a doubt that it was in fact the Lord reaching out in the first place. You don't believe He'll do the same for you, watch this. When Moses was tending sheep and minding his own business, verse number two says, *There the angel of the Lord appeared to him in flames of fire from within a bush. Moses saw that though the bush was on fire, yet it did not burn.*" Richard slammed his hand down on the podium. "Everyone out there at some point in your lives have said to yourselves, 'I was in an accident and by all accounts I should have been killed.' Or, 'The doctors said that kind of cancer should have ended my life.' Or, 'I was acting so carelessly with my body that it's a miracle I didn't get pregnant.' Or, 'I had so much to drink the Lord must have guided my car home.'" Richard clapped joyously. "You can't tell me God isn't still in the miracle-making business. There's something else you need to be aware of. Chapter three says, *So Moses thought, 'I will go over and see this strange sight —— why the bush does not burn up.' When the Lord saw that Moses had gone over to look, God called to him from within the bush, 'Moses! Moses!' And Moses said, 'Here I am.'*"

After dabbing his forehead again and purposely ignoring Dior, Richard moved across the platform as if setting the stage for a contemporary application. "God used a sign to bring Moses near then He called out to him specifically. When Moses heard his name, he acknowledged that he was attentive, present, and accounted for." Speaking into a cordless microphone, Richard put on a fearful expression while staring into a make-believe bush. "I'm here, what you want with me?" Richard whispered with feigned astonishment. He waved the Bible again, reading from verse five. " '*Do not come any closer,' God said. 'Take off your sandals, for the place you are standing is holy ground.'* See, He made Moses humble himself before receiving the message. *Then He said, 'I am the God of your father, the God of Abraham, the God of Isaac and Jacob.'* God was simply letting Moses know that He was Lord to his daddy, his daddy's daddy, and his great-great granddaddy too." Laughter filled the sanctuary. Richard even saw a smile trickle onto Nadeen's lips. "*Moses then hid his face, because he was afraid to look at God. The Lord said, 'I have indeed seen the misery of my people in Egypt. I have heard them crying out because of their slave drivers, and I am concerned about their* *suffering. So I have come down to rescue them up out of that land into a good* *and spacious land, a land flowing with milk and honey*—' Doesn't that sound just like God to give His people the best there is? He said He'd give them the home of the Canaanites: Beverly Hills, of the Hittites: Hollywood, of the Amorites: Rodeo Drive, of the Perizzites: the cobbledstone streets of Paris, of the Hivites and Jebusites: Park Avenue and Fifth Avenue. God said He'd make good on the best there was to offer." Richard was in his zone then; he placed the Bible on the podium stand then freestyled it from there. Nadeen always said that's when he was at his most persuasive. "If you don't mind, I'd like to recap just to make sure we're on the same page as Moses and God. The Lord was telling Moses and now I'm telling you, He has seen your struggles. He was there when the slave catchers beat on your ancestors. He was there when the police let the dogs loose on your kinfolk in Birmingham, Alabama. He was there when your supervisor passed you over for a promotion and the person who did get it was less qualified and three shades lighter. God was there when your friends lied on you. He was there when you got up out of Susan's bed then hopped right into Steven's bed. That's right, I said it. He was there when you promised to put down the crack, the cocaine, the pipe, the pills, and the porn. And He was there when you went back and picked them up again too." Richard had the congregation standing on their feet, praising and moaning. "Know that whatever the struggle is, God is there too. Furthermore, it's clear to me why the bush was on fire but did not burn. God was in the bush!" The ovation swelled. Phillip handed his friend a glass of water. Richard sipped until the cheers subsided. "When God is in it, there's always a chance to walk away without getting burned. Amen. He knew Moses' people were troubled, oppressed, and distressed just like He knows your struggles too.

Praise Him and serve Him, in your *brokenness*. When He gets your attention, church, and then calls your name, humble yourselves, listen to His instruction, and then do what He moves you to do. I've heard Him call my name and I'm going to respond accordingly. The deacons don't know about this, the elders either, but I had decided to put my money where my mouth is by writing a personal check for three hundred and fifty members to go with me on a fellowship mission to New Orleans to help them during their brokenness. I'm paying for the buses, gas, and hotel rooms. I realize it's short notice but for those who are able to make the worthwhile journey, we'll leave Thursday at midnight, arrive there in time for breakfast, and enjoy a long day of painting and repairing. We will then leave the Crescent City around noon on the following day. This is a pledge to help restore the damaged areas which the state and federal governments failed to protect and later have seemed to overlook." Richard caught a glimpse of the row where Dior had been sitting. When he didn't see her, he assumed she had skipped out after having either felt neglected or touched by the power of the message. It wouldn't take long before Richard learned not to underestimate Dior's extraordinary savvy for scandal.

While checking her makeup in the women's lounge, Dior identified a miniature admirer. Roxanne stood behind her, looking on at the woman she figured was responsible for the tense emotions wedged between her parents. The precocious eight-year-old wrinkled her nose after Dior refreshed her perfume with an exaggerated squirt from a travel-size bottle. Patiently waiting for the darling and littlest Allamay to let go of the words ready to seep out where two front teeth used to be, Dior turned and extended her hand for an introduction. "Well, aren't you the prettiest thing."

"I said the same about you but my mommy said you wasn't

all that pretty. Sometimes mommies make mistakes though," she asserted with a brisk head nod.

"My name is Dior Wicker and I'm guessing you are Roxanne Allamay?" Dior shook hands with the small child, seeing semblances of Richard throughout her face.

"You guessed right, Ms. Dior, but my friends call me Roxy."

"Can I call you Roxy?"

"If you want to be my friend," she answered with a wistful smile.

"Good, it's a deal. Friends." Dior checked her hair then motioned to say goodbye to Roxanne. The girl gazed at the woman, dressed perhaps a bit too casually for Sunday service. There was a question stamped on her tiny face. Dior leaned in closer, fearing she might say something that shouldn't be overheard by other women milling about. "Yes, what is it, Roxy?"

"I've been wanting to see you again because I wanted to ask you something. Well, I can't figure it out but I'm only a kid so there's a lot about grown-up stuff I don't know yet."

"If there's something on a young lady's mind, she should always come right out with it." Dior smiled cordially, believing she handled that fairly well for a beginner. Before giving it any more thought, Roxanne came out with both barrels blazing.

"Ms. Dior, why do you want to be my new mommy?" Roxanne's question caught Dior off guard. She stalled, while searching her mind for appropriate words that wouldn't upset her young acquaintance. It must have taken too long for the child's liking because she broke in another one. "Another thing, Herman's daddy called you a stank-butt gold digger but he isn't a real man because he can't keep a job more than a week at a time, so he cannot be taken seriously. Do you know Herman's no-good, always-begging daddy?"

"No, I don't think I've had the pleasure of meeting him. On

the other hand, he certainly thinks he knows me," she joked uncomfortably.

"Don't worry, you haven't missed out on a thing. Trust me," Roxanne assured her.

Mahalia entered the women's room on an investigative search for her younger sister, who at times hung out too long, listening to adults trading gossip. Roxanne jerked her head when Mahalia berated her for staying out of sight long enough to get yelled at by their mother.

"You know better than to run off like that, Roxy. I'm tired of having to look all over for you," she huffed, staring squarely into Dior's eyes with hateful intentions. "And don't ever let me catch you talking to her again or I'll beat you myself."

"What's the matter with talking to her?" Roxanne squealed.

"Shut up!" Mahalia snapped, grabbing her kid sister by the arm and proceeding to pull her out of there by hook or by crook until Dior raised her hand to stifle their exodus.

"Hold up a minute. Roxy asked me a question I didn't get the chance to answer," Dior said in a soothing tone. "You remember, don't you, friend, the one about me being your new mommy? Why don't you ask your daddy why he wants me to be his new mama?" Evidently shaken by the tone Mahalia used when warning Roxanne to stay away or else, Dior assumed Nadeen must have put the child up to it. Regardless, Dior was hurt by the interaction and saw to it that she wouldn't be the last one feeling the sting of embarrassment.

Mahalia made Roxanne promise never to speak of her encounter with the witch in the restroom because she recognized the gravity of Dior's insinuation. During the ride home, not one word was cast. Nadeen dealt with seeing Dior in another light, so close to home at that. Richard couldn't afford to make any wrong moves with Nadeen, knowing the end of his marriage was merely one lawyer phone call away. Roxanne was sworn to secrecy and brooding about the pact she was forced to conceal. Mahalia was lost as to why everyone was letting this outsider come into their lives without checking her. Roxanne was Dior's newest fan. Richard didn't have a leg to stand on. And her mother appeared to have thrown in the cards. Fueled by her parents' reluctance to straighten out Dior for getting involved with another woman's husband, Mahalia remained soured by the series of events leading them to this troublesome crossroad. She swore to God that she would get even with that tramp, if she ever got the chance.

# TWENTY-FOUR

## *Eggshells and Egos*

Two grueling days at the Allamay household had taken its toll. Everyone was on pins and needles. Mahalia stayed cooped up in her room but not like before when seduced by compilations of mindless teenaged chatter. Behind closed doors, she spent endless hours fuming with her mouth slammed shut. Richard had numerous problems of his own to worry about, too many to be aware of his eldest daughter's. He walked on eggshells after having been banished to the guestroom and wondering when and if he would ever be allowed to reclaim his side of the bed in the master suite. Nadeen held her tongue while taking it all in. She worked diligently at making strides to forgive Richard's *intimate relations* with Dior through daily prayer and intense personal Bible studies. Rose ran right over to visit her when she heard the strain in Nadeen's voice during a brief phone call. She wanted to say how she empathized but that wasn't entirely true. Her husband, Phillip, hadn't given his mistress carte blanche to pop up at his job dressed in nightclub attire and put her face in his then have the unmitigated gall to pretend it was all done in the name of

Godly worship. Rose didn't identify with or internalize her girl-friend's plight because they didn't belong to her. Despite her feelings of inadequacy, Rose stumbled onto a bridge fit for Nadeen's journey forward, a bridge to tread above her tribulations without having to endure yet another minute of indecisiveness. Not knowing what to do about anything that mattered had her trapped in a mean blue funk that would not cut her an even break.

"I have just the thing for you," Rose gushed eagerly, as soon as Nadeen greeted her at the door. She held up a stack of books and pamphlets bound by a purple ribbon. "You probably don't remember these; I almost forgot about them myself." Nadeen eyed the stack of literature curiously as Rose stepped in waving it excitedly.

"Now you've got me interested. Let's go on up to *my* room and see what this is you brought for me."

Rose chuckled. "Richard is still in the doghouse, huh?"

"Yep, for sneaking off and chasing flea-bitten mutts," answered Nadeen. "Come on in and lock the door."

Rose sat on the bed and untied the ribbon. "Think back on that women's retreat you took me to for my birthday three years ago. You remember the one in Los Angeles? We talked about it for weeks when we got back."

"Oh yeah, it was so good. What was it called?"

"Too Blessed to Be Stressed with Jewel Diamond Taylor!" A brilliant smile spread across Rose's full lips as she handed the first book to Nadeen. "This is my favorite. It's called *Keeping the Main Thing the Main Thing.*"

"That was such a great weekend, Rose. I came home so filled with the spirit. Guess I neglected to keep up with the take-home material. We heard some powerful prayers and messages from Jewel."

"And the testimonies from other sisters," Rose sighed,

thinking back. "Just when I thought I'd seen it all, another strong woman would stand up and share what she was going through. Real everyday struggles."

"Some people's everyday is rougher than others," Nadeen agreed. "Real struggles with sex, drugs, alcohol, and everything else imaginable." Rose broke out laughing when a particular thought entered her mind. "What is it, Rose?"

"And some things unimaginable too, even for me, and I'm a freak. That lesbian from Oakland raising three sons on her own—she was up against it."

"She should have decided on going the other way before popping out three kids," Nadeen joked before catching herself. "See, I'm sorry for that. I had no business talking about that poor woman."

"Me neither. She was just trying to find her way without losing herself in the process." There was a moment of hesitation in the room. Both of the women were contemplating the same thing. Nadeen voiced it first. "Rose, you think she ever found a way to deal with her sexuality and explaining it to her sons?"

"God, I sure do hope so. I wouldn't wish that on anybody. Not even the women I can't stand the most."

"Tell me about it."

Rose accomplished her good deed then dashed off to give her friend the room she needed to start over that bridge. Nadeen creased the pages of the book, reading the profound words of a woman who had to overcome a mountain of personal distress before she could help others climb theirs as well. "Keeping the main thing the main thing," Nadeen said to herself for the umpteenth time. "*My main thing is my family and keeping it together,*" she'd determined. "*If God says the same, I will.*"

After Nadeen filled her head with fortifying passages from the uplifting materials Rose provided, she opened the bedroom door and ventured out of her cave. It was unusually quiet throughout the house, even for a Tuesday evening. Roxy feasted on a cartoon marathon, as she did when the others were too busy to entertain her. Nadeen lent some thought to preparing dinner then remembered Richard mentioning picking up takeout earlier. "Hey, kiddo, aren't you getting hungry?" she asked softly from the mouth of the vast family room.

"No, ma'am, I'm just tired," Roxanne replied despondently. Nadeen picked up the remote lying on the coffee table and then paused the program. Now, sitting on the sofa next to her pride and joy, she threw her arm around Roxanne's shoulder.

"I don't like the way that sounded. Tired? What's got my baby so worn out?" Nadeen assumed Roxanne was utilizing the opportunity to pout simply because no one had paid her the level of attention to which she was accustomed. "Your father will be home soon. Maybe we could play a board game. How about Monopoly? You could even be the thimble."

"The thimble?" Roxanne sneered disagreeably. "If you let me be the banker that would really be something."

"Okay, there's a first time for everything. The banker it is. I'll go up and see if Mahalia wants to help me set up the board." Nadeen thought she would have received a round of riotous cheers but there wasn't one ounce of elation. "Uh-oh, what is it now?"

"Mommy, Mahalia's not interested in playing with me or you. *She's* the reason I'm so tired," Roxanne informed her, wearing the previous sneer as before.

"Has your sister been mean to you?"

"No, but she did make me do something I didn't want to."

"Ooh, that's not good. Why don't you tell me what it is and I'll speak to Mahalia and fix it."

"You can't. That's one of the things she's mad at me about.

The other one I swore not to tell." Roxanne wanted so desperately to blab about her conversation with Dior. But a promise was a promise. Nadeen understood that whatever she was holding inside had gotten the better of her. Pulling rank was one option of dragging the information out of her although it would bother Roxanne afterward and possibly put her at odds with Mahalia for breaking their pact. There was always a backdoor entrance to getting at the truth from stubborn little girls, and Nadeen had it down to a science.

"Okay then, since you swore not to tell me what I can't fix or the other thing that made your sister angry with you, the only thing you're able to share is what you were doing before the trouble started." Nadeen watched her child mull over the proposition carefully, not wanting to make any slipups and subsequently alienate Mahalia.

"Before Mahalia grabbed my arm and yanked on it, I wasn't doing anything but standing in the restroom and looking at Daddy's friend Dior comb her hair in the mirror. She didn't like that."

"Dior didn't?"

"Uh-uh, Mahalia. She didn't like it that I was standing there, talking nice to her, or the question she told me to ask Daddy."

Nadeen's blood turned cold. She turned her head away to shield Roxanne from her rage. Dior had to have been out of her mind involving an innocent child in the dangerous game she played with people's lives. Nadeen couldn't let another second pass without squeezing that question from the little girl's grasp. "Roxy, I need you to listen very closely because this is very important. There are a few things you are not supposed to tell and I just want to be sure you didn't forget them."

"No, ma'am, I didn't forget," she said assuredly.

"I don't know. Maybe you should remind yourself so that you don't," Nadeen pried tactfully.

"It sounded kind of silly when Ms. Dior told me to ask Daddy why he wanted her to be his new mommy."

Nadeen was as much confused as she was incensed. "His new mommy? Why would she say such a thing to you?"

"Maybe she didn't like it when I asked her why she wanted to be my new mommy. If Daddy likes her and she likes him back, they might fall in love and get married too, then I would have a brand-new mommy like my friends at school." Roxanne placed her tiny hands on Nadeen's to stop them from trembling. "Don't worry. Mahalia said you couldn't fix it but you'll always be the best mommy ever and my favorite one." Nadeen pulled Roxanne closely and held her there for the longest time, fighting the urge to find Dior's whereabouts and then see what she could break once she did. She didn't know Mahalia had been listening from just around the corner. Tears streamed down the girl's flat cheeks, effortlessly. She felt every damaging word carve holes in her heart.

Near the downtown canyon, Richard milled around the pickup window at Boscoe's, the neighborhood eatery where fried wings outsold other menu items five to one. He had purposely avoided the local greasy spoon for healthier links in the food chain. When Nadeen failed to mention dinner plans for the evening, Richard found himself groping for entrées the entire family would enjoy. Hot wings, southwestern egg rolls, and curly fries had once been a biweekly staple.

After placing a hefty order to go, Richard shoved both hands into his front pockets. He read the stream of words floating below the sports newscast merely to pass the time. An annoying itch dug in behind his left ear. When he went to scratch it, his gaze drifted from the television that was harnessed in the upper corner of the bar area. His heart rate pounded because of what he saw. Richard wanted to discount the jolt of emotion that rocked him. It was Dior, sharing drinks and laughs with a man, a young man closer to her age than Richard's.

Backing into the shadows behind a tall Boscoe's souvenir stand, Richard sought a better vantage point where he could observe the date in progress without being detected. Dior's tight tank top and painted on jeans offered a gratifying preview. Richard shook his head bitterly. Dior made no qualms about putting on display the resources she'd used to nab him. Her companion, a thuggish-looking wannabe gangster type in designer street denim, flirted with his urban bravado above the table and his hands beneath it. Dior seemed to rather enjoy the sleight-of-hand play. Richard assumed she had reached out for the comforts of the first unattached male who came her way. He stared at what he presumed was a likely rebound opportunity, a light-skinned hoodrat who was rocking thick, played out cornrows. Surely he couldn't have been qualified to take care of Dior, even if the man happened to be remotely interested in the art of pleasing women past getting his own kicks. Dior's tablemate removed his jacket to show off a detailed tattoo. Although Richard was too far away to make out the design, his swollen arms and muscular shoulders were easily detectable. Unfortunately, the unanticipated revelation produced a renegade thought that stomped on Richard's chest and dared him to react. Suddenly, he was looking at the hip-hop homeboy with grave suspicion and mounting jealousy. For a forty-year-old minister, Richard was in great shape, but his biceps paled in comparison. In a matter of seconds, he had begun to imagine this Mandingo-built stranger imposing his physical will on Dior. To make matters worse, Richard could see her loving every minute of it and writhing passionately with every stroke.

Rushing the table to confront Dior crossed Richard's mind. Throwing caution to the wind didn't appeal nearly as much when he contemplated the very likely outcome of Dior's street-wise suitor stomping on Richard's chest in the literal sense. He quickly cowered farther behind the plastic obstruction to pursue the path of least resistance, deciding to convey his disapproval of Dior's date over the phone. Growing more perturbed as the cell phone rang, Richard secretly watched while she rambled through her purse to get a hold of it. With a mind to torture Dior and ultimately ruin her evening the way she'd mangled his, he grinned sadistically until she read his name on the screen then immediately tossed her phone aside. Richard was beside himself. *How could she dismiss my call like I was nothing*, he thought. *She'd better step up, I know that much.* Clearly upset by the turn of events, regardless of any authentic justification for being so, Richard mashed down on the REDIAL button and waited.

Dior went digging into her leather handbag again. After she identified the caller, she twisted her lips then rolled her eyes to exhibit sheer displeasure. Richard blew gusts of steam from both flared nostrils at once. He'd witnessed a complete brush-off and still could not believe his eyes or her indifference. Whether it was a façade to impress her new friend or not, her actions left him feeling just about as worthless as yesterday's news. Richard was hurt, understandably so, and very close to blasting the woman he saw tossing him over like she did to the bothersome cell phone when he called. Had it not been for the petite hostess with his take-home order in hand, Richard would have ripped the lid off of Pandora's box.

He thanked the woman, took his family's meal, and headed out the door on a tear. Hating himself over the affair and how badly it affected his behavior came easily for Richard. Despising Dior for the role she played seemed to be a cinch too until his cell phone hummed two blocks from the house. Dior was summoning him now. He had been given a shot at painting her unimportant, demoting her to second-class status. If it were only that easy, he would have. "What?" he said with exasperated breathing.

"*What?*" Dior echoed harshly. "I'm returning your calls and you pop off with me talking about *what*? I must have the wrong number."

"No, you got the right one this time," Richard smarted. "Don't tell me you're tired of slumming already." Dior held her hand over the phone to muffle another conversation going on from her end. Richard was highly irritated by her tacky attempt to conceal it. "Dior?" he said. "Dior!"

"I'm—I'm here. Why are you treating me like I have two bucked teeth? Huh? What is the deal with you? Here I was thinking you wanted to see me and maybe talk things over but you're all funny actin'."

"Funny actin'? Maybe you can tell me how I should be actin' after seeing you and some rough-looking dude hemmed up at Boscoe's." Again, there was another stream of muffled noises on Dior's end.

"I told Kevlin that was you leaving the restaurant," Dior answered distrustfully. "He said I just had too much to drink."

"Who's Kevlin and was he right, about you drinking too much?" Richard asked, humiliated after having made both queries. Dior explained her association with Kevlin as one of convenience from time to time, mostly as a connection for party drugs. Dior neglected to mention how she also maintained an on-again off-again sexual relationship with the small-time dealer, however infrequent they actually hooked up. Because Richard wanted to believe Dior's version of the truth, he pouted instead of going clean off the deep end. "I didn't like seeing you with him. You deserve better."

"Like you?" she answered plainly.

"Would that be so bad? I mean, we've had some good times," Richard recounted as the garage door opened. "Real good times."

"Don't take this the wrong way, Richard, but I can't go back to that, not like it was. I'm tired of sitting at home and thinking about you doing the husband-daddy-pastor thing, I guess. I don't know which is worse, when you have to go or knowing that you can't come." Richard bit on Dior's sweet-and-sour act, instantly wishing his car was parked at her place instead of in his garage with Nadeen standing in the doorway scoffing at him.

"I know," he said, ending the call abruptly.

Nadeen weighed and measured his pitiful expression. Her conclusion was guilty as sin. It was difficult to accept what she saw, even though it was glaringly obvious. Richard was a man who could not shake free from the hold Satan used, binding him to Dior. Nadeen was reminded of similar situations, seasoned by her mother's voice. "Some things are worth fighting for. Others are barely worth fighting over."

# TWENTY-FIVE

## *Gimme One*

D ior placed a caller on hold when interrupted. She hadn't
seen Tangerine for weeks because of all the quality time
she had given to Richard. The radio diva voiced concerns regarding the last message she'd left on Dior's phone. When she didn't
receive a response, Tangie decided to make a personal visit to
Giorgio's to see what was going on for herself. "See there, heffa,
I hate it when you think you're too grown to check in every now
and then," Tangie spat playfully. "I always said if you want to
wash the weave, you got to dig way down to the glue. What's with
ducking me like you owe me money?"

The smile on Dior's lips glistened. "Hey, Tangie. I've been
meaning to get back at you but I—" she started in before getting
cut off abruptly.

"I nothing! We're supposed to be looking out for each other.
What if I was duct taped, bound, and gagged?"

"I'd wait for you to do your thing and call me when you got
through," Dior howled. "Shoot, I wouldn't want to be running to
the phone if I had it like that."

Tangie laughed once she imagined the scene playing out in her head. "Okay, you got me there. But that does not excuse you from hiding out." Another telephone line lit up. Tangie glanced at it. Dior waved it off.

"How am I going to catch up with you if I'm expected to answer the calls too?" She smacked her lips rudely then dove back into the conversation at hand. "I'm sorry and I will try to do better. Now that I have my situation under wraps, it shouldn't be a problem."

"Situation, meaning a male situation?" Tangie asked eagerly.

"Uh-huh, a freaky situation too," Dior added sensually.

"Leave it to you to roll up on something good enough to drop your girl on her head. I won't charge it to your heart unless he's got a freaky friend you haven't told me about."

Dior wrinkled her nose while trying to recall any discussions about Richard's close associates. "Nah, I don't think we've ever gotten around to who he runs with but I'll check on it for you. Yeah, that would be real cool if we double-dated."

"Don't play with me now. The man I've been schooling for a minute learned all of my tricks then up and bounced," she admitted scornfully. "You can't trust some brothas these days."

"Not with all your tricks you can't," Dior huffed assuredly. "Besides, you should save a few of your best stunts for your husband. That's what I'm doing." She realized the second her friend sampled that appetizer Tangie would be back in her mouth for the main course.

"Wait a minute, Dior." She leered suspiciously across the counter. "Why would you be talking about husbands unless you were in the market for one yourself?" Dior played dumb for as long as she could.

"I was just saying, you know how some people, and some times...ahh, forget it. There's been so much going on that I can barely keep track of it. I wanted to tell you about Richard but it never seemed like the right time, and now I'm thinking about kicking it with Giorgio again. I don't know what time it is. Just last night I hung out with Kevlin."

"Hold up. You're all over the place with this. First, you're getting married to some guy named Richard, who I haven't gotten a chance to stamp my approval on or run up under my hairdresser's gaydar. Avanté ain't been wrong yet. And you told me that thing with your boss was over and done with months ago. Your bed is crowded as hell, Dior. You'd better get a handle on it. And don't let me get started on Kevlin. He beat on you once, which is plenty for me. Uhhgh, this is so mess up. You make my head hurt."

Dior folded her arms defensively. "Forget you, Tangie. It's not easy being me and that's why I wasn't in any hurry to dump my dirt on you. I got this," she hissed angrily. "I'm a big girl, always have been."

"Could've fooled me," argued Tangie. "This is too trifling, even for you. Call me when you get off tonight. I'll come right over and step on this mess with both my size tens. Your tracks must be in too tight." Earlier, she regretted barging her way into Dior's personal affairs but now she was truly sorry for staying out of her friend's business for too long. "Real friends owe it to one another to keep a lookout for foolishness, regardless of who it comes from. You're asking for the kind of trouble you don't want. Think on it because you've got to let somebody go. Too many men is too many men."

"I said, I got this!" shouted Dior with both hands raised.

"What you're doing is toxic on so many levels. Oomph, I can't believe you."

*I can*, Nadeen thought, as she sauntered into the men's clothing store. "Dior, you'll have to excuse me. I'm not in the habit of doing this sort of thing but I felt conditions demanded it."

Dior's mouth popped open like a trapdoor although there was no escape route to disappear through. "Yeah, it is a trip you showing up at my job out of the blue."

Tangie was a longtime admirer of the pastor's wife when her membership resided at the Methodist Episcopal Greater Apostolic Church. Nadeen carried the title of "first lady" well and always dressed to impress. Tangie was taken aback, seeing the woman she'd held in such high regard wearing a jogging suit and sneakers like common folk. "Sister Allamay, it's good to see you. You might not remember me. I'm Tangie Green," she announced, oblivious to the reason for her impromptu visit. "I was a member at M.E.G.A. but moved my membership last year. I still miss the pastor's sermons though. Oh, and the choirs didn't let me down when it came to lifting voices up for the Lord." Tangie chattered on amicably while Nadeen's wicked gaze zoomed in on Dior's frozen sneer.

"If your friend was warning you against any further interaction with my family, you should listen to her," Nadeen offered as calmly as you please. She didn't have to get the whole truth from Richard. Dior couldn't have sunk her hooks that deep into him unless she'd allowed him to do likewise between her legs. "You do understand this could get extremely dirty. Danger is just the beginning when you stoop to sleeping with someone's husband. Richard and I have discussed it."

"Pastor Richard Allamay?" yelled Tangie in total disbelief. "That's the Richard you were talking about?"

Dior's eyes narrowed in a sinister manner. "And?" she answered curtly, after feeling abandoned on the battlefield. "If that's your attitude, you can get gone because I'm not in the mood to be judged by you or this." She pointed her index finger at Nadeen.

Tangie bowed her head, searching for the right place to stand in the midst of bad gone to worse. "Dior, you're my girl and I care what happens to you. You're right. It's not my place to judge but that don't make what you're doing any better. This is killing me. You lied when I asked if you were trying to know him like that. You lied."

"Don't you go throwing this in my face," Dior grunted. "You're supposed to be on my side."

"The pastor of all people, Dior? The pastor!" Tangie clamored disappointedly. "I told you how hard it is for Godly men to maintain with all the lonely church hoochies ready to come up off the panties." She glanced at Nadeen politely after taking it to the sheets. "No offense."

"None taken," Nadeen uttered agreeably. "I couldn't have said it better myself, Tangie."

"Thanks for nothing, *Tangerine*," Dior snapped. "I didn't think you'd bail on me, snuggling up to Richard's wife and whatnot."

"You knew I would blow my top when I found out about you and a minister," Tangie said assuredly. "That's why you've been hiding it from me and keeping it to yourself. Ooh, this is killing me."

"I feel you there, sister," Nadeen cosigned. "And thank you for trying to talk some sense into her. I've been respectable although disrespected. I've been prayerful and played for stupid. Now, I'm getting tired of being treated like I'm walking around with a tail." When she reached into her bag, Tangie scurried behind the counter. Dior panicked along with her but refused to take her eyes off Nadeen's, praying she hadn't snapped. "Relax. I didn't come here to take your life, Dior, despite having the right to. I have a proposition. Perhaps this is the time you should ask Tangie to go her own way." Tangie was happy to make herself scarce seeing as how she thought death was just around the corner moments before. Dior stepped in front of her friend's path, wisely blocking her exit.

"Uh-uh. She's staying. Anything you want to say to me, Tangie can hear it too," Dior announced soundly.

"Alright then, fine with you, fine with me. This is my first and final offer." Nadeen laid her checkbook down then opened it. She seemed confused when the other two appeared clueless. "Money, that is what you're after, isn't it?" she asked Dior, positively sure that it was. "How much would it cost to make this sinful relationship go away? Five? Ten? Fifteen thousand?"

Tangie licked her lips then gulped. "Dollars?"

"Of course I'm prepared to discuss something more drastic if necessary," added Nadeen earnestly.

"Money?" Tangie asked yet again, when she failed to comprehend the thought of Dior actually getting paid to stop doing something she shouldn't have in the first place.

"Sure, women like Dior are always in it for the money. I'm willing to make the arrangements tonight, before we've all gone too far and there's no turning back. Karma has a way of taking care of things once they've spun out of control, so to speak."

Tangie cleared her throat then tried to correct what she assumed was a grave mistake in character. "Sister Allamay, with all due respect, I think you're out of line. Dior has obviously wronged you but she is not interested in taking your money on top of sleeping with your man."

"You can go now, Tangie," Dior said without blinking. "Go on, I'll call you later." Tangie searched for signs of sanity while timidly passing between the women's sparing session. Her pace accelerated when there were scarcely any to be found. "Now then, back to the money. How much do you think Richard is worth?"

Nadeen came close to laughing. "For him, I wouldn't give a nickel a pound. To keep my family together, to keep Richard's legacy alive and growing through his ministry, I'd give all that I have. His last mistress accepted seven thousand and a Hyundai.

Oh, you probably thought you were his first ghetto-queen. Sorry to disappoint you. He's been with a filthy mutt and come home with fleas before." Nadeen did pay off Richard's kept woman, after she threatened to expose the affair in the presence of Nadeen's parents during a church retreat. Dior was younger and apparently greedier. She would likely want a great deal more than a Hyundai.

"True, I love money and would do just about anything to get paid, kick back awhile, and nest on it. Huh, you knew that though, or you would have made other plans to get rid of me. You rich chicks are something else," Dior countered craftily. "White or black, you're pretty much the same. Men run to me because of the things you can't do or aren't willing to for them. Richard loves being licked and he's just as generous when returning the favor. Whenever he gets hungry, I feed him and then I send him on home to you. There's no point in telling you what really floats his boat. You're too old and too big to pull it off anyway." She flung a dirty grin at Nadeen then laughed in her face. "Tell you what you should do: Save your money for the divorce. You won't ever be rid of me and I'll never stop giving Richard what he keeps running back for. It started out as fun and games, me and him. Now, I'm in it to my very last breath."

"Watch your mouth, child," Nadeen whispered somberly. "That might come sooner than you think."

No sooner than Nadeen left, Dior disregarded her threats of cosmic reprisal and the horror of reaping what she sowed. As far as Dior was concerned, Karma was the stage name of a stripper who worked the late shift at a raunchy dive bar on the south side. Dooney used to date her. *Nothing is going to happen to me that I don't want it to*, she thought. *As for Richard, he is different from what I'm used to. He's crazy for loving me. I'm crazy for letting him, although I wish I could love him like Nadeen does. Enough to come flapping into some other chick's job talking about get away from my husband or I'll pay you. What kind of stuff is that? I could learn to dig him that much, only difference would be, I'd bust out the check-book to have his other lady's head split wide open. Huh, bet I wouldn't have to pay that fee but once. I'm tired of dealing with housewives and headaches. I don't need Tangie to understand me or why I'm staying close to my meal ticket. She's already got a good job and a little piece of fame to hold her down. I want to be somebody too. Richard's my pass out of this life of scheming and dreaming. Once I'm out, I ain't ever jumping back in.*

A fog of reflection settled in after Dior realized she was in another deep pit of immorality, telling herself that she was purely going after what she wanted and how this was going to be different from all the seedy relationships she'd been involved in before. She winced when remembrance of the pain she'd caused other women came back like a swift backhand slap. The sting of getting in too deep paled in comparison to the thought of losing a good friend over her bad case of man-stealing blues.

Dior's watch read nine thirty when she pulled her car into the parking lot behind Tangie's apartment building east of down-town. She remained nestled in the driver's seat until the nerve she'd searched for on the drive over actually found her. Still somewhat cloaked with the veil of apprehension, Dior knocked against Tangie's door, wondering what her best and only friend felt about the lies she'd concealed and the married minister who kept her bed warm. Heavy-laden with reservations, Dior turned to leave just as she had arrived, with her tail tucked and head bowed. She cringed when someone approached the door from the inside of Tangie's apartment.

"Dior? What are you doing here?" Tangie asked quietly through a narrow gap in the doorway. She clutched at the silk leopard-print robe when it fell open, then she looked over her shoulder before returning her attention to her latest visitor's pitiful expression. "Uhhhh, you should have called first. But, since you didn't, I guess you should come on in."

Dior raised her head as if to thank Tangie for the invitation without actually having to say the words. She slinked inside, neglecting to notice that a number of candles burned throughout the living room. "I'm sorry for popping up like this, Tangie," she offered finally. "I would have called but I didn't want to risk you telling me no or worse."

"Worse?"

"Yeah, like you didn't want me in your space no more. I hurt you today. I know that." Suddenly, Dior peered around the room as if she'd just entered it. "What's with all these candles? You got something nice coming by?"

"Uh-uh, I got something real nice on pause."

"Ooh, my bad. I didn't even think to…I should just go." Dior took two steps toward the door. Tangie stopped her.

"Girl, stop trippin'. Cop a squat." She motioned toward the tan leather love seat then tossed another glance at her closed bedroom door. "You look like a trainwreck about to happen and as much as I like other people's drama, I can't just sit and watch it go down. Yes, I was disappointed when I learned that the Richard you'd been putting in work with was Pastor Allamay. Yes, it hurt that you'd been so secretive about it too. Shoot, I'd even called myself getting mad about it but then I realized that you couldn't tell me after I went on about married preachers being off-limits. I put you in a bad spot, making it nearly impossible to clue me in. Question is, what are you going to do about it now that the cat's out of the bag?"

Dior chewed on her bottom lip while remaining silent as if she'd been reminded of her rights to do so. Eventually, her lips parted slowly. Before she had the chance to address Tangie's worries, a half-naked stranger exited the bedroom wearing a bath towel snugly wrapped around his narrow waist. Dior was amply embarrassed but not nearly enough to turn away from the gorgeous hunk of bronze muscle whose patience had apparently worn about as thin as that bath towel. With both eyes affixed, she fought hard to keep her mouth closed. Dior was pleasantly surprised but even more so by the soured expression Tangie cast on the awkward situation.

"I know mama said she'd be right back, but it's gonna take a bit longer than I thought," Tangie said casually, as if that grown man was a child instead of six feet and two hundred pounds of dynamite. Dior's eyes scaled his broad shoulders and toned thighs, then she gawked at Tangie. "Be a good boy, Derrick, and stay in the bedroom until mama is finished with grown-folks business." When he pouted, she insisted on his obedience. "Go on now. I won't be long. If I'm not there in five minutes, you can start without me." As if their exchange wasn't peculiar enough, Tangie dismissed him when he neglected to excuse himself. "Derrick, don't make me have to tell you twice."

Dior's mouth fell open when the man retuned to the bedroom as instructed. "Tangie, you got to tell me where to get one of those. He's fine and he minds too. Give me some dap on that."

"Yep, every woman should have one."

"What's up with the role-play? The way you talked to him was crazy."

"A crazy little thing called love," she gushed. "Yeah, I met Derrick on the Internet. I cruised the Net for something different and there he was, advertising for a mother figure to help him sort out some abandonment issues. There I was looking for a man with a strong back, fully loaded and no strings attached." She chuckled lightly as if she'd merely stumbled over a good pair of shoes on sale. "Why are you looking at me like that? Huh, what the problem is?"

"I'm guessing there isn't one, at least not on your end." Dior shook her head then stood with her purse in hand. "I just need to know that you and me are still cool?"

"Cool as a fan if you'd hurry and bounce up out of here," she answered sheepishly. "Derrick ought to be good and worked up by now."

"Whew, I bet he is. Why'ont I let you get back to that."

"Goodbye would sound even better from the hallway."

Dior laughed as Tangie rushed her off then hastily slammed the door. She caught the elevator going down, wearing a subtle smile and the assurance that Tangie had already moved on from her disappointment after learning of Dior's relationship with Dr. Pastor Richard Allamay, PhD. Dior drove home, pondering whether Nadeen could manage to get over hers.

# TWENTY-SIX

## *Elbow Grease*

At one in the morning, five full-length tour buses cruised down the interstate toward Louisiana. Richard played cards with some of the older men on the last bus, trying his hand at bid whist and spades. Phillip enjoyed the gospel music CD someone played on a portable boom box. Every so often, he took time to stand over Richard's shoulder to heckle his skills as a gamesman. "Maybe you'd have better luck with the fellows up front rattling some bones," Phillip chided. Richard took another look at his cards.

"I started out up front with the domino players and I didn't have much luck up there either," he joked, to a load of laughter from the other players. "I'm starting to hope one of the other buses has a Go Fishing tournament I can get in." Richard's partner snickered at his next move.

"With plays like that, don't count on it, Brother Pastor. You might want to see if somebody brought a box of pickup sticks." Richard bowed his head and laughed, just like one of the guys. Phillip took notice and smiled heartily. He'd missed that side of his best friend, easygoing and easier to fit into any situation without much jostling to speak of. Somewhere down the line, the business of spreading the Word got in the way of enjoying his calling. If there was an avenue for Richard to recapture his youthful attitude about life and make the best of the present, Phillip wanted desperately for him to find it. The past was a point in time to look back on and learn from. Tomorrow would provide for itself. Richard's marriage and the success of M.E.G.A. resided within his ability to seize the moment and make it what he needed it to be. Richard was presently concerned with the cards he'd drawn and getting kicked off another game table. It seemed, for a time at least, Richard was not only living in the now but it agreed with him.

Sunshine peeked over the horizon as the New Orleans skyline came into view. The holy caravan eased along I-10 until morning drive-time traffic introduced it to gridlock. Many of the members stretched and yawned before lining up for the restrooms at the rear of the rented travel coaches. Nadeen, on the first bus with Mahalia and Roxanne, stared out of the window at the refurbished Superdome. She heard others whispering a similar sentiment to what she felt. *That's where all of those poor people had to go when no one came.* A strange calm entered her heart as the entire contingency stopped talking altogether, as if a spell had come over them. Memories of bloated bodies floating down the city streets, corpses of loved ones rotting on sidewalks, and scores of babies crying in a sea of television cameras came to mind.

Mahalia left her seat two rows back to sit with her mother. She wasn't surprised to find Roxanne nestled in Nadeen's arms. "It still hurts like it happened yesterday, doesn't it, Mama?" asked Mahalia, in a subdued tone.

"Yes, baby, yes it does. Yes it does." As they inched closer to the downtown off-ramp Nadeen tried to turn her eyes away from the football stadium, once the toast of the town. Like a ghostly graveyard, it sat there beckoning to be gawked at and prayed over. No one could have imagined the tragedies to unfold after the levees broke and before order was restored. The magnificence of the Crescent City was tarnished, leaving millions the world over to question how the U.S. government allowed it to happen, then responded in a passive manner that rivaled its initial indifference.

Roxanne craned her neck to look over the seat. Shades of sadness were evident everywhere her wide eyes roamed. "Mommy, what's happening to everybody?" she mumbled quietly. "It's like a funeral or something."

"Yes, Roxy, that's it. It's exactly like a funeral," Nadeen answered. "A terrible flood killed a lot of people who lived here. Our friends are very sad because it didn't have to be. They're crying because it was." Roxanne pressed her nose against the window as if she expected to see dead people.

"What if the flood comes back while we stay here, Mommy? Will people cry for us then?" Nadeen hadn't thought of that. It wasn't out of the question because the Army Corps of Engineers had yet to sufficiently fortify the levees since the last hurricane dumped Lake Pontchartrain into the city basin. After giving it further thought, Nadeen hugged her youngest daughter extra tight.

"I hope they will, Roxy. That'd be nice if they did." Mahalia placed her hand in Nadeen's, then laid her head on her mother's shoulder.

"I wish Daddy was here right now, I mean, on this bus with us," she whined sorrowfully.

Nadeen fought off a swelling sigh pushing its way past her chest. "That's funny. I was just thinking the same." She had also spent several hours wishing Richard could become the man she fell in love with again. He stumbled, as some men do. Picking hisself up and walking the straight and narrow afterward, that's what she needed to witness in order to close this chapter and await the next. Nadeen wasn't good at lying to herself. Richard's personally sponsored caravan to New Orleans wasn't anything other than a prideful attempt at atoning for his affair by throwing money and goodwill at it. Nadeen almost laughed at herself for trying to erase Dior in the same manner, minus the goodwill of course. She couldn't have cared less if Dior choked on a chicken bone and died on the spot. Nadeen couldn't say much more for the way she felt about Richard after Dior made her confession at the clothing store. It was one thing to imagine her husband's head buried in someone else's lap. It was another entirely to be told how much he liked it.

Half an hour later, the caravan parked on the edge of the Ninth Ward, where remnants of flooding were the most profound. Richard stuck his head in each of the buses to make a short speech. He reminded church members to be strong for the people whose lives they planned on infusing with a dose of normalcy. "Church, we've come a long way to rebuild, not only houses but spirits. Keep in mind," he added, "they've seen a number of groups come before us, many of them too saddened by what they've seen to do what was required. So, fix your faces and toughen up. A lot of folks are counting on that, including me."

After the buses unloaded the passengers, they pulled away to deliver luggage to their hotel in the French Quarter. Richard paid for that too. He was happy to offer his faithful members' muscle in an area beat down by circumstance and incompetence. Carlton Tatum sent a hundred gallons of paint, twenty boxes of nails, several slabs of lumber, and a dozen wheelbarrows at Richard's behest. What lacked now was the sweat equity necessary to repair the damaged houses. Homeowners deserved to bask in a

renewed hope; having a home with a face-lift was as good a way
as any to get that ball rolling. Nearly three hundred and fifty
men, women, and children gathered in the intersection, which
was once submerged beneath filthy floodwater and desperate
inhabitants trying to withstand the rising tide of death. During
breakfast, the local minister welcomed the horde in attendance,
prayed for a hard day's work, and then thanked them for making
the pilgrimage.

Soon after, the workers were separated into four groups.
Richard headed a men's only contingency that was responsible
for stripping rotted wood from external surfaces and then haul-
ing it to large metal Dumpsters provided by the city. Phillip was
in charge of the carpentry team, which cut, sawed, and replaced
the planks torn off by the first group. The painting brigade
came in behind them, applying fresh coats to the wooden homes.
Nadeen and Rose worked feverishly, organizing the women and
children to make lunch boxes and coolers stocked with Gatorade
and water. Like a well-oiled machine, they moved from house
to house, stripping, hammering, and painting. By the end of the
day, everyone met in the same intersection where they'd begun.
Neighbors came from miles around to witness a faction of determined visitors make a grand display of helping others to heal.

One television news reporter on the scene pulled Richard aside
on the heels of prayers and well-wishes from those they assisted.
"I have with me Pastor Richard Allamay from the Methodist
Episcopal Greater Apostolic Church in Dallas, Texas," he said,
beaming with a pleasant smile. "As you know, the city of New
Orleans has experienced difficulties getting over the storm.
There is a new mantra we've come to live by: *We are down but certainly not out.* Today there are blessings all around us. Over twenty
homes have received much needed attention. If you didn't know
better, you'd be hard-pressed to believe this neighborhood was

one of the hardest hit. Tell me, Pastor, what possessed you to bring all of this love and labor to our city?"

Richard, dressed in blue jeans and a dark and dirty golf shirt, wiped his brow with a soiled handkerchief. "God said to move, so we moved. We believe in remaining faithful in our brokenness, which is a constant reminder that trouble don't last always." After Richard's heartfelt sermonette, two of the young men dumped a cooler of Gatorade on his head, which was typically reserved for football coaches after engineering lofty accomplishments. Cheers rang throughout the intersection from church members and bystanders alike. Richard, now soaking wet and grimacing from gallons of chilled liquid, shivered as his friends and family laughed. "Whew, that's cold!" he yelled. "Next time, a simple pat on the back will do."

Nadeen toweled him off as best she could while Mahalia and Roxanne giggled by her side. Dior watched the newscast on the television in the hotel room Richard had stashed her away in. Her shoulders tightened at the sight of him being comforted by his family. She was only biding her time before that man and that job belonged to her. For now, she'd set the stage for a celebration Richard wouldn't soon forget. She went to the closet to select an outfit for the occasion, knowing the dutiful pastor would come tipping by as soon as he could. After agreeing to play it safe when Richard flew her into New Orleans, Dior saw fit to crawfish on the deal and sidestep the one she made previously. She'd reasoned that showing up wasn't enough to chase Nadeen away after her trips to the M.E.G.A. Church facility neglected to bring about her desired result. This time, she had to do more than simply show up: It was time to show out.

She made several calls to area hotels, searching for the one with the amenity she just had to have: Richard Allamay. Once she discovered where the congregation was staying, Dior made other living arrangements. She showered, changed clothes, then rang to have her luggage brought down. The young bellman with a tanned bronze complexion grinned politely when she opened the door. Her tight white slacks with a peach-colored halter top inspired the fair-skinned hunk to hustle. He moved double-time to catch the same elevator going down. "You sure you want to check out, miss?" he asked as the doors opened on the ground floor.

"I need better accommodations than this hotel has to offer." She stepped off with the handsome Cajun on her heels.

"If there's something I can do to change your mind, I get off in an hour." Dior whipped her head around to shut the door on what she saw as a cheap proposition. Then she leered at him with a discerning eye. She noticed his curly hair and boyishly charming good looks, recognizing that a man with his features could come in handy if she played him right.

"What makes you think I'd be interested in accepting a date from a man who's carrying my bags?"

"I feel you," he said, chuckling. "I can see why you might have preconceived notions about a lowly bellman. But I'm a medical student during the week, and I clean up real well." He blushed innocently after making a pitch at the prettiest guest he'd seen in a month of weekend shifts.

"A doctor in the making, huh? Well, that is a reason to give it a little more thought. Why don't you give me your cell number so you can swing by the place I'll be staying tonight? If you clean up as nice as you say, *Frenchy*, dinner is on me." He passed her a slip of paper with his cell and home numbers jotted on it. Dior read over them, then smirked at him amiably. "You sure do scribble like a doctor. I can hardly read this chicken scratch," she joked.

"So, you'll call me then?" he asked, flashing two rows of perfect teeth.

Dior read the name tag on his uniform. "Yeah, Armand, I'll call you. By the way, I tend to get very impatient so don't make me wait too long after hearing from me."

"No, ma'am, there's no chance of that," he answered, pushing the lobby doors open for Dior to exit. "Taxi!" he shouted urgently. "I'll be ready and looking forward to it. Be careful. Dressed like that, somebody might get you." He watched the taxi zoom out into traffic until it made a right heading toward the Navy Pier. Dior didn't have to guess what was on Armand's mind. She intended on having a similar effect on Richard when he saw her traipsing through his hotel lobby.

The plan she laid out in her mind could not have worked out better. Dior's taxi whipped in front of a line of buses idling against the curb. "This is the Marriott," her lady cabdriver announced from the front seat. Dior paid the woman, then climbed out onto the sidewalk with her designer bag on wheels. The sway in her hips insisted that every man in her path become aware of her presence. She was in a devilish state of mind with the goods to pull it off. The doorman raced to get her bag but she declined. "No thanks, I got it from here," she told him plainly. With a great deal of reluctance, he nodded then backed away.

Dior entered the lobby, which was buzzing with an anxious multitude forming lines for room assignments and keys. She recognized several of the people from the newscast she viewed earlier. Richard's attention was tied to a clipboard when she strutted toward the front desk to check in. Phillip saw the same young men who had drenched Richard captivated by something behind him. Phillip discovered what held the men in suspense. It was Dior's shapely profile.

The front desk manager worked diligently to find her space in his sold-out hotel. She flirted with him, batting her eyes and suggesting an upgrade to a suite would suffice if he couldn't locate a regular available room. "I'm sure you can come up with some-thing if you put your mind to it," she said suggestively, playing the diva in distress. In a matter of seconds, Dior was awarded a junior suite on the eighteenth floor. She thanked the manager then requested he have someone bring her bag to the room.

Phillip grunted slyly when she glided by, en route to the eleva-tor. Richard glanced up from his list then shot a stinging glare at her. His expression was textbook shock and awe. As if seeing her there wasn't bad enough, Nadeen passed Dior as she exited the gift shop. She stopped on a dime then spun on her heels. Dior kept right on going. Nadeen was so angry at Richard she consid-ered doing the same thing. Was there no end to his hypocrisy? she thought. She assumed he'd flown her in to be near him. Although Richard would deny it vehemently, Nadeen knew better.

She searched the lobby for Rose, who was cooling her heels in the lobby sports bar with a virgin daiquiri. "Hey, there you are," she said, practically out of breath.

"What is it, Nadeen? One of the girls sick?"

Nadeen frowned sadly. "You might say that, but not either of the ones you're thinking of. You can't guess who I almost ran smack into."

"Okay, I won't try then," Rose answered. "But I can tell it wasn't anyone you wanted to see."

"Apparently Richard has lost his ever-loving mind. Dior is out there and is dressed in skimpy paper-thin clothes too. You should have seen the way men were gawking at her."

Rose gasped at the implication. "Richard didn't?" she said, sensing that he had. "Nadeen, you know that girl ain't wrapped too tight. Maybe she came down here on her own. I wouldn't put it past her." Nadeen panted. Her eyes stared into the distance as if she could see her future and didn't care for the way it played out. "Hey, you alright?" Rose asked cautiously.

"No I'm not alright, but I'm getting used to it and that bothers me. I wished my day hadn't been ruined and I hate to take this up with Richard while the girls are here. It could and probably will get gritty."

"You need to tend to that. I'll keep an eye on Roxanne. Mahalia is already signed up for a streetcar tour and dinner with the young adult ministry. Don't worry about her. She'll do fine with her friends."

Nadeen huffed then rubbed her eyes with the heels of her palms. "I need some Visine and there isn't any telling what I'll need later on tonight. Thanks, Rose. I'll call you later."

"Go slow, Nadeen. If that woman did follow Richard here on her own, you need to know that too. Ain't no reason to rush into anything you can't take back or do over. I'll pray for you, and Richard."

# TWENTY-SEVEN

## Bayou Heartbreak

As soon as the last room assignments were doled out, Phillip glared at Richard. "I'm not trying to tell you when you're screwing up, but this is it."

"Man, I had no idea she would come here. I didn't have anything to do with this," Richard said. *This* would be referring to Dior traipsing through the same hotel where his family was staying. Richard wasn't ready to admit his continued infidelity. Phillip took a long look at his old friend, then shook his head and threw up his hands. Richard glinted at him. "You don't have to say it. I know it's jacked up. I sure hope Nadeen doesn't see her. She won't believe I didn't orchestrate this whole thing. Why would I ask for another headache when we're just smoothing over the last time Dior popped up at church? She must've decided on her own to make the trip," he lied.

"I'll tell you one thing, selling that story to Nadeen is going to take some doing. I'm on your side and I don't know if I believe it," Phillip confessed honestly.

"Thanks for your vote of confidence. I'm in it waist-deep,

huh? Keeping them separated—that's the only chance I've got to come out of this with Nadeen by my side. Got any ideas?"

"Yeah, a good one," Phillip answered. "Get prayed up; you'll need it. I'm out." He started out toward the elevators, washing his hands of the matter. Phillip was smart enough not to look back. Rose had warned him about getting into the middle of other people's marriages when lies were running through them.

Going it alone, Richard hurried into the men's room. He whipped out his cell phone then scrolled down the address book for Dior's number. Pacing erratically, Richard frowned as the voice mailbox picked up the call. "Dior, this is Richard! You couldn't have thought I'd be okay with you changing hotels like this. I purposely selected one where you'd be close enough for me to slide by and see you. This—this stuff you pulled is sick. Nadeen's going to have a fit! Call me and leave your room number." Richard flipped the phone shut then stared at himself in the wall mirror. He didn't like the image leering back at him. Phillip was right: He needed to get prayed up, but quick.

On the eighteenth floor, Mahalia carried an ice bucket to the vending area. She sang a carefree tune, glad to have completed a day of service for the less fortunate. Out of nowhere, Dior appeared with an ice bucket, chips, and a bottle of soda cradled in her hands. Mahalia gawked without any trepidation whatsoever. "What are you doing here?" she asked shrewdly.

"Oh, I thought I recognized you," Dior replied. "You're quite the protector, huh? Cute kid, don't get yourself hurt."

"I'd take the same advice if I were you," the young girl threatened. Dior turned her nose up then entered the first room on the next corridor. Mahalia read the room number then scampered back the way she came.

While banging on the door, Mahalia tried to calm herself down. "Mama, open up! It's me, Mahalia!" When there was no immediate response, she remembered having adjoining rooms. She dug into her pocket and pulled out the plastic keycard. Shoving it in hastily, Mahalia couldn't get it to work. "Come on! Come on!" she whispered heatedly. On the second try, the magnetic lock released. She opened the door, throwing the empty ice bucket aside. "Mama!" she started in again, rapping on the door separating their rooms.

"What's gotten into you?" Nadeen asked, startled and half dressed. "Let me get this robe fastened." She pulled it together before fastening the cloth belt around her waist.

Mahalia bent over, gasping for air. "Where's, where's Daddy?"

"Downstairs I think, why? What's going on?"

"I saw her, Mama. That evil witch Dior," she confirmed excitedly. "She was right out in the hall, on this floor!" Mahalia was confused by her mother's unruffled demeanor. "Don't you care? Aren't you going to do something about it?"

Nadeen sat on the edge of the bed, composed and contrite. She was so sorry for what her daughter had endured. Furthermore, she was convinced that Dior's guile was exceptional. "Sit down, Mahalia. I said sit! I know she's here. I passed her down in the lobby acting like she owned the place. Yes, I do care and will talk to your father as soon as he comes in." Mahalia pounced up angrily, obviously dismayed by what she heard.

"That's it?" she spat. "You're not going to break her neck?"

"That's not the way to handle a thing like this," Nadeen debated, not sure of what the best way was to go about it. She rubbed her chin with the back of her hand, contemplating everything that had happened since Dior's first appearance in their lives. Since she didn't have the answers Mahalia was eager to hear, Nadeen tried to assure her of an inevitable outcome. "Don't worry. This sort of problem usually works itself out in due time, you'll see."

"I'm glad one of us thinks so. When I get married, I'm not letting any woman terrorize my family. I wish Dior and every conceited cow like her was dead."

"Don't talk that way," Nadeen fussed, although she remembered telling herself the very same thing when she was about Mahalia's age. "Don't ever forget you're a Christian."

Mahalia moved out of arm's reach before flinging a stiff suggestion in return. "Don't you forget there's a funky-butt-skank sleeping with your husband!" She dashed out of the door to flee her mother's reprisal.

Nadeen shouted down the hall after her, "Mahalia! Mahalia, you get back here. Mahalia!" Nadeen was beside herself with grief. Her hands went numb as she untied her robe. She felt ill, having been chastised by her child and made a jackass of by her husband. Her only saving grace was the knowledge that Roxanne was out of earshot and ignorant to the facts plaguing her. She wished she could say the same for Mahalia, but it was too late for wishing all the way around. Something had to turn things in the other direction or she'd be faced with raising her daughters as a single mother with the aftereffects of a publicly scrutinized divorce. Nadeen dreaded that more than dealing with her present set of circumstances.

Richard made it to the room eventually. He was surprised to find the bathroom door locked when he attempted to open it and inform Nadeen of his arrival. "Hey, Nadeen!" he yelled, knocking on the door. "Nadeen, I'm here. It's Richard!" He placed his ear against it. He heard the shower running and his wife's voice.

"I know," she said begrudgingly. "I'm almost done."

Richard glared at the closed door peculiarly. He slipped off his shoes then his shirt. "Is everybody going crazy?" he thought aloud. When the bathroom door opened, steam rushed out and so did Nadeen. "Hey, baby, the door was locked."

"Let me see your cell phone," she demanded.

"My what?" he replied, stalling.

"Your phone, give it to me." Nadeen's teeth were clenched together like a rusty vise. "Hand it over."

Reluctantly, Richard waffled. "Here. What you want it for?"

Nadeen overlooked his question. She flipped it open then pressed the RECENT CALLS icon. "See, I'm kind of slow but I'm catching on fast. I asked for this," she said, returning his phone, "to find out what I needed to know before you fixed your mouth to lie about it." Nadeen turned away from him and toward the closet. She sorted through the hanging clothes, casually picking out an outfit for the evening. "So, now we both know you've called Dior since we got here. How could you?"

"Nadeen, I did not have any idea she would come running down here. Yes, I did call her but it was to ask her why she was doing this," he lied, partially clouded with truth. "I don't blame you for doubting me but Dior did this on her own. I swear it."

"Oh, Richard, there is nothing but doubt left," she answered, much too nonchalantly for Richard's taste.

"So you do believe me?"

"It's not me you have to satisfy this time. Mahalia bumped into your friend out in the hall. She came running to me, expecting a hellish response. I'd be the same way if it was my mother's marriage *being terrorized* by my father's mistress." She observed Richard, fiddling with the phone aimlessly. He couldn't look her in the eye. She recognized a broken man when she saw one, though she couldn't have anticipated one would belong to her. "I'm hungry. Why don't you get ready for dinner," she said finally. Richard nodded then eased off his pants. Nadeen dressed while he showered. She felt helpless in many respects, paralyzed in the face of what had become her life, her role as mother, protector, and wife. Her soul was uneven, capable of flipping inside out.

Nadeen searched for the words to prop it up then scrapped the idea altogether. She was even too tired to pray.

Richard powered off his cell phone then set it on the dresser. If Dior decided to return his call while Nadeen was on his arm, it might push her over the edge. Richard couldn't take that chance. He was already skating on thin ice with a three-hundred-pound gorilla on his back. Quality time with Nadeen never sounded so good. Richard slapped on a splash of cologne after he'd gotten dressed. Still finding it impossible to face the haunting expression hanging on Nadeen's face, he followed her steps to the elevator with his head bowed.

Richard was exceedingly thankful that his world had paused long enough for a nice, quiet, uneventful dinner when he escorted his wife into the four-star hotel restaurant. He counted on catching his wind and using the time to placate Nadeen. Richard, overloaded in the optimism department, suffered a ghastly setback when the hostess seated him and Nadeen two tables from an attractive couple who were enjoying their drinks as much as each other's company.

Richard noticed them first. He saw the pair chuckling with their heads tilted dangerously close, sharing a quaint meal with a window view of the Navy Pier. Richard recognized the woman right off; she was flirting with a half empty martini glass and her handsome date simultaneously. He made several attempts to shrug off what he saw but that was impossible. Even after Nadeen had followed his narrow-eyed stare then scoffed at his discovery, Richard continued to glance their way occasionally. He couldn't concentrate on the menu as he kept an eye peeled on Dior and that smooth-talking medical student she let carry her bags earlier. It bothered Richard down to his loafers to watch her. Dior called nearly ten restaurants to inquire about an Allamay party of two. All she had to do then was make the call to her handsome escort and set it off.

*Lord, who's going to raise my children if I kill this woman?* Nadeen thought at the outset. She was close to requesting another table on the opposite side of the restaurant but wisely changed her mind. Now that Richard was pushing his blackened snapper from one side of the plate to the other, she liked the seating arrangements just fine. Nadeen devoured a full order of jambalaya as she took in the show. Dior's new acquaintance was easy on the eyes but hard on Richard's stomach. He could not manage to eat a single bite. He'd determined Dior was having too much fun, placing her hand on her date's arm and throwing her hair every time she laughed at his jokes. Nadeen peeped that too but it didn't worry her in the least. Dior had her hands full with a younger man, one more her own speed, Nadeen thought. Whether he was married or not was of no consequence as long as he wasn't Richard. All in all, it was worth the price of admission to watch her husband squirm, although she hated the sight of Dior getting under his skin.

Four blocks away, Mahalia lagged behind the group of young adults surveying Bourbon Street. Everyone was amazed at the tight quarters and narrowed streets, vintage architecture, neon signs advertising live sex shows from the sidewalks, and numerous brass bands playing to standing-room-only crowds along the avenue. Mahalia appeared inconsolable when friends offered to cheer her up until she encountered a novelty gift shop with a litany of trinkets that interested her. She fingered an oddly fashioned miniature doll near the front counter. "Excuse me, ma'am, what is this?" she asked the shopkeeper.

"That a keepsake, what you might call a voodoo doll or spirit charm," the haggard old woman answered with a thick Arcadian accent.

"Voodoo?" Mahalia repeated, as her brow rose noticeably. "Do these dolls *really* do anything?"

The shopkeeper puffed on a pipe, then blew smoke out of her nose. "Some do, yeah."

"Well if I buy one, I'd need to know how to work it," she said, as if seeking permission to purchase it with evil intent.

The woman, who happened to be as wide as she was tall, slid off her chair then waddled down three steps toward Mahalia. Gazing upward at her potential customer, she nodded her full head of silver hair then puffed from her pipe again. "You wan' somebody hurt yeah?"

"Oh yeah. Real bad. Some people don't know when to leave a married man alone."

She looked at Mahalia strangely. "Not your husband?"

"No, ma'am, my mother is not dealing with competition too well."

The woman reached up to return the small toy sold to tourists, which was very likely made in China. "You won't be wantin' that toy then." She climbed a small ladder then pulled something down from a wooden box on an upper shelf. "This be your best tool of neee-go-ti-a-tion," she informed Mahalia.

The girl's face lit up like a full moon. "You telling me this is the real thing?"

"It called a remedy. Thirty dollars is all it cost for a friend in need." She chuckled enthusiastically, showing all three of her thick yellowed teeth. Mahalia bit on the offer to come away with the genuine article, handmade by a group of Creole women from a nearby parish. She paid the shopkeeper, received the instructions on how to put the remedy into action, then she dashed off for the hotel just as the sun set over the city.

Later, Mahalia called the hotel operator from a house phone in the lobby. She asked for room 1828. The phone rang four times then it rolled back to the operator. Dior was either out of the room or didn't want to be interrupted. Mahalia was on her way up to see if there was a DO NOT DISTURB sign posted on the door. She caught a glimpse of what resembled her parents having dinner together. A detailed look revealed another surprise: Dior sitting that close to Nadeen with all of her hair still intact. Keeping in mind what the shopkeeper said regarding the mojo charm, Mahalia practically skipped up to the customer service desk. "I'm with my big sister in eighteen twenty-eight but I think I lost my key," she said, sounding even younger than she was.

The front desk attendant, annoyed by the umpteenth child asking to replace a lost key, rolled his eyes. "Eighteen twenty-eight. Do you have identification?"

"Yeah, in the room," Mahalia smarted back at him.

"No identification? Whose name is the room under?" he questioned, after making a duplicate key then holding on to it. Mahalia wanted that key. She had to think fast or risk making the snooty employee suspicious.

Mahalia smacked her lips, now pretending to be just as annoyed as him. "Look, my sister Dior uses all kinds of names when she's relaxing after a tour. Let's see, she's gone with Johnson, Jones, Jenkins?" After each name offered, she watched the man holding her future in his hand. "When we're in London, she goes by Williams, Washington, or Wilkes."

"What about Wicker?" he said, helping her along so she would cease and desist with wasting his time.

"Wicker!" Mahalia snapped rudely. "That's our *real* name," she insisted believably. "Huh, that's brand-new. You understand how singers can be? Too dramatic for me," she added, after accepting the plastic duplicate. She walked past the restaurant again, to assure Dior was still occupied, then she caught an elevator going up. "Come on, slowpoke," she teased. "I've got to move, get in an' out." The doors opened on the eighteenth floor. Mahalia peered both ways as if preparing to dodge traffic. The coast was clear. She bolted down the hall, used the copied key to open the door. Once inside she tiptoed past the bed, sneering at a black lacy underwear and bra ensemble laid on a fluffy pillow like after-dinner mints. *I need something personal but I ain't touching that gold digger's panties*, Mahalia thought, as she circled around to the restroom.

In a designer toiletry bag, she found a toothbrush, floss, makeup, and other necessities. Sensing time was against her, a quick decision had to be made. Mahalia reached for several items but none of them seemed suitable. And then she saw it: a hair-brush with long strands sticking out every which way. She pulled several of them from it, placing each one into the plastic bag she got from the shopkeeper. "Perfect," she mouthed. Staring at her reflection in the mirror, she liked what she saw: a dedicated daughter with the nerve to do what her mother wouldn't. "Now we'll see who gets hurt when this hex kicks in."

# TWENTY-EIGHT

## *Humble Pie*

Dior staggered out of the restaurant arm in arm with her date. Richard looked worse than death warmed over as she left from her table. She almost stumbled into him then acted as if she didn't know he'd been there the entire time. It served him right; what had he been thinking, flying in the source of all his troubles? "See there. I told you she didn't come here to be with me," he grumbled to Nadeen, partly believing it himself because of her behavior. Chatter hadn't come easy for either of them during dinner. Richard managed to eek out a few words. "Pass the butter" was about the full extent of it. Nadeen played it slow like Rose suggested, holding on to the outside chance that Richard wouldn't have bet his marriage and career on a getaway with Dior.

After dinner, Nadeen poured cream in her black coffee then stirred in a leisurely manner so as not to be rushed. She ran her finger down the list of dessert items but humble pie wasn't on the menu so she ordered a slice of bread pudding instead. When it was delivered, she took her sweet time nibbling on it.

When Richard uttered for the waiter to bring the bill, Nadeen ordered a scoop of ice cream. Visibly torn over what had transpired, he smiled awkwardly. "Why are you dragging this out? It's like I told you. That woman coming here had nothing to do with me. As you just witnessed for yourself, she's doing her own thing." He was beginning to believe it more than he wanted to.

"If you say so, dear." Nadeen analyzed the way Richard spoke of Dior. He couldn't get himself to say her name. However, she could and she did. "I will have to say that Dior did look happy; maybe a tad bit drunk, but happy. It's a good thing if she's gotten over the crush she may have had on you. That tall drink of water that practically carried her out may have had everything to do with it." She continued stirring as Richard frowned. Nadeen grinned as the waiter returned with a small bowl of chocolate ice cream on a serving tray. She gestured that the bowl be placed in front of her jilted husband.

"No-no, *she* asked for this," said Richard, waving the gentleman to the other side of the table.

Nadeen nodded to the waiter. "Don't you pay him any attention. It's his, but he doesn't want to claim it. Pride, you understand." The waiter smiled politely then vanished.

"What are you talking about? I haven't eaten sweets in weeks."

"You've heard the old cliché about revenge being best served cold," said Nadeen, wiping at her lips with a white cloth napkin. "Well, there you go." She excused herself from the table, leaving Richard to his own devices. She had better things to do than sit and watch him sulk all night. Doing nothing was better than that.

Richard signed his name on the bill, charging it to the room. He couldn't wait to call Dior but there was no way Nadeen would allow him to retrieve his cell phone from the room then

roll out to check his messages. He tugged at the edges of the dinner receipt with his room number written on it. The waiter he'd
shooed away moments before straightened the table setting where
Dior spent the past hour. "Hey excuse me," Richard called out.
"The young lady with the man who was just sitting there, they're
with the group I brought down from Dallas. I'm supposed to
add their lodging to the master list but they checked in late. You
wouldn't happen to know their room number?"

The waiter put off his task to think on it. "The guy lives here
in town. He works over at the Belvedere Hotel. Are you sure she's
church folk? She drank like a fish," he joked.

"Maybe I should take this as a sign to preach on the topic of
sobriety come Sunday morning," Richard quipped, to inform his
would-be accomplice that he was a minister.

"It couldn't hurt. Let me see what I can do about the information you want."

Visions of Dior on all fours, moaning passionately, danced in
Richard's head in the same manner as before, when she was suck-
ing on chicken wings with Kevlin at Boscoe's. The tension in his
neck then was nothing compared to the stiffness he experienced
now. His fists were balled tightly when the waiter slipped him a
piece of paper with Dior's name and the number 1828 jotted on
it. "Thanks for looking that up," said Richard, as he rewarded
the man's efforts with a ten-dollar tip.

"Hey, thanks a lot, Reverend."

"Don't mention it."

Richard secured a toothpick from the reception area outside
the restaurant. He held it between his index finger and thumb,
waiting for the right time to use it. Three older sisters from his
congregation sauntered into the hotel with bags of souvenirs.
They complained about not getting any younger then called it
a night. Richard made small talk with two deacons who were

impatiently waiting on their wives to finish getting dressed for a night tour of the city's oldest cemeteries. Richard teased the men about losing their better halves among the monumental gravestones New Orleans was known for. "Make sure they don't accidentally get left behind when we push off tomorrow. You might have some explaining to do when you get home." All of the men laughed as their female companions approached, eager to get started. "Good night," Richard saluted calmly. He glanced at his watch. Twenty-nine minutes had passed by since Dior staggered off with her six-foot three-inch escort. Richard jumped on the same house phone Mahalia used earlier. He dialed the operator, asking for the room number he'd gotten from the waiter. Dior answered on the fourth ring. "Who was that man hanging on you!" he demanded to know. "Hello? Hello?" Richard grunted when he heard the dial tone buzzing in his ear. Dior had hung up the telephone. Phillip and Rose rambled by hand in hand as he redialed the operator. They stopped when he looked up. He placed the receiver down and stepped aside.

"Hey, Richard, where's Nadeen?" Phillip asked him. Rose knew where Nadeen was and didn't care if her husband did or not. "I thought y'all would be up and down Bourbon Street like everybody else."

"We ate an early dinner here. If I can get her on the phone, we might join you later." He took out the toothpick and began to fiddle around with it in his mouth. "I may as well go on up and floss while I wait on Nadeen." Phillip shrugged, Rose sneered. They mumbled silently as they headed for the French Quarter on a sightseeing extravaganza.

Richard darted over to the elevators right away. He pressed every arrow pointing up that he could find. *Dior wasn't going to play him any longer,* he decided. *Who did she think she was anyway?* Cavorting with other men on his dime was unacceptable. She was not going to give up the goods to some local hotel worker if Richard could help it. When the elevator door opened, he bolted inside. "Eighteen!" he said, mashing the button repeatedly. Watching the floor numbers on the digital readout was excruciating. "Get there already." The elevator doors opened to let him off. Richard marched out with long steady strides, past his room and toward the adjacent corridor. "Eighteen twenty-four, twenty-six, twenty-eight," he whispered, placing his ear to the door. There wasn't a sound from the other side. Richard balled his fist again then banged on the door like a madman. "Open up! I know you're in there!" He continued thumping on it harshly while shouting Dior's name. Eventually she opened it. Richard rushed past her, saliva collecting in the corners of his mouth. "Where is he? I'm tossing his yellow butt out."

"Where's who?" Dior barked, keeping distance with a straight arm between them.

"Don't think I'm a moron. Where's that dude you had the drinks and laughs with?"

"Oh Armand, he's gone. I didn't want to know him like that. He was just a nice guy I met. You were tied up, I didn't think I needed permission to hang out and I did not want to be stuck in my room the entire time, so I let him stop by the hotel for drinks." Richard chewed on her explanation. It didn't sit right with him. He zoomed into the bathroom, yanking back the shower curtain. He checked the closet and under the bed.

"What did you do with him?"

"I sent him home and why are you asking me that *with your wife on the next wing?*" Dior challenged. "You're a trip and my head is throbbing. What's in a kamikaze anyway?" Richard's chest heaved in and out slower now. He glared at the black lacy underwear she had on.

"Who is that for?" he asked suspiciously.

"For you, Richard—who else would I be going through all of this for? Armand wanted to hook up but I told him no. After I got your funky message, I almost changed my mind but then I went on ahead and left you three of them, telling you to come and see about me."

Richard was proud of her. She'd shunned another man to be with him. He leered smugly at Dior. "*Armand* wants some of this? I'll bet he does."

"You had me wondering if I came here for nothing. I'm tipsy, horny, and in need of attention. Oomph, I was about to get at it myself." She cast a fleeting glance at the oils and battery-powered gadgets resting on the nightstand by the bed.

Richard lunged at Dior, kissing her furiously. She moaned hungrily while unbuttoning his shirt with ten busy fingers. "Hurr' up, daddy. I got to have it. Ooh, I'm burning up." Richard flung his clothes on the floor then climbed on top of Dior. Her legs flew open wildly. Richard wrestled off her panties. His fingers roamed into her as he unhooked her skimpy bra with the other hand. Dior taught him that maneuver the second time he came running back to her. "Ooh yeah, you remembered," she cooed tenderly, reaching for a stack of condoms in the top drawer. Richard slapped her hand away then forced himself into her. She squealed loudly, clamping her heels around his waist. Dior threw her all into pleasing him. Ulterior motives added an extra incentive. Richard was grinding frantically with his eyes closed. Dior kept hers open so she could watch her plans unfold in the pale moonlight. The pastor was digging into her with reckless abandon, his back sweaty and bowed. Dior groaned heartily when she felt him swelling inside of her. "Come on and get it," she exclaimed heatedly. "Ooh, get every last drop. It's yours, daddy, all yours."

Richard pounded mightily. "Yeah, it's all mine. Don't ever give this to anybody else. It's mine, baby, all mine," he ranted until his muscles seized. He grunted and gasped. "Ohhh my God, you're so good to me."

"Uh-huh, always will be too." She wiped the sweat from his face with the bedsheet. "Go on and rest. You deserve it."

Richard didn't argue. He rolled off, basking in the mind-numbing climax that floored him. "Whew-wee, ain't nothing supposed to feel that good," he joked, drifting off to sleep.

Dior grinned satisfactorily as she propped two pillows behind her back. "Yes it is," she said, thinking of the tools she used to nab him. She planted a kiss on his shoulder, grinned again, and then pointed the remote control at the television. Dior went to wake him when the late news station reaired his interview and the subsequent dousing he received but she thought better of it. The longer he stayed there, the harder it would be to explain his whereabouts to his wife when he did find his way to her room. Nothing happened strictly by chance if Dior had anything to say about it. She set out on a mission, set her traps, and set up Richard to make a mistake he couldn't climb over. Even Nadeen had a breaking point, one of no return, she reasoned. With momentum on her side and the wind at her back, Dior figured Richard's lengthy disappearance and wrinkled clothes just might be the feather tipping the scales in her favor.

The alarm clock read 1:05 a.m. when Richard raised his head to look at it. He peered around the room, a stranger to the sur-roundings. Then it occurred to him: He wasn't in bed with his wife. "Ohhh, this is bad...very bad," he yelped.

Dior rubbed her eyes, squinting at him and feigning inno-cence. "What is it?" she grumbled.

"It's after one o'clock," he answered, stepping on his shirt as he pulled his slacks up to zip them. "Where are my drawers? Never mind. I've got to go." He dipped into the bathroom to splash water on his face. Dior sat up in the bed with a sheet draped over her breasts. She did her best to appear sympathetic.

"Is there something I can do to help, Richard?"

He tucked his shirttail inside his pants then opened the door. "I'll call you tomorrow. Get up and put the dead bolt on." He was afraid of Armand doubling back and getting some of what he was forced to leave behind.

Dior's bright smile illuminated the room. She hopped up and placed a second lock on the door at Richard's suggestion. In the bottom of the closet, she riffled through her luggage to find the double pack of Early Pregnancy Tests she remembered to bring from home. She hadn't been positive of her ovulation schedule the first time she let Richard in without a condom, but Dior had this date circled on her calendar. Having her trip to New Orleans sponsored by him was icing on the cake. With so much riding on Richard's inability to control himself in her presence, she would have gladly sprung for the ticket herself.

Richard slinked down the hall. There was no use in conjuring up a lie to dump on Nadeen. He'd really done it now. When he saw his bags sitting against the wall outside of his room, he stopped. Afraid to take another step, Richard sighed despondently. He was willing to beg and grovel on bended knee if it came to that. He rubbed at the corners of his eyes to remove any lingering evidence that he'd been asleep. Phillip was right; he should have prayed for God to lead him, then he should have followed.

Richard slid the plastic keycard into the slot to get in. A red light flashed. Richard looked up at the door number. He had the right one but Nadeen had the magnetic lock changed, rendering his key useless. "She actually went and put me out," he said to himself. "Nadeen, don't do this." He knocked gingerly so as not to wake up the girls in the next room or other church members staying on their floor. Richard drew in a calculated breath when Nadeen answered the door. Her hair was wrapped in a silk scarf. Her eyes were nearly puffed shut from crying.

"I set your things out," she said, void of all maliciousness. In the partially open doorway, she yawned casually. "Your key won't work because you're not welcome in my space anymore. I don't trust you. I've tried to deal with it, work with it, and get over it. I can't continue stacking your lies and trying to make something good come out of them. You need help, Richard. It's obvious you don't need me."

"What does this mean? What am I supposed to do?"

"You should have been asking yourself that question every time you left my bed and raced off to hers. Before I forget, your cell phone is in the zipper pocket. Dior left three messages. I listened to all of them. Now I see why you can't turn her down; she's willing to do anything you want her to. Congratulations."

"Nadeen, we've been together a long time. Baby, I know this doesn't look right but I…I…"

"Please don't tell me you can explain. If I pulled something like this, you'd try to kill me and you know it."

Richard couldn't argue with her. He would have violently assaulted everyone connected with Nadeen's affair. "I don't know what to say but…but…I…" he stammered, from his knees. "I'm sorry, Nadeen. Please believe me. I'm repentant. I'll let her go." She yawned again, staring directly through Richard and the seemingly rehearsed act to restore what he'd lost. Nadeen heard some of the doors on their floor open after Richard resorted to pleading. She slapped at his hands when he reached for the hem of her nightgown.

"I'm going back to bed. Get away from this door, Richard, and that's the last time I'm saying it before calling security."

Annoyed more than apologetic now, Richard hated Nadeen's

resolve to stay the course. "Wait a minute now. You're carrying this way too far, Nadeen. I said I was sorry!"

"You certainly know what you're talking about. You are sorry and by the way, Brotha Pastor, your shirt is inside out. Next time, get your little girlfriend to dress you better." Nadeen slammed the door, shut Richard out of her room, and then flopped onto the bed. Mahalia came in to see about her.

"I'm sorry, Mama. Don't cry anymore, you've still got us." Roxanne stood at the foot of the bed, awaiting permission to come aboard.

"My girls," Nadeen whispered, with them on either side of her. She pulled the covers up to her neck, held them tightly, and stared into the darkness.

# TWENTY-NINE

## *Not Yet, I Don't*

The following morning Richard ate breakfast in his room, the same one Dior abandoned at her previous hotel. Since it was his money that paid for it, he couldn't see letting it go to waste. Richard spent the remainder of the night wondering how he had allowed himself to be drawn in by Dior's schemes and led astray by his own carnal desires. He didn't want to be near her or anyone who might have known about what happened the night before. Being thrown out by his wife was the lowest point of his life. Richard kept hearing Nadeen's words resonating in his ears. "You certainly know what you're talking about. You are sorry," she'd said sullenly. There was no fire behind it, no spiteful rage to speak of. The love of his life had given up on him. He couldn't find it within his heart to blame her. If Richard could have taken back the past five weeks, he would have. Unfortunately, too many things had been said and done for that to be remotely possible. While checking out of his room, he realized that life didn't accept the slightest regret. Life was all about making the best of a bad situation and moving forward.

Cartloads of luggage were being packed into bus storage compartments as the vehicles idled against the curb outside the Marriott. Richard paid the taxi driver then grabbed his bags from the backseat. With egg on his face and painstakingly unsure of exactly who knew about his having been ousted, he set his bags on the sidewalk and lamented.

After several minutes passed, a smattering of church members began to exit the hotel. Two women boarded the first bus. Both of them neglected to speak to him. Soon after, several of them avoided eye contact completely. Others nodded out of respect but it was clear that the rumor mill had opened early on the weekend and the faithful were taking sides. From the outset it appeared Richard was behind in the polls. Then a ray of sun shone on his face.

"Good morning, Brother Pastor," Phillip said, with Rose two steps behind him. "Rough night, huh?" Richard chuckled lightly to keep from crying.

"I should have known you'd caught wind of it. Morning, Rose," Richard added, out of common courtesy, knowing full well she stood with Nadeen despite the bloodline she shared with him.

"Yep, and the wind is kicking up quite a bit of gossip," Rose informed him. "Question is, what are you going to do about it?"

Richard's eyes softened before he answered. "Everything in my power with God at the wheel." He awaited her response. It was a safe bet that she'd relay his sentiment to Nadeen as soon as she could.

"Oomph" was her stoic reply. She squeezed Phillip's hand then hopped on the first travel coach. Never had such a short dissertation sent Richard reeling like Rose's potent utterance. She'd conveyed her position soundly without saying a solitary word. It was very likely Nadeen would be just as decisive when refusing to mince hers.

"Is it worse than I thought?" Richard asked, praying it wasn't.

"Man, it's worse than you can imagine. Nadeen was in the business center at the crack of dawn booking three tickets to Georgia." Phillip patted him on the shoulder, knowing he needed a hug. "She still loves you. You've got to remember that when you're putting your marriage back together."

"My kids, Phillip, I can't have them not believing in me," Richard confessed.

"They're daughters, Richard. That means they'll never give up on you. Now, if you had to depend on two rusty-butt boys, you'd be better off moving in with me and Rose."

"I hear you, although I don't think Rose would have me."

Phillip considered the chances then grinned playfully. "No, probably not, but Rose isn't the conscience of the congregation. You're still our leader so you'd probably want to fix your face and handle your business in private. Buck up, here comes the gang." Phillip's gaze landed behind Richard. A frown weighed it down like an anchor. Nadeen raised her sunshades to read from a small sheet of paper she'd pulled from her purse. Her eyelids were red and swollen. It made Phillip sad to think what she must have suffered. Richard felt it too.

"Hey, y'all. Nadeen, I..."

"Not yet," she answered, in such a way that made Richard wonder if she would ever be ready or willing to discuss their marriage and family again.

"I understand." Richard manufactured a smile for Mahalia then reached out to help with her backpack. She sidestepped him, snatching her bag from his grasp.

"No thank you," she said, rushing her words. "I can manage." She sniffled, then followed her mother onto the bus.

"I could use some help, Daddy," sang Roxanne, dragging a carry-on bag like a reluctant puppy. Richard's heart melted inside his chest when she offered to share hers with him.

"I could use some too. Thank you so much, Roxy." He reached down and hoisted her off the ground. He squeezed his youngest child so hard, she wiggled to get loose.

"Ouch, Daddy, I can't breathe!"

Richard relaxed his grip immediately. "You made me so happy I got too excited."

"Well, the next time you help me, not so rough." She winked at him then giggled heartily. "Bye, Daddy. See you when we get home, if Mommy lets you in." Richard looked away when a wave of emotion swept over him. Roxanne exhibited the kind of love Richard needed to rebuild his life: unconditional love, giving for the sake of giving. If the other women in his household followed suit, he might stand a chance. On the other hand, Roxanne was only eight, uncorrupted by pain and fashioned in the image of innocents. In her eyes, Richard could do no wrong. Nadeen wasn't so naïve and Mahalia knew better.

During the eight-hour bus trip home Nadeen stared endlessly out of the window. Rose entertained Roxanne as best she could in the seats directly across from her. Mahalia prayed all the way. She wanted Dior dead. Among her sincere petitions begging for the heartless homewrecker to be wiped off the face of the earth was an unwavering plea for Dior to meet with a slow, horrible death so she would know what it felt like to drown in an ocean of agony. With every prayer Mahalia grew more determined, more engrossed in hate. She boldly summoned Satan for assistance and pledged her allegiance to him if he carried out her wishes. Although misguided, she meant every word.

On the third bus, less than half of the merriment that had ushered the men to New Orleans accompanied them home. Phillip overheard whispers questioning the pastor's extracurricular activities, how long he'd been giving in to his carnal man at the detriment of the inner one. There was nothing Phillip could do but hope the murmurs subsided instead of billowing into a heated fire of discontent. Phillip labored to find a decent moment of rest while vowing silently to stand by his friend. He was tortured nonetheless by restlessness.

In the first seat on the bus, Richard slept like a baby. Concern for his job was absent. The survival of his family was paramount. Everything else was a distant second. In the back of his mind, Richard assumed his tenure in the church was a lock. Phillip couldn't disagree more.

At nine thirty on Saturday evening, Richard settled the account with the bus drivers in the rear of the church parking lot. He glanced at his watch as the last few members started for home. Nadeen was the first to leave once they had arrived. She couldn't get away from Richard and the memories of a disastrous trip fast enough. The blame lay squarely on his shoulders. Now that the hotel and travel bills had been paid and the work M.E.G.A. set out to do completed, Richard faced a daunting task. Building an overwhelmingly successful ministry constructed for the purpose of saving souls was easy compared to saving Nadeen and the girls from the fallout over his impropriety.

Richard entered his ritzy subdivision, with mansions lining the landscape. He still found it hard to face himself. It was even more difficult addressing Nadeen. As the garage door opened, Richard breathed a sigh of relief. His wife's car was there and it hadn't been loaded down with luggage. He thanked God for however much time he'd been given to make appeals and amends. When he tried to jiggle the doorknob leading from the garage to the utility room, it wouldn't budge. Before he could question why Nadeen felt it necessary to shut him out once again, he heard a car approaching the house from the circular driveway.

Richard exited the garage. He squinted into the headlights of a blue airport shuttle van. His first inclination was to send the taxi away. Nadeen opened the front door as he rounded the van on the driver's side. "Hey, man, you can go!" Richard yelled angrily.

"No he can't either!" Nadeen battled back. "I called him and I say he stays until I get me and the girls loaded up." She was indignant and tired, too tired to see her journey forward stalled by the likes of the man who put himself ahead of her. "Might I remind you the police in this city have a long history of brutality against stubborn black men? They would love coming out to a house like this and dragging your butt across the lawn in handcuffs." Nadeen assured the driver of his safety when he declined to get out and retrieve the luggage from the den. "He won't mess with you or I'll see to it that the cops deal with him."

"Is this how it ends, Nadeen?" Richard asked, his eyes narrowing. "Huh? You'd really call the law on me when all I'm trying to do is stop my wife from leaving my home? I love you and don't want our marriage to fall apart over a senseless affair that didn't mean nothing to me in the first place."

Nadeen shoved Richard aside when the driver made his way toward the opened door. "Oh, you're a piece of work, Richard. What about all I've wanted? Didn't it occur to you how lonely and hurt I was when you'd come home late without a decent excuse as to where you'd been? Obviously being with Dior did mean something to you. Play that song somewhere else because I don't like the way it sounds."

Irritated, Richard watched as the van driver stepped into his house. "Hey, man, hold on. I'll get them. Just stay out there. This is my family and…" he huffed, glaring at the stranger. He waved the man off then followed Nadeen inside. "Hey. Nadeen, are you saying we can't talk about this?"

"When it was time to talk you weren't interested in hearing what I had to say. Now the shoe's on the other foot. As a matter of fact, you'd better watch your step before that shoe is up your behind. I'm not playing, Richard. If you want a fight, that's what you'll get." Richard felt as if he'd fallen off a tall building without a net. His marriage was plummeting toward a gruesome end.

"Okay, how about now? Look-look," he pleaded. Nadeen sorted through the mail she planned to take with her. "Since you put my stuff out in the hall, I haven't talked to Dior nor do I intend to. Believe me, now I see how dumb it was letting myself get too close to her."

"Now, now, now. *Now* is too late. Me, Roxy, and Mahalia are going to Atlanta on the eleven fifty flight. If you make us miss that plane, I'm prepared to use your platinum card to book a private charter. If you don't mind paying forty-five thousand dollars then I won't mind charging it." When he remained silent, she nodded her head assertively. "Thought so."

With luggage in hand, Richard eyed Nadeen as he followed her out to the van. "Where're the girls?" he questioned. His voice was shaky, and she peeked to see if he was crying. Even in her plight, she was still interested in his well-being.

"They're upstairs in the master bedroom. I wanted them out of the way in case you decided to get silly. They've seen and heard enough already. Oh and you'll need to talk to Roxy about using bad words."

"Bad words? Since when?"

"Since last week, but I've been too busy worrying about my husband's girlfriend to tell you about it. And, I found this when going through Mahalia's things." She unwrapped the small hand-carved charm Mahalia had purchased at the novelty store in New Orleans. Mahalia didn't deny getting it but she wouldn't admit as to why.

"That looks like some kind of voodoo trinket," he said, pulling at the hair tied around the doll's neck.

"Because that's exactly what it is," Nadeen griped smugly. She gestured to the driver that she would be along in a few minutes when he appeared to be getting antsy.

Richard jogged up the stairs then hurried down the hall to the master suite. When he opened the door, he found his daughters huddled together on the chaise longue. Roxanne smiled lovingly when she saw her father until Mahalia persuaded her to drop the pleasantries. "Don't forget, we're mad at him."

Roxanne stomped her foot then crossed her arms defiantly. "Oh yeah, I forgot."

"Hey, girls, I hear you're going to visit Gramps in Atlanta," Richard said, pretending to be at ease when it was apparently otherwise. "Roxy, come over here and give me a hug." The small child reserved her compliance, awaiting permission from her chaperone. Eventually Mahalia gave her the okay. Roxanne giggled as she sprinted toward her father's arms.

"I wasn't really mad at you, Daddy," she whispered in his ear. "'Halia tried to talk me into it."

"Oh, is that so?" Richard asked, enjoying another secret moment with his youngest child. "Who talked you into saying the bad words your mama told me about?"

Roxanne frowned after realizing she'd been ratted out. "Mommy told you about those three I learned from Herman Kelly?"

"Sure did, and we don't want to hear you saying those kinds of things anymore."

Roxanne smirked in a cavalier manner that surprised Richard as much as what she said next. "Well, that's nothing. Mommy can take those dirty words from me. I know two more good ones." She winked at Mahalia for increasing her vocabulary. "Bye, Daddy," she said, before leaving the room.

"I guess it's just you and me, kid." Richard offered as an olive branch. "Are we going to make it, me and you, I mean?" Mahalia hid her tears with both hands. She didn't want to leave without speaking to him, but the heartache pierced so deeply. Richard threw his arms around her. He squeezed tightly. "I know, kitten, I know. It's rough. Daddy messed up but I'll take care of it."

Suddenly she peered into his eyes like the woman-child she'd become. "Kitten? I can't remember the last time you called me that."

"Then it must've been too long. Let me walk you out. Your mother's in a hurry." They descended the staircase arm in arm. Nadeen stood at the base of it, imagining how beautiful Mahalia would be in a ball gown, escorted by her father. She reached out for her daughter's hand when they made it to the foyer.

"Come on or we'll be late," she muttered tenderly. "What did your father say about that thing you brought back?" Richard had forgotten about the trinket in his pocket. He pulled it out then held it in the palm of his hand.

"Mahalia, I know this is a rough patch in your life but things never get so bad that you run to black magic. Never invite Satan into your heart. It's too hard getting him out." Nadeen agreed, although he should have taken his own advice.

Mahalia tried to make sense of it, why he wagered his family on a diversion like Dior. "I just wanted her to leave you alone, Daddy. I prayed and I prayed to God but He didn't hear me. Even if He did, He didn't answer in time."

Richard brushed his hand against Mahalia's face. Her frailty was heartbreaking. "God heard you, I'm sure of it. You don't need things like this. He'll answer in His own time." Richard popped the head off the trinket, tossed the doll down on the floor at his feet. "See there, it's worthless."

He waved goodbye as they climbed into the van, all looking back at him through raised windows. "I'll call you, Nadeen. I love you!" he yelled, when they pulled out of the driveway. "Mahalia, take care of your sister. I'll miss you."

# THIRTY

## *Let It Shine*

**M**orning came too fast. Richard awoke in his bed, fully clothed and hungover from the bottle of champagne someone had given him as a gift for ten years of service to M.E.G.A. He never planned on popping the cork but losing sleep for two consecutive nights didn't appeal to him. Once he threw both legs over the side of the bed, he stretched and moaned. *My head is ringing,* he thought. *I'll do better after two cups of Nadeen's coffee.* He was using the bathroom with the toilet seat up when it came to mind that there was no one demanding it be lowered afterward nor would there be freshly brewed coffee on standby to help him meet the day.

Richard broke down mentally. He cried over his troubled marriage and waffling relationship. He recognized the work he had cut out, the long road ahead littered with phone calls to check on the kids, plane trips to Georgia, and prayers of winning his wife back on her terms.

After gargling three times with mouthwash, Richard felt convinced he'd rinsed the smell of liquor from his breath. Several times during his career, he condemned carousers and Saturday nightclub prowlers for dragging into the Lord's house half inebriated and hungover just as he happened to be then. *Pull yourself together, man,* he heard himself say. *You're the pastor of a prestigious congregation with thousands of followers. You are Dr. Pastor Richard Allamay, PhD. You still got that going for you. Phillip was right and you can't forget it.* Richard smiled at himself in the bathroom mirror, determined to play the part of a man holding it together.

An hour later, Phillip paced in the pastor's chambers, reading his wristwatch every thirty seconds. He put off calling Richard's cell phone, predicting his arrival in due time. The church auditorium was filled to the rim as usual although there was a strangely different vibe circulating. Two of the deacons, who neglected to make the road trip to New Orleans, pulled Phillip's coattail to get the real story once their phones rang off the hook. His answer was the same every time: "A slight misunderstanding occurred, but the pastor and Sister Allamay are doing fine." He actually believed they would patch things up eventually so it wasn't a total fabrication as far as he knew. One immediate problem existed however. If Richard did not show up in time for morning service and the television broadcast, Phillip was slated to fill in and preach in his place. The thought of that made him shiver.

"Richard! Boy, I'm glad to see you," Phillip hailed when the pastor sailed in. Richard looked shinier than a brand-new dime.

"It's good to see you too, Phillip," he answered plainly, as if his world hadn't been turned upside down.

"You can't believe how tickled I am that you made it. Second of all, how's Nadeen this morning?"

"She's in Atlanta. Nadeen took the girls there late last night. I'm sorry. I just assumed she told Rose."

Phillip was at a loss for words. "Uh-uh, we haven't heard. At least I haven't. I'm sorry too. You are able to preach this morning?" he added, praying for a favorable response. Richard adjusted his necktie. "Why wouldn't I be? Come on, let's go to work." Phillip followed the pastor out of the office, onto the elevator, and into the worship hall. When Richard paused a few feet from the pulpit, the deacon shrugged to question why. "Is there anything I should be aware of?"

"Like what?"

"Like Dior sitting in the front row naked?" The look on Phillip's face made Richard chuckle. "Ease up, Brother Evans, I'm only joking."

"Dear Lord, please don't let that happen today. My heart can't take it." He craned his neck to look over the audience. There was not one sign of Dior. He exhaled slowly. "Thank you."

Richard approached the podium like he'd done hundreds of times. However this one was very different. Absent was his wife, who'd served as a pulse of the congregation when he spoke. If she wrinkled her nose, he knew to back off. When her eyes appeared blank and glassy, she was probably one of a number who had begun to think about the afternoon football game, pot roasts, or other matters he'd rather not imagine.

Richard was smiling when he thought of Nadeen as a fine helpmate and he was lost to the fact that the choir had finished their second selection. He stood alone in a quiet auditorium. One of the camera production managers signaled at Phillip to do something, anything, to get the pastor going.

The deacon rose to his feet. He began to clap his hands, then he belted out the first song that came to his mind. "This little light of mine, I'm gonna let it shine. This little light of mine…" The minister of music almost had a hissy fit when the deacon led thousands of church members in a rousing rendition of a spiritual typically reserved for children's Sunday school. Eventually, he fired up the organ and joined in. Phillip was suffocating.

He felt breathless and faint. Richard simply continued standing there, smiling. "It's showtime, Richard. You got to pull it together."

Richard's lips began to move ever so slightly, as if he were coming out of a fog. He sang the song he hadn't heard in years, interested why the church was rocking enthusiastically. "Let it shine, let it shine, let it shine. Aaaamen. I'll take some of that old-time religion any day. Good morning, church. I have to apologize, guess I got stuck in yesterday, which is a whole lot better than being stuck in reverse." He winked at Phillip, to suggest he was back on task. "Can I get an amen?" Richard got more than that. He got a rim shot solo from the drummer. "I see one brother agrees; sometimes that's all a country preacher needs. Now, I must admit I'm a bit distracted this morning, church. Some of you might have heard rumors of what happened over the weekend." He paused again to watch Phillip, who he knew would be afraid of the truth coming out. "No, me and Sister Allamay didn't gamble away the church building at the casino crap tables. You might have heard the saying 'what happens in Vegas stays in Vegas.' Well, I'm here to tell you how glad I am we didn't go to Vegas, because there's a lot to share about what went on in New Or-leens. Church, be proud of the group who sat on those buses, cramped for hours at a time and forced to put up with me all the way to Louisiana and back." Laughter replaced looks of uneasiness. Nadeen was correct. Richard's light shined the brightest when he freestyled. "However, in between the fellowship and bid whist tournaments, we put in work. Three hundred and fifty members toiled in the sun and labored like they expected to get paid. Hallelujah. They pulled off rotted wood, hammered and nailed up new lumber, painted and perspired until the job was done. Hear me well, they put in work. I ought to know because I supervised." Again, laughter lit up the auditorium. "Of course,

I'm joking. I worked a little too. Be proud of your congregation because the Lord told us to move and we did. Faith is so hard to maintain during difficult times. This is one of them. Now then, what doth the Lord have to say about it? In the book of John, around about the third chapter and the sixteenth verse, it reminds us that *Faith is the substance of things hoped for and evidence of things not seen.*"

Phillip glanced at Richard peculiarly because the scripture he referred to did not correspond with the passage he recited. Richard was referring to Hebrews 11:1. During the pastor's sermon, Phillip counted six biblical errors. The elders noticed quite a few more than that. If Phillip hadn't been as well-versed on the Word, he would have overlooked the host of mistakes. Reasons behind Richard's strange behavior had to be addressed. After the service concluded, Richard shook hands with hundreds of members near the exit. As long as the line held, he remained.

Tuesday evening, there was an unexpected knock at Richard's home. He grunted from the upstairs bedroom that he was on the way down, as if the visitor could hear him. He staggered to the landing then took several careful steps to reach the bottom of the staircase. Richard flew off the handle when the insistent knocks continued. "I said I was coming! If that's not good enough for you, get on back to wherever you came from!" Had he not recognized Phillip's car when he glanced out of the front window, he wouldn't have opened the door. "Hey, Deacon," Richard uttered. "Well, come on in. And keep the mosquitoes out." He hiccupped then burped rudely. Phillip used the DVD case he'd brought to fan the foul odor.

"Uhhgh, how long have you been drinking?" he asked, shielding his nose.

Richard belched again then flopped on the sofa, wearing the

same clothes he'd put on the day before. "That depends on what day it is." Phillip gave his good friend the once-over. Richard didn't look good. He hadn't shaved or bathed in days. It made what the deacon had come to do a lot harder.

"Brother Pastor," Phillip started in.

"Uh-oh, you sound like a man on church business," Richard cackled. "Maybe I ought to get the Bible out."

*It couldn't hurt*, Phillip thought to himself. "Taking into account all that's gone on and what you're dealing with now, I hate to be the bearer of bad news." He shifted his weight then lowered his head. Phillip detested the secret meetings held to oust Richard from the top job at M.E.G.A. Church, now a multimillion-dollar enterprise mainly because of his stewardship. The elders convened an assembly of senior members to discuss grumblings of whoremongering and adultery attached to the pastor's name. A few of the men in attendance were on hand to witness Richard begging outside of Nadeen's hotel room to be let in. Phillip sat quietly and listened to them condemn the man he cared about, thinking it would have been easier to speak up had Richard gambled away the church building at one of those offshore casino boats. Arranging for Dior to meet him while on church business was far more unscrupulous in their eyes. Phillip couldn't argue against them.

"So what bad news do you hate being the bearer of?" Richard sniped. His eyes squinted distrustfully.

"The elders think you ought to take some time off, get your business in order, then come back and have a sit-down to talk about it."

"Uh-huh," Richard huffed, dismissing the entire idea. "The elders think that's what I ought to do? Well, I don't!"

"Try to calm down. It's a lot more complicated than that."

"I don't care how complicated they think it is. I'll decide when I need a break and for how long!" he shouted.

"Richard, it's not up to you. I'm sorry, but the decision has already been made to find a replacement in the meanwhile."

"Who's gonna fill my shoes? Is it you, *Brother Deacon*? You went after my job behind my back? Huh?"

"No-no," Phillip answered in record speed. He quickly remembered the collection of knots in his stomach when he thought he'd have to deliver the last message. "I'm not the right one for it."

Richard sat up with his forearms resting on his thighs. "They offered it to you though, didn't they?"

"Yeah, yesterday."

The pastor sprang to his bare feet. "You're telling me those old buzzards convened to toss me out?" Phillip nodded his head reluctantly. "How long they been plotting against me?" Paranoia surrounded Richard from all sides.

"It's not like that. Think of how things look. Dior shows up at the hotel, nobody could miss that. You got busted, Richard! You brought your sideline woman around your wife. What did you expect to happen?"

"The elders are all jealous. Mad 'cause they couldn't pull a fine young thing like Dior for themselves."

"That's nonsense, Richard. You should listen to yourself. As a matter of fact, that's what I want you to do." Phillip picked up the DVD case from the coffee table then tossed it at him. "This is a copy of last Sunday's worship service. It's one of the only remaining copies. We had to trash the others. They were useless." Phillip had Richard's attention then. It troubled him to be so direct but it had to be done. "Because of the erroneous information and the wrong scriptures you quoted during your sermon, the entire recorded program had to be destroyed. I wanted to pitch for you, really I did. When several of the sisters from the ladies auxiliary said they smelled alcohol on your breath afterwards, I didn't have a leg to stand on." Even though it was hard to take, Richard was ready to listen to everything Phillip had to say. "People are counting on you, Pastor, people like me who know what a great man of God you are. One who has fallen, but a great man irregardless."

Richard wore a beleaguered frown. "Oomph, some great man I turned out to be. My wife ran off and she took the kids. I've been trying to reach them at her parents' home, but they won't take my calls." He smacked his lips then eyed the DVD cover as if he was finally willing to examine himself. "Is it that bad?"

"Yeah," Phillip cautioned. "But it's not the end unless you cause it to be. Just take a break, go to your family even if Nadeen is too hurt or too prideful to take your calls. Patch things up, get her back here, and we'll work it out. The elders know they need you. But not like this. Not with the drinking and certainly not with Dior on your mind. Do what you got to do, Richard, or the Methodist Episcopal Greater Apostolic Church will have no recourse but to go in another direction without you."

Richard looked at the messenger from the corner of his eye. "*Recourse?*"

Phillip grinned then threw his hands up defensively. "That's their word, not mine." He stood up, then shrugged his shoulders. "When will you get back to me with your plans?"

"I'll let you know as soon as I come up with some." Richard shook hands with his best friend then hugged him like a long-lost brother. "Just when you thought it couldn't get any worse."

"Take care of yourself, Brother Pastor. I'm not ready to stop believing in you."

"That makes one of us," Richard jested. "I'll be in touch, Phillip, thanks again. They sent the right man to straighten me out."

# THIRTY-ONE

## *Clear Blue Easy*

There weren't any words, phrases, or expressions to describe the ghastly feelings flooring Richard after he viewed the DVD Phillip delivered. He understood why the M.E.G.A. Church leadership destroyed the evidence of this horrendous sermon. Richard wanted to ask forgiveness for dishonoring the holy Word of God on the heels of a champagne binge, but he didn't feel worthy. Serving the Lord in his brokenness was tougher than he thought. Richard wanted his family back, his life back, and the mental health he enjoyed before meeting Dior restored. He needed closure. He needed to end it face-to-face, to remove all doubt that he still wanted her.

A long shower invigorated him. A close shave made him feel like new money. His black Lexus sedan idled inside of the garage, purring to go. Richard tossed his cell phone charger and a number of toiletry items into a duffel bag along with a week's worth of jeans and sweats, then he slung the travel gear over his shoulder. He'd begun to pick up the shattered pieces of what used to be his life. Richard locked the doors and windows, then set the home monitoring system with a small remote control. He backed out of the garage, staring at the house his ego built. Although elegantly designed, it didn't hold the attraction it once had. *Empty vessels rarely do*, he thought while zooming down the driveway.

Minutes from Dior's neighborhood, Richard parked in front of a convenience store parking lot to gather himself. Dior was strong-willed, crafty, and had to be handled right. The direct approach was his best bet. He decided to march in, tell her how it was going to be, then bounce. *She'll be lucky to get a word in edgewise,* he thought. *I'm running things now and I wouldn't have been in this trouble if I had been from the jump.* Richard dialed Dior's cell phone. If she didn't answer, he was prepared to park down the street from her house and wait it out.

"Where you been, sugar?" she answered. Her voice sounded strained.

Richard chose his words carefully. "Hey, I'm about to run out of town for a minute. You mind if I stop by?" He said just enough to pique her interest, making it difficult to refuse his company even if she was so inclined.

"Yeah, that'll be cool. Hey, where…" she said, catching herself in the middle of overplaying her hand. She knew he'd been going through it because of the way he botched the sermon on television. She attempted to study along in her Bible like she had before. He was so far off the mark, she couldn't keep up. "Never mind, Richard, come on."

She spied on him from the window as he parked the car. Dior was surprised to see a spring in his step. A friend of a friend had informed Tangie of the latest church chat, which had Dior's name sprinkled all over it. Richard didn't have to tell her that he was in hot water with the elders and ditched by Nadeen. What she didn't know was how he planned to go about keeping his head above the tide. Regardless, Dior was prepared to go along for the ride.

"Hey, Dior," Richard muttered. He looked straight through her as if she wasn't scantily clad in tight cotton shorts and a revealing crop top. "Can I come in?"

"Why would I tell you to come over and not let you in?" she asked apprehensively. "Are you sure you want to be here?"

She posed a very pointed question. Richard grinned awkwardly. He didn't want to be there, not anymore. "Like I was saying on the phone, I'm going out of town for a while. I have some business to tend to in Georgia."

"I figured that's where Nadeen took the girls," she said knowingly. "Yep, I was going to call and see how you were managing things, but I didn't want to press." Dior didn't like the way the story was being directed. It was time to rewrite it to suit her happily ever after. "Come upstairs with me while I straighten up my bathroom."

"I really don't have time to watch you scrub your bathtub," he objected.

"How soon we forget. Before your wife ran out on you, there wasn't anything you wouldn't mind watching me do to my bathtub," Dior huffed arrogantly then strolled casually up the carpeted stairs. Richard stood on the tiled floor, reluctantly wishing he could have simply blurted out what an ignominious mistake it was to step outside his marriage, turn, and walk away. Dior was onto his strategy. She baited him to join her on the second floor. When he started up the stairs, she instituted her plan. She sat on the vanity chair, rearranging bathroom cleaners beneath the sink. "What's the matter, sugar? You don't want a foot massage tonight? Too much on your mind?"

He leaned against the doorjamb, peering into the bathroom. "Now you're talking. I've got way too much on my mind and going on in my life. The walls are crashing down around me, Dior. You're not even a member of the church and you know what's going on. Oh wait, that's right, you're the reason I'm fighting for my marriage and my job," he said, so-there fashion.

"You knew what you were getting into when you started with that perfume you bought me in the beginning. *Oh wait, that's right,*" she mocked, "it was your so-called token of appreciation. Dangling the carrot got you just what you wanted. The rabbit."

"Okay, so I thought it would be easier to manage. I was wrong."

"You can't put no handcuffs on love."

"Love? Who said anything about that? Love didn't have a thing to do with your changing hotels, now did it?"

"You're telling me that love didn't play a part in you flying me to another state so I could be next to you, a few tiny blocks from your wife and kids? Hello."

"Don't try to put that on love. Put the entire New Orleans trip on me being an idiot."

Dior was growing more agitated by the second. She stood up from the cloth-covered stool then opened the first drawer nearest to Richard. "Uh-uh, I can't do that." Dior swung her hips then rolled her eyes. "Ain't nothing changed with us."

"Everything has changed!" Richard grunted angrily. "I'm shut out of my life, people at the church are having secret meetings to shut me out of that, and it's all because I let my weakness for you get in front of what I really love. You screwed me, Dior, and I let you."

"You loved every minute of it too. Don't lie and say you didn't." She closed her eyes and pretended to be Richard, in the throes of passion. "*Ooh Dior, it's so good,*" she mimicked in a wimpy voice. "*I ain't never had it put on me like this before. You got me tossin' and turnin' in my sleep. Forget about the meeting at the church. I'd rather stay up in yo' sweet stuff."* Her rendition of Richard's pillow talk was highly insulting but that didn't stop her from pushing his buttons. "You can act like such a punk. I told you not to come if you couldn't stay but you kept on coming. I gave you several chances to walk away before the skillet got too hot. It's true what they say about getting out of the kitchen. Now it's too late. There's a bun in the oven." Dior rubbed her flat stomach then posed in the mirror as if she expected to see early signs of change in her figure. "Alicia Allamay, that has a nice ring to it," she howled. "Ooh, what if it's a boy? Alexander Allamay? Even better, we could be having twins. You know twins run in my family."

"Don't try to run one of those ghetto games on me," he said, feeling weak-kneed while feigning indifference. "I'm tired of being manipulated by you and the sooner you accept that, the sooner we can both get on with our lives." Richard didn't believe Dior because he couldn't deal with it being the truth.

"Man, you're just plain tired," she goaded him. "I got proof right here, somewhere. Where'd I put it?" Dior began fishing through the top drawer. "Keep on calling me a liar and I might name the baby after you, Dick." She laughed at his shoddy attempt at dismissing her. These were things Dior knew how to do: plan a pregnancy with someone else's husband and all the body slapping that led up to it. "Ah-hah, here is the proof. Clear. Blue. Easy. Uh-huh, told you I was pregnant." She waved the home pregnancy kit in his face.

Richard saw what he'd hoped to recapture flash before his eyes, except Dior kept sticking her nose in it. *She couldn't be carrying my child, she couldn't be,* he thought. *My luck cannot be that bad.* "Dior, get that out of my face. I'm not going to debate this."

"Because you can't," Dior teased. She raised her hands in the air then started her victory dance while continually harassing Richard with what she called "the proof."

"If I'm supposed to think my feet were the only ones in that tub of yours, you got another thing coming," he grunted nastily. "And I've warned you once to keep that thing away from me." Richard swung his hand to knock the cardboard stick from hers. When Dior ducked away, he caught her wildly across the face. Accident or not, Dior snapped. She raced into her bedroom. Richard heard her sniveling but couldn't chance falling for another in a long line of her tricks.

"I told you never to put your hands on me!" she screamed hysterically. "Richard!"

He rounded the top of the banister, looking back. Richard's heart saw a woman distraught over a misunderstanding and an affair that fell apart on her. His eyes saw her trembling hands gripped around the pistol she aimed in his direction. Richard cowered against the wall. "Whoa, Dior! Put the gun down!"

"I promised I wouldn't ever let no man put his hands on me again and get away with it. Look at my face, Richard! Look at it!" A red welt ran over the top of Dior's left cheek.

"It was an accident. You have to know that." Richard's chest swelled as Dior lowered her aim momentarily. He lunged forward, grabbing the gun barrel with both hands. Dior scuffled mightily to keep her finger on the trigger. Richard grunted as he fell against the banister with a tight grasp on Dior's hands. They wrestled heatedly. He growled. She cussed and sputtered. They both went tumbling down the stairs. Two thunderous shots fired. Dior screamed.

Richard came crashing down hard on top of her at the base of the stairs. Moments passed without either of them moving a muscle. Eventually, Richard groaned. He clutched at his chest and shoulder. He climbed off of Dior, searching his body for gunshot wounds. It was nothing short of a miracle; both shots missed him. There wasn't an ounce of blood anywhere. Richard peered at a couple of golf ball–size holes in the wall, inches from the place he'd made his stand.

"You almost killed both of us," he complained. "You're crazy, certifiable. Uhhhhhgh! I must have…busted my knee." He looked Dior over then kicked the gun from her reach.

"Ouuch," she sighed tenderly. "My whole body is tingling and my head is ringing. Just help me up. Come on now, I wasn't gonna shoot you."

"You shot at me, twice!" he argued.

"Ahhhh, okay, I was mad. Now I'm sore all over." Dior tried to extend her hand to Richard. "Ouuch! Come on, help me up." She raised her eyes to rest on his. Dior didn't like the way he was standing over her, like a grim pallbearer. "What's wrong?" she asked, feeling a shooting pain in her back. "You've got to help me up. I can't seem to move." The moment she realized that's why Richard was staring at her with dim-lit eyes, Dior panicked. "I can't move, Richard. Wait…why can't I move?"

His eyes rounded with a reflective gaze. He choked back a horrible gasp then stumbled toward the telephone to dial 911. *Okay, okay,* he thought nervously. *I've got to get an ambulance here in a hurry. Dior looks bad. Her legs are sprawled out like that man Phillip killed in the car accident. Dior needs an ambulance or she's going to die.* When Richard picked up the phone, he had every intention of begging the operator to get the nearest rapid-response vehicle to Dior's address. Paralyzed below the neck, she groaned about excruciating throbbing in her legs and feet. Richard assumed they were phantom pains typically experienced after victim's limbs were lost or had become inoperable. Richard held the phone in his unsteady hands, willing to bet everything he owned that Dior would never walk again.

He took a deep breath. Streams of sweat poured into his eyes. Each time he closed them to wipe it away, he kept seeing Nadeen's face. She was sneering at him disappointedly for getting himself caught up in a situation where everyone lost. He saw Mahalia's sullen expression as the police carted him off to jail. Richard's heart skipped a beat when Roxanne's last giggles tickled at his ears. He imagined her visits to prison, year after year, until she found better things to do with her time than to look in on a man she once thought could do no wrong. Phillip's words played in his mind too. "They're daughters, Richard. They'll never give up on you." Richard wondered how long his friend's perception of truth would stand up against a felony assault rap with a maximum sentence. He rocked back and forth, agonizing over doing the right thing and self-preservation. Contemplating his fate as well as Dior's, he recognized that this unfortunate tragedy provided the exit he wanted from her life. *What if I can't do anything to help her,* he said to himself. *What if the paramedics get here and it's too late? I can't just leave her lying on the floor like some wounded animal in the streets. Do something, Richard. Do what you're supposed to.* He stood there, listening to the dial tone and playing the odds of Dior's death if he neglected to call emergency personnel and nobody happened to find her for hours, if not days. After he'd held the phone for what seemed like forever, Richard jumped when the phone began to beep impatiently.

Once he'd compared two probable endings, he returned the receiver to its base then swept perspiration from his face with the back of his hand. *I'm sorry, Dior,* he said silently, while wiping the telephone down with a dishtowel to remove his fingerprints. He stared around the house in an odd fashion, skulking about aimlessly like a desperate man who'd broken into her house only to discover there wasn't anything worth taking.

Richard was drowning in a sea of uncertainty. For a man who spent most of his adult life plotting his future well in advance, he had no direction or designs on how to proceed with fleeing the scene of a criminal act. "I am sorry it turned out this way for you, but I was never supposed to be here," Richard said, limping to Dior's side. "I was never supposed to…" he reiterated before he broke down and wept.

Dior was woozy, bordering on incoherent. Her eyes rolled back in her head as she witnessed Richard using his shirttail to open her front door. "Please don't leave me like this," she cried. "Richard! Don't go!" The last thing she remembered before losing consciousness was her lover's cowardly retreat in the face of peril.

Richard gassed up his luxury sedan and then hit the first interstate he came across heading east. He tried to follow the traffic laws to avoid suspicion, all the while reading his rearview mirror for highway patrol cars closing in on him. Richard told himself more than once how it had to be that way. He had to leave Dior or risk giving up his freedom and his family forever. And, although there were no guarantees of reconciliation with Nadeen once he made it to Atlanta, Richard was no longer above begging and pleading. He was up for whatever it took to get her back, whatever and then some.

# THIRTY-TWO

## *Burning Bridges*

D ior woke up screaming. She was frightened by a loud hissing noise that sounded like a den full of snakes. Her eyes flew open as the alarming noise grew even louder. "What's that?" she whined. "Somebody! Somebody help me! Anybody!" Droplets of water pelted the front window as if thrown by angry hands. Dior's insistent panting stopped when she realized she had been terrorized by the sprinkler system, set to spray the shrubs every other morning at five a.m. *Ouch, I hurt all over,* she thought. *I've got to get up.* She lifted her head from the white ceramic floor but couldn't move any part of her body below the neck. "Uhhgh, what's the matter with me?" Dior grunted. Suddenly her dark eyes focused on the bullet holes in the wall, inches above the staircase railing. "Wait, wait, where's Richard? Richard!" she yelled, remembering the terrible fall and everything that led up to it. "I know you didn't leave me. You didn't leave me and your baby. You couldn't have." Dior flinched each time the sprinkles splashed the window as if it were a delayed reaction to being squirted in the face with a child's water gun. "The first thing

I do when I get up is yanking that sprinkler control box off the wall in the garage," she snarled. "Help!" she hollered as loudly as possible. "Somebody help me! Why won't somebody help?"

Dior continued to yell at the top of her lungs until she grew too tired. Thirty minutes passed; no one came to her rescue. Scared and alone, she sniffled miserably. "Help me, somebody. I fell and I can't get up." She replayed her words after they reminded her of a television commercial that made her laugh. However, there was nothing to laugh about when it was her who'd collapsed on the cold hard tile. *Why am I stuck to this floor and what is that smell?* she thought. *Ooh, it stinks. It smells like somebody used the restroom.* Dior wrinkled her nose again, blowing breath through her nose to spare herself the pungent odor. As she opened her mouth to verbally complain of the foul smell, she made a startling revelation. The stench was emanating from her snuggly fitting shorts. She huffed to keep from crying at the thought of losing control of her bowels. Disgusted and frustrated by her debilitated state, Dior couldn't fight off the tears pouring from the wells of her eyes. She whimpered uncontrollably, feeling less than human. "I'm sorry!" she said, wincing at the pain she felt in her hip. "I'm sorry, Richard. I didn't mean to scare you like that. I'm sorry, God, and I mean it this time, not like before when Isis died and I thought it should have been me because it was my fault. That was guilt talking for me. This time, I'm really sorry. I'm sorry with all my heart," she blubbered. "Please believe me. I put that on everything I love, God. Everything!" She sniffled and wagged her head from side to side. "I'm sorry! What else you want me to say! All I'm asking is for somebody to help me get up since you won't give me the strength to do it on my own. Do you hear me, God? Do you hear me!" Tormented, Dior waggled her head from side to side. "Ahhh, I'm so cold. I'm freezing down here, God. The Bible says you help people in need so I'm asking, I'm asking for one more chance to do right. Please," she added much softer than before.

As Dior's energy waned, she began to fade in and out. Trapped in a semi-sedated state, she remembered things she'd forgotten too many years ago to matter, or so she thought. Sitting in a fourth-grade classroom, she scowled at Mrs. Wellston, a snooty white woman who'd gotten stuck in an urban school district that had turned black too fast for her to land a cushy and less challenging position in the suburbs like many of her contemporaries. The prim and proper teacher had Dior's best interest at heart when telling her, *"Good looks will only get a pretty girl so far. You'd better concentrate on your multiplication tables and stop letting those mannish boys look under your dress. Soon enough they'll start trying to get under those fancy dresses your mother obviously overspends on. Now, get back to work before I have to call your mother and report your unladylike behavior."* Mrs. Wellston would have slapped the taste out of her mouth had Dior actually voiced what was hidden behind that nine-year-old's sneer. "I like boys and they like me back. Maybe if you had some really cute ones trying to get at what's under your ugly old dresses, you wouldn't care about who I'm letting look under mine."

Dior also recalled hard times and hardly getting by with enough food to eat. One night, Billie Rae had to pull a double shift at the lounge. Dior couldn't have been more than eight years old at the time. During a midnight snack run, she couldn't find anything to eat that didn't require cooking, so she devoured half a pack of frozen wieners. Her tiny stomach swelled so badly, Dooney thought it was going to pop. Dior moaned as she lay on the floor of her house, remembering how it felt worse than death then. "What kind of mother stays out all times of the day and night, leaving two children to do for themselves? Not anyone I want to be like," she scoffed.

Grunting erratically from the phantom pains, Dior bellowed

that she was sore all over at once. "Ouch, ouch, ouch. I hurt so much. Please send somebody to see about me." As the hours faded by, the sun shone through the windows in the back of the house, opposite from the spot where she lay at the mouth of the foyer. "I'm going to get up from here one day," she cussed. "And I'm going to settle up with all those tricks who messed me over too. That superfreak Marta Mills, who stole my boyfriend and date to the junior prom. I'm coming for you, Marta! I hope you're fat with a million babies and no husband to help you feed them nasty crumb-snatchers. Ooh!" Dior yelped, when a cord of pain spiked in her back. "Don't think I'ma let this little setback stop me from putting my foot up that conniving-flunking-the-twelfth-grade-twice behind of yours, Marta. I'm not forgetting about the dirt you threw on me either. I won't. You'll get yours." Dior laughed heartily when she remembered hearing rumors three days following the prom that Marta contracted a subsequent bad case of gonorrhea from the ex-boyfriend she stole. "Ha-ha, that's what you get!"

When the sun eased over the horizon, Dior shifted her mental energies toward the men in her past. She named each of those who shared what the snooty teacher warned her about giving up years before. There was Byron, the finest ninth grader ever to keep a full beard neatly trimmed on a daily basis. Eric and Travon came after Byron, although Dior couldn't determine in which order she'd slept with them. Charles and Patrick came sometime later, in the summer of her senior year. It wasn't necessary to recall which of those she had first because she did them together. Dior accepted the threesome on a dare when her girlfriends chickened out. Sorting names, faces, and intimate details became cumbersome. She kept losing track somewhere in the thirties so she rounded up to an even forty male conquests, as she put it. Having contracted three different sexually transmitted diseases during her fast and feverish flings, Dior figured treatable offenses were the cost of doing business. Other girls she came up with, some who slept with far fewer men, weren't as lucky while paying the cost of doing theirs.

The very moment that absurd hissing started up again, Dior's eyes opened wildly. She panicked just as she had on the previous morning. "What's that! Who's there!" she scolded it frantically. "I'm in here. I have a...I have a gun!" She raised her chin as far as she could then she made an attempt to search the floor for the pistol she used to threaten Richard. Failing to locate it, Dior assumed the pastor had swiped it during his disappearing act. Dehydrated and desperate, Dior howled wearily. Her lips were crusty and split. She'd grown tired of swallowing saliva and her throat was sore and itchy. "I'm so thirsty. So thirsty," she muttered silently. "And I want a bubble bath. I could drink a bubble bath."

Dior was in the middle of making a mental list of things she couldn't wait to eat and drink once rescued. She heard a rustling sound behind a magazine rack placed near the sofa. Her eyes stayed trained on the metal rack. *Please, let it be the magazines shifting,* she mouthed. *Ooh, there it is again.* Dior shrieked as a green salamander shimmied from behind the stack of periodicals. "Go back, go back," she panted, but it kept on crawling toward her in a slow and curious manner. The six-inch reptile came even nearer to get an up-close-and-personal view. She wailed helplessly when the lizard mounted her chest then waved its long head at her. Dior was afraid to blink. She was literally nose to nose with the predator and afraid to breathe. She was afraid of it clawing her eyes or making a play to get into her mouth. While a host of negative scenarios rummaged through her mind, Dior swallowed hard. Since it required less energy to whistle than to scream, she puckered her severely chapped lips and blew. Surely enough, the salamander raised its head, stuck out its tongue, then dashed off as quickly as it appeared.

Proud of the way she'd chased off her live-in reptile, Dior imagined voices cheering her efforts. *I must be hearing things*, she thought. Dior raised her head to peer at the drapes covering the windows. She did hear someone outside. "I'm here!" she said, much lower than she did two days ago. "I'm in here! I'm still here!" she asserted. The couple who lived across the street didn't hear her weakened voice. They continued walking their ridiculously large poodle with the French salon hairdo. Dior screamed their names but it was no use. Her voice was worn, too timid to be heard from passersby out on the sidewalk. Dior drifted into a deeper pool of sadness with each passing hour. She felt dizzy when the sun fell on the third full day. She remained calm as best she could, although she kept getting confused over how many days she'd been lying on the very same spot. Slipping in and out of consciousness over the next few hours, she contemplated how the bridges she burned and the bad roads she traveled down all led her back to this place. She heard her cell phone ring but there was no way to determine who called or if anyone was looking for her. "I should have been a better friend to you, Tangie," she whispered. "If I had, you'd come looking for me. I know you would. I would, if we were tight…really tight."

If Giorgio or Suza had called from the clothing salon, she wasn't aware of it. Actually, there were several calls demanding Dior show up for work or else. Giorgio wouldn't think of firing her. He merely rattled her cage to elicit a response. If she hadn't broken things off, there was a good chance he'd have stopped by to check on her.

Reconciling her life was a tough nut to crack with a weary mind. Dior's hair stretched out on the hard and dusty floor. She scrubbed her head against the grout lines indented in the tile.

"Ouch, ouch, my scalp itches. It must be filthy. Filthy." Dior began to cough insistently. Her throat was raw and scratchy. She gasped, then sighed. "Why am I still here? I don't deserve this. I don't." Saddened by the thought of dying alone, Dior was ashamed. *I know I'm not all bad, God, but it seems like every good thing I did, I paid for it somehow,* she thought silently, in as much of a prayer as she knew how. *Please find room in your heart to forgive me even though I don't have it coming. You don't owe me nothing. My brother, Dooney, he deserves to see heaven. I won't hold it against you if he makes it in. He went about his business scratching and clawing ever since the day my momma spit him out. I passed up some good jobs, I passed on finishing college, passed up on having kids because I didn't want to spend the rest of my life raising them all by myself. I know I'll have to answer for each of the abortions, but what can I say. Condoms break from time to time and so do promises to do right. What I'm saying is thank you for my brother and my mama despite what she thinks of me. I'll never be much in her book. It's alright though. She's as good as gold in mine. I'm not sure what it takes to be saved or if it's too late for me. Hey, is heaven as beautiful as they say? I hope it is. Good people should have a nice place to go after putting up with the rest of us. God, look after Dooney. See about getting him a mansion, a robe, and a crown like that song he likes. A mansion . . . one with a big yard and a barbeque grill. He'd like that.*

Dior couldn't tell if she was in her right mind most of the day. She swore that her mother came to visit with platters of food. Then she found herself staring up at the same ceiling as before. She imagined eating her favorites, but it was sorrow that filled her stomach now. There were so many things to regret. Dior wanted to apologize to Billie Rae for all the years she neglected to visit before Dooney talked her into it. *"I should have written you more, Mama, like Dooney did. He'd show me your letters and even read a few to me when I hung around long enough. I'm sorry for being mad at you when you worked two jobs to keep food on the table and us in nice clothes. I understand now that you did the best you could, the best you knew how to raise two kids on your own. It's funny, you weren't too much older than I am now. Oomph, picture me with two babies,"* she rambled on. *"Ohhh, I'm so hungry. I wish I'd never looked down my nose at your hamburger casserole when it turned out green, Mama. I was just a kid then. I was just a stupid kid. I'm so sorry for hurting your feelings."* Dior felt a gas bubble pushing its way up her esophagus. Instinctively, she laid her head to the side to spill the vomit onto the floor. She had nearly choked during the last episode. Strength to survive another rough one didn't exist.

Nine o'clock the next morning, Dooney parked against the curb outside of Dior's house. He could hardly contain his excitement when hustling to the passenger-side door. His mother waited impatiently for her son to show off his chivalrous charm. "See there, that's that good home training paying off," Billie Rae joked as he escorted her up the walkway toward the front door. She straightened the new outfit Dooney had sent ahead for her release day. It was a dazzling cream-colored Chanel pantsuit. "So, how do I look?" she asked nervously. "Maybe Dior could make some time for a mother-daughter day at the spa. I don't have to report to the halfway house until four thirty."

"I know, Mama. Relax. Dior ain't no fool. She'll do what's right to make up for lost time. Now calm down before you ruin the surprise. It took all I had in me not to call and tell her you were getting out today." Dooney rang the bell. When no one stirred inside, he stepped off the porch to peek in the window, but there was no movement. "Huh, I thought she'd be here when she didn't answer at the store this morning. I hope she don't have company, or it's about to get real awkward up in there." Dooney used his key to unlock the door. "Wait a minute, Mama. Let me check." He tiptoed inside cautiously. "Dior," he sang loudly. "Please don't be naked…with some dude." He took three steps before a repulsive odor sent him reeling. In the past, Dooney had committed his share of crimes, but never murder. Yet he still recognized the smell of death.

Anxious to see Dior, Billie Rae wandered inside the house. "What's taking so long? Why are you taking off your shirt?"

Dooney feared he'd have to cover Dior's body. "Mama, go back," he growled, shoving her toward the exit.

Refusing to be moved aside, Billie Rae's motherly intuition was piqued. "What's the matter, Dooney! What's wrong?" She darted past him and then immediately regretted that decision the moment her eyes discovered Dior's body sprawled on the floor. Dior's eyes were open wide. Her pupils were stone-gray and dilated. Urine and feces saturated her clothes. Dior's hair was matted with dried vomit. Billie Rae clutched at her chest then fell to her knees. "No, no, no. Please God, no!" Dooney glared at his twin's demise with his face taut and strained. By the looks of things, she'd taken her last breath more then twelve hours ago. Viewing the dreadful scene was heartbreaking. Billie Rae lifted her daughter's shoulders off the hard tile floor then laid Dior's head on her lap. She'd dreamed of holding Dior in her arms when her daughter had visited lockup at Azalea Springs. She finally got the chance. "My darling baby. I'm here now, Dior," she moaned tenderly. "Oh dear God, what have I done? She needed me and I came too late. My baby needed me."

Dooney raced through the house to search for clues. When every conceivable nook and cranny turned up empty, Dooney sprinted down the stairs. He paced the floor like a caged animal, collecting himself, plotting retribution. His growl began as a low, guttural groan, pitched from the depths of his soul. "Ahhhhh! They killed my sister! Somebody took her, Mama! Then they left her to rot." He knelt beside Billie Rae to comfort her. "Don't you worry about it, Mama. I'm gonna find out who did this to Dior and then I'm gonna kill him."

Billie Rae held Dior's face in her hands. It appeared that she hadn't heard any of her son's violent rants. She raised her eyes to the ceiling as if she was looking for something. "Dior told me about this man with a family who wanted to marry her. Maybe he changed his mind."

"I don't care how long it takes, he's a dead man," Dooney vowed adamantly. "I'll dig until I get the scoop on him. You hear me? He's dead!" Grief-stricken and blinded by thoughts of revenge, Billie Rae nodded her consent.

"Dior said his name was Richard."

# THIRTY-THREE

## *Everything and Nothing*

Richard threw his legs over the side of the bed. He rubbed his eyes and yawned. Unlike the first three days he'd awoken in an Atlanta hotel room, this was going to be a good one, he'd decided. After having driven 750 miles in sixteen hours only to be put off by Nadeen continually, Richard had something to smile about. The night before, his wife agreed to see him over breakfast and discuss what, if any, chances existed for reconciliation. Begging and pleading had finally worn her down. For the first time in almost a week, Richard felt as if his life was getting back on track.

Showered and dressed, he called Nadeen's cell phone to inform her that he was on his way to the restaurant. She refused to be alone with him because that would lessen the control she needed to hold on to, along with her sanity. Tiny steps, Richard concluded as well, were as good as any toward making the journey back home.

When his repeated calls forwarded directly to Nadeen's voice mail, it was clear that her cell phone was powered off. Fearing she'd had second thoughts, Richard dialed her parents' home. Mahalia answered on the second ring. "Simon residence."

"Good morning, Mahalia. This is Dad."

"Oh, hi, Daddy," she said, her voice light and easy. Richard sat on the corner of the bed wishing his was too.

"Hey, is your mother sleeping in? I tried calling her but the phone isn't on."

"Well, she's probably still in the air. I don't think her flight landed yet."

Richard leaped to his feet. "Flight? What flight? We were suppose to meet this morning, here in Atlanta."

"I'm sorry, Daddy. I thought you knew." Mahalia bit her bottom lip, realizing her mother had purposely left without telling Richard.

Richard was frantic. Just when it appeared he could begin picking up the pieces of his shattered life, Nadeen decided to pull something like this. "Did she say anything? Like where she was going or why?"

"Uh-uh. She hasn't said much since we've been here. Then last night she got a phone call. It must've been important because she stayed on the phone for a long time in Grandpa's study. Then she came out crying. I thought y'all had another fight or something." Mahalia heard her father trying to sort it out in his head as he sighed deeply. "Daddy?"

"Yeah, baby?"

"I don't know if this will help but I saw the papers she printed from the airline's web page. She's going home. Her flight lands at noon, I think."

*Dallas?* he thought. *Why would she do this after I came all this way?* "Okay, thanks, Mahalia. Kiss Roxy for me. I'll figure something out. I love you, kitten."

"I love you too, Daddy."

By the time Richard had packed and checked out of his hotel room, he was mentally spent. Too many questions loomed without the answers needed to rest his troubled mind. He raced to Hartsfield International Airport, leaving his Lexus in long-term parking. The shuttle ride to the gate seemed to take forever. It allowed him too much time to think. What if she learned about Dior? What if he was wanted as a prime suspect? What if there was another emergency Nadeen felt compelled to address without including him? Again, he felt stretched and pulled in several directions.

After obtaining a seat on the next flight to Dallas, Richard knew he'd implode if he didn't at least try to get some answers before boarding that plane. He stood inside a small coffee shop across from his gate. Nadeen's phone rang several times now, indicating she was either on a call or avoiding his. In either case, he couldn't speak with her. Richard's chest swelled as he inhaled a steep dose of courage. He scrolled through entries in his address book until Phillip's name appeared. There was silence when the deacon answered. "Hey, man, I was wondering when you'd reach out to me." He omitted using Richard's name, in the event his conversation was overheard.

"Yeah-yeah. Sorry about not getting back to you sooner. I've been too tied up with family business to deal with church affairs. Look here, has Nadeen been by or called Rose this morning?" Silence played loudly for a second time. "Phillip?"

"I heard you. I just don't know how to answer that. Been too busy dealing with the call I got from the police last night and then another one this morning."

"Police? What do they want with you?"

"You ought to know. If you don't, then you should." Phillip was letting his friend know he should watch what he said over the phone. "I haven't returned their calls because I didn't want to get involved. I know too much."

"Too much about what?" Richard grunted quietly. "Please tell me what's going on down there."

"It's all about *her*. She was found dead in her home two days ago. It's been all over the news. The Dallas Police Department put a homicide investigator on the case. They're calling it murder."

"Murder! Good Lord, no." Richard blew a thick stream of anxiety into the air. "This is all wrong. Any cops mention me by name?"

"No, at least not the ones who've called here, but it's only a matter of time. There's been talk. Word gets around pretty easy when a high-profile minister's mistress is murdered."

Richard cringed when he heard that word again. "As far as you can tell, who's doing all the talking?"

"Church members mostly, those who didn't like what went down in New Orleans between you and Nadeen after *she* showed up. Good thing you've been in Georgia since before it happened, huh? Otherwise you might need a good lawyer."

"Yeah, good thing. I've been here going on four days." Richard sensed his friend was helping to bridge an alibi to throw at the police when they caught up to him. He rubbed his face in one long swoop, then eyed the line forming to board his flight. "Thanks, Phillip. I've got to go now. I knew I could count on you."

Phillip was bothered by Richard's questions as much as he was by the answers he'd given. What upset him the most was the lack of surprise in the pastor's voice when he said Dior had died. Richard already knew, and that crushed Phillip. "Go with God, friend. Let Him lead you."

"I will. I will."

Dooney sat in his truck parked down the street from the Allamay mansion. He'd been there off and on since learning two days ago that Dior's mystery man was the pastor of Dallas's largest predominantly black congregation. A man with that much to lose stood a lot to gain by killing his mistress. Fueled by pain too deep to live with, Dooney was willing to give his life in order to end Richard's. Tangie explained how Dior became obsessed with marrying the minister and that she'd even had a standoff with Nadeen over the affair. Dooney made Tangie promise to never tell the police that he was investigating the case himself or that he'd stolen Dior's cell phone from the crime scene. He'd seen how officers often botched things only to let criminals with high-priced lawyers walk away without as much as a slap on the wrist. He was determined to seek retribution.

At a few minutes past one o'clock, an airport shuttle pulled into the circular driveway at Richard's house. Dooney eased down in the front seat. He placed his hand on the chrome-plated automatic resting on his lap. His fingers tingled when the van driver stepped to the passenger's side to open the door. Adrenaline pumped through his veins when the thought of enacting vengeance played out in his head. While peering over the dashboard, he saw a woman climb down with a shoulder bag. Dooney shook his head furiously when the shuttle driver hopped behind the wheel then motored out of the subdivision. "No, no, no," he growled. "Where's the dude?" Dooney slammed his hand against the console when Nadeen entered the house, alone.

He yelled when his cell phone hummed. "What!"

"This is Tangie. I'm sorry to bother you, Dooney. I know you must be a wreck too."

"You don't know the half of it. Mad bad for going off on you," he apologized. "What you need?"

"I should be asking you that. The police have been dogging me to set up a meeting but I keep telling them I don't know anything. This woman, a sergeant I think, wants to know who Dior was kicking it with other than Giorgio. They cleared him yesterday."

"I knew he didn't do nothing the minute I stuck my lie detector in his face in the back of his shop. That fool cried like a baby when I started asking about him and Dior. He didn't ever care that I was ready to blow his nose clean off if he answered wrong. Alls he cared about was losing my sister. Ain't that a dirty trick. The man had me feeling bad for him. He said she dumped him for that preacher. He really thought they'd get back together, though. Even wanted to help with Dior's funeral arrangements, after I came at him foul. She should have stayed with him. Then none of this would've happened."

Tangie sniffled as she offered new information. "Uh, this lady cop who came by said they found Dior's gun under the sofa yesterday. I don't know how they missed it the first time." Dooney was angry because he failed to locate it before calling the police. "She said there were two sets of prints on it, Dior's and other's on the barrel. Dooney, the police need some help on this. It's so hard stalling when they don't have any leads. You gotta let me tell them about the pastor. I know you wanted to talk to him first, but I can't sleep or eat or anything because Dior is gone and I'm doing nothing about it. Maybe the police could find him faster. Maybe they can make him…ohhh, I didn't know I could miss her so much."

"Me neither," Dooney answered in a voice so tender it made Tangie break down and cry. "You got to be strong for her, Tangie. Don't worry about holding back if the law comes around again. Tell 'em what they want to know, all of it. You did yo' thing. Dior would be proud of you. I know I am."

"Okay," she whispered thankfully. "What about you? What are you going to do now?"

Dooney thought about it while stroking the lie detector he'd brought along as judge, jury, and executioner. "I got a hole in my soul and I aim to fill it. Go on and do what you have to. That's all I got left."

"What do you mean, Dooney? Dooney?" Tangie realized he'd disconnected the call. She picked up the business card offered by the homicide detective working Dior's case, felt sorry for Dooney, and then prayed.

# THIRTY-FOUR

## *Damaged Souls*

Dooney checked in with his mother hours after speaking with Tangie. He apprised Billie Rae on the latest developments, the harassing detective, and the news about Dior's gun. Billie listened to her only remaining child quietly while she analyzed the information he'd come across. Dooney seemed relentless in his pursuit to even the score. His mother wasn't so sure anymore. "Dooney, this changes everything. Maybe this Richard didn't mean to kill Dior. You know she had a bad temper."

"I don't care, Mama," he shouted. "My sister is dead and I told you I was gonna get him."

"And my daughter is gone. I'm not making small of that. It just seemed so cut and dry when we found her body. You were hurt and I was hurting too. Yes, Dior passed away but we don't know how it happened."

"It don't much matter to me. Somebody caused it," he argued. "When I run up on Richard Allamay, I'll know right off whether he's the one deserves to join Dior."

"Come home, Dooney," Billie Rae pleaded. "Come on home so we can talk." As he deliberated, another shuttle arrived from the airport. Dooney slid down in the front seat like he'd done before when it parked in front of the mansion. This time, his patience paid off. Richard exited the van by himself, with a duffel bag under his arm. "Do you hear me, son?" Billie Rae was saying. "I said for you to get back here, where we can hash this out."

"Ain't nothing else to say. Bye, Mama."

Dooney watched Richard enter through the front door. He jogged up the street with his automatic tucked in the waistband of his jeans. After circling to the backyard, he hopped the brick fence surrounding the cement patio. He saw his mark standing in the foyer and Richard's wife coming down the stairs to greet him. Dooney decided it was the perfect time to crash their homecoming.

"Nadeen, I've been calling you all day," said Richard, wearing a tired expression. "Why didn't you pick up?"

"You should be the one to question me? Since your secretary called me last night talking about my husband might want to clear his name I've had nothing but questions." Nadeen thought she heard something in the other side of the house but ignored it. "So, you're going to make me ask why the police want to come by here and question you *about a murder case!*" Her eyes were so red and glassy, Richard tried to control her voice by lowering his.

"Slow down, Nadeen. Slow down. I haven't seen you in days and the first thing I get is this?"

"Maybe I should wait on the police and see what they can get out of you," she spat, venom dripping from her lips. "I want answers, Richard. Did you have anything to do with what happened to Dior?" Richard froze when a stranger sauntered out of his kitchen with a shiny gun pointed at him.

"Yeah, I've been waiting to hear about that myself. Move over there and sit down," he instructed Richard. "You too, lady." Richard swallowed hard but Nadeen seemed unmoved by the intrusion into her own home. "Now that I got your attention, you're gonna tell me why you killed my sister."

"Your sister?" Nadeen asked, looking the man over carefully. "Lord have mercy."

"Dior, she told me she had a twin," Richard sighed.

Dooney walked closer to the sofa, where the others huddled. With calculated steps, he started a death march leading to Richard's feet. He cocked the gun, then held it against the pastor's forehead. "It's about time you got to telling."

"Okay, okay — wait," Richard uttered, his hands raised in the air. "I went to see Dior, but I didn't kill her. She — she got mad when I told her it was over. I tried to leave but she pulled a gun on me." His eyes blinked rapidly, unsure which blink would be his last. "And — and I reached for the gun. I grabbed the barrel and the thing went off, twice. We both went tumbling down the stairs. I thought she'd shot me. I thought I was dead. Honest, I didn't do nothing to hurt her."

"The coroner said Dior was still alive after the fall severed her spinal cord. Why'd you leave her there!" Dooney questioned heatedly. "She died like a dog because of you." He steadied his trigger finger to fire.

"Because I was scared!" Richard whined, staring wildly into his attacker's eyes. "I was scared."

"Uh-huh, bet you real scared now?"

"Please don't shoot him, young man," cried Nadeen. "Please don't kill my husband."

Dooney clenched his teeth. "Give me a good reason not to after what he did?"

"Because he's not worth it," she answered emphatically.

Richard's eyes grew wider still. "If you murder him, your life would be ruined too…and this man is not worth that. He's not worth another damaged soul."

Richard gasped when thunderous knocks sounded at the front door. He shrugged when Dooney asked who that could be. Nadeen knew most assuredly. "Don't you know? That's who the Lord sent to save you from making a grave mistake." She didn't ask permission to answer the door. Instead, she reached out her hand toward Dooney. His eyes danced erratically back and forth. "Let this be the best thing you ever did for your mother. Put that gun away and sit down."

Richard was shocked when Dooney lowered his weapon. He leaned against the sofa cushion and breathed a heavy sigh of relief. "Thank you, God. Thank you."

"Oh, you think it's over?" said Dooney. "What until your company leaves; I'll be right back on that…"

"Yes sir, officer," Nadeen said, loud enough to be overheard in the den. "My husband is home." Dooney slid the gun beneath the sofa, figuring that's where the police had the hardest time finding Dior's. He watched Richard as Nadeen returned to the room with two plainclothes detectives. Her demeanor was unbelievably casual considering what she'd moments before experienced. "And this is Mr. Wicker, a friend of the family."

The female officer placed her hand on her weapon. "Wicker? That's the same name as the deceased."

"He's her brother," said Richard. "He's only here to make sure I do the right thing." Richard gave a full statement, detailing his affair with Dior and everything he could remember about the night in question. Surprisingly, he managed to recall Dior's voice begging him not to leave her helpless on the floor. Dooney and Nadeen sat side by side, listening to each word, tortured by one after the next. Before the police took Richard into custody,

Dooney understood how a man in his position could have suc-
cumbed to fears of the unknown. Dior was right about him;
Richard wasn't made to behave in the ways he did when with her.
He wasn't the man she needed or the one he thought he wanted
to be. Nadeen sat alone, dazed and confused. Richard was the
husband she never knew.

# READING GROUP GUIDE

1. Should Nadeen have divorced Richard when she confirmed suspicions about another woman?
2. Did Richard have immediate intentions of sleeping with Dior after meeting her at the clothing salon?
3. Why do you think Richard risked his marriage and career to become intimate with Dior?
4. Was Nadeen's threat to pay off Dior a rational decision?
5. Did Tangie do enough to discourage Dior's simultaneous affair with two married men?
6. Was Phillip out of place for fighting Richard in the conference room?
7. Was Rose negligent as a friend to Nadeen for keeping quiet about the revelation Phillip shared in strict confidence?
8. Did Mahalia's voodoo charm have anything to do with Dior's tragic fall?
9. Richard had several opportunities to break up with Dior. Why wasn't he able to do it?
10. During Dior's last days, what did she say that affected you the most?
11. Do you think Nadeen would have taken Richard back if Dooney hadn't shown up?
12. Do you think Dior got what she deserved in the end? Why or why not?

# ABOUT THE AUTHOR

*Essence* bestselling author VICTOR MCGLOTHIN is a former bank vice president who nearly forfeited an athletic scholarship due to poor reading skills. Ultimately, he overcame that obstacle and later completed a master's degree in human relations and business. Victor is also an online columnist of *Victor Said?*, a real brotha-to-sistah look at relationships.

Living in Dallas with his wife and two sons, Victor is hard at work on his next novel and movie projects.